THE GOOD VAMPIRE'S GUIDE TO BLOOD & BOYFRIENDS

Jamie D'Amato (she/they) is a queer, autistic writer and sticky-note enthusiast based in Louisville, Kentucky. She writes quirky, heartfelt novels for teens and young adults. Jamie has her BA in communications and design from Northeastern University. She is passionate about queer and feminist issues as well as disability and neurodivergence, and her writing tackles those topics with compassion. Outside of writing, she loves crafting and cosplay, analyzing media on Tumblr, playing so-called "casual" simulation games, and geeking out about story structure and craft. You can always ask her about her latest travels or her dog, Luna.

THE GOOD VAMPIRE'S GUIDE TO BLOOD & BOYFRIENDS

Jamie D'Amato

MICHAEL JOSEPH

PENGUIN MICHAEL JOSEPH

UK | USA | Canada | Ireland | Australia
India | New Zealand | South Africa

Penguin Michael Joseph is part of the Penguin Random House group of companies
whose addresses can be found at global.penguinrandomhouse.com

Penguin Random House UK,
One Embassy Gardens, 8 Viaduct Gardens, London SW11 7BW

penguin.co.uk

Penguin
Random House
UK

First published in the United States by Wednesday Books,
an imprint of St. Martin's Publishing Group 2025
First published in Great Britain by Penguin Michael Joseph 2025
001

'Visible World' from Crush copyright © 2005
by Richard Siken. Used by permission of Yale University Press.
Design by Michelle McMillian
Title page art © Shutterstock
Printed and bound in Great Britain by Clays Ltd, Elcograf S.p.A.

The authorized representative in the EEA is Penguin Random House Ireland,
Morrison Chambers, 32 Nassau Street, Dublin D02 YH68

A CIP catalogue record for this book is available from the British Library

HARDBACK ISBN: 978-0-241-73201-4
TRADE PAPERBACK ISBN: 978-0-241-76417-6

Penguin Random House is committed to a sustainable future
for our business, our readers and our planet. This book is made from
Forest Stewardship Council® certified paper.

MIX
Paper | Supporting
responsible forestry
FSC
www.fsc.org   FSC® C018179

To the sad gay kids

Please note that the novel overall includes non-graphic references to a past suicide attempt, non-graphic small animal death via vampire, and descriptions of panic attacks.

THE GOOD VAMPIRE'S VAMPIRE'S GUIDE TO BLOOD & BOYFRIENDS

1

FUNERALS FOR SQUIRRELS

BRENNAN'S JOURNAL

For plausible deniability purposes, everything contained in this journal is hypothetical, theoretical, and/or fictional. Yep.

Questions

- Who turned me?
- Blood: Animal? Human? How much? How often? Regular food, too?
- Other vampires? Other supernatural???
- Nocturnal? Sleep?
- Garlic? Sunlight? Silver? Holy water?
- Sparkles?????
- <u>IMMORTALITY???????</u>

It took Brennan Brooks forty-eight hours, six coffees, and approximately eight thousand pages of reading to come to the conclusion that there were too many goddamn books about vampires, and none of them came with an instruction manual.

In the far corner on the "silent study" third floor of Folz Library, Brennan sat on the carpet in the folklore and mythology aisle at the center of a tornado of books, stacks rising up into towers. He wore a flannel over an old band T-shirt and was currently testing whether vampires needed sleep or needed to shower by—you guessed it—neither sleeping nor showering. Signs pointed toward not needing sleep and desperately needing a shower, but more observation would be needed.

In Brennan's experience, there were no problems that books didn't have answers for. Unfortunately, being turned into a vampire during an accident you didn't fully remember did not have its own *For Dummies* manual.

But Brennan had no trouble sinking into a fog of research, lost in a book about vampirism in Serbia and Bulgaria, which was fascinating but ultimately useless. His throat burned with a persistent thirst, his head throbbed, and every sound and smell was like a tidal wave. The soft snoring of some poor soul already behind on work for the semester was like a chain saw, the rhythmic squeak of a library cart like a piercing alarm, footsteps coming to a stop—

A shadow darkened the text and Brennan squinted upward, blinking away the dissonance of being rudely ripped back to reality.

"If you don't mind my saying so" came a rich Southern lilt, light with amusement, "I think you're missing a few key texts in the genre."

Standing at the end of the aisle with a library cart, a guy arched a brow. Brennan processed what he must be seeing. The mess of books, not subtle in their titles of *The Vampyre, Vampires and Vampirism, Les Vampires, The Legend & Romance of the Vampire,* a dozen other things featuring the words "vampire," "blood," "monsters," and so on. Brennan half-heartedly covered the book he was reading with an arm and blinked up at the fluorescent lights.

"Um, what?" Brennan said.

"Vampires, yeah?"

The boy had curly brown hair, delicate features disrupted by bushy brows, and light skin a bit more tanned than Brennan's ghastly pale. He smiled, encouraging, and it was familiar. Brennan couldn't place it. They must have had a class together, or crossed paths on campus. He looked like if Timothée Chalamet had a less punchable face. Maybe that was it?

Brennan squinted at the guy. "You have recommendations?" His voice was scratchy, his mouth dry. He was thirsty again. He cleared his throat.

The boy kept smiling, but it was sly. "It looks like you're lacking in the trashy YA romance department. No *Twilight Saga*? Or have you already read it?"

Brennan deflated and avoided rolling his eyes, narrowly.

"No, I have not. I don't think that will help with this particular project. Thanks, though." He returned his attention to his pile of destruction.

He meant it as dismissal, but the boy left the cart at the end of the aisle and crossed toward Brennan and the stacks of books between them. He wore a ringer T-shirt with the logo for a coffee roastery, and the bitter, nutty smell of espresso lingered on him. He had one AirPod hanging from his ear, buzzing with some indie-sounding music Brennan could hear but didn't recognize. He smelled too good to be normal, which meant Brennan was *really* thirsty.

"Come on, where's *The Vampire Diaries*? *Vampire Academy*? *House of Night*?" he continued, and at Brennan's increasingly blank look, added, "Or at least—*Interview with the Vampire*?"

"Okay, I *have* read Anne Rice," Brennan defended himself. "But I don't think half-naked werewolf love triangles are going to help me right now."

"Fine, if you don't do it for the research, do it for the experience."

"I'll keep that in mind," Brennan said, and didn't bother hiding his amusement.

Brennan took in the brown curls, the freckles, and once again it niggled at the back of his brain that he'd seen the kid before—spoken to him, even. The memory was barely evading his grasp, like a dream slipping away as the morning alarm went off.

As soon as Brennan turned on the scrutiny, the boy straightened up and took a step back, pink spreading over his cheeks. "Gosh, here you are trying to work and I'm prattling on about *Twilight* and distracting you."

"No, it's okay," Brennan caught himself saying, then shut his mouth with an audible click.

Really, he shouldn't be encouraging this—distraction. He had work to do, questions to answer, and none of that would be helped by an (admittedly cute) boy talking to him about *Twilight*. No, no, nope.

While Brennan debated how to politely tell the boy to leave him alone until he figured out whether he was at risk of snapping and murdering someone, the rhythmic sound of high-heeled footsteps approached.

A girl with a pencil skirt, heels, massive dangling earrings, and blue hair came to a stop and leaned around the edges of the bookshelves.

"Cole, we have a homesick freshman situation in 202B and I'm really not equipped for these things like you are," she said.

The boy—Cole, though the name didn't answer the tugging question of familiarity—straightened, whirled around with the energy of *Brennan who?,* and gave the girl his full attention.

"Don't worry about it, I'll get it. Will you put on the kettle? I'll be down in a minute."

The girl nodded with relief and strode back the way she came.

And that was when Brennan realized why Cole was so fucking familiar.

"You're the Hot Library Blanket Guy!" Brennan said. Then he wanted to sink into the ground and let the earth reclaim him.

Cole winced and then put on a tight, polite smile. "I think technically the adjective used in the Sturbridge U memes group is 'cute,' but . . . yep. That's, uh, that's me."

Brennan was mortified, but heat didn't flood to his cheeks like normal. Did he even blush anymore? His pen was still in his hand, the notebook in his lap. He jotted his question down.

Cole's eyes—brown, Brennan noted—flitted between Brennan and the notebook. His lips pinched inward. He smoothed his shirt, and the smell of roasted espresso wafted toward Brennan.

"Sorry," Brennan said. "I'm easily distracted. I just—" He paused, unsure. "We talked once. I knew I recognized you somehow. It was a while ago, I don't know if you even—"

"I remember," Cole said. He gathered the books he'd set aside and propped them on his hip. "Of course I do. But, look, let me let you get back to your thing. Blanket duty calls."

And as quickly as he'd pulled Brennan out of Serbian mythology, Cole left him to it.

He stayed in his corner in the stacks for a while longer, trying to delve back into Bulgarian folklore, but found his attention drifting while he read the same sentence over and over again.

Because Cole said he *remembered,* in a tone like, *obviously,* like he stayed up at night talking to his friends about what a loser this guy was from this one random library encounter. He'd never be able to return to the library again. He'd end up wasting away in front of his computer in his room and would die as he lived, alone and ashamed.

Brennan closed the book, cutting off *that* stream of thought.

Dr. Morris would call this catastrophizing. Cole probably didn't think about that night half as hard as Brennan was right then.

It had been such a small thing, really.

It was last semester, not long before everything happened in March and Brennan had forfeited the semester in favor of therapy. He had been sitting at the library, as he tended to do, and he was depressed, as he tended to be. He buried himself in homework—a giant essay for his History of Capitalism class. Not exactly a *calming* topic. He'd been working himself up to a frenzy, typing fueled by rage and what he could now call his deep-seated emotional regulation issues. He could recognize *now* after months of therapy that he was refusing to process his emotions, but at the time he'd thought he was just *that* invigorated by the atrocities of late-stage capitalism.

So when someone had leaned a hip against the desk he'd been working on and said, "I don't know about you, but typing that angry usually means you need a break, a snack, a nap, or some combination of the three," Brennan had barely pulled away from his essay before he broke like a dam.

Cole wasn't Cole yet, just the Cute Library Blanket Guy—a campus celebrity from the university's Facebook meme group who helped random students through various crises with blankets, stuffed animals, stress toys, and warm beverages. He was a library aide, but he'd turned into something of a campus urban legend.

He'd taken Brennan's little breakdown in stride, took him to a storage room that had been done up as best as a library storage closet could be: besides the boxes of paper and office supplies that circled the small space, there was a shag rug on the floor, a few of the cozier, egg-shaped chairs stolen from the downstairs study lounge, and a crate serving as a table that held an electric kettle.

"What, you just have this back here?" Brennan had asked.

Cute Library Blanket Guy opened a tin from one of the shelves and said, "Tea or hot chocolate?"

The tin was full of assorted tea bags and drink mixes, and the guy was looking through them thoughtfully.

"Coffee?" Brennan said.

"Man after my own heart," Cole had said, and Brennan remembered vividly the secret smile he'd given him then. Really, if not from the Southern drawl, Brennan couldn't believe he hadn't recognized him based off that smile.

But once he'd offered Brennan a blanket and a mug of shitty instant coffee, Brennan had just—unleashed it all. Word-vomited about college not being what he'd expected and having no friends and *also,* what the fuck are we supposed to do about the wage gap when Congress has been dragging their feet about fifteen dollars for the last decade, and does it even *matter* when we're all specks in the universe who are going to die either way?

He'd been so embarrassed at the outburst he'd said most of this into his hands, shielding his face from the world. He didn't want to be perceived, and Cole respectfully asked questions where appropriate and agreed when he could and just. Listened. His mug said MY WEEKEND IS BOOKED with an illustration of stacks of books, and his hands looped around it delicately.

Cole had listened, and nodded, and sipped his coffee while Brennan talked and drank his own and refused to make eye contact. After his rant, he caught his breath and realized that Cole hadn't had to say anything and he already felt better.

"Wow, I need to go back to therapy," Brennan had said in conclusion.

Cole snorted a laugh and then covered his mouth with his hand in apology. "Maybe so," he said, and Brennan still only looked at him in quick, mortified glances, but he could hear the smile in his voice. "Either way, if you ever need some space to relax that brain of yours, this space is usually free. If it's ever locked, you can find me, I'm—" He'd coughed. "I'm around."

And that was when Brennan's anxiety had finally taken the reins, because this guy *worked here* and had better things to do than listen to Brennan whine about his first-world white-boy bullshit problems. He shot up from his seat and put the mug on the crate like it burned.

"Right, that's very generous, thank you," Brennan rushed out. "I'm here a lot, I'm sure I'll see you around. But I should go."

And so he went!

That was it, really. A one-sided encounter that Brennan sure as hell wouldn't be posting about on any Facebook groups.

So then, why did he feel like shit about it? Dread sunk in his stomach, a *Titanic* leaking anxiety.

Rooting himself back in the present, Brennan closed his laptop and started shoving his notes and computer away. The library now was as empty as it had been that night, but this time there was sound drifting up from downstairs—voices, laughter, keyboards clacking.

Brennan shouldered his backpack and headed out, across the second floor, around a student snoozing over an art project, down the stairs, and into the main area.

A quick scan showed it wasn't crowded, and he spotted Cole with a girl who was burrito-wrapped in her blanket and literally crying into Cole's shoulder.

"Like, does she hate me that much? Why else would she just fuck off the day after moving in?"

Brennan hesitated at the door, social norms telling him not to eavesdrop. His curiosity won out, as always.

"Well, did you tell your RA?" Cole asked.

"She said it was nothing," the girl said. "But it's been days now. What if something happened to her?"

Brennan froze. A girl, missing, the day after students returned to campus. Also known as the day Brennan was turned into a vampire during a car accident he didn't fully remember.

Taking a deep breath, he tried to clear his head from the fog that descended when he went too long without snacking on some poor squirrel. He was so thirsty his throat felt like a rash, which was getting fucking old, to be frank. He'd accomplished nothing yet except new levels of thirst and anxiety.

As if sensing Brennan's gaze, Cole looked up from across the way and spotted Brennan. His head tilted ever so slightly, and Brennan did what he did best: he ran.

BRENNAN'S JOURNAL

More thirst = senses go haywire? Everyone smells like a ~~goddamn~~ smoothie.

RANT

How many ~~fucking~~ woodland creatures do I have to kill to stop being so ~~goddamn~~ thirsty?

Nothing seems to help. It dulls the ache for a while but doesn't satiate it.

I have a hypothesis, but I'm going to consider some other options before I start having an existential crisis about something that might not even be the case.

~~Fuck~~.

Substitutes?

· Coffee—miraculously, helps temporarily

To test

· ~~Coconut water?~~
· ~~Iron supplements?~~

Sturbridge's campus was full of open spaces and greenery, lots of shady trees and curving pathways, and that was part of why Brennan had chosen it: it had a storybook charm that Brennan had fallen in love with. But over a year in and he'd still never felt part of the story—just a visitor, a side character. It was a beautiful backdrop he didn't belong in.

But he loved jogging through the lush forests that surrounded the campus, with their meandering paths and steep inclines. In early high school, when Brennan had his first experiences with existential dread–induced insomnia and couldn't sleep, with nothing else to do, he started jogging. It helped, mostly. He guessed some of the stuff they say about endorphins must have been true, because if he pounded the pavement hard enough, all the oppressive problems of the world scattered away from him. For at least a little while.

But this? This could barely be called running—he was *flying*.

Everything was faster and sharper, each step launched him farther, and each movement was steady and instinctive even as he moved at a speed he knew he'd never run before. That possibly no *human* had ever run before.

How fast can I run? Another question for the journal. *How fast can a human run? The average person? An Olympic athlete?*

Once he was far enough away from campus to not encounter a stray jogger, he skidded to a stop. He processed a skittering sound up a tree, a blur of motion. Instinct took over, easy as breathing, and he dove at the squirrel and then bit down and—

Look—Brennan used to escort spiders in his apartment outside because he didn't want to kill them. He was a vegetarian. Two days ago, if someone had asked him, like, *You wouldn't attack a wild squirrel, right?* he would have been confident in the answer. But life was full of surprises.

It was sweet relief with a quick chaser of deep shame, next-level post-nut clarity where afterward he was left to clean up the mess he'd made. Except the mess in this case was a lifeless squirrel body.

Brennan did the same thing that he had done with the two squirrels and one rabbit he had drunk the blood of in the past two days: he knelt down and started digging. It felt like the least he could do.

He eased the squirrel's limp little body into its grave, sweeping loose dirt over it until it was buried. For good measure, he plucked a few wildflowers from the brush and put them on the patch of upturned soil.

"I'm sorry," Brennan said. He stood up, brushing dirt off his hands and knees.

Brennan pushed forward. He hadn't realized it, but his feet were leading him to the bridge he'd promised his mom and two therapists he wouldn't return to.

Begrudgingly, he would admit they had been right, considering it was where he'd been hit by a car and turned into a vampire, but explaining as much to Dr. Morris would probably get him back in the psych ward.

The sight of it—the small, arched stone bridge over a narrow bubbling creek, the path leading to a dead end of thick brush—used to bring him comfort. It was his place, far enough from campus and deep enough into the woods that he could be alone, think, get away.

But then everything in March happened, and now it loomed, shadowy and foreboding.

The narrow wood path widened ahead, and the rushing stream grew louder. Following the widening path would take you to the highway, despite the road barely being wide enough for a car. There, if you knew where to look, hidden by a cluster of maple trees, was where the bridge was nestled.

Brennan retraced his steps from that night. He'd been walking to the bridge then, too.

He slowed to a stop.

Because now, as he emerged into the clearing, he saw a car parked just before the little stone bridge, and a dark head of hair bobbing around the very area that Brennan remembered so vividly. The car, too—a blue pickup truck, rusted and beaten half to death. Recognition sparked and Brennan knew this was the car that had hit him.

Instinctively, Brennan dropped to shield himself from view. Very few hikers or bicyclists made it out there. That was part of the old appeal, when Brennan had wanted to be alone. In the year since he'd found this place, he'd never run into another person.

Until now. And she was hovering over the spot where Brennan was *pretty fucking sure* he had died two nights ago.

The person had a small, feminine frame with long brown hair, and she was bent down like she was looking for something on the ground.

Brennan was strategizing how to inch around to watch without her seeing him when he felt a vibration in his pocket.

"BACKSTREET'S BACK, ALRIGHT!"

Brennan jumped, and the girl flinched, as Brennan's phone buzzed to life. He dove for cover too slowly, as her head whipped toward the sound and she stared right at him. She had a round face and pale skin, and Brennan committed it to memory as the Backstreet Boys ruined his only lead on whatever was happening to him.

In a heartbeat, the girl threw herself into her car. The engine started, and Brennan rose from his weak hiding spot to peek at the car roaring away.

Brennan bit back a curse as the car disappeared down the road and whipped his head around to make sure he was alone now, for real. The vibration and noise from his pocket died down.

A few yards away, there was a murky smear of a stain that Brennan *knew* was blood. He knew because he could *smell* it. He knew because it was *his* blood from the other night. It was right at the spot of impact, right where he'd been standing.

There were skid marks from tires. Brennan could almost hear their squeal, the rumbling engine.

"BACKSTREET'S BACK, ALRIGHT!"

Brennan scrambled for his phone. The only person who ever called him was his mom, who worked a Very Important Job that kept her Very Busy, and who would call campus security if Brennan dodged more than one of her calls after everything in March.

His mom's picture in the caller ID made his stomach clench in an anxiety-guilt hybrid. Instead of processing that, he answered.

"Hey, I have class," Brennan said, which was not a lie. He should have been in class ten minutes ago, had he not been fleeing the library.

"Oh, don't worry, I only have a few minutes, too. I have a meeting with a big Harvard guy about me speaking for the environmental conference and of course *today's* the day the coffee place runs out of the *good* recycled paper cups and is using *plastic.*"

"Wow, talk about Murphy's Law," Brennan deadpanned.

"It's really that kind of day," his mom agreed, his sarcasm so far over her head it was intercepting a flight to Boston Logan. She added, almost as an afterthought, "How are you? How do I make it video again? I want to see your face."

Ah, yes. That was Brennan's mom. Meredith Brooks, big-shot academic-slash-activist, running around yelling about the rising oceans and industrial carbon emissions, trying to save the planet. That part was awesome. Always busy, always between meetings or classes, environmental scientist first, mom second. That part was less awesome.

Brennan grimaced and checked in his phone's reflection to make sure there was no trace of blood on his face. Which was not something he'd ever thought he'd have to do before FaceTiming his mom.

It took a solid minute for his mom to get her own camera on, and then it was their two rectangle images set over each other, with his mom's perfectly maintained blond hair pulled into a neat ponytail. She was all tan and strong, natural energy. It was no wonder she did well in the environmental space. She was so put-together.

And then there was Brennan. With his patchy-bleached hair, pale and gaunt with shadows under his eyes, he *looked* like a depressed, zombified shell of a human, which was scary-accurate considering his possibly-not-alive status.

"Oh good," she said, paused, took in Brennan. Then, "You need a haircut."

He *did* need a haircut. But would it even grow out anymore? Another question for his journal. Not quite as high a priority as some others.

"Yeah," Brennan said. "Soon, yeah, I'm just getting used to the semester."

"Tell me about it," his mom said, and Brennan prepared for her to start monologuing. "Kirigan pushed off all the freshman courses to me, and was so condescending about it. But I do really enjoy the younger classes, helping them build that foundation. . . ."

Brennan tuned her out, focusing instead on the sound of wind rustling the trees. His mom had finally accepted a tenure-track professor position a few months after Brennan started college. Now she was enmeshed and thriving, though still a relative newbie. He was proud of her, obviously, but he couldn't help resenting her a little. He spent his entire life moving from place to place because she didn't want to settle down, and as soon as he moved out, she changed her mind.

People would tell Brennan that it took a special kind of person to get a master's and two PhDs while being a single mother. Brennan disagreed—it took *two* kinds of special people. The first, a self-absorbed, book-smart mother, and the second, an overly self-sufficient latchkey kid cursed to grow up with attachment issues.

"—I'm really just trying to take it a day at a time," she finished. Brennan hummed along to confirm he was listening, which he was not. "But anyway, you're keeping up with school? Getting ahead on your readings?"

"Of course," Brennan said. He'd started reading chapters as soon as his textbooks were available, but even that head start wouldn't buy him much time with everything else going on.

"And how are you doing?"

He hated this question from her. She always asked it with the demeanor of checking something off her to-do list.

"I'm doing well," Brennan hedged.

His mom scanned him from the screen, her face so close to the camera that he couldn't see anything around her. She had two doctorates but didn't know how to hold a phone so Brennan didn't have to look directly up her nostrils.

"That's so good to hear," she said, and her voice was thick, and no, *no*, if she started crying Brennan would hang up—

"I'm so glad you're doing well," she continued around a sniffle. "You know how I worry and how much last semester scared me." She started crying. The camera showed her chin from below, perfectly highlighting her trembling lower lip.

"Oh, Mom, I'm—I'm really doing well. This semester will be different, I know it," he said, instinctively going back to the mantra he'd been telling himself a few days ago. Now it felt like a bold-faced lie.

"I just want you to be happy and do well, okay? I can't go through something like that again."

That one hit Brennan right in the gut. Somewhere, the Dr. Morris in his head was saying something about narcissistic, emotionally immature parents, but Brennan couldn't hear her. He stood up, needing to move, pace, run.

"You don't have to worry about that," Brennan said. "I'm on top of things. Look, I should go—"

"Okay, me, too, but you know you have my credit card for anything you need, you don't have to ask."

He made it a few feet before something else caught his eye, something bright pink in the grass to the side of the road.

Brennan crouched and picked it up. A pink scrunchie. No tags, no labels, nothing distinguishable. But it was something. It might have even been the thing the girl was looking for. Why, though? What did she want? What did she *know*?

"Brennan? Did you hear me?"

Brennan shoved the scrunchie in his pocket. A problem for later. More questions for the journal.

"I don't need anything," Brennan insisted.

She was already paying his rent since he'd lost his tutoring gig last semester. He knew she had money now and they were in a realm of living comfortably, but clipping coupons and counting quarters to get groceries when your mom forgot to (and then went to an out-of-town conference without you) was a habit that died hard.

"You need to *eat*. Coffee doesn't count. Order some DoorDash on me. Any night of the week. You look like you're starving. I must look like a terrible mother."

She hung up, and Brennan stared at the CALL ENDED screen for a moment too long.

He went through a slideshow in his mind of reasons he loved, respected, and was proud of his mother. She was a hard worker, she instilled a value of knowledge in him, and sometimes when he was a kid she'd pull him out of school to take field trips to the zoo or the aquarium or the library because she always said life outside of the classroom was as important as life within one.

And with that appreciative disclaimer out of the way, he allowed himself to shift to the stormy cloud of negativity that he *really* felt. He let the anger drive his feet as he headed home.

That was one thing Brennan couldn't stand about surviving his attempted suicide in March: everyone wanted to relate it back to them. He had barely processed his own feelings about trying to off himself before he had to juggle everyone else's—the concern, the worry, the *How can I help?*s and the *But you're better now, right?*s. All he wanted to do since then was move on, but with each passing month, people kept wanting to hear that he was doing better, that he was *good*.

But to be honest? He'd been fucking better.

Except no one wanted to hear that. Hell, Brennan didn't want to hear it, either.

Brennan's throat returned to its natural state of severe burning, and that was when he sped past the angst and bullshit and focused on something else his mom had said.

Because Brennan knew what it felt like to drink water when you were hungry.

When he was twelve, he had his first existential crisis, and spent days and nights mainlining Gatorade and familiarizing himself with every popular idea of life after death. He didn't realize he hadn't eaten for a week until he passed out in front of thirty unforgiving seventh graders while presenting a book report on *The Book Thief.*

Drinking the blood of animals felt a lot like that. Enough to soothe the ache for a moment, but not enough to stop it. And Brennan had a theory about what *would* satisfy the craving.

Worse, that voice of the girl crying in the library rang in his head. Someone had gone missing around the same time Brennan woke up and realized he was a vampire. Brennan *maybe* needed human blood to live, and he *maybe* had a block of lost memory between getting hit by a car and waking up in his apartment, a totally reasonable eight hours during which to commit murder.

In typical Brennan fashion, he briefly contemplated suicide. In a cool, totally low-key and logical fashion, thank you very much. But he guessed somehow, somewhere along the way, *some* of the therapy must have worked, because not being alive wasn't an appealing option. At least, it was less appealing than being—*undead.*

And really, just that feeling was novel. As someone who tried to kill himself six months ago, "optimistic" wasn't a word he freely associated with himself, but this semester he'd been almost hopeful.

The guilt and the angst were par for the course. But trying to do something about it? Having hope? Wanting to keep fighting? To keep *living?*

That was pretty new to Brennan. He'd only just gotten those things back.

Brennan shuffled back toward the bridge and sat down on it with his back to the rocks like he used to do. He squeezed his eyes shut. Did eight counts of a breathing exercise he'd learned from the therapists at the in-patient facility he went to after his attempt. Opened his eyes.

He reached into his jacket pocket and pulled out the journal he now stowed there at all times.

If Brennan dared to want to exist on this planet, he'd have to drink human blood. Which meant morally gray situations and committing minor felonies, things Brennan generally tried to avoid.

He couldn't drag anyone else into this shit the way he used to drag people into his moods or make his mother worry. This was his problem, and he'd figure it out on his own. And he'd do it *well*: if he had to be a vampire, he'd be the best damn vampire this side of the prime meridian.

Because yeah, of course he had a plan.

It might even work.

2

THE BLOOD PACT

MICHAELSON HEALTH SCIENCES BUILDING

Open Hours
- Building proctors at both entrances 7 a.m.–9 p.m. M–F
- Building proctor only front entrance 10 a.m.–5 p.m. weekends
- Locked doors after hours
- Janitors 12–1 a.m. ~~every night~~ every weeknight
- Deep cleaners 10 p.m.–?? Saturday nights

Key/Passcodes?
- 9/10 6:59 a.m.–proctor uses key to get in, code to disable security. What is code???
- 9/11 7:02 a.m.–99 something can't tell
- 9/12 7:00 a.m.–okay actually 09 something?
- 9/13 6:58 a.m.–091298 *hacker voice* we're in!

MORALITY & ETHICS
Under consequentialism, stealing blood will prevent me from potentially harming/killing others. ~~So that would be okay.~~ Except no, wait, because stealing the blood will prevent people who need it from getting it. Or prevent life-saving research. So it's bad.

Utilitarianism: only benefits me and the people I am able to resist killing with my teeth, which I would say isn't in itself commendable.

Under altruism, the answer may actually be suicide, since cutting me from the equation means no death, no stealing, and no depriving science or doctors of blood. So. Uh. Not the most fun conclusion.

Absolutism would say I would already be fucked for stealing, let alone stealing something that could save lives. Kant would kill me with a wooden stake and no hesitation: under Kant, killing vampires is probably a Universal Good action. How comforting, to be on the Kantian Bingo Card.

Hedonism would say it's okay because it brings me pleasure/relief. That doesn't make me feel much better about the situation. Hedonism isn't the peak of morality.

Moral relativism: okay, this one might work! Moral value is relative to context and culture. In this case, uh, I guess the culture of vampirism means that drinking human blood is. Less bad? I'm not convinced, but it's better than nothing.

Aristotle's golden mean would say there's a middle path to virtue. So, uh, maybe if I steal blood this once but am super good elsewhere it can balance out my karma or whatever? That's … not so bad. Maybe I can do that.

Brennan had had one required biology class in Michaelson Hall his first year at Sturbridge University. The building was modern, all floor-to-ceiling windows and curved walls, everything sleek and new and smelling like a hospital. It was the building they showed on all the brochures, yet the majority of Brennan's classes ended up relegated to the less modern, more run-down humanities buildings around the edges of campus. The ones that hadn't been updated in a while and always smelled like mildew and eggs. Ugh.

If he hadn't known much about Michaelson before, now he knew too much. Because if Brennan knew how to do anything? It was motherfucking *homework*.

He knew how many entrances there were, how many windows opened, and at what time the proctors stationed at the main entrance changed shifts.

He had a crude map of the few security cameras, easy enough to avoid by using a back entrance attached to a stairwell that would take him where he needed to be without being caught on camera. Wasn't there something about vampires not being on film? Or photos? Or was it just mirrors?

Whatever, it was too late now; Brennan's watch read 6:55 and he was loitering under a tree, Michaelson on the other end of the landscaped greenery of the quad. The lawn, often populated with Frisbee players and picnickers and studiers, was empty save for a scampering squirrel.

Brennan shivered in the crisp air—muscle memory, maybe? Could he still *really* get cold?—and pulled his windbreaker tighter around him.

The thirst was brutal. His body felt feverish—not in temperature, but weak and dizzy. And there was the constant driving *urge* that felt like he was barely holding himself back, like he was one inconvenience away from breaking.

A figure appeared in the distance, walking on the paved pathway toward Michaelson, and Brennan jolted. That was the proctor—and he'd almost missed him.

His senses, still blaring and confusing, jumbled together into a cloudy haze that Brennan blamed on thirst. That was his hypothesis for now, at least, because the worse he burned to drink, the harder sounds became to distinguish from one another, a wall of noise closing in from all directions.

He launched forward, taking a long path around the quad to approach the back entrance he needed. At that time of day, it would be unlocked, unmonitored, and unoccupied for a small window of time.

Then all he had to do was follow the smell of blood.

Brennan moved with purpose, like a bloodhound with his nose to the ground. His body moved like it had learned ballet without telling him, perfectly balanced with each delicate, impossibly light step. He needed to write *that* down. Maybe this schtick had some perks, after all.

He came to a classroom door and glanced around again before entering and closing the door behind him. It wasn't even locked.

The scent flooded him instantly, grabbing Brennan right by the neck with the overwhelming instinct to bite.

That still-foreign feeling of his fangs dropping down filled his mouth.

Brennan nearly teleported to the giant freezer across the room, ignoring the tables and desks and whiteboards with elaborate diagrams, because Brennan knew, he'd seen enough movies and had enough context clues to be certain that was it—

He flung the freezer open to trays of blood in vials and plastic packs.

Really, if they don't want their blood samples stolen, they should keep them more secure, Brennan thought, and he was about to bite into the plastic then and there when he heard voices and footsteps. His senses must have been really dulled for him not to notice until then, but he launched into action, loading as many packs of blood into his backpack as he could reasonably steal.

And, fuck, he'd really meant to pilfer a little, few enough not to draw attention but enough to tide him over. But he had no idea how long a pack would last him, and he tended to be thirstier than he'd hypothesized, so screw it.

He tucked the packs in as carefully as he could in his haste and zipped the bag closed. He shut the fridge doors, returned to their undisturbed state.

The footsteps were in the hallway now, and he'd only have a moment to put distance between himself and the newcomer. Which meant no more *thinking*: act, dumbass.

He threw himself across the room to open the door. Footsteps shuffled outside.

Brennan turned in a whirling circle to take in the room. Even if he wasn't caught in the act, there was a decent amount of blood missing—he couldn't be seen at *all*.

He sized up the door, then turned with greater dread to the window.

He leapt to it, pushed it open, poked his head through.

The coast was clear—no witnesses.

And it was just the second floor. People survived that all the time, right?

He backed away, adjusted his backpack.

And then he launched himself out of the window.

He rolled when he landed, swift and practiced. Like jumping out of windows was an everyday occurrence. He kind of wished someone had seen—it was probably badass.

But more pressing was the *smell* wafting from Brennan's backpack, and the burning thirst that pulled at him. Brennan gave in to the smell, the instinct, and let his body take over.

He grabbed one of the pint bags and bit down right into the plastic, and then the blood was sliding down his throat and the feeling was absolutely unreal. Like, the satisfaction of scratching an itch, eating your first bite of vegan cheesecake, and having a screaming orgasm, all tied into one. Like all of his nerves were lit up in satisfaction, relief.

He drained the pack in seconds, like one of the frat boys shotgunning beer at the parties some freshman-year friends had convinced him to attend—except those boys had ended up choking and gagging into the sink, whereas Brennan lifted his head and his world came into full Technicolor for the first time.

The prickling feeling, like shards of metal piercing his skin, smoothed over, his senses calming into something vivid and *real*. Where the noises around him had been a cacophony in his head, they faded into the background, and he felt at peace in his own brain for the first time since getting hit by that car. The tight itchiness of his skin was soothed, like aloe on a sunburn, and everything around him came into focus in stunning clarity. He'd put his own life into 8K resolution, and it felt—

Powerful.

The world was in stunning clarity, sharper, and that was when Brennan realized too late that he was not alone.

The murky smell of weed.

A rapidly increasing heartbeat.

Brennan lifted his head from the emptied blood bag and saw Cole— the cute library blanket guy—leaning against the wall, a lighter in one hand and a joint between his lips, just before his jaw fell open and the joint fell from his mouth.

It might have been comedic if Brennan wasn't amid about fourteen different crises.

Brennan's fangs were still bared, bulging against his lips. He willed them away but they remained stubbornly visible.

"Um," Brennan said, going completely still, as if that might activate some secret vampire invisibility power. No such luck. *Fuck*. "Hi."

He realized there was blood on his lips and moved to wipe his mouth with the back of his hand. Cole flinched back at the movement. Reflexively, Brennan threw both his hands up in surrender.

"I'm not gonna hurt you! I— Hold on."

He concentrated on making his fangs go away. *No more blood here! The situation has passed! Go to sleep!* It felt akin to talking down an inappropriate boner, a thought that added insult to injury.

Brennan summoned the memory of the garlic scampi his roommate, Tony, cooked last week, how the acrid smell had permeated through the walls and ruined Brennan's research cocoon, and at *last,* the fangs receded.

The first good thing Tony's cooking had done for him, thanks very much.

"This looks bad, probably, right? I'm gonna say this probably looks bad...." Brennan trailed off as Cole slowly, deliberately rubbed his eyes with closed fists and blinked hard. "Would you believe that I'm a talented acrobat and this is an unbranded Capri-Sun?"

"I—You—" Cole stammered, then settled on, "Fangs?"

Well. So much for secrecy. Brennan was never a good liar.

"Okay, so," Brennan said, palms out like he was talking to a skittish animal, "I'm maybe a vampire."

The words hung in the air for all of a minute before Cole started laughing, light and confused, until it morphed slowly into a horrified *what the fuck* that pulled Brennan from the tidal wave of panic in his brain.

"What the fuck!" he said, laughter edging toward something unhinged. "Is this a joke?"

Brennan's life? Yes. Absolutely, on a cosmic level.

He said, drawing out each word, "I don't think so."

"You don't *think* so?" Cole's voice went progressively higher, but he was frozen to the spot on the stoop leading into Michaelson. "Either you *are* a vampire and you *did* just jump out of a window and drink a pint of donated blood, or you *didn't.*"

Fuck. Shit. He went through a litany of curse words in his head but carefully said none aloud. His mother would be proud.

"I know it sounds—ridiculous, okay, but it's a developing hypothesis.

This is still new to me. That was actually my first time drinking human blood. A week ago, I didn't even eat meat!" Brennan's brain and mouth were moving too fast, and he knew he was rambling, but he needed to fill the silence. "My mom made me watch a documentary about factory farming when I was in high school and we went vegetarian together."

Okay, no. This was irrelevant and Cole was looking at him like he was insane. *Read the room, Brooks.* Brennan cut himself off and stopped pacing, foot tapping restlessly in place instead. He faced Cole and silently pleaded for him to say something, *anything.* Cole was stock-still, mouth twisted in a strange wobbly frown.

"So, the library. With the vampire books?"

"Research," Brennan confirmed.

Cole plucked up the joint he'd dropped and lit it with the urgency of someone who didn't know what else to do. He shook his head a few times, apparently at the entire situation. Brennan couldn't blame him. *He* still didn't know how to process this.

Cole took a long drag. "You're telling me vampires are real," he said, gesturing with the hand not holding the joint.

"In some form? Yeah, I'm coming to that conclusion. It's not like *Dracula* or *Twilight,* the rules are all weird and—I mean, most importantly: I don't sparkle."

"Disappointing." Cole sniffed.

Brennan huffed a laugh before he remembered to resume panicking. What would Cole do? Who would he tell? Brennan barely understood what was going on himself, and now this random blanket-toting, joint-smoking Southern gentleman would run to call the nearest priest as soon as he was sure Brennan wasn't about to maul him.

Cole finally moved to take in the empty street. God, he was probably making sure there were witnesses so he didn't get murdered. The streetlights flickered off as the first rays of sunlight rose above the line of maple trees and brownstone apartments. It was barely September, but an early-morning chill was settling over the college town.

"I hate to even ask . . ." Cole started.

"Go ahead," said Brennan. "I doubt I have the answer either way."

"Should I be scared?"

Brennan choked down the acrid smell of smoke, curled and uncurled his fingers. He looked helplessly back to Cole, who sucked on his joint and stared Brennan down through narrowed eyes like that alone would give him answers.

I hope not, Brennan almost said, and then, *I don't think so,* but neither of those seemed good enough.

"I'm figuring it out," he said instead.

Cole laughed. "Well," he said, almost to himself, "if you're stealing donated blood, then at least I know you're not, like, attacking humans in the streets in secret."

"That's the goal, yeah."

"That's not so bad," Cole decided, tilting his head and taking another long, deep hit.

"Cole!" A voice called down from the open window Brennan had jumped from. "I can smell you smoking down there, are you gonna come help me or what?"

Brennan's eyes cut to Cole, ice crackling down his spine.

"Did I not mention?" Cole whispered. "I'm helping my friend with some stuff for the school's blood drive."

Of course he was.

"What, are you making friends down there?" A head of dark, curly hair peeked out the window from above.

Brennan flinched away, hoping to conceal his face. Even if there wasn't blood on his face, and his backpack wasn't visible from her viewpoint, she had a good view of his bleached hair and could probably pick him out of a lineup, if it came to that. God, he hoped it wouldn't come to that.

Cole turned over his shoulder but kept his eyes on Brennan as he called up, "Always, Marisela. I'll be right up!"

With Marisela disappearing into the building, Brennan swallowed hard as Cole considered him. This kid, in the wrong place at the wrong time, could make or break Brennan's life as a vampire before it had even really started.

"Here's the deal," Cole said, conspiratorial, leaning forward with a secret in his eyes. All Brennan could do was follow, drawn like a magnet. "I won't tell anyone, as long as no one's getting hurt."

"But?" Brennan prompted.

"But," Cole said, "in exchange . . ."

Brennan braced himself. This was real blackmail material. He could want anything.

Cole grinned, wicked, and said, "You read *Twilight*, and give me live updates."

Brennan blinked. "You're kidding."

Cole shrugged, seeming awfully pleased with himself. Brennan wasn't sure whether to be relieved or deeply, deeply concerned.

"Yeah, uh, how high are you?" Brennan asked.

"I believe it's 'Hi, how are you?'" Cole said, giggling, which was an answer to Brennan's question in itself. "So, whaddya say? Deal?"

Cole didn't go so far as to reach out a hand to shake—maybe that was too much trust, even when stoned—but it felt like an important offering. A lifeline.

Brennan took it gladly.

Sometime after stealing blood from a blood drive, making a back-alley deal with a campus cryptid, and walking home, Brennan's phone vibrated in his pocket.

He didn't open it until he got home to his place, passed Tony playing *Apex Legends* on his Xbox, and dropped his backpack at the foot of his bed. He flopped dramatically onto his bed face-first, and after a long moment, finally checked his phone.

His stomach dropped right out from under him.

1 unread text

[Unknown Number]
We know about you.

3

BACHELORETTE NIGHT

[Unknown Number]
We know about you.

Brennan
Who is this?

[Unknown Number]
111 North Elm St. Saturday 11 a.m.
Be there. Ask for Sunny.

BRENNAN'S JOURNAL

ENHANCED STRENGTH & SPEED, ADDENDUM
Accidentally ripped the third floor Ryder Hall bathroom door off the hinges while opening it. I'll totally deserve it if a priest stakes me in my sleep; I'm terrible at being a vampire.

I put in a work request for the door breaking. Sorry to the underpaid staff that will have to fix that.

Test
- Use light bulbs or fragile things to train down passive strength? Like those dogs who hold eggs in their mouths???
- Buy stress ball??

It had to be Cole.

Or, Cole had told someone else.

Sure, Brennan had been a little sloppy with a few incidents of sudden thirst, but sloppy enough that someone else had found out so soon? Sloppy enough for that person to have blackmail material?

He spent all day riling himself up about all the ways his undead life was going to come to an abrupt end, wasting another day's tuition and disappointing his mother by paying absolutely no attention in class yet again. He analyzed every encounter he'd ever had with Cole. Why would he act all innocent if this was the end goal? It didn't add up.

He worried and scribbled furious notes in his notebook and worked himself near a panic attack once or twice until finally, it was time.

It was *Bachelorette* Night.

His new roommate Tony had invited him to watch, of all things, *The Bachelorette* with him and his friends. It was some sort of weekly ritual of semesters past, and this was the kickoff for that fall. Apparently, they drank wine and made bets and took it pretty seriously. Tony didn't seem like the kind of guy who watched *The Bachelorette,* but Brennan was desperate enough for potential friends that he had been clinging to the polite invitation as a social life raft for the semester.

Brennan emerged from his room only after he heard the TV switching on and Tony's friends catching up and settling in. He had been holed up all day researching how to buy blood on the black market and exactly how unethical was it, in the grand scheme of capitalism? So he wasn't exactly on high alert when he shuffled out and peered into the living room.

"Okay, Nick has absolutely no banter," Tony said around a mouthful of popcorn.

He had a half-full bottle of Tito's on the coffee table in front of him, and he still seemed stone-cold sober. He was the only one avidly paying attention to the TV, which was playing a show that was *not The Bachelorette*—it was brightly colored and everyone had ridiculous accents that sounded more like people making fun of British people than actual British people. On the coffee table, missing a few slices, was an intricately latticed apple pie.

"If she even *looks* at Jake T. I will set myself on fire," announced a girl from beside Tony, shaking her head. She was Latina, her frame slight, wavy dark hair cut at her chin. She held a glass of wine primly by the stem, the flush on her face betraying that it was not her first.

Draped across the couch next to the girl was a boy with his head in the girl's lap, legs sprawled over the arm of the couch. One hand was fiddling with one of those cube fidget toys.

It took Brennan a solid minute to process that the boy on the couch was *Cole*.

Before he had time to about-face out of *that* situation, they all seemed to notice Brennan's appearance at once, and he winced as their heads swiveled toward him.

Well. Shit.

Cole's eyes fell on him and his mouth quirked in a silent, almost amused greeting.

"Ayyyy!" cheered Tony.

"You're late!" said the girl. He recognized her voice now, the slight accent—she was Marisela. From the blood drive. *Fuck.* She didn't seem to recognize him, or at least didn't let on if she did.

Cole stayed quiet, but he pushed up to sit like a normal person and watched Brennan. His hair was a mess, flat from where he'd been lying and sticking up in all other directions. Brennan didn't allow himself to find it charming, but it was a near thing.

"Late joiner's fee is . . . two shots? What do you think, Mari?" Tony asked, and Mari gave a nod of approval before throwing back the remnants of her wine.

"You gotta get on our level," Mari agreed.

Cole defended weakly, "It's a Monday, go easy—"

"It's the *rules,* dude," Tony said, and then he pushed off the couch to thrust a plastic Star Wars cup toward Brennan. Brennan didn't need vampire senses to smell the vodka.

The liquid sloshed around in the cup, and Tony's defiant expression said he was serious about enforcing the rules.

And, well, Brennan had been wanting to figure out if vampires could get drunk.

"This is peer pressure," Cole pointed out.

Not to mention that he still needed to get a read on whether Cole was a lying traitor or not.

Two birds, one stone.

Brennan swiped the cup from Tony's hand and threw it back while Tony and Mari whooped.

It barely burned going down, which was new.

"Peer pressure claims another innocent soul," Brennan announced, and offered a bow before joining the party in the living room.

Tony poured Brennan another drink, the TV went to commercial break, and Brennan took a spot on the floor instead of squeezing onto the couch.

Everything was sharper with fresh blood in his system, like his world had come into focus or switched to high definition. But it wasn't overwhelming. The sounds of the neighboring apartments—a blender on high, a radio playing Nicki Minaj, a group playing Dungeons & Dragons—were still there in the background, but he could tune them out like turning dials on a radio.

Brennan suffered through the last fifteen minutes of the show, the unidentifiable sexy singles "recoupling," while Tony periodically announced that something one of them said meant everyone had to drink.

Finally, Brennan took a chance on a half-baked idea, just as he realized with utter certainty that vampires could, indeed, get drunk.

"Never have I ever," Brennan said, "unironically enjoyed the Bachelor franchise."

"This isn't even *The Bachelor,*" Tony protested.

"My sincerest apologies," Brennan deadpanned. "What are we watching?"

"*Love Island*! Have you not been paying attention—"

"Um, Tony, you'd better drink," Mari pointed out, taking a gulp of her wine.

Cole had summoned a glass from somewhere and drank, too.

"Oh, so we're doing this?" Tony asked. "I can smoke all you bitches."

He took a pull from the Tito's bottle. Then, "Never have I ever gone to therapy," Tony said.

Brennan's stomach swooped until he saw both Mari and Cole taking sips. He took his own and avoided eye contact.

"Way to be emotionally well-adjusted," Cole said.

"Oh, I am *not,*" Tony said.

"Maybe you should, I don't know," Mari said, "*try therapy?*"

"Never have I ever . . ." Cole started, "pulled an all-nighter for school."

"Boring," said Tony.

Mari and Brennan both drank.

"Um, how have you *not?*" Brennan asked. Getting caught up in a project and realizing six hours had passed was a typical Tuesday night for him in high school.

"If it isn't done by ten o'clock, it doesn't need to get done until to-morrow," Tony said. "I need my beauty sleep."

"Same here," said Cole.

"Yeah, so you can bake up a bribe and get the professor to give you an extension," Mari said.

"There's nothing wrong with forming a good relationship with your professors," Cole said. "I can't help it if my brownies are worth giving extensions for."

Mari cleared her throat and said, "Never have I ever . . ." She paused, eyes cutting to Tony in a failed attempt at discretion, then continued, "cheated on someone."

Tony drank. "In my defense, it was high school. I was a little boy then."

"You're a little boy now," Mari countered. She was squinting at Tony like she had given him a test, and he'd failed.

Brennan's turn. Okay. Cool. Casual.

"Never have I ever"—he pointedly didn't look at Cole—"blackmailed someone."

A beat passed that seemed like forever, the TV blasting a commercial. Then Mari drank. Her eyes locked with Brennan as she took a long sip.

Brennan risked a glance at Cole. He was watching Brennan with a pinch at his brows, but his gaze jerked away as soon as Brennan looked. Cole focused on Mari instead and, mercifully, did the asking for Brennan.

"Who did you blackmail?" he challenged. "And why didn't you tell me about it?"

Mari examined her fingernails. "It was nothing, really."

"Well, now we definitely need to know," Tony said.

Brennan kept silent. His heart was in his throat and if he opened his mouth they'd surely hear it.

"I found this guy selling test answers in high school," she said. "But he was an office aide, so I held it over him to get unlimited hall passes and late passes."

"Bro, I am quaking," Tony said. "You're the baddest bitch. You've girlbossed all the way to the sun—"

"I have one," Cole interrupted, and it was the loudest and most present he'd been all night. Brennan got the impression he didn't interrupt much, and it made Mari and Tony quiet. "Never have I ever stolen university property."

Brennan clenched his jaw so hard he thought he might break it. Cole was being discreet and looking at everyone, but it was clear he was watching for Brennan's answer. He gave it honestly, taking a sip. Tony and Mari drank, too.

"Damn, Mari!" said Tony. "Here I thought you were, like, a law-abiding citizen."

"Oh, fuck off." Mari rolled her eyes. "I stole a couple of blue books last semester for finals week." She shrugged, then jutted her chin out. "I'm not at all surprised that *you* have a story, though."

"Obviously, me and the boys stole the Lucky the Bulldog statue before finals week freshman year."

"No way," Cole said.

"That was *you?*" Mari gasped. "Administration was pissed! *I* was pissed. I got a B on my bio exam and I always thought it was 'cause I didn't get to rub his nose before class."

"Oh, a B, the *horror*—" said Tony.

"Wait, where is it now?" asked Cole.

"Proudly in Epsilon Epsilon Phi's trophy room, god help him," Tony said, and made a sign of the cross over his chest.

Brennan remembered to breathe again with the spotlight off him, glad to let Tony recollect his shenanigans as long as he wanted. But of course—

"Anyways, what about you, Brennan?" Tony asked.

On one hand, he appreciated that Tony was trying to include him. On the other hand, *fuck.*

Brennan floundered under the weighted gazes from all three of them. The alcohol sloshed in his stomach in warning.

"I stole the key to the top floor of Smith," Brennan said, and it wasn't a lie. Smith's tenth floor was a fancy event space with floor-to-ceiling windows and open spaces for tables or dancing. It was mostly reserved for fancy highbrow events for big donors, which meant the best view on campus was eternally locked and restricted. "I used to go there to hang out."

To stargaze and people watch and get away from everything on campus that left him feeling overwhelmed and alone. He'd bring snacks and drinks, sitting on the floor and watching campus from above, making up stories about the people who passed. He didn't feel so lonely that way.

"Not anymore?"

Brennan blinked away the memory. Cole's head was tilted with the question, and he wasn't watching Brennan like it was a test anymore. He seemed interested. Maybe a little sad.

Suddenly Brennan regretted saying anything, regretted having tried to hang out with them at all. It was far from the first time Brennan had started what sounded like a fun story only for it to turn dark and depressing and uniquely embarrassing.

"I got caught last semester, they took the key back," Brennan said, simple, like it was no big deal. But it had actually been a *big* deal to him, at the time. The top floor had been his safe space to think and be alone and let the vastness of the universe comfort him instead of scare him. But he'd slipped up and ran into a janitor, and that was the end.

Maybe two weeks after that, he went to the woods to the bridge to nowhere and made the big attempt.

"Too bad, that would've made a great party spot," Tony said.

Mari jumped in with her next Never Have I Ever, but her voice went out of focus as Brennan's thoughts turned loud and fast and the world tilted sideways. It was the classic, unfortunately familiar feeling of folding into himself: spiraling. The physical sensation of depression and anxiety washed over him like a wave.

This was ridiculous. What was he doing here, playing these games and pretending these people were his friends, pretending he could be normal? He wasn't normal before he became a bloodsucking monster, so he sure as hell wasn't now. Brennan knew it. Cole knew it, too.

Brennan set his drink down when he realized his hands were shaking. The ringing in his ears turned louder. He stood up from the floor and barely mumbled an "excuse me" before fleeing the room.

Coffee, he thought, coffee was a distraction. Coffee helped. Step-by-step helped. He could hide himself in the kitchen, blessedly out of view from the others but not separated by a door. He heard some whispered concern but couldn't let himself focus on it. Mari and Tony were probably lamenting what a weirdo he was. Cole was probably telling them everything, that he was a monster, that he had the audacity to think he could handle being a bloodsucking creature on his own—

Coffee filter, he commanded. His limbs didn't want to cooperate.

The absolute worst thing—the thing he refused to think about or process until he was confronted with undeniable evidence that it was true: vampires tended to be immortal. That was their whole schtick. They drank blood in exchange for endless life.

Endless.

Life.

He moved for the filter, put it in the machine.

The world is big, filled with billions of people, all with a finite time on earth to make their lives matter. It was something that kept Brennan awake at night through the end of high school and most of college so far, when the heavy weight of understanding his place in the world settled over him in a dark curtain.

What did anything *he* did matter?

Coffee grounds from the cabinet, lid off.

This was the problem with majoring in history. He knew how much got lost in it. He would, too. Another unremarkable person in a sea of billions that exist now, have existed, will exist.

How was he supposed to do that *forever*? He wasn't even sure he wanted to commit to the normal seventy-odd years.

He dropped the canister. Coffee grounds spilled across the tile floor. Brennan stared at the mess, immobile. He didn't feel capable of cleaning up. No, easier to stand there, staring, letting his head go straight into that particular void of his brain he called *Do Not Fucking Touch*.

He realized, a beat too late to be helpful, that he wasn't breathing, and, and, maybe vampires didn't need to breathe, Brennan had yet to test that theory, but, but, Brennan, *he* definitely needed to breathe, right then, probably, for his sanity maybe, but he couldn't.

"Brennan?"

Great, fucking fantastic, really. Him a-fucking-*gain*. Cole kept stumbling into Brennan's worst moments, all concerned and charming and possibly lying his ass off.

He must have thought Brennan was a monster. He *had* to, the way he saw him that morning, blood on his lips.

He shook his head, shaking off his immobilization. "I'm sorry, I—" Brennan gasped. "I can't be here right now."

"I wanted to see if you were okay—"

"I want it on the record that you have, consistently, the worst fucking timing," Brennan spat.

He spun around, moving for the door and not letting himself look at Cole as he pushed past to make his escape.

"Hey, breathe," Cole said, reaching out to touch Brennan's arm, to stop him, and Brennan flinched away like his touch would burn him, and it *would,* right then, to his fucking core—

"Just don't, Cole," Brennan said, and he didn't think he'd ever heard his voice go that low and cold before. He fucking hated it.

But it got Cole out of his way.

He didn't remember slamming the apartment door behind him, or going out into the evening air, but somehow he ended up riding out the rest of his panic attack against the side of the building, tucked out of sight, running through every grounding method Dr. Morris had ever taught him.

Things he could see: a bird in a tree, like the ones he'd been drinking, and a couple laughing across the street, people who would become dust while Brennan lived on.

Things he could hear: too much. The laughter, and the birds, but also a dozen TVs and Bluetooth speakers in the surrounding apartments, all buzzing in his ears.

Okay, Dr. Morris would say he could recite something, a poem, maybe, but the only thing he could think of was the part of a poem that goes, *Nobody's going to save you. . . .*

He leaned weakly against the brick wall.

He'd survived worse.

The good news was, Brennan thought weakly, six months ago something like this would have driven Brennan straight to thoughts of doing something destructive. Anxiety never went away, the too-logical voice of Dr. Morris reminded him. It was okay to have attacks, to have bad days.

But it didn't stop the wave of exhaustion that came over him as soon as he could breathe again, collapsing to sit against the wall, tilting his head back and closing his eyes. He needed a nap. Or the coffee he'd set out for initially.

He sighed, almost huffing out a laugh at the whole situation. He was such an *asshole,* he realized, now in the post-panic-attack clarity that always came with that deep shame. That feeling that something was wrong with him, that he broke down in the first place, that he let himself yell at Cole who, really, outside of Brennan pointing fingers at him, had done nothing but try to help.

He should give Cole some space after all this. You can only see a person at rock bottom so many times before losing patience, and surely Cole was at the end of his. Brennan would have to avoid him at the library. And, well, he could avoid *Bachelorette* Night. Cole would be glad for it, and Tony and Mari had little reason to care either way.

He considered going for a long walk or waiting until everyone left before returning to his room with his tail between his legs. But the exhaustion of all the panic and anxiety Brennan had been shoving down for a week (fuck it, his whole *life*) was catching up to him, and the call to collapse in his bed was strong.

Or maybe, the Dr. Morris in his mind coaxed, *you could apologize instead of running away.*

Brennan hated the Dr. Morris in his mind.

He pushed up from the ground, dusting off his jeans and going up the porch steps. Just as he reached for the door, it swung open, nearly smacking Brennan in the face.

"Oh, shit, sorry," Cole said from the doorway, because of course it was him. His hands, one wrapped around a pack of cigarettes, fluttered in the air around Brennan, like he wanted to make sure he was okay but was afraid to touch him.

"No, you're fine, I was—I mean," Brennan said helplessly. His brain was fried, okay? Which was why he followed that up by blurting, "Did you send that text?"

Cole blinked. "What text?"

He reached for his phone, tapped until the text was on-screen, and held it out to Cole.

Cole leaned forward, his free hand moving to the phone to stabilize it. His fingers brushed Brennan's, and that made something horribly fluttery go off in his chest. Cole's eyes scanned the screen, the blue light illuminating his freckles. It seemed unfair that he looked so handsome while staring at something that could ruin Brennan's life.

"I didn't send that," Cole said after a moment, one hand to his chest, all *scout's honor.* "And I didn't tell anyone about you. I promise."

"What about Mari? She saw me earlier outside Michaelson—"

"Mari didn't even notice any blood missing. Besides, if she had a problem with you, she wouldn't send weird texts about it. She'd tell it to your face."

Cole offered a smile but concern pinched his brow. Just like that, Brennan felt ashamed for even thinking it could *possibly* be Cole. The balloons in Brennan's stomach popped and deflated and he was left with empty, guilty aftershocks. He scrubbed a hand over his face. He wished he could collapse into bed and sleep for eight years, but then, he couldn't sleep *at all* anymore.

"I'm sorry for coming off as a total dick, like, all the time," Brennan said.

Cole snorted, waved his pack of cigarettes toward where Brennan was blocking his way.

"Not a *total* dick," Cole corrected, "and not all the time."

Brennan stepped aside to let Cole out of the doorway, but let the door click shut behind him. Suddenly, returning to his room with his tail between his legs wasn't good enough.

"I'm serious," Brennan said again, while Cole sprawled out on the cobbled porch steps and lit the cigarette. "You were trying to help. I was an asshole."

The smell of the smoke turned rancid up close with his stronger senses. It was kind of gross.

"You obviously needed to be alone," Cole said. "That's, uh. Valid."

He took a long drag, looking up at Brennan, and Brennan wanted to sit with him. Instead he pushed his hands into his pockets and leaned against a column next to the porch, keeping a careful distance from Cole but making it clear he wasn't running away.

Cole asked, "That was a panic attack?"

Of course Cole was going to be, like, *cool* about it. Cole was the Cute Library Blanket Guy; he probably volunteered with the elderly and rescued kittens from trees in his spare time. It made Brennan feel more like complete shit.

Brennan always felt like he was on display when he was around Cole. It was like being naked, and unfortunately, not in a sexy way. Cole saw Brennan's worst parts, and Brennan barely knew Cole beyond the perfect, glorified meme version of him.

"Yeah," Brennan said finally. "I've basically been on the verge all week."

"Do you get them often?"

Brennan gave in and sat on the steps, below Cole and with two feet between them. He took in the night sky. It was a nice night, all things considered. The first traces of autumn painted the leaves with red and brown and gold, intercepting clear skies and bright stars. *Ursa major,* he greeted, *Orion.* When he was younger he had loved astronomy, but the vastness of the universe had long since brought Brennan panic instead of comfort.

"No," Brennan said. If nothing else, Cole deserved an explanation. "Only when things are really bad. I almost had one earlier today so this was kind of—inevitable. Like, built up." He turned his head, trying to sneak a glance at Cole. "Do you?"

Cole didn't seem bothered. "I have friends who do. It's normal."

"More normal than vampirism," Brennan guessed.

This, surprisingly, made Cole's face twitch from its relaxed mask, but Brennan couldn't for the life of him identify the quirk of his mouth around the cigarette.

Until Cole said, "Oh, so we're addressing this now?"

Brennan blinked. "You're acting like you *want* to."

"Of course I want to!" Cole burst, like he'd been waiting for the opportunity, lowering the cigarette as he shifted to face Brennan. "How is it more weird for me to talk to you about your life than to keep acting like I don't know you're *literally* a vampire?"

It was a decent point, but Brennan was more taken aback by the outburst, that Cole was even capable of it.

"I didn't mean for anyone to find out," Brennan tried. "You weren't supposed to know."

"But I *do* know. I can't *un*know," Cole said. "So tell me. Who'd you kill? What vampire curses have you unearthed? Whatever's bugging you, you don't have to keep it a secret. Not from me."

"It's not a big secret or anything! It's that text, and the meetup. I had a whole breakdown about it, but I'm feeling much better after express-ing myself and would love it if we could move on."

"Yeah?" Cole said. "Well, I've been hearing these rumors."

Brennan's stomach dropped.

"About?"

"There's this freshman girl missing. People are getting all up in a tizzy about it. Does this have something to do with your vampire stuff?"

Brennan bounced his knee anxiously.

"I might have overheard you in the library the other day."

"No shit," Cole said.

"But I swear, I had nothing to do with it! That I know of. And I know that's not extremely convincing but just know I'm trying to figure it out. I'm *going* to figure it out."

Cole tilted his head, studying Brennan, and hummed. Brennan couldn't handle waiting for him to form a response so he kept talking.

"If you thought I could be involved, why didn't you tell anyone about me?" Brennan asked, crossing his arms. "That was my end of the deal."

"Oh. Well." Cole reached into his pocket with his free hand and emerged with a fidget toy that he focused his attention on. "I didn't really think you were involved. You don't mean any harm."

Brennan's mouth opened and closed again. The first time the thirst had hit, even *he* hadn't been sure he wasn't going to hurt someone. He settled on asking, "How do you know?"

"That night we met? The first time in the library last year?" Fidget toy forgotten, Cole's piercing attention was back on him, and Brennan didn't know what to do with it. He waited a beat too long before realizing that was the end of Cole's answer.

"When I whined to you for hours about all my stupid problems?" Brennan finished. That didn't seem like a good reason to trust someone.

Cole's eyebrows raised in such disbelief that Brennan wondered if his own memory was betraying him. That night only came to him in flashes. His own emotions and depression were his strongest memory, far more than what he actually said, or what Cole had said, for that matter.

"You mean when you talked to me about all the people you cared about and all the ways you wished the world were better?" Cole corrected. "It was the kindest and most thoughtful rant I ever heard, and that's saying something."

Brennan blinked and tried to absorb that information, almost expecting Cole to fizzle away as a half-baked fever dream. But Cole stayed, shadows cloaking his face.

"I don't think I remember our conversation the way you do," Brennan said.

"You don't have to. But that's why I . . . trusted you to do the right things, I guess."

"That's a pretty big leap."

"I was right, wasn't I? You're doing pretty good from what I've seen."

Brennan resisted the urge to laugh out loud. He didn't *feel* like he was doing well. It felt like he was one misstep away from crashing and burning.

"Why do you want to get involved?" Brennan said in a rush. "It would be easier for everyone if you stayed away from this."

"Because, well—" Cole's cheeks flushed pink, which was all sorts of interesting, and he said, "It's kind of cool, obviously."

Brennan repeated, "It's *cool?*"

Cole rolled his eyes, like he thought Brennan was fishing for compliments. "Come on, man, it's objectively freakin' cool."

Brennan gaped at him. Cole offered Brennan his cigarette and Brennan was *dying* to ask him questions.

Because maybe Brennan wanted to even the playing field. If he learned about Cole—if he could know as much about Cole as Cole did about him—maybe that sharp feeling in Brennan's stomach whenever Cole was around would soften. Maybe it'd be easier to look him in the (soft, warm, chocolate-brown) eyes.

"Smoking's bad for you," Brennan said weakly. He made a mental note for the future—*Vampires and smoking? Vampires and cancer?* God, each question had grounds for a dozen books, hundreds of academic research papers, and Brennan would never scratch the surface.

Cole gave him an amused smile, lifted his cigarette in a *cheers* motion and said, "Yeah, but I look so mysterious and cool doing it." And his eyes crinkled all bright and carefree and Brennan didn't understand him, not at all. But he wanted to.

He *shouldn't*, he knew, because it *would* be easier not to be friends. He had a lot to figure out, and his life was growing increasingly complicated by the day. And Brennan still didn't get what Cole wanted out of this.

But it could be nice, Brennan's traitorous brain said, *to have someone who knows. Someone to talk to.*

"What about this is cool, then?" Brennan asked, and his mouth kept going without his go-ahead. "I mean, you did recommend *Twilight*, so if it's like, a *thing* for you I'm gonna have to let you down easy. . . ."

Cole gasped, then let out a sharp, delighted laugh and shoved Brennan's shoulder with his fist in a way that sent a warm spike up Brennan's stomach.

"Oh my god," he sputtered, still laughing, "I *told* you, it was for the cultural experience!"

Brennan couldn't help smiling under that warmth of *you made him laugh* and *he doesn't hate you.*

"But, I guess you're not totally far off," Cole said, and this time it was Brennan's turn to sputter and gape.

"Please enlighten me," Brennan said.

"Well, I mean—I read."

"Yes."

"I read *a lot.*"

"So, you have a kink for vampires . . . ?"

"Shut up, oh my god, you're so—" Cole said, but he was laughing even as he looked like he wanted to punch Brennan. Then he shrugged, dropped the cigarette, and kicked out a foot to stomp it out. "How do I explain this?" It was a true rhetorical question, thoughtful, to himself, and it was endlessly endearing.

Cole sat up, scooted so he was fully facing Brennan in a precarious balance on the stairs, tucking his feet under him. He reminded Brennan of a kid settling in for a bedtime story.

"On my eleventh birthday, when I didn't get a letter inviting me to some magical boarding school, I cried," Cole said, all earnest eyes and conspiratorial smile. "And then I turned twelve and didn't get dragged away to Camp Half-Blood, or find a portal to another world in the back of a wardrobe." He started to move his hands while he talked, and Brennan tried to keep his eyes from tracking them. "And then each year went by and I didn't discover any developing magic powers, or some hidden underground world, or a dark history or—*anything*, any of the stuff that I thought would make me . . . I don't know, like, *special*, or whatever."

He rolled his eyes at the word, like it was embarrassing. Cole paused, and Brennan was watching him, breath caught in his throat. Brennan acutely understood that gut-wrenching feeling of realizing you weren't special, and Cole had summed it up so succinctly.

"I mean, obviously, it's not about me," Cole said. "But aside from the scary stuff, it's kind of like . . . proof that there is magic in the world. And *then* it's like—you know, if vampires are real, then maybe ghosts are, or werewolves, or witches, anything." Cole smiled at Brennan as he concluded, "Like, I just met one person, but the world got a whole lot bigger. And *that* is cool."

As Brennan processed, Cole poked at a particular divot in the steps with too much interest. And Brennan realized, with a resounding internal *Duh,* that Cole was putting himself out there, too, wasn't he? He was, at least, trying to.

Brennan grinned and extended friendship in the best way he knew how.

"I'm happy to aid in fulfilling your middle school vampire fantasies."

Cole had fire in his eyes but a smile on his lips, his shoulders relaxing from where they'd been set in a tense hunch. "Oh my god, as if you don't get off on the whole broody, tortured soul aesthetic!"

Brennan jolted out a laugh that was equal parts offended and de-lighted, because Cole was *fast,* wasn't he?

There were probably real reasons, somewhere, for Brennan to shut down on the interest that was building. But for the life of him, he couldn't find a good excuse.

By the time Brennan and Cole went back inside, Tony was dozing with his head on Mari's shoulder, snoring softly while Mari sat perfectly still, focusing on the TV despite it being on the Netflix home screen. Mari seemed somewhere between annoyed and charmed.

She looked up when they arrived and glowered. "Not a word."

After Tony crawled off to bed, the last of the pie was wrapped up in their fridge on Cole's insistence, and Mari and Cole left to walk home. Brennan wasn't thirsty again yet but he still wanted to check that the freezer in his closet was undisturbed. It was small but not cheap, but thanks to his mom's credit card and overnight shipping, he had a place to keep the blood. He'd even added a heavy lock to keep the freezer shut.

When he went to close his bedroom door, something blocked it from closing. There was something tucked against the doorframe that he hadn't put there.

Cold seeped into his skin. Someone had been in his room. Or at least at the door. The person sending the text? Could this be another threat?

The anxiety deflated instantly when he turned back and saw a tattered paperback book just inside the door. He reached for it and laughed.

Twilight by Stephenie Meyer.

A sticky note was on the cover, next to the classic pale-hands-holding-an-apple visual:

A VITAL CULTURAL EXPERIENCE, it said in neat block letters, BUT MAYBE RESEARCH?

It didn't need a signature for Brennan to know who it was from.

And. Like.

Goddammit. He was really going to read *Twilight*.

4

ORIENTATION

[Unknown Number]
Ummm wait hold on!
I forgot to ask
Are you going to the meeting??
From the text?
This is Cole btw

Cole
I got ur number from Tony

> **Brennan**
> Hey. I think I'm gonna go.
> I don't have a lot else to go on right now.

Cole
What if they're like vampire hunters??
Or they want to experiment on you???

> **Brennan**
> I'll be careful. I have some time to prepare.
> I need to learn something from them.

Cole
Okay well maybe we should do what mari and I do

for tinder dates, we do code words and check-in times
and stuff so we don't get murdered

Brennan

Um. Yeah. That's a great idea, if you don't mind.

BRENNAN'S JOURNAL

Blood Rationing
- 16 oz per pint
- 1 packet per week??? = ~2 oz per day? Or 8 oz twice a week?
- ~~Less with more animal blood??~~
- Regular, consistent dose instead of waiting—helps manage sensory overload, distraction by peoples' pulses. Needs more experimenting.
- Maybe I can do 1 oz per day? Worried about running out, stealing more. This isn't sustainable. ~~Shit.~~
- ~~Four~~ Three pint bags left

The address, it turned out, was for a trendy-looking café in Boston, about an hour on the university shuttle into the city and then twenty minutes on the T away. It was, if nothing else, comforting that it was public. He couldn't be murdered in public, right? But he was the genius going to meet a group of unknown people who might or might not be watching him, far away from anyone who knew what was going on, so maybe he should be getting a second opinion.

Brennan had had an ongoing mental play-by-play of every terrible outcome that could come about. Popular ideas were vampire hunters poised with stakes and flaming pitchforks, or comically Dracula-like vampire clans come to kidnap him in their quest to desecrate humanity. And Sunny, that had to be a code name, right?

A tentative part of him wondered if, just maybe, he might meet a potential ally. A lead. A friend. Because while he was adapting, living off of stolen blood wasn't sustainable.

This was how his days were going:

Each morning he microwaved a shot glass's worth of frozen blood and took it like medicine, and so far, it was effective in keeping his thirst in check. Notably, the buzz of caffeine quieted the thirst, too, so he'd embraced his inner New Englander and started toting around a large iced coffee from Dunkin. And while he didn't burn in the sunlight, he squinted in the light like never before and wore sunglasses far more often than he used to. He went to classes and tried to keep his mind and senses from wandering while he tried to absorb a fraction of the material.

He fended off calls from his mom. She continued to offer her worries and concerns in between rattling on about her own job and life, and she continued to tell him to use the credit card, as if her giving him money now made up for being a broke workaholic throughout his childhood. She reminded him, as she had all summer, that he could take a semester off "if things got a bit much."

Well, Mom, he didn't say, *everything has officially gotten a bit much.*
He read *Twilight.*

It was . . . exactly what he expected. Not great in terms of literary value or cheap thrills, nothing illuminating in terms of vampire research, but informative about the vampire craze he'd missed out on as a kid.

He went to the library, an escape from a constantly garlic-scented apartment. He went at night, when the quiet let him focus. He'd ended up deep down a rabbit hole of local secret societies, trying to figure out who might know about him. Mostly it seemed like conspiracies, but, hey, no stone unturned.

Cole had run into him in the stacks again, and Brennan gave his review of *Twilight* thus far.

"They don't talk a lot," Brennan said, "they just kind of"—he waved a hand in the distance between them—"angst at each other. It's not really romantic."

"Right!" Cole said, lighting up. "He's kind of creepy. Like, first relationships suck but. Talk about ignoring red flags."

Mostly, though, Brennan waited.

The meeting approached. Saturday, eleven in the morning. It didn't seem like a good place to launch a vampire-hunting ambush. But still, Brennan needed to be prepared for anything.

BRENNAN'S JOURNAL

Weaknesses
- Garlic—yes, obviously, established.
- Silver—burns like a motherfucker. Also, seems like the only way to break skin.
- Side note, I bleed, somehow. It's gross, black, thick, and oozy and doesn't look like blood. Vampire blood?? Research later.
- Wooden stake—would probably kill anyone? But might be part of making vamps "stay" dead? Not something I'm equipped to experiment with right now.
- Fire—Fire hurts. In related news, water is wet.
- Holy water—TBD, ordered some on the internet.
- Rushing water / rivers—nothing, at least, not the little creek in the woods nearby. Maybe bigger bodies of water are bad?

Maybe I should go to the meeting equipped with a bowl of Tony's marinara. It would do the job, worst-case scenario.

BRENNAN'S PHONE

Cole
You on your way??

Brennan
On the commuter line now.
I'll let you know if I die.

Cole
Not dying is preferred!

Brennan
You can't always get what you want.

Brennan's backpack held a jar of marinara sauce, a silver pocket-knife, and an oven mitt to wield it.

He fit right in. The magic of Boston being a city of students meant that he was basically invisible, another white guy with a backpack.

The café was unbearably trendy, all exposed brick and string lights and leafy plants on every surface. The menu was written on a chalkboard. The little storefront was crowded, the outdoor tables full of students talking or studying, the inside just as bustling behind the big glass windows.

If there was a vampire and/or vampire-hunter ambush planned, this wasn't a great place for it. It was very public, and very full of girls taking pictures of their food for Instagram. Brennan's rampant nerves settled down infinitesimally.

His daily dose of blood kept his senses in check, but he felt much duller than when he'd drank a lot. He'd have to note that one ounce a day wasn't enough. Even if lights and sounds weren't piercing anymore, there was still this dry itch under his skin that served as the constant reminder that something was wrong with him.

He scanned the room for anyone who might stand out while he waited for the host. Everyone looked . . . normal. A group of girls studying, a couple outside with a dog under the table. No one who screamed "vampire adjacent." If Brennan blended in, anyone could.

When the host returned, Brennan asked for Sunny. A part of him hoped she'd have no idea who he was talking about, so he could leave quietly and write the texts off as badly timed spam mail. But his (dead?) heart skipped in his chest when the host immediately turned to lead him across the restaurant.

He followed her through the café. She beelined through the small main space and went to a door with a sign that said DO NOT ENTER. Brennan braced himself again to be ambushed or murdered, and when she opened the door, she revealed—

A private room. A large circular table with endless plates of food and pastries. It must have been one of everything on the menu: brioche French toast with fresh strawberries, spicy shakshuka with crusty bread, spinach and feta quiche, a pear tart, chocolate mousse cheesecake.

More importantly, two girls, just as college-aged as everyone in the building. One had pale skin and dark hair, the long limbs of a model. She wore a crop top and cargo pants straight out of an Instagram ad, and was taking pictures of the food. She expertly dual-wielded the latest iPhone in one hand and a DSLR camera in the other. The other girl had brown skin, a pixie cut with coiled curls, and a binder so full of papers it probably equaled her in body mass.

The host quickly went back to her post, leaving Brennan hovering over the table when the girls looked up in perfect unison.

"Oh good, you found us." The girl with the binder smiled. She set down a chocolate croissant and wiped her hands on a napkin, standing up to offer a handshake.

Brennan blinked, taking in her straight-out-of-the-nineties bomber jacket and earnest smile. Brennan shook her hand. She gave his a firm shake, a bit aggressive, and immediately began an enthusiastic ramble.

"We can never agree on where to do these things, and for the record"—she leaned forward, waggling her eyebrows—"I wanted to do laser tag. But we agreed that was more of a second meeting thing. For now, we figured we'd let Sunny get us brunch with her fancy Instagram superpowers. Sound good?"

Sunny didn't look up from her camera, the click of the shutter punctuating the moment of silence as Brennan took in the scene.

"Not that I don't love this energy, or, like, free food, but"—Brennan looked between the two girls—"what the hell is this?"

Sunny took one more picture of the food before peering at Brennan with a thoughtful frown.

"Oh shit," said Sunny. "He's the one who didn't RSVP." Her nose wrinkled.

"RSVP to *what*?"

Binder Girl pouted. "Don't you use Facebook?"

"I mean, I *have* Facebook," Brennan said. "But it's kind of like a phone book nowadays, I don't really keep up with it—"

"Wait, I *finally* figured out Facebook and you're telling me it's already uncool with the kids?"

Brennan grabbed his phone and started to pull up the long-abandoned Facebook app with 99+ notifications on it. Clearly, they weren't going to give him answers, so Facebook it was.

"I told you we should have DM'd him on Insta," Sunny was telling Binder Girl. "I have a checkmark, he'd listen to me."

He scrolled past useless notifications from friends he hadn't spoken to since high school until finally, he saw what they must have been referring to. He gripped his phone so tight that a crack split down the glass screen, catching himself just before his vampiric strength fully crushed it.

bloodsucking memes for immortal non-teens (new england clan)

Brennan put his fingers to his temples while staring at the newly cracked screen, the name alone giving him a headache. This was, apparently and unfortunately, his life now.

"If he didn't RSVP then he didn't get the welcome pack, Nel," said Sunny.

"Oh, gosh, you must have had one heck of a confusing week," Binder Girl (Nel?) was saying, digging through her backpack under the table and pulling out a thick folder. She pushed it toward Brennan, obstructing his view of his phone. "I have physical copies on hand for this very reason!"

He sank into one of the open seats and cautiously took the folder. It was bright red and had a neat label in the upper corner that said VAMPIRE ORIENTATION.

"That's not the reason," Sunny corrected with a wry smile. To Brennan, she added, "Physical copies are all she knows how to do. Nellie's still figuring out how the internet works. She just learned what a PDF was two weeks ago."

"It's the moving picture one," Nellie said with such pride that Brennan hated to burst her bubble, but Sunny had no such hesitations.

"That's a GIF, sweetheart."

Nellie huffed in frustration. "I don't get why it matters."

"So, making sure I have this straight, you guys are *vampires*?" Brennan said, his heart picking up speed with something like hope. "Vampire Orientation" meant they were here to *help,* right? His headache deepened, temples throbbing.

Sunny and Nellie looked at him then and it was like a university stock image with purposefully diverse models, both girls perfectly put-together and beautiful with twin smiles and amused eyes, like they were charmed by his disbelief. They didn't *look* scary, or dangerous. They just seemed like people.

"I'm Nellie. I do community outreach," said Nellie. "Sunny does surveillance, which is a fancy way of saying she stalks people on social media."

"I'm very good at it," Sunny added.

Before Brennan could respond or really process either of those introductions, a new figure approached and loomed over the table.

The newcomer was short and plump, white with a round face. Her arms were crossed in front of her stomach like she was trying to make herself smaller. She was wearing winged eyeliner and a frumpy sweater.

And, more important: she was, without a doubt, the person he had seen at the place he had died. Driving a car that had possibly killed him. Her hair was darker now, an inky black straight from a box, but it was her, he was sure of it. Brennan shot up from his seat, alarm bells going off in his head, but he managed to bite his tongue while she scanned the table, eyes flickering over Sunny, Nellie, and finally Brennan. When they locked eyes, he could tell there were complex calculations going on behind hers. Whatever it added up to, she didn't seem satisfied.

"You must be Dominique!" Nellie said, springing up to give her an enthusiastic handshake.

Dominique crossed toward the table with slow, small steps, casing the room like she was looking for exits.

"It's just Dom," she said.

It was so pretentiously mysterious that Brennan couldn't help it. He snorted. Nellie shot Brennan a dirty look, but Dom's mouth curved into an amused closed-lip smile.

And somehow, her smiling like they shared some secret was what pissed him off enough to say, "We've met, I think. You were driving the car that killed me."

Dom arched an eyebrow. "And you were the idiot standing in the middle of the road that made me crash into a tree."

"Come on, guys," Nellie cut in. "I totally want you guys to get to know each other, but we do have an agenda I'd love to stick to."

Brennan narrowed his eyes at Dom and she stared back, unperturbed. Reluctantly, Brennan took his seat at the table. Dom followed suit.

Nellie clapped her hands together in the universal camp-counselor signal to begin a meeting. "Great, now we're all here, let's get started."

She launched into an impassioned speech that somehow sounded exactly like the speech Brennan's RAs and orientation leaders had given in his freshman year of college. Lots of stuff about *a scary time of transition* and *stepping out of your comfort zone* and *community* and *we're here as a resource.* Sunny sat silently next to her, sipping her iced coffee while scrolling one-handed through her phone.

With Nellie's intense focus not on Brennan, he finally turned to the folder she had given him, which was near bursting with little pamphlets that could have been cutting-edge designs in the '90s, with the WordArt and Comic Sans. There had to be hundreds of them, and dozens of others folded up like zines. They must have been added over time, because each one seemed to reference another ten or more pamphlets, forming an endless chain of leafing through papers. Heaven help him, he was gonna make an organization and filing system the second he got home.

So You're a Vampire; Now What?

The Modern Vampire's Guide to Drinking Blood Safely and Politely

What Your Clan and Clan Leaders Can Do for You
(and What You Can Do for Your Clan!)

And on and on into specifics that Brennan had yet to even consider in all the pages of questions in his journal. His head throbbed faintly. Did Advil work on vampires? Or was he thirsty, yet again? It was exhausting trying to keep up.

On his phone, the Facebook group had post after post about vampirism written by, allegedly, vampires. The number on the screen taunted him. There were thirty-two people in the New England vampires group. So many, but also, so few. It gave Brennan the strange warm feeling in his stomach he'd gotten when he first learned about bisexuality, then depression, and then anxiety. The deep comfort and the deep-seated dread of not being alone in the world.

There were a few frequent posters in the group, including Sunny and Nellie and a few others spread out in Maine and Vermont. One post mentioned a blood drive and blood collection, another advertised that some old, powerful vampire was doing a meetup. Nellie and Sunny posted a lot about when they'd be in different cities—Providence, Port-land, Boston, and beyond in an endless rotation.

"—and that's why it's so important to have trust and transparency within the vampire community," Nellie said, finally stopping for air. "Did you get a chance to look at the pamphlet 'Finding Your Clan'? It's about the types of clans, the different laws and cultures, and how to transfer if you want a different lifestyle." She waited expectantly but was met with blank faces. Brennan, of course, hadn't read it, and Dom was picking at a hangnail, barely paying attention.

Nellie's mouth twitched into a frown, and Sunny didn't even look up from her phone to put a manicured, placating hand on her shoulder for a second before grabbing her coffee again.

"So, just for housekeeping purposes," Nellie said, "the New England clan is an *urban* clan. We stay under the radar, and we don't attack hu-mans, ever, at all, period."

Brennan nodded, because, yeah, definitely, he was on board with not murdering people. But then—

"Um, sorry," Dom interrupted Nellie's latest ramble and Brennan's racing thoughts. "So that's it? You guys keep it secret, drink donated blood, and act like everything's normal?"

"Well, I wouldn't say *that's it,*" Nellie said. "We also provide com-munity and resources—"

"I'm supposed to keep quiet and act like my entire world didn't ex-plode? Like I couldn't kill someone with my bare teeth if I wanted to?"

Brennan flinched.

"Come on," Dom continued, "tell me about the dark powers, the freaky shit!"

"Well," Nellie started, neatening the papers in her binder, "there are other clans you could transfer to if we aren't able to meet your needs."

"Meaning that there are clans that *do* kill people?" Brennan said. He shuffled through the folder of pamphlets, trying to find the one Nellie had mentioned.

Nellie and Sunny exchanged looks.

"You can read up on it later," Nellie said, gentle but firm.

Sunny finally put down her phone and leaned forward to look closer at Brennan. She was intimidatingly beautiful, with perfectly understated makeup. Her eyes flashed a warning. Brennan was reminded again that these were vampires, capable of things he didn't understand yet, and he swallowed hard.

"Obviously it seems strange from a human perspective," Sunny said, far less gently than Nellie. "It's an option, for some vampires."

"But not in the city!" Nellie interjected. "The pamphlets have a map of borders and clan laws by area, but the point is, we don't kill here, and we all have to protect each other by following that."

He finally found the "Finding Your Clan" pamphlet. It unfolded thrice as much as he expected, like a tourist's map. There was a complex map, first of the US and then of New England, all sorts of color-coded borders labeling different jurisdictions. But what Brennan wanted was below it, a description of vampire clans.

A quick scan gave this information:

- Urban—live among humans . . . sustenance from clan-run blood drives . . . maintain secrecy
- Nomads—travel from city to city . . . hunt bits at a time in unclaimed cities and rural areas . . . rules to avoid overhunting and threats to secrecy
- Colonies—traditional . . . established fortresses of vampires and thralls . . . captive human farms and thralls provide sustenance

Brennan's stomach turned, and he slammed the pamphlet closed as if that would make the information go away. His head was spinning in that unpleasant, too-many-thoughts, loud-brain way. His therapist would say—his therapist would tell him to—

"If you . . . did something," Nellie said, slow and careful, and Brennan couldn't look away from the orange paper of the pamphlet, "when you first turned, it's okay. If you're honest about it now, we can handle it."

He stood from his seat, pushing away abruptly with a loud scrape that had even Dom looking up from her fingernails.

"You realize that none of this is *normal?*" Brennan demanded, his chest getting tight, like the room was getting smaller, hotter. "You're talking about human beings! You're talking about *murdering* human beings! Like, *people.*"

"Brennan, let's not get confrontational here," Nellie was saying in a placating therapist's voice that only annoyed him. "We want to be open and honest, even if you make mistakes."

"Mistakes? An overdue library book is a mistake, biting and killing someone isn't a mistake."

He didn't know how to convey the importance of that, the fact that they were talking casually over brunch about covering up baby vampires' first kills. Of course, vampires were dark creatures; that was their whole schtick. Of course murder would seem like nothing, the lives of humans minuscule in the scale of their long lives. How old were Nellie and Sunny, really? How many humans had they bitten? Underneath their deceivingly human exteriors, were they monsters?

Was Brennan a monster, too?

A choked sob pulled Brennan from spiraling, and Dom started to cry, curled in on herself. Nellie and Sunny regarded both of them like fires to be put out. Brennan swallowed around a thickness in his throat, taking in the way Dom's shoulders shook, the way she held back whimpers like she was used to crying quietly.

Maybe she was as lost and confused as Brennan, but her expression wasn't one of horror—it was guilt.

And Brennan knew then that Dom had killed someone. Whether it was the girl missing at his school or not, he would have to find out. The thought made him sick to his stomach—both at the realization, and his own guilt as he watched her cry. Was he being an asshole, or was he the only one being rational?

Even worse were the worried gazes of Sunny and Nellie. He couldn't stand it. He could never stand others' concern, even when it was justified.

"Let's take a walk, Brennan," Nellie said, voice as cheerful as before. But she caught Brennan's eye with the sort of intent that said he didn't have a choice.

He didn't, really. Either walk away and forfeit the treasure trove of knowledge he'd finally found, or pretend he was fine with murder to appease these new and fashionable vampires.

Brennan bit back a groan, proud enough to resist sounding like a kid complaining after getting in trouble with the teacher, and grumbled, "Let's."

5

HANGRY

BRENNAN'S PHONE

Cole
Please confirm if you are dead (💀)
or alive and well (🏃)

Brennan
🏃

....

bloodsucking memes for immortal non-teens (new england clan)
SOON-HEE KIM

Hello vamps and vamplings,

Nellie and I will be doing our normal rounds again this month.

Check out the schedule attached to see when we'll be in different areas of New England. Set up any meetings for questions/concerns/etc for when we're in your area. DM me, not Nel, she's still trying to figure out the phone I got her.

As always, dates are subject to change if something urgent comes up.
Sunny, xxx
3 comments / 12 ❤

> NARRISSA: you two owe me a round of laser tag still, I need revenge on Sunny for last time

   >> SOON-HEE: bet. i'll book us the arena.

> QUINN: extra big shipment this month, the 8th for pickup works for me! See you then!

·················

QUINN MILLER

We're still seeking volunteers to join the committee planning this year's annual NEW ENGLAND VAMPIRE BALL! The vampire ball is the one night each year where the New England clan can gather in person and party our faces off, so join me in making this a night to remember!

Either way, save the date for this March 1, 2025 to dance the night away with your fellow vampires!

12 comments / 28 🖤

> MAX: wouldn't miss it for the world

> EDMUND: um you better put me on the planning committee, no way we're getting a terrible DJ like last year

   >> CRYSTAL: Agreed, let's do live music. So much classier.

   >> QUINN: Love this energy! Please DM me!

Brennan had been to three elementary schools, two middle schools, and five high schools in almost a dozen different cities, and if there was one thing he'd learned, it was how to recognize when someone with authority was going to give him a talking-to. Many a well-meaning school guidance counselor had tried to check in on the new kid who moved around a lot, but by the fourth move, Brennan had realized the best approach to school was to be invisible and stay out of people's way. By age twelve, he'd gotten skilled at dodging concerned questions from adults, and with his good grades, they let him.

Nellie walked next to Brennan in silence as they left the café and walked down a busy street. The jumble of conversations and noises from traffic made Brennan's headache stab a steady rhythm into his temples. He felt like he was being walked to his execution, and each passing moment of Nellie's silence made it worse.

She turned down a less busy side street and Brennan followed, weaving around a group of students in Boston University gear eating tacos from a truck. She turned once more and stopped near a quiet subway entrance.

"Is this where you kill me?" Brennan joked. But also, did not joke. He wondered how quickly he could get to the silver knife if Nellie *did* try to kill him. He still didn't *know* these people, and they talked so easily about death.

"You're hangry," Nellie said.

"Uh." Brennan blinked. Nellie started digging inside her jacket. "What?"

"Hangry? Did I say it wrong? Sunny taught me that. Hungry and angry. You need blood."

Brennan shook his head. He'd been taking his daily rationed amount, and he hadn't felt anywhere near approaching the overwhelming thirst that had taken over before.

"I'm not *hangry*. I've been drinking."

"Not enough."

As soon as she said it, Brennan knew she was right. His senses had been dull and slow, in between asleep and awake. His head had been out of sorts in a fog he'd thought was anxiety for days, but when he thought about it, the haze *was* different, had a sharper edge to it.

"I was rationing," Brennan defended. But the thirst, now that he'd identified it, burned. And Nellie had picked up on it effortlessly. The idea that Brennan could handle this on his own suddenly seemed absolutely batshit, but the idea of accepting help terrified him even more.

Nellie's hand emerged from her jacket with a simple metal flask, and she presented it with an encouraging smile. Brennan felt frozen. What if this was a trick?

Something about her reminded him of one of his old half-friends triumphantly presenting a flask of cheap vodka with a grand flourish back when they were freshmen. Something about the familiarity of it—or the sharp smell of blood filling his nostrils as Nellie twisted off the cap—relaxed him.

He took the flask, and he drank.

It never stopped being strange, how utterly *not* strange it was to drink blood. Each time, in the moment, felt right. Warm and thick and sticky and delicious, consuming him with the fervor of a child with chocolate. It was only afterward that the shame would kick in, the reality of *You just drank human blood, you absolute freak* ringing in his head. (Intrusive thought, his therapist would say. Recognize it, but don't engage with it.)

Even with the shame, it was impossible to deny that Nellie had been right. A few swallows, and he felt a warmth settle over his body like a cat stretching out in the sun, the fog in his head clearing until everything was crisp and sharp and *real*. Brennan nearly gasped with it. It was like the first day of not feeling like crap after a weeklong depressive slump: he hadn't realized how heavy he'd felt until the weight lifted.

"Good stuff, is this organic?" Brennan tried for a joke as he handed the nearly empty flask back to Nellie. His hands fell to his sides with nothing to hold and fiddle with, and he felt bare and exposed under Nellie's watchful eyes.

She kept looking at him, concern twisting into wide eyes and dawning horror.

Brennan cleared his throat. "Thanks."

The lack of thanks was not what Nellie was afraid of.

"You were starving," she said. "You didn't RSVP or get the welcome package, so you didn't know about the blood caches."

Brennan kicked at an empty can on the ground to avoid her earnest, dark eyes. He kept having to remind himself she wasn't human. (He wasn't, either.)

"I wasn't completely on my own, I—" Brennan paused, shrugged. "—I knew a guy."

"What kind of guy? Do you need us to cover anything up?"

The ease with which she made that offer threw him.

"No, it's not—it's just this guy that volunteered with the school blood drive? You don't need to worry about it. I can take care of myself."

"Don't downplay it, Brennan," Nellie said. She lifted a hand and let it drop, like she wanted to comfort him but knew better. "We messed up. I mean, we usually get to new-turn orientations faster, but Travis didn't get the paperwork in on time."

"Travis?"

"Travis is, like, Vampire Jesus," Nellie said, waving her hand dismissively, as if that wasn't the single most interesting thing she'd said all day. Brennan made a mental note to add that to his growing list of questions. "He's the oldest and most powerful vampire in the New England clan, and he always has some sob story for why he *had* to turn someone even though we have strict rules in place for population control and—"

"Sorry, Travis is the person who turned me?"

Nellie blinked. "Yeah. You and Dom. We don't allow new turns often, but yours were special situations."

"What are special situations?"

"Well, like yours. If someone would otherwise die and turning them is a second chance at life. There are some exceptions for turning loved ones or friends. All of this is outlined in the pamphlets, and there's typically an approvals process. Travis tends to ask forgiveness instead of permission."

A second chance at life? That was a weird way to look at ruining Brennan's life. Brennan didn't know how to process that he now had a name for the person who turned him. That girl, Dom, was like . . . a vampire sister. Nellie and Sunny were vampire bureaucrats. It was a lot to unpack.

"Does Travis lead the clan with you guys?" Brennan asked.

"Oh god, no." Nellie laughed. "Well, he used to, ages ago, but now he does his own thing."

"Can I meet him?"

"That's not the best idea," Nellie said. Before Brennan had the chance to protest, Nellie continued, "But look, one of our stations is near here. I can show you how the blood caches work, and then you can go, if you want. None of us are going to force you to do anything."

Brennan wanted to say no, gazing longingly at the steps leading down to the subway. But he also took in Nellie, a person who needed blood to survive, like Brennan. Like Brennan always had, technically.

"Fine," Brennan said.

Nellie pressed her lips together, not satisfied, but maybe a bit appeased, and she tucked her flask into her bag before leading the way out of the alley.

"It's only a few minutes' walk," she said, conversational, and in the same breath, "You really didn't hurt anyone this whole time?"

Brennan flinched like she'd slapped him, his steps faltering while she turned to look at him over her shoulder. "*No*. I'm not—I'm not a *monster*."

Unless I am, a part of Brennan's brain offered, thinking of the girl who had gone missing the day he turned. But before he could go down that line of thinking, Nellie's eyes went fierce and narrow and when she spoke, her voice was low with warning.

"Watch it with that word," she said.

Oh my god, Brennan thought, *there's vampire discourse.* His life was a nightmare.

But more importantly—

"There's this girl missing at my school," Brennan said instead. "Was it vampire-related? Should I be worried?"

"I'll make sure Sunny looks into it," Nellie said. "That's her jurisdiction. She makes sure no one suspects vampires in anything."

"But what about the girl? What if Dom killed her?"

What if he *killed her?* No, nope, no.

"Brennan, this stuff you're stressing about? That's what we're here for! We're your clan. We've got your back."

Nellie weaved confidently through the streets of Boston, turning down increasingly narrow side streets until she approached a quiet corner occupied only by a bodega with the windows boarded up, a man rolling a joint a few yards away, and a drink vending machine nestled into a narrow alley.

"There are hiding spots in discreet areas of each of our main hub cities," Nellie explained, leading him toward the vending machine.

"So stock up for a month or so when you're here. We usually recommend about three pints a week at first"—she scanned him appraisingly, then knelt next to the vending machine, feeling around underneath for something—"but you're tall, so, maybe more. Anyway, that's eight ounces a day, or a pack every two days."

Brennan nodded along with a dazed confusion, like he was getting released from the hospital or getting directions in an unknown city.

"Where do you . . . ?" Brennan started, afraid of the answer.

"Back in the day we paid off some Red Cross lab guys to mark some tests as not-fit-for-donation and pass them off to us. Nowadays, Quinn runs a blood-drive operation out in Connecticut."

She must have found what she was looking for underneath the vending machine, because a panel along the side popped open to reveal a sizable pull-out compartment. She tugged it open with practiced ease, and Brennan followed the movement to see a freezer loaded with hospital-grade packs of human blood, dusted with frost.

Brennan paced a short length, trying to process what exactly a "blood-drive operation" entailed. But one thing was clear, and the pit of anxiety in his stomach from the café rose back up in protest.

"Oh, great, we steal from the Red Cross. That's at least a step up from the murder."

"It's not murder, it's *survival,*" Nellie said.

She stepped away from the freezer and gave a jerky nod toward it, gesturing for him to load up. Brennan looked over his shoulder, but the alley was quiet and hidden, devoid of prying eyes. He took fifteen to last him a month, and layered them carefully in his backpack while Nellie watched.

"What you said back there," Nellie said, jutting her chin in the general direction of the way they'd come. "I get it. Some people have different views on vampirism, and it can seem scary."

"Differing views is an interesting angle," Brennan said, zipping his backpack shut, "considering that murder is pretty objectively bad and not, like, a *viewpoint*—"

"I'm trying to say," Nellie cut in, "with what we are, we can still be *good.* We can choose that."

Brennan scoffed. "While covering up that Dom, like, flipped and killed someone? And standing by while people are"—with a shiver, he remembered, *human farms*—"like, wandering around killing people?"

"Not everyone sees things the same. I don't like it, either, but we've got millennia of politics at play here. I've been a vampire for over ninety years and I've never killed a human. Sunny's been a vampire for three centuries and she definitely *has,* but it's far in the past so it doesn't matter."

There it was again. The horrid question he'd been trying quite hard not to overthink. But now, it wasn't library research, folklore, or fiction. This was a real vampire, telling him this. He couldn't ignore it this time.

With a forced casual tone that Nellie probably saw straight through, he asked, "We're immortal?"

Nellie nodded.

His stomach dropped out from under him. He knew, in his heart, but it was one thing to assume and another to hear it confirmed by someone who ostensibly knew what she was talking about.

Brennan could feel himself about to spiral and jotted that down as something to panic about later. He hadn't thought he'd live to be nineteen, and now he would be nineteen for-fucking-ever. It was the kind of thing he would want to talk to a therapist about, but he couldn't exactly call up Dr. Morris and cry about the woes of being newly immortal without her giving him some new, colorful diagnoses.

Nellie smiled sympathetically, like she could smell his panic with some sixth sense. God, maybe she *could.* She closed the freezer door, replaced the panel carefully, and pushed it into place with a sharp click. Just like that, it was a vending machine again.

Now, her full attention on Brennan, she continued, "The point of an urban clan is that our past mistakes don't matter, as long as we move on from them. We get to live out the lives we should have lived as humans. We get to exist in the world, as people. We get to feel normal. That's what we're offering. If you want it."

Brennan's heart felt like it was in his throat, because that *was* what he wanted. But he couldn't really trust them, could he?

"It's just a lot," he said. "Obviously."

Nellie nodded. "It's a hard transition. You're through the worst of it, physically, but mentally—*yeesh.*"

"Well, don't sugarcoat it."

"I know you don't have much reason to trust me, but, hey, we have nothing but time! I can earn it. And, if you need to talk, I'll be here. As a friend, a mentor, or"—she gave a little shrug—"as a licensed mental health professional."

Brennan blinked. "Isn't it weird to be friends with your therapist?"

"We're vampires, hon, a lot about us is weird. I'm just saying, you can ask me anything." She added, with pride, "I'm on Facebook now!"

Everything in Brennan yearned to bombard her with questions, to take this offered alliance and run with it. He wanted to ask, *Do you have powers? Will I have powers?* and every other question in his journal. He couldn't lie to himself—no amount of research would ever match the wealth of knowledge in that one Facebook group, let alone what expertise the other vampires themselves could offer. She had answers, she had support, and she was offering it on a golden platter. He felt far too much like he was being bribed to the dark side, and he had no reason to trust they were the good guys.

"I need to think about it," Brennan said. He was drafting Venn diagrams in his head already.

Then she went in for the kill, striking when she saw a moment of hesitation like a master salesman.

"Look, we're in Boston once a month, sometimes twice. You can think about it, look through the information, join us next time. We're not going anywhere."

We're not going anywhere. He knew it was meant to be supportive, but it just reminded him of the dizzying confirmation of his immortality and he was flooded with the fight-or-flight reflexes that sent him out of the café. He took a shaky step back from Nellie.

"I'll think about it," Brennan repeated.

The scary part was, Brennan was pretty sure he'd already made up his mind.

Curiosity, meet cat. I'm sure you'll be very happy together.

6

ANYTHING GOES AT THE WAFFLE DEN

A Pamphlet

5 Ways Your Clan Can Help You + 3 Ways You Can Help Your Clan

By Nellie Adams

A vampire's clan is an important and time-honored tradition that serves as a network and support system in today's modern age. (For more information about the history of clans, refer to the pamphlet "Vampire Law History, Volume 16." For more information about efforts to modernize urban clans, refer to "Vampires and Connection in the Digital Age: The New Wave of Urban Clans.") Clans can support vampires in a number of vital ways, but it's just as important that vampires give back to their community.

What Your Clan Can Do For You

1. Orientation
Turning can be a difficult transition. We help new turns navigate vampire life to find their best self. (For more information about navigating vampire life, see "Finding Your Best Vampire Self, Living Your Best Vampire Life.")

2. Protection

As part of the clan, you are protected both from other vampires and from humans. We ensure secrecy is upheld and address any rogue situations. At least one leader of each clan has a significant power rank to be able to protect from larger threats that may emerge. (For more information about how your clan leaders are equipped to defend the clan, read "Lead, Guide, Connect: The Clan Leader Handbook.")

3. Blood Supply

Through decades of deals and through the hard work of our bloodbank operators, we are able to maintain a consistent flow of blood to prevent thirst and unwanted biting. (For more information about managing thirst, see "The Modern Vampire's Guide to Drinking Blood Safely and Politely.")

4. Community

Being a vampire can be a lonely experience, but peers in your clan can offer support, understanding, friendship, or mentorship. You don't have to go through anything alone. (For more information about mentorship opportunities, see "Apprenticeships and Arcane Arts: Finding a Mentor.")

5. Individualized Coaching

Your vampire clan leaders are here to guide you through this experience. Regardless of your skill or interest, there is a way for you to get involved. More important, if you are unsatisfied with your experience in the clan, we can discuss options. (For more information about changing clans, see "When Your Clan Isn't a Good Fit: Requesting Transfers" and "Finding Your Clan: Vampire Lifestyles to Suit Every Need.")

What You Can Do For Your Clan

1. Support Your Fellow Vampires

As you become part of the community, others may turn to you for help, advice, or companionship. It's important to have solidarity with your fellow vampires and support them in their endeavors. (For more information about meeting fellow vampires, see "Get Connected! Engaging in the New England Vampire Community.")

2. Uphold Secrecy Expectations

We all have to do our part in protecting our existence as an urban clan that coexists with humans. Please familiarize yourself with our secrecy expectations by reading "New England Clan Bylaws, Part 12: Maintaining the Veil of Ignorance."

3. Volunteer Your Time

There is always a way to intersect your unique skills and interests with the unique needs of our clan! From helping organize events and talking to new turns to mastering the arcane arts and researching ancient relics, there is always something exciting to be done! See your clan leader about opportunities in your clan and neighboring ones.

The pamphlets were going to be the death of him.

There was no way to organize them. There were more than he'd thought, and some of them unfolded a dozen times and had pop-ups and foldouts. A few had notes on Post-its, or scribbles in the margins. Some seemed to be directed toward very specific situations that Brennan couldn't imagine happening twice. Worse, the majority of them looked to have been reproduced on the world's shittiest copying machine, shadowy and difficult to read. It was an academic's nightmare, on par with the loss of the Library of Alexandria.

Brennan didn't know where to start with a system. There was no rhyme or reason to the titles, so alphabetical was out. One little brochure spanned a variety of subject matter, so dividing by topic wasn't viable. They all referenced one another without any page numbers or table of contents and— He needed to start over.

First he had to interpret the hieroglyphs that were his "orientation" folder.

It was late at night, late enough that the library and the two terrible food joints were the only places open. Naturally, he was at the library.

It was nearly empty, and blessedly quiet. He'd glanced around, half expecting to see Cole talking down a depressed freshman around every corner, but couldn't spot him. Then he'd found the most isolated corner of the stacks he could hide in, sat down on the floor, spread out the maze of booklets, and started reading.

He didn't know how much time had passed when a voice pulled him out of his headspace.

"'So You Want to Date a Human'?"

Brennan got whiplash from jerking toward the voice so quickly. Cole was leaning against a cart of books, reading a stray pamphlet with delight. He continued, "'A Vampire's Guide to Interspecies Relationships and Sex—'"

Brennan shot up from the ground to snatch the pamphlet from Cole's hands. He nearly took them both out in the effort, but caught himself just in time, pressing the pamphlet protectively to his chest.

"Please don't touch things," Brennan said, "I have a delicate system here and . . ."

He trailed off as he belatedly processed that he was too far into Cole's space. He could feel his warmth, hear his pulse. Pink crept into Cole's cheeks and washed over his freckles. The line of his jaw was frankly unfair. Brennan's brain turned to static.

Brennan stepped back, static bursting into silence and replaced with one thought. *He's cute.*

"My *deepest* apologies," Cole said, and was he playing up his accent or was it just coming through thicker than normal? "You're clearly running a well-oiled machine; I wouldn't want to get in the way."

The tornado of pamphlets and zines and printouts stared them down. Brennan cracked.

"If I stare at these pamphlets any longer I'm gonna start imagining them talking to me."

Cole's lips quirked in the beginning of a laugh. "It just so happens I was thinking the same thing about the books I'm supposed to be shelving."

"Sounds like we both need a break," Brennan said. "Or mental help."

"Both," Cole agreed, then gestured at Brennan's spread of information. "Like, where do we even *begin* to unpack this?"

"The vampire meeting was interesting."

"Clearly."

"Now I'm trying to organize their ungodly collection of 2000s Microsoft WordArt pamphlets into something resembling an index."

"Naturally."

"That's basically where I'm at." He paused. "What's your damage?"

Cole laughed. Brennan did *not* melt at the sound. "I have to shelve the rest of these before I can leave."

"Right," said Brennan.

"And I don't want to."

"That's tough." Then he crossed over to the cart of books, scanned the spines, each clearly labeled with numbers and letters. At this point, Brennan probably owed Cole one, and he could use a distraction. "Can I help?"

Cole placed a protective hand on the books on the cart. "You don't have to do that, it's my job." Brennan plucked a book from the end of the stack and scanned the shelf for its home. "Besides, it's not alphabetical, it's—"

Brennan slotted the book into place and Cole's mouth shut with a click. A beat passed and Cole inhaled a shaky breath. Brennan worried he had somehow offended him.

Behind him, Cole spoke, voice low, "You know the Dewey decimal system?"

Brennan turned. Cole was eyeing him with a strange intensity that made his skin prickle the same way it did under the sun—strange, but not unpleasant.

"I practically grew up in libraries." Brennan shrugged. "They were the one thing that was the same no matter where we moved."

It was why libraries always felt like a safe space—why here, at night, he and Cole alone on the floor, he dared to let Cole know him.

Brennan peered back at the books and focused on the task at hand, methodically scanning the cart and shelves. Cole stepped up beside him and reached for a book, shifting it back and forth in his hands.

"You moved a lot as a kid?"

Brennan huffed a dry laugh. "Yeah, you could say that. As a kid, as a teen. Basically until I came here."

"That must have been hard." Cole joined Brennan in shelving. Brennan kept his attention on the books so he wouldn't get distracted by the heat of Cole's eyes on him.

"I read a lot," Brennan said. He meant, *I was lonely*.

"Me, too," Cole said. "I had this little group. Me, Mari, and my brother, Noah. We grew up together and we'd trade and take turns reading books."

"Like a little book club." Brennan smiled.

"Yeah." Cole went a little quiet, took a little too long staring at a book's spine, before he added, "But then in high school, Mari started getting busy with all her APs, and Noah started hanging out with these, like, cliché bully assholes. I joined the school book club, but it wasn't the same, and eventually I got used to reading on my own."

"Like the rest of us losers," Brennan joked.

They shelved books for a few minutes, Cole moving the cart down the aisle as they progressed. Brennan liked the easy monotony of it. Straightforward, repetitive, absolute, a predefined system that Brennan could easily fall into. He could almost be absorbed by it, and ignore the annoying flutter in his chest whenever his eyes caught on Cole's hands for a beat too long, which was happening more and more often. What could he say, the guy had nice hands.

Brennan went to break the silence. "You know—"

"Um, actually—" Cole started.

"Oh," Brennan said. "You first."

"I was just gonna say," Cole said, mouth twisting sideways as he considered his words, "if you need someone to talk to about all the vampire business, you know, my metaphorical door is open. What were you gonna say?"

Brennan suppressed a smile. Somehow, they were on the same page. He had set out to do this thing right—on his own. But Cole already knew, and maybe Brennan needed a second opinion. Or a friend.

"Just, uh . . ." Brennan started. "Kind of a lot happened with that meeting. I don't know how to make sense of it. Do you . . . ?" He didn't know how to finish the sentence without sounding pathetic. *Do you wanna hang out with me?*

Cole didn't miss a beat. "I'm off as soon as I finish this cart."

Brennan glanced down. There were only a few more books left.

"Okay," Brennan said, grabbing one of the remaining books. "Then let's get waffles."

The Waffle Den was a twenty-four-hour breakfast dive outside of campus, alongside a Walmart, a gas station, a cannabis dispensary, and a single stoplight.

Small-town charm with access to urban adventures, the Sturbridge University marketing bragged. It was a pretty way of saying they lived an hour away from the nearest hospital.

Most people who went to the Waffle Den were either intoxicated, on their way to intoxication, or recovering from intoxication; it fulfilled a need for both late-night munchies and morning hangover cures. It always smelled like burnt coffee, pancake batter, grease, as well as cigarette or marijuana smoke, depending on the time of day.

"I love this place," Cole said. "It's the closest thing to a Waffle House y'all Northerners have."

And that was exactly why Brennan liked the place.

"I lived in Ohio for my sophomore year of high school," Brennan said. His mom had gotten a job at the University of Cincinnati. "I had a study group that met at the Waffle House every week." It was the closest he'd gotten to having real friends in high school. At the end of the year, when his mom's contract was up, she had them up and move again.

"Sounds like me and Mari and Noah." Cole smiled. "We used to wreak havoc on that poor Waffle House. I befriended the waitress. I wonder how she's doing."

They got a booth. The place was small and mostly quiet. A lone cook shuffled along, flipping things on the griddle behind the counter, while one punk-looking couple at a table, all leather and brightly colored hair, talked quietly.

A grouchy woman in her forties took their order, brought them coffee, and returned to a book of crossword puzzles. Finally, Brennan got Cole up to speed.

He told him about the meeting, the café, Sunny and Nellie, and the other new vampire, Dom, who had almost definitely killed someone. Which everyone except Brennan seemed to be fine with.

"How am I supposed to be cool with that?" Brennan finished.

Cole sipped delicately at his latte and eased it back on the table, tilting his head.

"Maybe it was self-defense," Cole suggested.

Brennan's own coffee—which he'd taken to drinking black since turning—had been quickly drained. He turned the mug back and forth in his hands.

"Maybe," Brennan said. "But she could also be a ruthless murderer." He brought his fingers to his mouth in a pantomime of a vampire's fangs that probably looked more like a walrus.

"You said she was crying. It sounds like she's a person who made a mistake."

"A *mistake* is like, 'Oh no, I accidentally spilled coffee on the book you loaned me,' not, 'Oh no, I accidentally chomped down, drained your blood, and killed you.'"

"She clearly feels bad about it. I bet she's just like you, trying to figure this thing out and be better."

Something about the idea of that girl being *like him* sent a shiver down his spine. That was exactly what he *didn't* want. Even if they were both vampires, that didn't mean they had anything else in common.

"What about that girl? The one who's missing? What if she's involved?" Brennan said.

"Well, there's no reason to think vampires were responsible besides the timeline, right? So why take it out on Dom when you don't know anything for sure?"

"How can you assume the best about a complete stranger?" Brennan accused.

Cole shrugged. "Hurt people hurt people."

Brennan pushed his coffee mug to the side. "What?"

"Hurt people hurt people," Cole said. "It's something my teacher used to say. People don't just *do* bad things out of nowhere. People hurt people because they've been hurt."

Brennan frowned. "That doesn't mean they didn't still *do* the bad thing."

"All I'm saying is, you could give her the benefit of the doubt."

"It's a miracle you haven't been murdered in the streets," Brennan said. "If someone told you they had puppies in their van, would you look? Do you have any email affairs with wealthy faraway princes you want to tell me about?"

"I don't think it's *naive* to think well of people," Cole said, and his voice had a steely edge that made Brennan bite his tongue. *Naive,* he'd spat out, and Brennan realized he'd hit a nerve.

"I don't think it's naive," Brennan said quickly. "I just—don't get it, I guess."

"Get . . . being positive?"

"Yeah."

"That's fucking depressing."

"Well, I'm fucking depressed!"

Cole's eyes went wide, and then he burst out laughing. "You know, I don't think I've heard you curse before."

"I usually keep it in my head. My mom is a professor, so she is very much of the belief that cursing is a lack of creativity or precision, or something like that."

"And here my mom didn't let me curse 'cause it was impolite, now look at me. Cursing left and fucking right like a goddamn sailor."

"Doing it creatively and with precision, too," Brennan said.

"You just need practice."

Cole shifted in his seat, bringing one foot up on the booth so he was curled with one knee tucked to his chest. Brennan had never seen some-one so unable to sit properly in a chair.

"Your mom's a professor. Does she teach here?" he asked.

"Nah. New Hampshire," Brennan said, souring. "Dartmouth."

"Damn. Impressive."

"Yeah," Brennan said, but it was hard not to let bitterness creep into his voice. "She's very good at academia."

"Oof, and lemme guess, not so good at parenting?"

Head hung down, Brennan said, "Jeez, do I radiate mommy issues?"

Cole laughed again, sharp and loud.

"No! No, that's how my dad is, so I caught the vibe. If I were to describe him, I'd say he's"—Cole wiggled his fingers—"'very good at business.' Same tone."

"Oh. Well. Yeah." Brennan shrugged. "School was always her priority." With some years of therapy, Brennan was starting to accept that.

Cole lifted his coffee mug in a mock toast. "To shitty parents and generational trauma."

Brennan clinked his empty mug against Cole's and smiled.

The waitress returned to drop off their food and Brennan salivated. Their plates were full of oversized waffles, eggs, bacon, and hash browns. Even though he drank blood now, there was still something about the appeal of diner junk food.

"My brother used to put the hash browns, bacon, and eggs on the waffle, fold it in half, and eat it like a taco," Cole offered as he started to dig into his food.

Brennan paused, took in his plate, imagining it. "Was it good?"

Cole shrugged and drowned his waffle in a syrupy death. "I have no idea."

It seemed as good an opportunity as ever to find out. He piled everything onto his waffle, folded it, and took a bite. He put the taco down and chewed thoughtfully.

"It's pretty good," Brennan agreed, and only then noticed the stricken look on Cole's face, as if Brennan had produced a copy of *Twilight* and ripped it in half right in front of him.

"What?" Brennan asked. "Did I not do it right?"

"No that's—exactly how he did it." Cole blinked a few times until the faraway look in his eyes went away. "You should give the other vampires a chance. Dom included."

Brennan's brain tripped over the change in topic. "Uh," he said. "Okay."

"Because if she does mean well, and you don't give her a chance, *you're* the one fucking up. And if you turn your back now, you might not get a shot to change your mind. I'd give a chance to someone who doesn't deserve it over losing them for good, any day."

Cole was too kind and good to be hanging out with Brennan, but he refrained from voicing the thought. Something in the pinch of Cole's lips said he was speaking from experience. Brennan wanted to understand it—he was starting to worry he wanted to know *everything* about Cole—but instead he nodded and tucked into his food.

The conversation turned light again, Brennan telling Cole about the nightmarish pamphlet situation while Cole laughed and asked questions. It felt surprisingly normal, just two college kids at a waffle joint at three in the morning. No secrets or elephants in the room.

This was what making a new friend was like, Brennan realized. He'd forgotten.

"Oh, I forgot to mention," Brennan said as the diner's door shut behind them and they stepped back into the cool night air. The quiet parking lot was illuminated by a single streetlight and the glowing Waffle Den sign. Cole's shoulder brushed his. Brennan reached for his bag and shuffled through it. He found what he was looking for, and presented it to Cole.

"I finished *Twilight*," he said. "It was . . . illuminating."

They stood toe to toe, Brennan shoving his hands in his pockets, Cole fiddling with the pages of the book. Brennan couldn't help leaning forward, like Cole was pulling him into his orbit.

"Yeah? It was actually helpful?"

"Oh, definitely not. But super informative about the *Twilight* craze I missed out on," he deadpanned. "Answered so many questions I did not need answered."

Cole's lips parted into a grin. Was Brennan imagining it, or was Cole leaning forward, too? Not *for* anything, not with intent, but in the slight way you do when you want to be closer to someone. Brennan hadn't experienced intimacy in a hot minute, and he wasn't entirely sure he was breathing.

"I'm glad I could do that for you?" Cole laughed. Brennan got a swoopy feeling in his stomach like the first time he'd ridden a roller coaster: *do that again.* "Does that mean you want *New Moon,* or no?"

Brennan blinked away the haze in his mind of *Oh no he's cute* and said, "Yes, absolutely."

Cole kept smiling and Brennan would read every trashy vampire novel in the world to keep it that way.

"You could come by the library tomorrow and I'll get you a copy?"

"Okay," Brennan said. "I'll see you then."

BRENNAN'S PHONE

"Sturbridge University Meme Center" Facebook Group

NOT A MEME!

Incoming freshman Evelyn VanMeter has been MISSING since September 4 after moving in. Her roommate, family, and the school have not been able to get in contact with her and we're trying to get answers! Does anyone know anything???

[In attached photos, Evelyn smiles into the camera. She has a round face, dark hair. In one photo, she has a pink scrunchie around her wrist. In the other photo, the pink scrunchie pulls her hair back.]

BRENNAN'S JOURNAL

~~Well.~~

~~Fuck.~~

7

A BETTER LOVE STORY
THAN TWILIGHT

BRENNAN'S PHONE

r/sturbridgeuniversity

u/micahlandau

Anyone else noticing dark omens at Sturbridge University?

I apologize if this is not the right forum for this kind of thing, as I'm not typically a Reddit person, but I don't know where else to turn. The *Sturbridge Post* student group all but laughed me out of the room and the official university news won't even meet with me. But something is going on at Sturbridge and no one seems to notice, or care.

It started with a girl breaking a handheld mirror in my ancient history class. Afterward I was on a walk through the forests outside Sturbridge and found a dead squirrel just off the walking path. It was almost deflated, thin and flopping, and it had puncture marks. Like it had been sucked dry. Then another, a few yards away. Suddenly, I felt an intense dark aura all around me, but I couldn't see anyone or anything that could be causing it.

When I got home, I did a tarot reading inquiring about the bad energy and got a really concerning reading that implied a powerful force is hovering over Sturbridge that threatens the existence of the world at large, a force which can only be conquered through the powers of love and enlightenment.

I've seen signs like this before, but I can only hope it's not what I think it is. I'm stashing a few hidden protective and luck charms around campus, and I burned some sage in my apartment, but I'm not sure what else to do.

Has anyone else been noticing dark signs?

>> u/easyalpha: ah, so you're the reason westside village stunk of sage all day yesterday

>>>> u/czarob: I literally thought I was going crazy. That's one mystery solved, I guess.

>> u/clownbe: OP, are you actually being serious right now? I'm not sure if this is satire or fiction or if you're very much on the wrong subreddit for this. Maybe r/nosleep if this is a fictional exercise, and r/witchcraft or r/occult if you're serious.

....

Brennan
[link]
Have you seen this?

Sunny
Unfortunately, I see everything.

....

Brennan
~~Hey Dom, it's Brennan, from the brunch,~~
~~and I wanted to apologize for~~
~~I guess we're stuck together since we're clan mates now and so~~
~~Hey, how are you? No more murders I hope?~~
Hey Dom. It's Brennan, from the meetup the other day.
I figure we should try to get along. Can we start over?

Dom
I would have done the same thing. It's forgotten.
I'm guessing we're both going through a lot of
the same shit right now.

> **Brennan**
> Yeah, maybe. It's definitely been a lot.
> You were turned by the same person as me,
> right? Travis?

Dom
Yeah.

> **Brennan**
> How did it happen?

Dom
Probably not a good conversation to have
over text. Or sober.

> **Brennan**
> Rain check, then.

Dom
Sure. We can get together and talk
shit sometime.

> **Brennan**
> ~~You seem surprisingly normal~~
> Okay, that could be cool.

Slowly but surely, Brennan developed a routine. He'd go to the library late at night with nothing else to do, and Cole—sometimes shelving books, sometimes talking a freshman down from dropping out—always made time to stop by wherever Brennan was camped for the night. They always at least chatted for a few minutes about whatever they were working on. Other times, when it was quiet and Cole didn't have so much to do, he'd sit across from Brennan and they'd talk for ages without realizing. Cole always had stories about shenanigans in the library. Brennan allowed himself to let his guard down.

"Alright, fair's fair," Cole said one night.

Brennan was halfway through *New Moon* and debating Cole on the merits of Team Jacob, his pamphlet organizing forgotten. They were at a table instead of the floor for once, books and papers strewn across it, Cole working on homework while Brennan flipped through pamphlets. He was still too nervous to let Cole help him, at least until he got through reading it all himself. He didn't know what secrets they held that could scare Cole off. Under the table, Cole's ankle was nudging Brennan's in a way that was *probably* accidental but *definitely* distracting.

Cole continued, "I'm making you read my trashy romance, you can make me read anything you want. Hit me with your angstiest poetry recs." He made *gimme* motions with his hands, like, *bring it on.*

"I'll have to think about it," Brennan said. "I need to look at my bookshelf and decide whether to give you something I actually like, or subject you to something appropriately terrible as payback for *Twilight.* Like Rupi Kaur."

"Oh, I actually read Rupi Kaur! *Milk and Honey* was great."

"Oh god," said Brennan. He nudged Cole's foot with his own. "Say you're joking."

"I thought it was nice! I liked the illustrations." He feigned defensiveness, but he was biting back a smile.

Brennan shook his head slowly. "Now you're definitely getting a serious recommendation. Maybe homework, too, for that comment."

"Sure thing, Professor," Cole said, and winked.

BRENNAN'S JOURNAL

NELLIE ADAMS

I know
- She's a vampire clan leader with Sunny. Friends (?) with Sunny. Terrible with technology.

Questions
- Why is she clan leader? What does she want?
- Is anybody really that nice?

Research
- No social media outside of Facebook, or else they're under a different name.
- No other relevant internet record. There are too many Nellie Adamses.
- Facebook is just interacting with the New England vampire group. She's pretty

popular, actually, going off the comment threads, and is constantly telling people to reference the pamphlets ~~even though there's fucking thousands of them~~

- WAIT, UPDATE: Scouring the internet for an ungodly number of hours looking up every record of a Nellie Adams in Massachusetts finally paid off!!! Found an archived article from Harvard University's student newspaper highlighting the first few Black women to graduate from Harvard undergrad. Guess who ~~the fuck~~ is there, looking exactly like she does now, in a photo taken in 1963? Totally wild.

SOON-HEE (SUNNY) KIM

I know
- Also clan leader with Nellie? Possibly second-in-command, or maybe just quieter.
- Good with tech and social media. Some sort of influencer, according to Nellie. Let's see!

Questions
- What exactly does she do?
- How does a vampire become social media famous? Like, shouldn't that be against the rules? Secrecy and stuff?

Research
- Wow, okay. @KeepItSunny on Instagram, with 200k+ followers. Fashion, food, makeup, lifestyle, that kind of stuff. She looks very glamorous, and is living her best life. Her Instagram account is one of the ones that makes you want to kill yourself a little bit. Or is that just me?
- Also active on Facebook, but where Nellie's interacting in the comments like it's a chat room, Sunny's posting the bigger announcement and administrative posts. Like, "we're restocking the blood bank on State Street tomorrow," or "don't forget to fill out this form to let us know if you kill somebody" and the like. (I'm paraphrasing, obviously, but that's the vibe.)
- WHOA—In one comment, she mentions growing up in Korea...in the 1700s. So. Around 300 years old, and better at social media than I'd ever hope to be. And way better than Nellie who said she's over 100? I don't get it, but there's a lot of this that doesn't make sense.

DOM

- My age, ish? Lives in Boston, I'm guessing, because she didn't head to the commuter rail with me after brunch. Possibly was avoiding me after I freaked?
- Turned around the same time as me, by the same person.
- When? Where?
- Possibly, probably, might have killed someone.

TRAVIS

- Turned both me and Dom.
- Most powerful, oldest vampire in the New England clan.
- ??????

BRENNAN'S PHONE

Brennan

So, what's the deal with Travis?
The guy who turned me?

Nellie

Oh. He's a bit of a loner. He lives out
in the forest near your school. —N

Brennan

Can I meet him?

Nellie

Not a good move at the moment. —N

Brennan

You don't have to keep signing your messages,
Nellie, I know it's you.

Nellie

You didn't the first time! I have to be sure. —N

Sometimes, Brennan helped Cole shelve library books, or else Cole did it himself while Brennan sorted pamphlets. For now, he was numbering each of them for reference, but it was becoming increasingly clear that the information needed big-picture reorganization. He kept adding to his notebook, endless pages of discoveries and questions and notes.

One time, Brennan brought coffee from the hipster place near his and Tony's apartment, and Cole commented it was his favorite place. So naturally, the next time he went over to the library, he got his normal black coffee and added a vanilla latte for Cole. It was an afterthought, really, but when he presented it to Cole, he lit up like a freaking Christmas tree.

"You better watch yourself buyin' me coffee, I might fall in love with you," Cole said, Southern accent extra thick, accepting the coffee and bumping their shoulders together. And Brennan realized, a bit belatedly, that he had a *crush* on Cole. A fucking middle school, little-girl, pathetic crush.

"We can't have that," Brennan said. "I'm married to my work."

Regardless, from that point on, if the coffee shop was open when Brennan was heading over, he got coffee for both of them.

BRENNAN'S JOURNAL, THE BACK PAGE

COLE

These little tidbits of knowledge about him keep leaking out everywhere when I'm trying to work on vampire stuff and I don't know what to do with them, so they will go here.

- Snobby about coffee—favorite place is Stino's on campus.
- Skateboarded in high school. For some reason, this really fits him. Him wearing a beanie and carrying a skateboard everywhere he went. ~~God.~~
- Snorts when he laughs, if he laughs hard enough. ~~It's cute.~~
- Not good relationship with parents? Uncertain.
- Knows library janitors by name. He smokes with them sometimes.

BRENNAN'S PHONE

Dr. Mom
I saw you have a B in your Social Theory class.
Is everything okay?

Brennan
I'm fine.

....

Brennan

You can ask me questions about it if you want

Cole

oh you mean like

an interview

with a vampire?????

Brennan

That was awful but I respect that you saw

an opportunity and took it.

They were sitting somewhere in the stacks, shelving cart forgotten a few feet away, when Cole finally took him up on it.

They sat on the floor opposite each other across the aisle, their backs against the bookshelves, the books that had originally distracted them spread open on the floor. Brennan had to remind himself that Cole was like this with everyone, the fierce undivided attention. Brennan just wasn't used to it, was all, which was why his gaze made him feel warm.

"You're sure you don't have any telepathy?" Cole asked, narrowing his eyes at Brennan in faux suspicion.

Brennan leaned his head back against the bookshelf and peered through his lashes at Cole, trying to force his thoughts to become clear.

"Nah," Brennan said. "Unfortunately not."

Cole made a disappointed little sound and played with a fidget cube. That was another thing Brennan was learning about Cole—he always had something to do with his hands, and often an extra fidget toy to offer to Brennan if ever he wanted.

"Can you turn into a bat?" Cole asked, then *giggled.*

"Can I—" Brennan startled out a laugh. "Can I turn into a *bat*?"

"I know, it felt silly as I said it."

"Don't you think I would have led with that?"

"No, I certainly do *not* think you would have led with that!"

They both laughed in the privacy of the stacks. Brennan loved the quiet, the warmth of their laughter, because it felt so normal. Despite the topic, when Cole and Brennan were talking at night in the library, Brennan felt like he was just a normal kid, flirting with the cute librarian.

Not that he was flirting.

But he wasn't. . . . *not* flirting.

It was objectively a terrible time for romance, and Brennan knew that, so he didn't bother entertaining the idea. But he could soak up the nice moments of normalcy for as long as they lasted.

The library was empty, *really* empty, for once, except for the few other library aides manning their various stations across the building. Cole stopped fidgeting with the cube and put his hands in his lap, sitting up, legs crossed, full attention on Brennan. Brennan straightened, self-conscious where he sprawled out on the floor.

"Have you told anyone else?" Cole asked quietly. "Your parents?"

Brennan averted his eyes, wet his lips, pressed them together. He hadn't told *anyone.*

It was hard to talk about anything personal without going back to March. Like, if Cole asked what Brennan wanted to do postgraduation, he'd end up telling him that he didn't plan that far ahead because he hadn't expected to live past eighteen.

He didn't know how to explain to Cole that he didn't want his mom or Cole or *anyone* to worry about him because of all the stuff in March.

So he said, "Nah, my mom's a vegetarian, she'd disown me."

Cole frowned, like he knew Brennan was deflecting and wasn't sure whether to call him out on it.

Brennan seized the pause to fumble for a distraction. "Oh!" Brennan said, snapping his fingers and going to his backpack, digging through for a thick volume he'd pulled from his personal bookshelf. "I brought that anthology, if you still wanted it."

"Dude, of course I want it. I think I can read a couple poems after I put you through *Twilight.*"

Brennan presented the poetry anthology to him. It was an old copy a teacher had given to him when he said he wanted to learn more about poetry, now worn and dog-eared, littered with highlights and notes in the margins from years of revisiting.

"Oh, dope," Cole said. He said things like that, unironically. *Dope. Sick. Tight.* It was probably the least attractive thing about him, and it was *still* somehow charming.

Cole made grabby hands until Brennan passed the book over, and Cole immediately started leafing through the pages. Brennan tried not to flinch at Cole looking at his angsty notes from high school, but Cole was grinning like it was Christmas morning.

"This is so fucking cool, Brennan, thanks," Cole said. He had a way of saying things with a level of sincerity that cut straight to your soul. It made Brennan want to light himself on fire.

"It's no big deal," Brennan said, because it seemed like the thing to say, and because admitting his angsty poetry collection was his pride and joy would make the whole thing even more horrifyingly personal. "Anyway, the ones with a star in the table of contents are the ones I think you should start with. Like a starter pack."

"I'm gonna read it cover to cover," Cole said. "Scout's honor." He held up three fingers in a salute.

"Oh, you *would* be a Boy Scout," Brennan accused. Cole had the whole *always be prepared* thing down pat with the small pharmacy he kept in his backpack.

"What does *that* mean?" Cole asked, indignant.

"I don't know, you're very . . . polite? Very"—he waved his hand around vaguely—"prepared."

Cole cast him a mischievous smile. "I'll have you know I was actually a *Girl* Scout."

Brennan sputtered for a minute and said, "You were not!" He bubbled with laughter and that buzzing *tell me everything about you* feeling he was used to getting around Cole. He leaned forward, propping his chin on his fist.

"Okay, yeah, I was an *honorary* member of Mari's troop," Cole said. "But I went all the way through Juniors!"

Brennan's brain, a useless thing set on destroying him, conjured up an image of an elementary-aged Cole with a Scouts vest and cookies to sell, all smiles and enthusiasm and messy hair. Brennan wondered if Cole was as effortlessly friendly and bright then as he was now.

BRENNAN'S PHONE

Brennan

He tries to kill himself???? That's the climax???

And it's supposed to be??? Romantic????

Cole

I'm sensing you finished New Moon?

Brennan

What a train wreck!

Give me the next one!

It was too easy to fall into the routine of researching vampirism as if it were for a class, as if the pamphlets were a frustrating textbook and reorganizing them his tedious assignment. He could look at it with a clinical distance that way, as a subject for research rather than something that actually affected his life.

Dr. Morris would say he was doing the same thing he did with his mental health. But what was so wrong about that? If Brennan could process his emotions without actually having to feel them, he'd count that as a win, thanks very much!

And then there was Cole.

"'Would I ever learn the outcome of that other fight?'" Brennan read.

Cole, who had Brennan dramatically reading *Eclipse* by Stephenie Meyer on the walk to Brennan's place for *Bachelorette* Night. It was one of the rare days Brennan had come to the library in the daytime instead of in the middle of the night, Cole having picked up a day shift from a coworker. Cole was still nursing the coffee Brennan had brought him, listening along and steering Brennan away from obstacles while his eyes were trained on the words. They would be early by more than an hour, and Brennan was experiencing a threatening mixture of anxiety and excitement at the idea of being alone with Cole in his apartment.

"'The odds of that didn't look so great. Black eyes, wild with their fierce craving for my death'—okay, wow, dramatic—'watched for the moment when my protector's attention would be diverted. The moment when I would surely die.'"

Cole tugged Brennan's arm to keep him from walking into a trash can. Another thing Brennan was learning was that Cole was a touchy friend. A hand on the shoulder, the arm, the back, all these casual touches that made Brennan melt into goo.

"'Somewhere, far, far away in the cold forest, a wolf howled.'"

Brennan paused and stared at the words. "That's the end of the pro-logue. What was the point?"

"It's *ominous*. It sets the scene, Brennan."

Beyond the pages of the book, campus was bustling in full autumn swing. All the trees had their New England fall colors on, but the weather was still nice enough for students to be hanging out in the quads with their blankets, hammocks, and Frisbees.

"It's pointless. And melodramatic, considering readers have no con-text for what's going on—"

Cole halted and shot Brennan a glare laced with amusement. "If you don't respect the *Twilight Saga*, you don't deserve it." He reached to grab the book from Brennan, who held it up and away from Cole, who was *just* too short to steal it from him.

"Ha! I knew these extra three inches would come in handy."

Cole stopped reaching for the book and crossed his arms. He gave Brennan a once-over. "Only three inches, huh?"

Brennan deliberately did *not* pass out. During his half second of floundering, Cole hopped to grab the book out of his hands.

Except—

His hand slipped against the pages and Cole hissed and the sweet smell that lingered under Cole's skin exploded into the air and that fa-miliar tug pulled at Brennan, mixed with panic because he was in a quad full of people and—

Brennan inhaled. The smell was sweeter than homemade cookies baking in the oven, warmer than freshly brewed coffee. But it wasn't all-consuming like it had been before.

Brennan exhaled. And he was neither lunging toward Cole nor away from him. Senses piqued, adrenaline rushing—but he'd drunk today.

"The Modern Vampire's Guide to Drinking Blood Safely and Po-litely" recommended half a pint per day, or a pint every two days. When Brennan had been rationing, he'd been lightly starving himself. Oops.

He glanced around. A girl sitting on a blanket with her laptop and a stack of books, a couple passing by holding hands, a group of guys kicking a soccer ball. He could hear each of their pulses if he focused hard enough, but none of them spared him a glance.

He wasn't freaking out. He was in control. Finally.

"You still keep Band-Aids in your back pocket?" Brennan asked.

Cole was bracing himself, pinching his forefinger with his other hand, a smudge of blood on his fingertips. And Brennan never thought he'd be into fingers, or blood, but there he was, wanting to lick them clean.

"Um, yep. Yeah, I do," Cole said, eyeing Brennan like he still wasn't convinced Brennan wasn't going to eat him.

Fuck, Brennan wasn't convinced himself. Heat rushed to his cheeks. He still wasn't sure how vampire blood worked, so he wasn't sure if he should be worried about blushing. He ducked his head and crossed behind Cole to dig in the back pocket of his backpack, where Cole seemingly had a small over-the-counter drugstore: painkillers, cold medicine, allergy medicine, lactose relief, menstrual relief, even a few multivitamins.

Brennan laughed at the extent of it, grabbing the variety pack of Band-Aids and zipping the pocket closed again. "Is this some sort of small business?"

"No, but I like to be prepared."

"You're not even lactose intolerant."

Cole whirled around, still holding the paper-cut finger. "I don't menstruate either, hon, and I don't take women's multivitamins." He blinked, then amended, "Well, not all the time. They do wonders for your nails and hair."

Brennan stepped closer to Cole, tugging his hand toward him.

"I guess I like being the person who can help when someone's like, 'Does anyone have an Advil?' Or, a pen, or a charger, you know?" Cole trailed off as Brennan cradled Cole's hand in his own and unwrapped the Band-Aid. He couldn't have been bleeding that much, but blood was still smeared across the tips of his fingers. Cole's hands were smaller than Brennan's, delicate with long fingers, like a pianist's.

Fuck. Brennan still wanted to lick them, and not even in a vampire way.

Brennan put the Band-Aid on, and when he finally tore his eyes away from Cole's fingers, Cole was watching him intently, head tilted like Brennan was one of his calculus homework questions.

"What?" Brennan asked.

He was still holding Cole's hand, standing too close to him. He dropped Cole's newly bandaged hand and stepped back, face burning, then circled back behind Cole to return the pack of Band-Aids. Why hadn't he passed Cole a Band-Aid to put on himself, like a normal person? God, he got *one* badly timed crush and completely forgot how to act like a person.

"Nothing, just . . ." Cole shrugged, the backpack shifting with the movement. "You blush blue."

Brennan's whirlwind of self-deprecating thoughts slammed to a stop. "What?"

"Well, I mean, I think . . . ? It kinda makes you look sickly, to be honest, but I think that's what it is?" He paused. Turned around to face Brennan again. "Am I making you blush?"

Brennan slapped a hand over his cheek, as if he might feel evidence of the traitorous color.

"Shit, how noticeable is it?" His brain shuffled through all the times he may have blushed in front of someone in the last few weeks and whether they may have noticed something weird about him. But then, he'd only blushed recently around Cole. "Would you see it and be like, 'That guy's a vampire'? Or would people just think I'm about to puke?"

Cole giggled. *Giggled.* "Not noticeable, unless you're looking for it."

They resumed walking, side by side, and Brennan felt like he could think again once Cole's unwavering gaze was off him. They left the crowded quad behind them, the path narrowing. But then—

"So you've been *looking* for it?" Brennan asked.

"I've gotta take the clues I can get."

They turned down the street toward Brennan's place down the block.

"You make it sound like I'm some sort of mystery."

"I feel like," Cole started, and that was another one of his things. He added these qualifiers to his statements, watering things down with *I feel*s and *I think, maybe*s. "I don't know, you can be kind of hard to read, sometimes."

Brennan had been told the same thing by his mom, two teachers, and three therapists. Dr. Morris traced it back to his mom and his childhood, as therapists often did, and said he was too used to being independent. It was a nice way of saying he started being depressed and lonely when he was ten years old and hadn't stopped since.

"Well, that's awkward," Brennan said. "Because at this point you know more about me than my mom does."

"I really doubt that. Because she doesn't know about the vampire thing?"

"It's a pretty big thing, wouldn't you say?"

"Yeah, sure, of course, but . . ." They approached the porch entrance to Brennan's apartment, nestled in a row of cozy brownstones. Cole stopped in front of the door and shoved his hands in the pockets of his hoodie. "I mean, I know you're a vampire, I know you read angsty poetry, I know you're a nerd for systems and organization and that you like *Twilight* even though you won't admit it—"

"Okay, *that's* blatantly untrue—"

"But I don't know what goes through that head of yours. I don't know how you *feel*."

Brennan hesitated, lingering a few steps behind Cole, still on the ground in front of the stone stairs to the door. "About what?"

He had a hypothesis.

Cole shuffled his feet, facing the door. Brennan took in the curls on the back of his head, the headphones around his neck, his short, lean frame.

Brennan desperately wanted Cole to address the elephant in the room that was their flirtation, but more than that, he *needed* Cole *not* to. Because if Cole asked Brennan how he felt about him, he might just be honest, and he might just do something reckless like kiss Cole's perfect face. Which was getting harder and harder to view as a Bad Idea.

Brennan took the two steps up and stood next to Cole in front of the door. Brennan traced the curve of his jawline with his eyes while Cole stared forward, mouth twisted in thought.

Their shoulders brushed when Brennan moved past him to unlock the door.

He pulled it open as Cole said, "I mean, I don't know, I guess . . ."

They stepped into the apartment and Cole trailed off into silence at the sight of Mari and Tony sitting on opposite ends of the couch, arms crossed over their chests, both looking straight ahead where the TV was dark and lifeless. The ice in the room was tangible.

"Don't you guys have class?" Cole asked, and for a second he almost seemed disappointed. Like he'd expected them to be alone, too. Like he wanted to say whatever he'd been about to say half as much as Brennan had wanted to hear it. But it was gone in an instant, evaporating into concern. "What's wrong? What happened?"

Tony opened his mouth to respond but Mari shot him a glare so cold he slumped back into silence immediately.

"I fell asleep while we were studying. Well, *I* was studying, Tony was playing *Call of Duty.* And *Anthony* here didn't wake me up for my four thirty class because he wants to ruin my life—"

"I just thought you could take a sick day and rest—"

"—and sabotage my perfect attendance, my scholarships, my *career*—"

To Cole and Brennan, Tony said, "She already emailed the teacher and got an alternate assignment."

"And now we're sitting in silence until it's *Bachelorette* time so I don't commit manslaughter before I can graduate summa cum laude," Mari finished, and offered an unhinged smile. "Does anyone want wine?"

No one dared accept the offer as she stormed toward the kitchen. Cole caught Brennan's eye with an apologetic look before following Mari.

Tony queued up their trashy reality show of choice on the Xbox. He was deflated and noticeably quiet, so Brennan shuffled farther into the living room.

"That seemed . . . tough?" Brennan tried.

Weeks of living together, and Brennan still didn't quite know how to communicate with Tony. Cole was easy, and with Mari, he could talk academics, but Tony's brand of broeyness wasn't something he knew how to approach. He half feared Tony saying something misogynistic along the lines of *bitches be crazy.* But Tony surprised him.

"Look, I know she cares a lot about school and the rules and stuff, but she's been working herself to death. She needed to sleep."

Brennan had gotten the impression Tony was interested in Mari, but he hadn't realized Tony actually *cared* about her. Before he could figure out what to say, Mari's voice spoke up, distant but clear even through the kitchen walls. He didn't mean to eavesdrop, but his hearing, bolstered by a refreshed drinking regimen under Nellie's instruction, tuned from Tony to Mari like changing radio stations.

"It's not even about that. I get that he cares, it's just, the irresponsibility. The lack of accountability. You know?"

Brennan blinked and refocused on Tony, whose expression was that of a kicked puppy.

"Um," Brennan said.

This was *so* not his business. But they were, if not quite friends yet, then candidates for friendship, and maybe this was the kind of thing you did when you were maybe-almost-friends with someone.

"Like, he barely apologized. He just kept making excuses," Mari was saying from the other room.

Brennan pinched his nose and exhaled. Maybe he shouldn't eavesdrop, but he didn't need vampiric powers to tell Tony to apologize.

"Maybe," Brennan started, "and I'm brainstorming here. But maybe it's more about the accountability. I know you had good intentions, but you messed up her schedule, so . . . own up to it and apologize some more." Brennan sighed. "You *did* apologize, right?"

Tony avoided his eyes. "She knows that I'm sorry, or whatever."

"But did you *say it*? The words? 'I'm sorry'?"

"Possibly not," Tony mumbled.

Brennan nodded toward Mari and Cole in a silent *Then go.* Tony looked like he'd been drafted to fight a war as he made his way to the kitchen.

Brennan stared at the TV screen, where another show that wasn't *The Bachelorette* or *Love Island* sat ready to play. How many of these were there? Brennan feared he might find out.

He waited a few moments before Cole, Mari, and Tony emerged from the kitchen. Mari was taking a call, and lingered by the door muttering "yes" and "okay" into her phone. Cole and Tony took their now-designated spots on the couch.

Brennan searched both of them for evidence of carnage. "So? What happened?"

Tony shot a double thumbs-up as he kicked his feet onto the coffee table with a grin. "All good."

Brennan looked to Cole for a second opinion. Cole shrugged like he didn't believe it himself. "All good," he agreed.

Brennan slid into his designated spot on the floor. Cole sat behind him, his knee brushing Brennan's shoulder in a way that was too distracting. Maybe Brennan had done some good for once, solving problems instead of creating them.

The feeling lasted all of a second, and then Mari hung up her call and pocketed her phone, saying, "Well, that was fucking weird."

"Me apologizing is *not* that weird," Tony started.

"No, Dr. Huong called, and apparently we were missing a bunch of samples in the last batch from the blood drive," Mari said.

Brennan's breath caught in his chest. "Wait, what?" He tried to keep his curiosity casual, but he was anxious to get an idea of what exactly they knew.

"Yeah, seriously!" Mari said. "What kind of freak would steal blood from a university?"

"I'll tell you who," Tony said, with enough confidence that Brennan convinced himself for a millisecond that it was over, the jig was up. "Vampires."

"Oh please," Mari said. "It's some shitty prank. Or something for rush week. Did your friends upgrade to blood sacrifices since you left the frat scene?"

Mari pocketed her phone and joined them on the couch with a bottle of wine, not bothering with glasses. Brennan feigned disinterest even as anxiety roiled in his stomach. Did they have suspicions? Or was this just gossip?

"Come on, vampires is the natural line of logic. My nonna always said she met vampires in her youth. Are you calling Grandma Esposito a liar?"

Mari sighed and took a swig of wine before passing it to Cole. "Cole, can you please tell Tony that vampires aren't real?"

"I would never disrespect Grandma Esposito like that," Cole said, accepting the bottle of wine. "Speaking of vampires, if Josh C. doesn't get kicked off this episode I'm giving the fuck up."

Cole caught Brennan's eye and tilted his head back as he took a drink. Brennan followed the motion with his eyes—the arch of his neck, the bobbing of his Adam's apple. Tony clicked play and Brennan tried not to blush blue when Cole shot him a smile.

Brennan was endlessly grateful for Cole's help, but anxiety lingered in the back of his mind even as conversation devolved into discussion of the show. Even if they didn't know when exactly the samples went missing, Mari had seen Brennan the morning he'd stolen them. He had to hope she wouldn't connect those dots.

But when he cast a glance in her direction, he caught Mari studying him with narrowed eyes and a tilt to her head for a split second before she averted her gaze.

Brennan stayed quiet the rest of the night.

8

VAMPIRE JESUS

BRENNAN'S JOURNAL

Travis
- Turned both me and Dom.
- ??????
- Nellie & Sunny don't like him (?)
- Located in woods near school.
- "Eccentric." "loner."

THE BRIDGE TO NOWHERE

Dom hit me with her car in the middle of the woods, and Travis turned us both. Is it so wild to think I might be able to find him through the power of sheer will and determination and staking out the forest like a stalker?

Sturbridge Forest—About twenty-five square miles just across the highway from Sturbridge U and the tiny town of Sturbridge itself. One stoplight in the whole town. Paths for biking and hiking all through the woods.

The bridge is three miles southwest of Pike's Point.

The bridge, though? Isn't on any map. Google Earth glitches out in the forest, and the roads on Maps only show the major hiking trails. And the bridge is down a side road.

I guess, for the sake of research, it might be important to note that the bridge is also where I attempted suicide. I never knew who found me, assumed it was some hiker, but. I don't know.

What matters is that someone (Dom?) hit me, and someone else (Travis?) turned me. And Travis might be able to fill in those gaps, so I have to talk to him. Whether Sunny and Nellie want me to or not.

Stakeout
- 11/02 nothing
- 11/03 a pair of bicyclers, no cars
- 11/04 nothing
- 11/05 nothing
- 11/06

The sound of tires on dirt cut through the forest like a knife and Brennan jolted out of his reading haze. He was sitting on the bridge, at the peak of its arch, leaning back against its stone rails with his legs outstretched in front of him and reading *Eclipse*.

His stakeout had been less than successful thus far. Except for a pair of bikers who looked like they'd gotten lost, Brennan hadn't seen any trace of activity. The paths that led here were all narrow and shrouded by trees, the whole area hidden in plain sight.

But an engine grumbled, and tires kicked up dirt, and Brennan leapt to hide himself from view on the other side of the bridge, hidden by trees.

The car rolled into view, and Brennan stilled.

There was a flash of light from the headlights, and it was so reminiscent of the night he was hit that for a moment he was back there, standing in the dirt, seeing the flash and thinking, in slow motion, *Well, shit,* before impact.

His heart was racing and he couldn't breathe. Because after the light flickered over his eyes, he saw *the* car. The one that hit him. Dom's.

The car crossed the narrow bridge and came to a stop on the other side, right before the thick overgrowth blocking the path. The engine stopped, and the headlights turned off. It was starting to get dark, especially in the shadows of the forest.

The driver's door opened. An inky black bob emerged, attached to a short, round frame. Brennan peered around the tree that hid him, the rough bark pressing into his palms.

Dom, wearing all black but definitely, undeniably *Dom,* slammed the door closed and walked toward the overgrowth. She checked over her shoulder as she locked her car, turned back to the overgrowth, and lifted a hand as if to knock.

But Brennan, shifting a half step to the right to get a better view, stepped on an uneven spot and the *crack*ing snap of a branch burst through the air like a firework. Dom whipped toward the sound like a predator hearing its dinner, and Brennan couldn't even stumble back into hiding before she was looking right at him.

"Brennan," she said, not quite surprised. She turned away from the dead end and hovered near the door of her car. "Why are you creeping around the woods? You look like a stalker."

Brennan could ask the same thing, but anger and confusion and anxiety bubbled up in his stomach until what came out was "Why are you still driving the car that killed me?"

Dom had the nerve to roll her eyes. "What was I supposed to do, get rid of it over a dent?" she asked. "Besides, you're not dead."

Funny enough, there was still a decent crater on the car's front bumper. Blood could be washed away, but the dent couldn't be totally smoothed over. Brennan shivered and resiliently did not vomit.

"What were you doing in the area, then?" Brennan asked. "And how did Travis end up turning us?"

Dom glanced over her shoulder at the dead end.

"You want to ask him yourself?"

Brennan took in Dom in all her new Goth glory, took in the overgrowth behind her, the trees and bushes winding together in intricate braids. It was almost unnatural. It was almost *magical.*

"You're kidding me," Brennan said. "How?"

Dom shrugged, then turned and knocked on the thickest tree trunk. Banged on it, really, with a tight fist. Brennan closed the distance between them, passing her car and standing a few feet behind her, looking over her shoulders.

"You know him? That's why you're here?"

"We've kind of been friends since I turned," Dom said, like it was to be expected. "Now come yell with me, the asshole probably fell asleep."

She banged harder against the wood and took a deep breath to shout out, "*Travis!*"

This was the best lead Brennan had gotten in a while, and he had nothing better to do, so then they were both banging on the tree trunks and shouting for Travis.

After a few calls, Dom changed to, "*Hey, asshole!*" and Brennan started laughing, and that was when the trees started to shift.

They unwound from one another like vines growing in a reverse time lapse, stretching apart and away in intricate patterns. Cole had said that vampires made the world feel more magical, but this was the first time Brennan felt it. The plants curved to the side, opening like a curtain in a wide arc that led to an impossibly huge clearing.

It was an expanse with wild tall grass, littered with hunks of metal, trinkets, and lawn ornaments, a few tires and lawn flamingos scattered about like sprinkles. Across the field was a structure that could generously be called a shack, next to an equally ramshackle greenhouse and two chicken coops with approximately eight thousand chickens toddling about a fenced-in area, clucking and doing their chicken thing.

Standing halfway between the structures and the entrance was a man with a mess of dirty blond hair in the kind of not-quite-dreads that white people get when they just don't wash or brush their hair for an ungodly amount of time. From a distance, he cupped dirty hands around his face and shouted,

"VAMPLINGS!"

The guy with the blond dreads—who, Brennan was realizing, was Travis, the oldest and most powerful vampire in the New England clan—started toward them, moving with a pep in his step and a wide grin. He wore denim overalls and nothing underneath, giving the illusion of a sexy farmer costume.

"Hey, lil dudes," Travis said once he'd gotten close enough not to shout.

Brennan tried to keep his jaw shut over the fact that this was the Vampire Jesus who had turned him. And he was a literal hippie, with an accent somewhere along the lines of Australian, who said the word "lil" out loud, on purpose.

"Dom! I wasn't expecting another friend, but the more the merrier, right?"

The Australian accent was wrong somehow, a bit too strong, like someone doing a Steve Irwin impression.

Travis went for a hug from Dom. Brennan couldn't quite believe that Dom hugged him back. Travis turned to Brennan right after and held open his arms.

"Are you a hugger? I'm a hugger," Travis threatened.

"Please, god, no," Brennan said, and it came out panicked enough that Dom and Travis thought it was a joke and laughed it off.

Travis settled for punching Brennan in the shoulder and saying, "It's good to see you in one piece, brother! You were pretty banged up last I saw you."

Brennan was too busy taking in Travis to process the bundle of fur that pushed its way through the tall grass until it launched itself at Brennan.

Some sort of Lab with sandy, shaggy fur jumped on Brennan with its front paws, tail wagging violently. She nudged a wet nose into his stomach and Brennan relented, petting her and laughing in delight, vampire lord forgotten. Brennan's mom had never let them have pets since she wasn't around enough, but he'd always wanted one.

"Rosie, down!" Travis called, and the dog dropped down but continued to wag her tail and nudge her head against Brennan's legs.

"It's okay," Brennan said, scratching her behind the ears.

"Come on, come in!" Travis said, waving them down a path of slightly flattened grass that led to the shack. "I have tea on and joints rolled."

They walked through the scattered bits around the yard, like a graveyard for destroyed sculptures. A garden gnome with the head kicked in. Metal sheets, twisted up and cast aside; yard signs for elections, battered and scattered; a light-up reindeer from some Christmas decoration with one leg removed.

Ahead of them, the shack of a house was slightly left-leaning, shingles falling, lots of spots on the building patched up with planks of wood and sheets of metal or plastic. The coops and the greenhouse were in better shape than the actual house. As they passed, Brennan noticed the greenhouse was full of cannabis plants. The thick and musky smell of weed and incense was overpowering even from afar, and the chickens clucked in a cacophonous chorus, and Brennan didn't know how Travis or Dom could *stand* it.

Once they started moving, Rosie ran ahead, running through the fields and barking happily. An old-school doghouse was set up under a tree a ways away from the house and coops.

"Now, it's no castle," Travis said cheerfully, moving a tarp that acted as a front door out of the way so that the group could sidle through the narrow space. Brennan squeezed through, afraid to touch anything wrong in fear of the whole structure crashing down.

"I love what you've done with the place," Dom said, voice deadpan. Travis's Cheshire Cat grin went impossibly wider.

"You noticed the new stop sign?" Travis asked like a kid at show-and-tell, gesturing behind him to a large road sign that still had dirt clinging to the bottom of the post.

"Really brightens up the place," Dom said.

"I thought so, too," Travis said, oblivious to Dom's sarcasm. He waved for them to follow and turned around.

The house was impressive, in the horrifying way a hoarder's home would be. Every surface was covered with *stuff*. Magazines. Books. CDs, tapes, notebooks, newspapers, boxes full of papers and envelopes. A tremendous amount of weed. Gallon-sized ziplock bags of it, and containers full of rolled joints, and grinders and all the associated gadgets, left around each corner of the shed-sized home. There was a small kitchenette to one side, with a mini fridge, stove, and microwave.

How the hell did this place get electricity? The whole building had to be a fire hazard. Brennan wasn't a neat freak by any means, but this left him itching to grab a couple of garbage bags. How could so much *stuff* exist in such a small space?

Travis pushed a pile of books onto the floor, off a couch that had likely seen better days judging by the stains, burns, and rips across the fabric. It creaked dangerously and leaned a few degrees to the right. Travis gestured in invitation at Brennan and Dom. Dom took a seat easily while Brennan hovered near the door and decided he'd be better off not touching anything.

The dog, Rosie, followed them inside, squeezing through the narrow space to sit directly on Brennan's foot. Brennan patted her head. She looked up at him with adoring eyes. Brennan's heart melted.

Travis reached to grab a pill bottle and shook out a joint, looking at Brennan with his ever-present grin.

"Talk about fun surprises. I never get visitors, but I always love meeting new turns. What brings you here?" He raised his pointer finger to the edge of the joint and it lit with a spark and a flare. Brennan tried not to look too impressed as Travis offered Dom the joint and she took it. Travis elbowed her good-naturedly. "Besides the free weed, hah!"

Brennan awkwardly leaned against the mini fridge, the only surface he was confident wouldn't collapse. He focused his attention on the dog in front of him instead of the two vampires, threading his fingers through the fur on her neck.

"I wanted answers," Brennan said. But he had about a thousand more questions than when he'd set out for the forest.

"Ooh, fun, *fun*," Travis said. "Can't guarantee I have 'em but I can sure try!"

Brennan wasn't sure where to start. Dom offered him the joint and he shook his head. He wanted to keep his head clear. She shrugged and passed it back to Travis.

"How old are you?" he blurted.

"Oh," Travis said. He feigned checking his watch, emphasizing his bare wrist. "Well, today's Saturday, so . . . Um, I don't know, a bajillion?"

Brennan tried to school away his disappointment but he was sure it was visible. What was the point of him coming if Travis wasn't going to tell him anything valuable?

"I'm somewhere in the mid–six thousands," Travis answered. "I lost track in the eighties."

"Which eighties?" Brennan tried to imagine Travis in the 1980s, the 1880s, the 1780s. He was going to give himself a headache.

"Precisely." Travis pointed at Brennan. "Good questions. Keep 'em coming, you've gotta be curious. If you work real hard, someday you can have all this."

Travis gave a grand gesture around the shack and Brennan was honest-to-god unsure whether it was sarcastic or not. He hoped with sudden ferocity that he would never live to be six thousand and *anything*. The thought was unsettling, so he cut to the chase:

"How did I turn?" Brennan asked. "What happened that night?"

Travis took a long hit and exhaled the smoke back toward Brennan. Brennan fought the urge to sneeze.

"Well," Travis said, "our girl Dom here hit you with her car, swerved into a tree, and stumbled out of the wreck looking for help. Luckily, I smelled the stench of a bloodbath from a mile away and found you guys."

The word "bloodbath" sent a chill through Brennan, because it was hard to imagine being the center of a bloodbath, bleeding out on the ground, *dying*.

"You were in pretty rough shape, so it was either let you die or turn you, so I made an executive decision."

Brennan took a deep breath to calm himself and asked, voice carefully level, "And Dom?"

"I was hurt, but not as bad as you," Dom said. "Then I thought I killed you, so I was kind of a mess."

"I couldn't stand seeing the lil lady sad, so I offered her the chance at a new life, too."

"Didn't exactly read me the fine print though, did you, asshole?" Dom said, elbowing Travis and accepting the offered joint. She was smiling, though, something Brennan wasn't used to seeing on her.

"Please, you love it," Travis said.

"I do."

"Why us, though?" Brennan interrupted the vampire pride parade he couldn't relate to. "People die every day."

"You were in my domain," Travis said, like it was simple.

"Your . . . domain," Brennan repeated.

"All the woods north of Sturbridge."

"And you guys," Brennan continued, "are . . . friends?"

"Yeah!" Travis said, giving one lazy jazz hand as if to say, *Ta-da!*

"It's nice to have a mentor who's a bit more low-key," Dom added. "Nellie is a bit . . . enthusiastic."

"Plus, Nellie's way hardcore into the urban schtick," Travis said, nose wrinkling at the sentiment. "I never got the whole pretending-to-be-human thing. No point in pretending to be something you're not."

Dom was nodding along, eyes bright for the first time since Brennan had met her. Annoyance flickered through Brennan. He wasn't *pretending* anything. He was trying to keep vampirism from ruining his life.

"Hey, does she still have all those pamphlets?" Travis laughed. "You know, back in the old days vampires used to be fearsome. Now people think we're *lame*. Or, worse, *sexy*. The sparkly vampire thing is the worst thing that's happened since Vlad slaughtered the whole eastern castle colony."

Every word out of Travis's mouth left Brennan with a thousand more questions. Castle colonies? Vlad? Old days of vampires?

"I know the beginning of all this is pretty crazy," Travis said, which was as unhelpful as it was uninformative. "But you'll figure out in your own time what being a vampire means."

When neither Dom nor Brennan seemed satisfied, he took a long pull from his joint.

"Don't overthink it," he said. "Trust yourself. Trust your handy new vampy instincts. Do what feels right, and you won't do anything you shouldn't. Well, I mean, I don't know your life."

"That's your advice?" Brennan said. "Follow your instincts and hope you don't accidentally murder anyone?"

Travis grinned and leaned forward conspiratorially. It came across as condescending, like he was taunting kids with candy. But Dom leaned in for the secret and Brennan couldn't help the curiosity that kept him from running away from all the madness.

"Here's something Camp Director Nellie won't talk to ya about," Travis said, stubbing out the roach of the joint in a mug that acted as an ashtray. "Have you drank from a human?"

Brennan's stomach dropped and he studied his hands where they were folded in his lap, avoiding Dom's gaze, his kind-of friend who had still, possibly, killed a guy, and Travis, his possibly deranged vampire-creator.

But Dom didn't answer. Travis continued, "You can drink from some-one without turning them. And without killing them. And that shit"—he gave a little chef's kiss to dirty, calloused fingers—"is better than any drug I've ever had."

Rosie moved from her perch on Brennan's foot and ran to Travis, whining. Brennan couldn't have said it better himself, thanks, Rosie!

"Is it dinnertime already, Little Rosebud?" Travis asked, and hopped to his feet, leaving Brennan still reeling from the information. He went to the mini fridge and Brennan sidestepped to get out of his way, while Rosie followed Travis with an excited wiggle.

Travis produced a bag of blood from the fridge, ripped open a corner with his teeth, and poured it into a bowl. Then he put the bowl on the floor and Rosie began licking it.

"No way," Brennan said. "The dog is . . . ?"

Travis brushed his hands on his overalls and patted Rosie's haunch while she eagerly drank blood from her bowl.

"She's been my loyal companion for something like a century now," Travis said. "Ever since Sunny and Nellie took over leading the clan. I retired to my domain in the woods, just me, Rosie, and enough weed and blood to go around. Can't complain."

Brennan swallowed around his dry throat, and the walls of the small shack somehow seemed closer than they'd been a minute ago. Now that he listened closer, the dog didn't have a heartbeat. She was eerily silent.

Brennan wondered why an immortal being would choose to be alone, save for a vampire dog, in a shack in the middle of nowhere. But it occurred to him that maybe Travis hadn't chosen this. That maybe everyone he'd ever loved had died and now Travis was the only one left to share war stories with new vampires and waste away.

While Brennan was pondering mortality, Travis had started answering one of Dom's questions, and by the time Brennan tuned back into the conversation he seemed to be on a rant about the glory days of vampirism.

"—and Nellie probably talked smack and made nomads sound like a bunch of assholes," Travis was saying, "but let me tell you, traveling the world with Sunny and Shea was the best century of my life."

He paused, a faraway look in his eyes at the memory.

Travis had said not to overthink things, but that wasn't something Brennan was capable of. He thought too much about *everything*. It was, according to his therapist, probably why he was depressed. In that moment, in that gross house that stank of weed and mold and god knew what else, Brennan felt disgusted with it all. Travis felt like a stark reminder that he wasn't *human.* None of them were, or would be again.

The part of his brain that sounded like his therapist was already troubleshooting, suggesting ways to cope as the familiar wave of panic and self-hate rose in his stomach.

Acknowledge the intrusive thought, then dismiss it. Except, that didn't make his lack of humanity any less real. It wasn't an intrusive thought if it was objectively *true.*

Focus on your breathing and surroundings. Any of that would remind him of the people around him, the stench, the dog without a heartbeat, the sound of Travis's voice around words he couldn't focus on.

Brennan's eyes snapped open as his swirling thoughts settled on the question he'd been afraid to ask all evening: *What about Evelyn?*

"—some war with the Germans, I don't know, I was on a bender for most of the 1900s after '28—"

Now that the thought was on his mind, he couldn't bite it back.

"There's a girl at my school who went missing the day we turned," Brennan interrupted. "Evelyn VanMeter."

Dom went still and stony. Travis looked at Brennan with amusement.

"Uh-oh," Travis said, delighted, "he's smarter than he looks."

"What do you know?" Brennan pressed.

For a long moment, Brennan wasn't sure whether anyone was going to answer, Travis smoking and grinning, Dom staring at her black-polished nails in her lap like they held the answers. "Evelyn was my sister," Dom finally said. "She was in the wreck with me."

Brennan's blood turned to ice. If Travis couldn't save her, then she must have died in the wreck. Unless—

The memory of Dom crying at brunch, the same round face and dark hair on Evelyn's missing-person flyer, struck like a lightning bolt. He remembered the pink scrunchie on the ground, yards away from where the car had actually struck, now shoved in a drawer in his room. Dom's sister—Evelyn—had died, and two new vampires emerged.

Brennan felt like a balloon was about to burst in his stomach, like he couldn't breathe, or was breathing too much.

"Tell me she died in the wreck," Brennan said.

"She was in the wreck with me—"

"And that's how she died, right?" Brennan pushed, pleaded.

"My leg was broken and you were knocked out and bleeding *so* much. She went looking for help. She found Travis. He turned you to save your life."

"And you, because you asked him to."

His disgust at Dom's choice must have been obvious, because Travis jumped in.

"Please, you think you were better off as a human?" Travis said. "Give it a few centuries, you'll be thanking me."

Brennan could barely comprehend the idea of existing in a few centuries, let alone being happy about it.

"Who killed Evelyn?" he demanded.

Dom studied Brennan, eyes darting across his face, silent.

"Oh, cute. You think it might have been you," Travis said, stroking the fuzz on his chin. "Don't worry, kid, you're still a vampire-virgin, unless you're biting a crush we don't know about."

"How. Did. Evelyn. Die."

"Travis turned us. It's, like, a whole ritual. After, he brought you to his place until he could get someone to bring you to campus. He doesn't leave the woods. And then it was just me and Evelyn."

"And you killed her."

Dom's expression was pained. "I went into frenzy. I was a new turn, and there was still so much blood."

Blood from *him*. From where she *hit him with her car and cursed him with this fucking existence* and then *killed her sister*.

"I . . . I need to go," Brennan said, standing up too fast.

Travis said, "Aw, come on, vampling, we can all get along—"

"You think I don't feel bad?" Dom stood to match him, nostrils flaring, eyes fiery. "You think living with that is easy?"

Brennan ignored her, heading to the tarp door only a pace away, mind a perfect storm.

"But you," Dom spat, "acting like you're so much better, like you've never made a mistake or like—like you don't drink blood like the rest of us! Pretending you're so perfect. I think that's pathetic."

Brennan paused in front of the doorway, back to Dom and Travis.

"Hey now, Dominique, let's try to be—" Travis started.

"You know, you're right," Dom said. "You should go."

As the tarp flapped closed behind him, Travis called out, "Come back and visit anytime!"

9

VAMPIRE LASER TAG LEAGUE

BRENNAN'S PHONE

Brennan

Did you know about Evelyn?

Did you help cover it up?

Nellie

Yes. It's our job. —N

Brennan

You and Sunny.

Nellie

And Travis, in this case. —N

Brennan

Why?

Nellie

Accidents, missing people. We have to cover them up,
or they'll lead right to us. —N

Brennan

How often do accidents like these happen?

Nellie

We minimize it. —N

Brennan

What does that mean?

Nellie

We have population control, restrictions on turning people, restrictions on killing, and penalties in place for this very reason. To protect both humans and vampires. —N

　　　　　　　　　　　　　　　　　　　　　　Brennan

　　　　　　　　　　　　Well maybe that's not good enough!

Nellie

I'm sensing frustration that might be misdirected?
Do you want to schedule a therapy appointment? —N

　　　　　　　　　　　　　　　　　　　　　　Brennan

　　　　　　　　　　　　　　　You know what? Yes.

The address for his one-on-one with Nellie led him to a side entrance down an alley that led to a retro arcade. The carpet was a bright swirl of colors to distract from the stains and smudges, and there were rows of old game machines spread out in a wide-open, tall-ceilinged warehouse.

Next to the entrance, there was a silvery cafeteria with an Instagram-ready wall of neon signs. Sunny was perched at one of the tables with her MacBook, long hair loose around her face, typing furiously, but she spared Brennan an arched eyebrow in greeting before returning to her task.

Brennan scanned the arcade—a kid and her parent, two college students on what might have been a date, and a lone figure staring down a Skee-Ball alley with the ball clutched to her chest.

Brennan approached Nellie and watched as she prepared to pitch, reeling back and mimicking the motion of throwing the ball underhand a few times without releasing it. She wore big hoop earrings, a fanny pack, and a colorful shirt that had a similar pattern to the arcade's carpets.

"Hold that thought, Brennan," she said without looking over her shoulder. "I need to get this shot."

He didn't know how the game worked, but the numbers at the top of the machine were high, and she only had one ball left. Nellie wound her arm back, and this time released the ball to skid across the alley and hop straight into the smallest hole marked with 1000.

The machine trilled with electronic music and started spitting out tickets. Nellie jumped and squealed.

"A perfect game of Skee-Ball!" she announced, clutching her tickets and beaming at Brennan.

"Impressive," Brennan said, and offered a smile in return, nowhere near matching her enthusiasm.

"Do you wanna play *Street Fighter*? I find it's great to talk about things that are stressing you out while playing *Street Fighter*."

"I can't say I've played before," Brennan said, with the sinking feeling that he didn't have a choice in the matter.

"You'll pick it up," Nellie said, tucking her tickets into her fanny pack around her hips and beelining toward the machine in question. Brennan followed.

The machine pretty much explained it: a joystick for moving, an array of buttons for attacking, two sets of controls for two players.

"Why do I get the feeling you're about to annihilate me?"

"I'll go easy on you," Nellie said, but there was a glint in her eyes that agreed with me. "So, tell me: how are you doing? How are you adjusting? How are things?"

She inserted coins to start the game without taking her attention off Brennan.

"That's a complicated question," Brennan said.

The game started, and Nellie turned to assume position with hands on the controls. Brennan mirrored her. They chose characters, and they immediately started beating each other up on the screen.

"I've got nothing but time," Nellie said, and finished Brennan's character with a roundhouse kick to the face.

Another round began, and with Brennan's hands busy button-mashing, the words flowed out easily. Brennan usually needed a few sessions to get comfortable with a new therapist, but something about them both being vampires, or Nellie looking his age, or the fact that he had been stewing in his own angst without therapy for about a month, made Brennan let loose.

He started with the Dom stuff. How she admitted to killing her own sister. Then it spiraled.

He told Nellie he was terrified of being immortal.

He told Nellie he was afraid of fucking up irreparably.

He told Nellie he still hated himself most of the time.

He told Nellie about Cole. About the library. How Cole was the only person who knew about him.

Nellie, for her part, was a good therapist, all while destroying at *Street Fighter*. She asked questions at the appropriate times, called him out on negative language and biases.

When he finally stopped rambling, Nellie spoke.

"As a side note, I'm gonna have to get you to fill out some forms about the people who know about you. Just housekeeping, Sunny will keep an eye on them."

Brennan frowned, still smashing the buttons of the game.

"That sounds sketchy. Keep an eye on them how?"

"Nothing worse than what Facebook or the US government does already."

"Oh, great, so full-on surveillance then?"

"Nothing invasive, don't worry. She makes sure nobody makes any information public, or does anything to endanger any of us. You're not putting your friends at risk."

"What about you? Are *your* friends and family on the vampire FBI watch list?"

"I never told my family about me, and all my human friends who once knew have died."

There was a lot to process there, and Brennan stumbled in his button-mashing. It was easy to think Nellie was the same as him—she looked like any other college student, if a bit more retro, and that could easily pass as hipster. But she was decades older than him. She had stayed the same while the people she knew grew old and died.

"You never told your family?" Brennan asked. He couldn't imagine telling his mom, but he also couldn't imagine her *never* knowing.

Nellie curb-stomped him a final time in *Street Fighter* and the game ended. Brennan faced Nellie, but Nellie remained with her head bowed toward the controls.

"My sister had such a bright future, and I knew if I ever told her, she would have given it all up to try to help me. And my mother already gave so much for me and my sister. I couldn't give them the burden of the truth." She inhaled sharply, blinking rapidly and forcing a smile onto her face. "I stayed in their lives for as long as I could. But then my little sister started maturing, and my mom's hair started graying, and I stayed the same."

"What did you do?"

"I left."

"You left."

"I estranged myself, over time. Answered calls less, visited less, then stopped until I was just writing them letters. Even that was hard, because they wanted to hear that I was having children and settling down and doing the kinds of things I'd never be able to do. I stopped writing, too, eventually."

"And that was it? You cut off contact?"

"I went to see my mother in the hospital when she was dying. She thought I was an angel. I wished I hadn't gone. I have a niece who's still alive, my little sister's kid, and I have Sunny keep an eye on her for me, from a distance."

"Those are the only two options? Keep it a secret and lose your family, or tell them the truth and keep them?"

"Not quite . . . Vampires with beginner levels of power can make minor adjustments to their appearance—like Sunny, she changes her hair color all the time, and she makes her eyelashes longer without extensions. So it'd be possible to, I guess, synthetically age to keep up the facade of normalcy."

"Why didn't you? Don't you have powers, or something?" It felt so science fiction to ask, but that was the world he lived in now: full of strange and impossible things.

"No, I've never had powers. I don't know if I ever will."

Brennan didn't know how to ask the question. Powers weren't covered in the pamphlets, as far as he could tell.

"Why not? I mean, how do you . . . get them?"

"Vampires gain power for each human kill, Brennan. That's why I don't have any, and why I don't think you ever will, either."

"So. The more people you kill, the more powerful you are."

"Yes. Or people you *turn*."

He guessed going from human to vampire counted as death, too. "That's a pretty messed-up rewards system."

"Exactly. Urban clans don't allow kills, and we don't train vampiric powers. If you ever have an inclination, I can happily provide you pamphlets about transferring to a nearby colony, but—"

"I'm good, thanks."

"Good." Nellie produced more quarters from her pockets. "You want to play another round? Tell me more about that cute librarian."

"I don't think I said he was cute."

"You actually said it twice."

"I resent that," Brennan said, but he waved for Nellie to start up another game.

He told Nellie how Cole had helped him steal blood from the school, how he was a university-renowned heartthrob, about the *Bachelorette* viewing group, about Cole's infuriatingly gravity-defying curly hair.

He told Nellie how Cole knew all his vampiric secrets and how, except for that first day, Cole was never afraid of him. Which was refreshing, when Brennan spent most of his time being afraid of himself.

After Brennan realized he'd been rambling about Cole for ten minutes and finally shut his mouth with a click, Nellie said, "It sounds like Cole has been a major source of comfort in all this."

Brennan's cheeks warmed and he focused on beating up Nellie's game character. "I guess."

"Do you think you'll pursue that relationship?"

Brennan sputtered. Nellie's character finished him in the moment's distraction.

"I don't—I didn't say that. And no. Of course not. He and I are, like, the textbook definition of 'bad timing.' Of 'it's not you, it's me.' I can't. He deserves better."

"Have you considered that maybe he should be part of this conversation? Doesn't Cole get to decide what he deserves?"

"You don't get it. He's literally the kindest person on the planet. He sees the vampire thing as a quirk. He doesn't see the whole picture."

"You have to decide, then," Nellie said, "if you're willing to show him or not."

"Yeah, and when he runs away screaming, we'll have our answer."

Nellie paused the game and faced Brennan, and his skin prickled under the attention.

"I've noticed you talk about being a vampire the same way you talk about being depressed. You assume they're the worst things about you."

Brennan blinked. "They are."

Nellie sighed. Not the answer she wanted. Was he missing some other fatal flaw she thought was more significant? Or did she really expect him to have some sort of pride in the things that actively ruined his life?

Before she could respond, an alarm jingled on Nellie's phone. The ringtone was retro 8-bit style, and the phone she produced was an early 2000s flip phone. Nellie frowned at it.

"That's time, unfortunately."

As she spoke, a shadow darkened the *Street Fighter* machine and footsteps slowed to a stop a few feet away. Sensing someone's eyes on him, Brennan turned around.

Dom leaned against a pinball machine across the aisle, most of her hair chopped off into an uneven chin-length cut. Her nails were chipped black and she wore a black hoodie, black jeans, and a beat-up pair of combat boots. She was either in mourning or embracing a Goth aesthetic that didn't totally fit her.

She offered a nod in greeting, but eyed Brennan warily.

"Dominique! Right on time," Nellie said as *Street Fighter* turned to GAME OVER, and crossed to stand next to Dom, putting a hand on her back. Dom stiffened.

"I said I'd be," Dom mumbled, studying her fingernails with interest.

"Dom has a one-on-one with me next, so I figured you could hang out for a bit and we could do some group bonding after!"

"Are you serious?" Brennan said. "After everything we just talked about?"

"Yeah, no," Dom said dryly. "I prefer not to hang out with judgmental assholes."

"You guys!" Nellie scolded. "We are a clan and we have to stick together. If we don't have each other's backs, we have nothing. It's important to set aside our differences and come together. Do you think you can do that?"

Brennan's eyes bounced between Dom and Nellie. Dom was getting ambushed with this too, judging by her clear discomfort.

"Right," Brennan said. "Sounds . . . great."

He lingered for a second more before nodding an uncertain goodbye and beelining over to Sunny, her fingers still flying over the keyboard with a rhythmic clacking. Brennan pulled out the chair opposite her, and it scraped loudly against the linoleum floor of the cafeteria. He collapsed into the seat and watched Sunny work for a minute.

"What exactly do you do?" Brennan asked.

Sunny didn't look up, and her typing didn't waver.

"Instagram, mostly," she said. "But I dabble in TikTok. Selfies, makeup, fashion, sometimes food—"

"I mean, for the"—he glanced around and dropped his voice, despite him and Sunny being the only people in the cafeteria section—"vampires."

Sunny rolled her eyes. "Security."

"What does that *mean,* though?"

Sunny stopped typing and turned her attention to Brennan with an exasperated sigh.

"Someone finds out about vampires and tries to plan an attack," Sunny said, raising her left hand, her pink shimmery polish catching the light. She brought up her right hand as if balancing options on each side, and said, "Security." She lifted her left hand again. "Someone sees something suspicious and posts on a Reddit forum." Her right hand went up. "Security. A wannabe investigator thinks they're on the verge of breaking a big story. Security. A vampire acts against clan law and needs to be put in their place. Security. Make sense?"

She returned her attention to her laptop.

"So you, what, kill them?" He remembered what Nellie had said about powers and added, "Or wipe their memories?"

"I take care of it."

"*Okaaaay.*" Then, "You have powers?"

"Yes."

"Which means you've killed people. Or turned them, I guess."

"Yes."

"And now you're leading the clan."

"Alongside Nellie."

"How did that happen?"

"Brennan," Sunny said, once again shifting her attention from work to him. "You know how Nellie's always saying 'You can ask me about anything' and 'I want you to be able to talk to me' and mom stuff like that?"

Brennan nodded.

"Notice how I don't say things like that."

"Yeah?" Then, "Oh."

"I'm very busy. I have two unaccounted kills to deal with and a minor ongoing surveillance campaign. If you need a history lesson, talk to Nellie."

"Fine. I'll ask Travis."

Sunny paused, eyes narrowed, going stiff enough to send alarm bells ringing in Brennan's head. "I'm sure he'd be *more* than happy to relive his golden days with you, but I don't think that's a good idea."

"Why not?"

"They say never meet your heroes? Well, you shouldn't meet your maker. Not when it's Travis."

Interesting. Even with whatever surveillance she had going on, she didn't know he had already met Travis.

"What does that mean?" Brennan pressed.

"He's unstable, alright? He's weird, and gross, and you only get that powerful from killing a *lot* of people over *thousands* of years. He's not a good influence. So don't, okay?" She huffed, shaking her head at her laptop screen. "But unless you need me to kill someone, shut someone up, or boost something on Instagram, I need to work."

"One more question," Brennan tried, "and I promise I'll shut up."

Sunny raised an impatient eyebrow and nodded for him to spit it out.

"Why do you care?" Brennan asked. Sunny's frown deepened, so he fumbled on, "I mean, you've killed people, so I'm guessing it's not for the moral high ground. You don't seem to like *people* in general. Why are you running an urban clan?"

Sunny cocked her head, less inquisitive and more calculating, like Brennan had surprised her.

"I do it for Nellie," she said. "Before her, I didn't have a purpose. Now I do."

With that, Sunny returned to her work.

Brennan looked over his shoulder, where Nellie and Dom were playing a racing game and chatting, then turned back to the table.

He reached for his journal and bided his time. He still wasn't sure about the clan, but there was no chance he was going to miss out on vampire group bonding. Whatever that meant.

"You're serious?" Brennan asked.

He'd seen Nellie slip money to one of the employees for this. Sunny had even put down her laptop, tied her hair into a high ponytail, and walked with extremely serious purpose.

Nellie turned away from the racks of plastic guns and vests, whirling toward Brennan with her hands on her hips. One of the vests was already draped over her shoulders.

"Oh, I'm *dead* serious, Brennan Brooks," she said. "You better armor up."

"You guys can team up, since you're new. Nellie and I each go solo," Sunny said. Brennan wrinkled his nose and sized up Dom, who seemed as unenthused about teaming up as Brennan was.

Nellie added, "We give Sunny a limit on shots as a disadvantage."

"I'm very good at laser tag," Sunny said solemnly.

"Battle royale, three hits to down, sound good?"

Dom, who had been off to the side with her arms crossed, caught Brennan's eye and raised an eyebrow. *Are we doing this?*

Brennan shrugged and grabbed a gun and a vest.

Nellie slipped another bill to the employee who opened the door to the arena for them.

"You're the best, Lee," she said.

"You'll post like you promised?" grunted Lee. "We got a huge surge after the last time."

"Already got my caption picked out," Sunny said, fingernails clicking against the screen of her phone.

"Good. Just don't break anything, okay?"

"That only happened once," Nellie said.

"You ripped a door off its hinges."

"What else was I supposed to do? Sunny was gonna kill me."

"That was the only time Nellie's beaten me," Sunny said.

Lee grumbled something about "No property damage," before closing the door behind them.

"Lee's sister is the vampire who runs the blood bank," Nellie explained. "She hooks us up sometimes. Makes sure the cameras go off while we're playing, so there's no need to hold back."

"Except for property damage," Brennan added.

"Eh," Sunny said, "we're good for it."

Brennan took in the arena. It was massive and elaborate, themed like a space action movie somewhere adjacent to Star Wars or Star Trek. The base level was full of red sand, decorated like a Martian wasteland. Big scraps of junk metal and random materials were scattered throughout as cover, and at the opposite ends of the battlefield were two bases. They were designed like space stations or massive spaceships, with multiple floors, entrances, and windows. Playing in the background was ambient music that tried too hard to sound like Star Wars without infringing on copyright.

A bell rang, and Nellie took the gun slung around her shoulders into her hand, shouted, "Ninety seconds to start!" and then sprinted toward one of the bases. She was wicked fast, red sand kicking up behind her.

Beside him, Dom was as unimpressed as ever, her face carefully bored.

Sunny studied them both, calculating. "I don't go easy on people."

"I wouldn't expect you to," Brennan agreed. Sunny sprinted off toward the same base as Nellie with deadly speed.

Dom's single arched brow was the only sign of amusement. "I guess this one's ours," Dom said, nodding to the other base.

Brennan couldn't help starting to strategize, brain kicking into full gear. They'd need to be on the defensive, surely, which meant finding a decently defensible area of the base to occupy.

"We shouldn't split up," Brennan said. "We'll need to cooperate if we want to survive."

"I'm pretty sure they're gonna destroy us either way," Dom said.

"Yeah, probably," Brennan agreed. Then, "We should seek higher ground."

"Yes, sir." Dom mock saluted.

They took off toward the base, a huge rocket with three levels and a lot of hiding spaces. They weaved through an elaborate set, different rooms with big machines and flashing lights. Brennan didn't stop until they reached the top level, where there was one small room designed like a control center: a big control panel in front of a swiveling captain's chair with a view of the whole arena below. There was one entrance and one large window, so they sat on the floor back-to-back. Brennan watched the door to the room, and Dom checked the window for any sign of movement.

"So, have you done this before?" Dom asked. She sounded like she couldn't care less about the answer.

"Only once, in, I don't know, sixth grade," Brennan said. "My mom didn't like me playing with anything resembling a gun."

"Wow, and you did anyway?" Dom said, somewhere between dry and mocking. "What a rebel."

"Ha, yeah. It was some kid's birthday party and he invited the whole class. I kinda killed the vibe reciting my mom's gun control lessons to a group of unforgiving twelve-year-old boys who just wanted to shoot lasers at each other."

Dom laughed. The sound was light and soft, and with his back to her, he realized he hadn't really seen her laugh. He couldn't even imagine it.

"I'm guessing you didn't do too well?"

"Hid in the corner the whole time. After my attempted lecture, I got chosen last for teams, and I was so afraid of messing up and being a burden, I did nothing."

Dom was quiet. Then, a buzzer sounded.

"I guess we're starting," Dom whispered. "Eyes open."

A moment of stillness and silence passed, and Brennan started to realize why Nellie and Sunny liked laser tag so much. It was different as a vampire. He could see more, hear more, move more quietly.

"This is weird, right?" Brennan asked.

"What?"

"We're immortal, undead vampires. And we're playing laser tag. I just . . . didn't see this one coming."

Dom snorted. "Yeah. I didn't expect a lot of things that happened this year."

Brennan didn't know how to respond, knowing that Dom had killed her own sister. That Dom was happier being a vampire than Brennan was, even though she had done something so terrible and permanent.

"Your sister," Brennan said, and Dom cut him a glare that said he was approaching dangerous territory. "Were you close?"

Dom chewed on her lip for a minute. Then, "She was my best friend."

Pew! Pew!

In the distance, the tinny electric sound of a gun going off pierced through the background music. A small trill of victory music sounded in response, then distant laughter and yelling. One of them had hit the other.

"I have eyes on Nellie," Dom said, shifting behind him to stand at a crouch near the window. "She's approaching the base."

"Do you have a clear shot?"

"No."

"Then we wait."

Laser tag with a group of vampires was intense.

When Nellie found them, she got a shot in on Brennan and Dom got a shot on her, and then Nellie had reared back and literally cartwheeled back from whence she came. With Sunny approaching the base, they abandoned their post to give chase.

They practically flew, with all the speed and strength of their vampiric abilities, and the thrill of a hunt sang in Brennan's veins like the harmonies from his favorite song.

They chased Nellie right into a dead end. Brennan pointed and shot.

Pew!

Nellie's vest trilled with the confirmed shot. She had one more life left on her, which meant she had gotten a hit from Sunny earlier. The lights on her vest flashed with the cooldown period that protected her from being shot multiple times in quick succession.

"Sorry, Mom," Dom said, and trained her gun on Nellie, waiting for the lights to stop.

Nellie kept her gun up and aimed, swinging it back and forth between Brennan and Dom.

"Don't do this," she said. "You need me if you want to beat Sunny."

They might. Brennan looked to Dom for her thoughts.

In their moment of hesitation, Nellie let loose a stream of *Pew pew pew pew pew*s and both Brennan's and Dom's vests lit up. Nellie cackled, and Dom shot her right back. Nellie's vest made a sad tinkle of notes that meant she had died.

Nellie collapsed to the ground with a dramatic flourish. "Sunny will avenge me!" she cried, coughing weakly to illustrate her death. "She's got two lives left."

"So do I," said Dom, then turned away from Nellie, brushing past Brennan to march back toward the lookout.

Brennan dove for cover, narrowly avoiding landing on his face next to Dom on the second floor of their base. Somewhere across the way, Sunny lingered in the shadows with deadly aim. Dom had been hit, and now they were each hanging on by one life while Sunny still had two.

"If we survive this," Dom said, shouldering her gun and preparing to move, "we're getting *so* drunk."

They stood together, stock-still, around a corner that led to a dead end. A few paces behind, Sunny's footsteps tapped lightly on the ground. She knew she'd caught her prey; why not take her time?

This was it. Brennan was going to die.

"Dom," Brennan said, "it was an honor to fight alongside you."

"We can get out of this," Dom said.

"No," Brennan said. "But *you* can."

He dove out from behind the corner to where Sunny stood, weapon poised. Brennan sliced through the air, desperately taking aim, watching as Sunny did the same, firing a shot. Everything was moving in slow motion. He narrowly dodged one of Sunny's shots, but another one followed just as quickly. Brennan fired again—

Sunny's vest lit up, and so did Brennan's.

Sunny immediately leapt away, using the cooldown time to put distance between herself and Dom.

Brennan was out, but Sunny was down to one life. They had a chance.

Brennan's vest announced his death. Dom marched up to him.

"That was pretty brave, kid," she said.

"Kill her," Brennan said. Dom nodded solemnly, then started running.

10

THE THINGS WE WANT

Instagram

KeepItSunny ✅
[A group shot in front of a space-station set, with Sunny, Nellie, Brennan, and Dominique shaping their hands like guns in a Charlie's Angels kind of pose. Sunny and Nellie are glamorous and posing. Brennan and Dom are mid-laugh.]
I never lose. (Except for when I do.)
@laserblazeboston

··········· ·········

Nellie
Don't take it personally! Sunny's a sore loser. —N

                                    Brennan
                Can you promise there won't be an attempt on my life?

Nellie
Hahahahaha —N

They'd spent the whole train ride melodramatically reenacting the game and laughing over the look of shock on Sunny's face at being defeated. When Dom was about to get off at her stop, she had asked, "So, you wanna come get drunk, or not?" And, with the train doors threatening to close, Brennan had gone against every instinct and hopped out after her.

They had won, after all.

They were two drinks in and still slightly damp from running through the pouring rain from the train to Dom's apartment in Roxbury. They both had been soaked to the bone, but cold no longer seeped into Brennan like before. He had felt the rain wash over him but wasn't bothered.

She'd led him up three flights of stairs, down a narrow, mildew-scented hallway to a small apartment. Then she'd beelined to a bottle of whiskey and force-fed Brennan two shots before letting him sit at her rackety kitchen table.

The apartment was small, messy, and lived-in in a way that could generously be called cozy. Stuff covered nearly every surface: dishes were piled in the sink and on the coffee table, papers and unopened letters littered the kitchen counters. A few had big red stamps on them flagging missing payments.

Dom returned from the fridge with a pint bag of blood. She got to work mixing shots of blood into their drinks, and Brennan reluctantly admitted it was a genius idea.

"You do this a lot?" Brennan asked. "Getting drunk on a Monday with your friendly neighborhood vampire?"

"Getting drunk on a Monday, sure. I usually do it alone, though."

Brennan grimaced. "Sounds healthy."

"What's it matter? We're never gonna die. It doesn't matter if I take care of my stupid liver or keep a stupid job or pay my stupid rent."

"That's a pretty extreme form of nihilism to adopt."

"Oh, do *not* go philosophy-bro on me. I'll kick you out, I swear to god."

Brennan lifted his hands in surrender and tried the drink. The sweet tinge of blood warmed his chest at the first sip, a subtle flavor underneath the alcohol that lifted the whole cocktail. Brennan made a note to try spiking his coffee.

"Besides, it's not nihilism," Dom said. "It's not like, nothing matters and everything sucks. Nothing matters, so I can focus on what I care about, and stop giving a fuck about what I don't. It's *freedom*. It's a chance for a new start."

"I love that for you," Brennan said dryly, "but I can't say I feel the same."

"Yeah, you don't exactly give off well-adjusted vibes, to be honest with you." Dom raised her eyebrows and took a long sip of her drink as if to say, *But that's none of my business!*

It was true, but hearing someone say it did not feel great. He tried hard to at least have a mask of normalcy, but he was always being reminded that mask had cracks in it.

After a moment, Dom excused herself to the bathroom, leaving Brennan alone in the living and kitchen area. Not wanting to snoop but deathly curious, Brennan turned away from the kitchen and crossed to the living area, which had a small TV and a stained, beat-up couch that looked like it had last been clean in the nineties. The walls were bare except for the photos next to the entryway. A few were framed, with smaller ones tucked into corners of the frames, but most were pinned and taped up haphazardly in a growing collage.

Brennan scanned the photos, taking them in. There were Dom and Evelyn posing in front of a roller coaster, Dom looking happier and lighter than he'd ever seen her, her hair still long and wavy before she'd chopped it off. Evelyn looked like her, the same skin and long hair, the same jut of her nose, the same round face. There were Dom and Evelyn over and over again, sometimes looking younger and more baby-faced, sometimes closer to the detached-looking girl Brennan knew. The two at a concert, at a fancy restaurant, at a bowling alley, at the beach. The younger girl, alone, flipping off the camera and laughing. In almost all of them, Evelyn wore that pink scrunchie.

At the base of the photo wall was a cardboard box full of more frames, photo albums, and loose papers that Brennan could only assume were more photos. Next to the box, a photo frame was on the floor, face down, a glass shard poking out from beneath.

Curiosity won out and Brennan lifted the frame. The glass cover of the frame was shattered inward from the center, like it had been struck. The photo showed Dom and Evelyn, both much younger, with a couple that must have been their parents. Dom couldn't have been older than fifteen or sixteen. It was a posed shot, with forced, closed-lipped smiles and stiff spines. The photo radiated unhappiness.

"Anything interesting?" Dom said, her voice close behind Brennan. He nearly jumped out of his skin and turned around to face her.

"I, uh." Brennan went to make an excuse, but, "Yeah, a little."

"You can ask me things. I'm an open book."

Brennan raised an eyebrow. "Are you? I thought I was a 'judgmental asshole' earlier."

"Oh please, you think I'm a murderer."

"You *did* kill someone."

"And you *are* a judgmental asshole, so I guess we're both right."

For a moment, Dom glared at him over her glass and Brennan wondered if he maybe shouldn't be alone with a murderous vampire, even if he was one, too. But then Dom snorted a laugh and the tension shattered, and Brennan allowed himself to relax.

They settled on the couch and Dom took the shattered frame from Brennan's hands, looking down at it.

"You just seem . . . pretty okay with the vampire thing considering it made you . . ." Brennan had the social capacity to not say the *bite and kill your sister* part out loud.

"Let's get this straight," Dom said. "I loved my sister more than anything. She was my everything. She was the only good thing that came out of my parents' shitty existence. And I'm always going to remember—" She stopped, staring back at the picture. "I'm gonna live with what I did forever."

Maybe Brennan wasn't the only one terrified of what *forever* meant for them now.

"You know I can't even mourn her? Or mention her? Nellie and Sunny swept it under the rug like she never existed at all. You're so high and mighty, but you have *no* idea—"

Dom broke off with a shaky sigh, gripping the frame so hard he thought she might break it further.

"But I can't change that she's dead, and hating myself won't bring her back or change the fact that I'm a vampire," said Dom. She set the photo face down on the coffee table among a pile of old magazines. "I'm powerful for the first time in my life. And she would want that for me. That's what Travis says. If vampirism is the only thing that comes of her death, then it has to be a good thing. It has to. Otherwise it's just . . ."

"A punishment," Brennan finished the thought. His chest squeezed unpleasantly, so he shut it up with a long gulp of his drink.

Dom pursed her lips at him. Maybe Brennan was drunk, but this might have been the first time Dom looked at him with understanding instead of contempt. Like they could be on the same team, and not just in laser tag.

"Is that why . . ." Dom started, speaking carefully. "I mean, why do you hate it so much?"

It seemed so obvious, the question was absurd. It wasn't in the fucking plans, for one, and it was an unfair, random wrench in what was supposed to be Brennan's first normal semester. And who would *want* to be technically dead, surviving on drinking human blood?

Not to mention, it seemed like another thing wrong with him. Another thing that made it feel impossible for him to relate to or communicate with his peers, another slew of symptoms to deal with and problems to solve. He'd always been afraid of being a monster, and now he *was* one.

But he was afraid if he said that, Dom might not understand.

Or maybe he was afraid she *would*.

"I guess I mostly miss Italian food," Brennan said, and finished his drink.

11

ONE EASY THING

BRENNAN'S PHONE

Dr. Mom

What do you mean?

You always come home for Thanksgiving.

Brennan

~~Yeah, and we usually just order Chinese food.~~

~~Do you really need me for that?~~

I'm way behind on school things! I need to focus on that.

You know how it is.

Dr. Mom

How behind are you? Is it serious? Maybe you

should set up meetings with your academic advisor,

and each of your teachers.

Brennan

I'll be okay. I just need to stay on campus.

Library access and all that.

Dr. Mom

Okay. No repeats of last semester, promise?

Brennan

Yep.

BRENNAN'S JOURNAL, THE BACK PAGE

COLE

Reasons not to like him???

- Obviously, <u>Twilight</u> is an absurd waste of time and is objectively terrible.
- He's distracting when he laughs.
- Or smiles.
- Sometimes he drinks his coffee with the lid off and gets whipped cream on his upper lip and it makes me want to light myself on fire.
- He waves to me from across the library shamelessly and I get secondhand embarrassment.
- When his hair is messy and there's a curl sticking up and I'm not allowed to smooth it down, that is also very distracting and frustrating.
- Southern accent is deceptively charming.

BRENNAN'S PHONE

Sunny
I'm deeply sorry in advance about Nellie

Brennan
What? What happened?

Sunny
I upgraded her flip phone to a smartphone. It seemed like a good idea at the time.

··················

Nellie
[a blurry, too-close photo of Nellie's chin from below]
How to send text on iphone
Text Sunny
Send text to Sunny
How to wi-fi
What is wi-fi

Brennan
This is Brennan, not Google.

Nellie

Text Brennan

My bad Sunny got me a new phone and I'm still

figuring out how to youth it send send send why isn't it

sending oh god it's still listening hold on

　　　　　　　　　　　　　　　　　　　　Brennan

　　　　　　　Well. At least you're not signing your name anymore.

Nellie

Sincerely, Nellie send send message send wait Sunny

can you help me send this it's not working

By the time he walked through the wide doors of the first floor of the library, he was already overwhelmed. He hadn't really thought this through—midterms were this week, so everyone was in hell. The library was crowded, students gathered in groups across every piece of available furniture and counter space, chattering about group projects or complaining about homework. The air was ripe with the stench of body odor, energy drinks, coffee, and, most likely, tears.

Brennan himself wasn't in the best shape with classes, that hadn't been a lie. Even with all the extra hours from not being able to sleep, school felt impossible to focus on in the scheme of things going on in his life.

He didn't know how to find Cole in this mess, if he even should. Cole probably had his hands full enough on a night like this without Brennan's own angst. He hovered in the entryway, cracking his knuckles, debating turning around. But he'd come here for a reason.

Right as he thought it, his eyes fell on Cole, who was kneeling next to a baby-faced freshman girl wrapped in a blanket and crying openly. Cole was talking calmly and soothingly to her and offering a steaming mug of something. Brennan's heart panged with equal parts concern and affection, because here was Cole, the Cute Library Blanket Guy, in action. But he had dark smudges under his eyes. His curly hair looked especially wild, like he'd been running his hands through it, like he did when he was bullshitting his way through a procrastinated essay while Brennan finished shelving as an apology for distracting him.

He entered the library, trying to keep the noise from overwhelming him as a tight pain started to form in his temple. He needed to focus on *something,* so he focused on Cole. If he let his instincts take over, he could zero in on the conversation from afar.

"—and I know Jane is reasonable, she's really an old friend, she'll grant the extension, sweetheart—" Cole was saying, and only *he* could pull off calling a stranger "sweetheart" as something soothing instead of creepy. It was either the Southern charm or the rainbow pin on his denim jacket.

Brennan lingered a ways back, until the freshman gave a sniffle and a watery smile. Cole turned to leave, visibly deflating as he did, cheery mask slipping. He looked . . . exhausted.

Brennan went to make his presence known but a girl with blue hair beat him to it, looking frazzled with a pen stuck behind her ear and a stack of books weighing her arms down. Brennan paused and listened.

"Take a break, Cole. Go shelve the three hundreds and then go home. That's an order."

"You're not actually my boss," Cole said, but he didn't seem to have much fight in him.

The girl turned to wherever she was lugging those books, gave Brennan a bored once-over, and disappeared.

Cole perked up a little when he saw Brennan, but Brennan didn't know if it was real excitement or the same polite mask as with the girl earlier.

"God, Brennan, it's good to see you. Do you mind talking while I shelve?" Cole said, already walking toward the staircase to the stacks. "It's been so busy, and we're behind on everything, and I kind of procrastinated on an essay due at midnight, so the sooner I get done shelving, the sooner I can go work on that—"

Cole was talking so fast, Brennan felt winded trying to keep up, following him up the stairs two at a time. Brennan almost tripped over a pair of girls crouched over a laptop together on one of the landings.

"Okay, slow down a sec."

Brennan reached out against all better judgment and put a hand on Cole's shoulder to get him to stop for a second, and it worked. Cole paused on the top step and turned toward the touch.

"Just breathe," Brennan said. "Slow down. Are you alright?"

Cole blinked. His eyes went to Brennan's hand and then back to Brennan's face in a slow, sleepy processing of events. If he had to guess, Cole was running on two hours of sleep and an ungodly amount of caffeine.

His mouth took over and blurted, "Cole, you look *tired.*"

Cole blinked up at him for a beat, dark circles under his eyes. He inhaled one shaky breath, and then his lower lip quivered, and that was the only warning before he burst into tears.

He immediately buried his face in his hands, bowed head and shaking shoulders, and Brennan tried to keep up with the rapidly changing emotions.

"Oh my god," Cole was saying into his hands, shaking his head, but his shoulders were still trembling. "Oh my god this is so embarrassing, I'm *fine.*"

Brennan's hand was still on Cole's shoulder and his other hand fluttered awkwardly, hovering, uncertain. He wanted to pull Cole in to him, to hug him until he stopped shaking, but he wasn't sure he was allowed.

He finally gave in to the urge to comfort and wrapped an arm around Cole, which, in practice, didn't feel that awkward. He tried to rub a hand up and down his shoulder in a way that he hoped was comforting, and he must have been somewhat successful because Cole fell into his chest like he was waiting for the invitation.

"I'm sorry," Cole said again, sobbing and dripping snot on Brennan's shirt. "I'm fine, I'm really fine."

"Yes, I'm seeing all the trademark signs of a person who's fine," Brennan said, which was probably not the right thing to say, but Cole snorted a small wet laugh.

Brennan looked around the crowded library. It wasn't like Cole was the only college kid on the verge of a breakdown during midterms, but he was sure Cole didn't want to be on display, with the way he kept his face buried in his hands and turned his whole body into Brennan's side.

"Hey, let's go to the break room, yeah?" Brennan said.

Cole sniffled loudly and his red face emerged from his hands at last. He nodded and Brennan led the way, Cole keeping a loose hold on Brennan's arm that Brennan was hyperaware of. Was Cole's touch always this hot?

No, bad *Brennan,* he scolded. He needed to ignore his ill-advised crush and help comfort his friend and act like a normal person for once in his goddamn life.

Brennan hoped things were still where he remembered them. He pushed open the door to the storage room and held it open for Cole, who passed up the table and chairs in favor of flopping on the ground with a fair amount of drama. Brennan went to the box labeled in Cole's scratchy all-caps EMERGENCY COMFORT STASH. The Cute Library Blanket Guy origin story.

Within five minutes, Cole was wrapped up in his favorite blanket— the fleece one with a scattered pattern of dogs with speech bubbles that said "fuck off"—and holding a steaming mug of cocoa. The mug, a gift from Tony, said SEXY LIBRARIAN in gaudy lettering. Brennan made the cocoa with water instead of milk, because Cole was a weirdo who preferred shitty watery packet hot chocolate to anything of real substance. By the time Brennan was sitting on the floor across from him, legs crossed and hands in his lap, Cole had stopped crying.

"It's just, obviously midterms is a stressful time for everyone, but the library is like . . . Everyone is stressed, all the time, and everyone needs my help, and I'm trying to—to *be* the library blanket guy, right? With the smiles and the hot cocoa and all." Everything came tumbling out of Cole in a rush. "But it's so exhausting when I'm trying to take care of everyone else. And, really, I don't *mind,* but it piles up."

While Cole was busy taking care of everybody, was there anyone taking care of Cole?

God, was that what Brennan had been doing, too? Accepting all of Cole's kindness and not offering much in return? He'd come here today, as all days, for selfish reasons—just wanting to see a friend. But maybe Cole needed a friend in all his shit, too.

"What do you need? Advice, or sympathy, or . . . ?"

Cole sniffled up at Brennan, dangerously close to crying again.

"Honestly, Brennan, I needed a little bit of hospitality and you have more than provided." He pulled the blanket more firmly around his shoulders in illustration. The lilt of his accent was thicker around the edges.

"I only did what you do for, what, eight people a day?"

"That's my job," Cole said. "And it's far less often than that."

"Then it's my job to make you your shitty cocoa and let you rant if you need to."

"You didn't come here to deal with me being *like this*. You must have your own stuff going on, you had the vampire support-group meeting this weekend, right?"

"Oh my god, Cole, just let me take care of you!"

Cole's jaw clamped shut and he gave a wide-eyed blink. Brennan startled at his own exclamation, and then they both started, in the most sophisticated and composed way possible, *giggling*.

"Sorry," Brennan said, "That was weird. It's been a long day."

"It's been a long week," Cole agreed. "And it's not weird. It's sweet. You're sweet."

Brennan pushed down the warmth that was flooding his chest and face and melting his insides. Inexplicably, he said, "Well, shucks, me?"

Cole snorted. "Yeah, you're pretty . . . good, for a vampire."

"That's the goal, I guess," Brennan said, picking at a thread on his jeans. Then he flickered back into problem-solving mode. "Now, you mentioned an essay due at midnight?" Brennan checked his phone for the time. "You could bang something out in two hours, or at least ask for an extension. I can handle a little shelving if you need to work on that."

Cole blinked up at him from inside the burrito of his puppy blanket. It was unbearably adorable. Brennan averted his gaze and eyed a cart of books by the door, sizing it up.

"Or, I mean, depending on your stance on academic integrity, you can handle the stacks and I can tackle the essay," Brennan joked.

Cole grabbed a nearby stuffed animal and chucked it at Brennan. He ducked swiftly, because, well, vampire instincts.

"I doubt you've ever lacked academic integrity in your life," Cole accused.

"Yeah, I don't know why I joked about that, I don't play around with plagiarism."

"Then I guess you should get stacking."

Brennan turned to leave but the sound of shuffling made him turn. Cole had tripped over himself trying to get up while still wrapped in his blanket, but he managed to cross the small space and wrap a warm hand around Brennan's wrist. After not seeing him for two weeks, having Cole this close was making Brennan dizzy.

"And hey," Cole said. "Thank you."

BRENNAN'S JOURNAL, THE BACK PAGE

Cole writing an essay next to me
- Restless. In between bouts of typing, stares down the screen while a fidget spinner goes in the other hand. He's in some sort of zone.
- Oral fixation. Sipping cocoa. Chewing his pens. Biting his lip. Licking his lips. I think they're chapped. Maybe I should stop looking at his lips.
- Even when we're doing our own things, it's comforting to be in his orbit. Is that pathetic? Am I pathetic?
- He glanced over at me and smiled and, can confirm, I am completely pathetic.

After Brennan finished shelving the books—a methodical process he honestly enjoyed, since it let his brain go on autopilot for a bit—he sat on the floor next to Cole, writing in his journal while Cole finished fast-drafting his essay. He'd started out with some sort of goal, but somewhere along the lines ended up in the back pages, one elbow-brush away from doodling Cole's name in hearts like a third grader. Their knees pressed together. Cole's foot tapped incessantly.

Brennan was still scribbling out notes when Cole finally slammed his laptop shut with a long sigh, slumped over sideways until his head was on Brennan's shoulder, and said, "Done."

Brennan closed his notebook to shield it from Cole's view, and then held his breath to not move the new weight on his shoulders. Cole's hair smelled like coconut. The wild curls tickled Brennan's chin. He wanted to smooth them down. Brennan ignored his warming cheeks.

After a moment, Cole said, "We're having a party this Friday for Mari's birthday, before Thanksgiving break. You should come."

"A party invite? I'm honored."

"Shut up," Cole said. "Say yes. You can invite your friends, too."

"I don't have a lot of friends, except the vampires."

Cole arched his brow.

"Seriously?" Brennan said.

"It'd be super dope to meet them, honestly."

Brennan's brain raced through a thousand reasons why that was a terrible idea, but his mouth ignored them all and said, "I can ask them."

Really, Cole could have invited him to a back-alley drug deal, and Brennan would leap to accept.

Cole smiled. The tears and stress from earlier were gone, leaving behind the bright-eyed enthusiasm Brennan had missed.

"Dope," Cole said, and Brennan wanted to kiss the terrible word out of his mouth. "Either way, you owe me some vampire gossip. I feel way out of the loop!"

Brennan surged with gratitude and said, sly, "You ever imagine laser tag with a bunch of vampires?"

"Shut up!" Cole said, then, "Say more right now!"

And Brennan told him the whole story, but when he told it like this, all overdramatic and trying too hard to make Cole laugh, it didn't feel so scary. In hindsight, it was funny, hanging out with old and powerful vampires who cared too much about arcade games and social media. His life seemed unfathomable to his own eyes, but in the library at night, he almost felt normal.

Brennan returned home late to Tony waiting up on the couch in his pajamas with his arms crossed like a concerned mother whose child had stayed out past curfew.

"Uh," Brennan said, kicking his shoes off. "Hi?"

"What were you doing out so late?" Tony asked.

Brennan stopped in his normal getting-home movements, slowly hanging up his jacket and turning toward Tony.

"I was at the library with Cole," Brennan said cautiously. Was this a confrontation? What did Tony know?

"I wanted to talk to you," Tony said. He stood up from the couch and crossed until he could face Brennan, who was frozen and debating the merits of flight versus fight.

"Sure," Brennan said. His voice came out surprisingly even.

"There's no easy way to say this," Tony said. Brennan dug his fingernails into his palm. Tony exhaled a sigh. "So I'll just say it."

Brennan waited a beat before Tony spoke again.

"I want to shoot my shot with Mari."

The words hovered in the air like static for a long moment before the relief registered and Brennan's body slackened from the tension that had gripped him.

"You want to ask Mari out?" Brennan laughed. "Awesome. Congrats. What, do you need my blessing, or something?"

Tony's brows furrowed. "Are you sure? I mean, Bro Code is, like, super important to me. And I know you're always, like, *awkward* whenever she and Cole come over."

"I'm awkward all the time," Brennan defended.

"Yeah, but especially then."

"Wait," Brennan said, brain catching up with the rest of Tony's words. "You think I like Mari?"

"Don't you?" Tony almost seemed offended that Brennan didn't.

"Oh my god. No. I don't have a crush on her. Ask her out. Seriously, go for it." He must have suffered some sort of stroke, because he tacked on a "bro" and then lightly punched Tony's shoulder. He immediately wished he hadn't.

Tony laughed, then squinted at Brennan for a long few seconds before it dawned on him.

"Wait, *Cole*? I didn't realize you were . . ."

He trailed off and Brennan prickled with worry that Tony would be weird about this.

Tony held out his fist for Brennan to bump. "Right on," Tony said. Cautiously, Brennan returned the gesture. "Sexuality and gender are spectrums or whatever. You do you."

Somehow, coming from Tony, that meant a lot.

"Right," said Brennan. "Thanks. And good luck with Mari."

"Same to you with Cole, bro," Tony said. "I won't lie, I thought you were gonna be a weirdo when we were first figuring out housing. And you kind of *are* a weirdo. But you're a good dude."

Brennan was certain Tony intended it as a compliment, but he couldn't help feeling slightly insulted. He appreciated the gesture, though, and respected that this, for Tony, was friendship. He slipped around Tony and crept toward his room.

"Have a good night, Tony."

BRENNAN'S PHONE

COLE MCNAMARA HAS INVITED YOU TO ATTEND "MARI'S 22 BIRTHDAY BASH!!!!"

You were invited by Cole, alongside 84 others.

Hey y'all! This Nov 20 is the 22nd birthday of our lovely Scorpio queen, Marisela. As 22 is the sacred taylor swift birthday, it shall be treated with the same sanctity as 18 and 21. RSVP, invite your friends, we will have a keg but BYOB, and DM me to help organize!!!

14 comments / 64 ♥

> MARI: I disagree with the taylor swift thing but will accept any excuse to binge drink .

> TONY: get ready to RRRRAAAAAAAAAAGE!!!!!!!!!

••••••••••••••••

You have created a group chat with: Soon-Hee Kim and Nellie Adams

Brennan

Okay don't be weird about this.

But there's a party this Friday and the cute guy I want to

make my boyfriend would really like for you to come.

Sunny

whipped.

Nellie

Yes exclamation mark I'm so excited exclamation mark wait

I meant the symbol don't

Sunny

it's been a while since I've been to a classic college party,

I will come.

Brennan

Okay. Cool. Cool cool cool.

Sunny

you were hoping we were busy?

Brennan

Nah, I'm stoked for my vampire clan to meet my

human not-boyfriend, it's actually ideal.

Nellie

Why isn't it doing the! Question mark

Okay what the duck now

Duck no I said duck oh my god forget it

Sunny

oh hon. you'll get there.

....

Regarding Rumors of a Missing Student
From the Sturbridge University President

Dear Students,
We understand there have been some concerns and rumors

*regarding an incoming freshman who has been away from campus.
We want to emphasize that student safety is of the utmost
importance at Sturbridge University. In the spirit of transparency,
we have made contact with the family of Evelyn VanMeter and
understand that she is well, but withdrawing her enrollment. Please
respect the student and her family's privacy during these times. If
you would like to learn about campus safety regulations and . . .*

.....,......,.......

Brennan
[link] This your doing?

Nellie
I told you we'd take care of it!
Also comma I figured out exclamation points!

Brennan raised his plastic cup over the sea of people, pushing through
the blockade between him and the relative freedom of the living room.
Brennan didn't know how he'd made it this far in the semester without
seeing the apartment Cole and Mari shared. The living room was Pinterest-
level aesthetic, decorated with string lights and framed photos everywhere,
complete with a sky-blue couch with an array of blankets and throw pillows. Now, though, the room was dim and sticky with beer that sloshed
out of cups. Squeezing this many people into a two-bedroom apartment
was definitely a fire hazard, the air thick with sweat and booze, but Brennan had long gotten over being overwhelmed by it. The alcohol helped
with that, let him focus on one thing at a time instead of the cacophony of
everything. He was tastefully tipsy, everything softened around the edges
from the shots Tony had bullied him into when he'd arrived.

He peered through the crowd, searching. Nellie and Sunny had
let him know they were on their way, and Brennan was doing his god-
honored best to not think too hard about the fact that he'd invited a
couple of vampires into a house party of drunken college students.
What could go wrong, right? He slurped his drink (jungle juice, dangerous) and didn't need to find Cole in the crowd, because suddenly he
appeared in front of him with Mari close beside him.

"Brennan!" Cole shouted, enthusiastic and giggling and, oh, drunk already. "We're getting drinks!"

Mari slid up to the counter dividing the kitchen and living space and started pouring a too-generous shot of vodka into her plastic cup, ignoring Brennan. Cole hovered in front of Brennan, relaxed and grinning, a step into his personal space, chin up to look at Brennan with the height difference.

"Hey," Cole said, like he hadn't already loudly greeted him.

"Hey," Brennan said, soft and private.

"One of you fuckers do a shot with me," said Mari.

Not so private, then.

Ten minutes later, they found a cozy, unoccupied corner of the room in which to hover, Brennan trying not to make eyes at Cole until Mari excused herself to refill her drink.

The apartment door opened a few yards from their spot, letting in a sliver of harsh fluorescent light from the hallway, and Brennan's eyes shot over to see Nellie and Sunny arriving. Nellie's hair was different, with extensions to give her long braids, and she had a miniskirt ensemble that made her look like not just a college girl, but a trendy, cool one. Sunny had her hair in a slicked-back ponytail, big cargo pants, a crop top, and big hoop earrings, like she'd come from a photo shoot. She probably had.

Nerves and excitement sloshed around in Brennan's stomach with the jungle juice. The vampires were here.

Cole followed Brennan's gaze and gasped when he landed on Sunny and Nellie.

"That's them?"

He sounded so earnest and enthusiastic Brennan couldn't help teasing him. "Want an autograph?"

"Maybe. That's KeepItSunny on Instagram! She's *real* Instagram-famous. She's a vampire?"

"She's like, the scariest vampire I've met so far," Brennan said. Cole's eyes lit up like a kid's on Christmas morning.

"Aren't you gonna introduce us?" he asked, looking up through his lashes and letting his Southern accent out like an absolute asshole. He knew exactly what he was doing.

"What could go wrong," Brennan said, taking Cole by the wrist and doing his best to weave through the clusters of people toward the door. The feeling of Cole's skin under his fingers made him more lightheaded than the alcohol.

Nellie caught Brennan's eye and shot a hand up in an enthusiastic, high-reaching wave, and she and Sunny moved to meet him.

At least, he thought, with the party as a buffer, they couldn't talk about the whole *vampire* thing. He could only imagine the questions Cole might ask if he cornered Nellie or Sunny alone tonight.

Why, exactly, had he brought this on himself again?

Brennan let go of Cole's wrist and didn't have time to miss the contact before Nellie pulled Brennan into a hug. He startled forward into the embrace and stiffly but gratefully reciprocated.

"Brennan, this is amazing!" Nellie said as she released him from her grasp. "I haven't been to a classic party in *ages*!"

"It's really quite frat-party-like," Sunny said, a step behind Nellie, phone out of sight for once. Brennan couldn't figure out if that was a good or bad sign.

Brennan made the awkward introductions, but it only got more awkward when Nellie turned her sights on Cole.

"So *you're* Cole!" Nellie said in an overexaggerated mom way, giving Brennan a transparently meaningful look. Brennan's face burned.

"Allegedly," Cole said in greeting. "Though it makes me nervous when you say it like that."

"Don't worry, I've heard only good things," Nellie said. Then, "Extensively good things—"

"Let's get drinks, Nel," Sunny interrupted, while Cole gave Brennan a sidelong glance of amusement. Thank god for Sunny.

"Oh my god, *yes*," said Nellie. "I wanna do a keg stand."

"Let's work our way up to that," Sunny said, tugging Nellie away by the hand. "We'll catch up with you guys."

As soon as the space in front of them was vacated, Tony appeared and did a series of dramatic lunges, pointing at Brennan and Cole.

"Finish those drinks!" he shouted, thumping his chest, doing his weird lunge dance. "Chug, chug, chug!"

Brennan laughed, but Cole went for it, and Tony kept chanting, "Chug, chug, chug!" like a goddamn cartoon train, until eventually Brennan joined in and all their drinks were drained.

"Fuck yeah," Tony said, stance relaxing from his strangely intimidating ritual, clapping Brennan on the back. "Go get refills! WHOO!"

He disappeared into the crowd, and as he did Brennan realized he was wearing a cape. In his wake, Mari approached with a full plastic cup, swaying slightly, watching Tony go with an unreadable expression.

"Is he smashed already?" Brennan asked.

"I might be," Mari said somberly.

"Frat-boy party habits die hard," Cole explained. "Have you been drinking water? Let's go get you some water—"

"This ain't my first rodeo, bro," Mari said, swaying forward in her heels.

"She only calls people 'bro' when she's drunk," Cole told Brennan, and took Mari by the arm to head toward the kitchen.

From there, the night went by in a blur of sweat, pop music, too-sweet mixed drinks, dancing, and talking. Brennan rotated between friends, and every time he looked across the room he saw Cole mingling with a different group. Brennan didn't know if Cole truly knew that many people, or if he was making an effort to befriend every single person who could be crammed into the apartment. Neither option would be surprising.

Nellie and Sunny hung out with him most of the time. Sunny inevitably returned to being glued to her phone, and Nellie chattered his ears off about different parties she'd been to over the decade, Sunny occasionally chiming in to add details Nellie forgot.

Tony had apparently taken it as his personal duty to make sure everyone got properly smashed, continuing to wander around and randomly yell at people to "CHUG CHUG CHUG." Often he'd head to the kitchen and start a round of shots.

Tony dragged Brennan into a round of a drinking game, and he shouted and rooted for him each time he made a shot like he actually cared about him. Nellie tackled his side in a strangely aggressive hug to celebrate a good throw on her part, and as soon as she released him, a harsh hand was on his shoulder, and then Mari tugged him aside into the relative privacy of the hallway to the bedrooms.

"Listen here, Brooks," Mari stood in front of him, her tough demeanor undercut by glassy eyes and a slight sway to her stance. "I don't know you, and I don't like you."

"Oh," Brennan said. "Awesome. What is this?"

Mari poked Brennan's chest hard. "This is a shovel talk, genius. Cole freaking likes you, god knows why, and you need to know that if you hurt him at all, in any way, I know where you live and will not hesitate to cut off your di—"

A rising clamor from the kitchen had the whole party peering over to see Tony starting the keg stands, hoisted up with help from two guys and soaking himself with beer when the hose got loose. The guys set him down and he stripped his beer-soaked shirt off, grinning and taking a bow.

"Oh for fuck's sake, this *night*," Mari said, throwing up her hands, then turned on her heels and stalked away.

"Good talk," said Brennan.

Brennan scanned the party and caught sight of Cole and Nellie sitting on the kitchen counter, leaned together in a hushed conversation with serious expressions on both their faces. It took everything in Brennan not to either barge over or run away screaming. He could listen, if he really tried, despite the music and chatter. He'd gotten quite good at it, actually. But that was the point of inviting the vampires: he trusted Cole and Nellie enough to allow these parts of his life he'd wanted to keep separate to collide.

Tony and Sunny waved him back over to the game table. Brennan let himself stop thinking for a change, and the night went back to the pleasant haze it had been before.

At one point the makeshift dance floor that had formed in the living room found Tony, shirt still off, with Mari grinding up next to him.

"Good for her," Sunny said absently.

Cole and Nellie found them again, and a half-formed list of questions popped into Brennan's head—*What did you ask her? What did she say? Are you afraid of me? What's going on in your brain, please and thank you?* But Cole didn't hesitate to press into Brennan's side, throwing an arm around his shoulder. The anxiety melted out of Brennan's mind, replaced by embarrassingly sappy thoughts about how *well* they fit together.

Another round of drinks, and somehow, Nellie started on the topic of modern poetry. Brennan was drunk enough to end up on a rant, with Cole, Tony, and Sunny watching in amusement.

"Listen! I get it! I love that she made poetry feel more accessible! She was a gateway drug to poetry for a lot of people and I love that for them! But you cannot look at me and tell me honestly that *Milk and Honey* was *good poetry* so help me god—"

"Alright, Mr. Know-It-All," Nellie challenged. "What accessible entry-level poetry do you have up your sleeve?"

"You *mock* me," Brennan said, because they probably thought he was too cool to have limericks memorized for no reason at all but, in fact, he did.

And, well, maybe Brennan was drunker than he thought—it had been awhile, with all his vampire stuff, since he'd really relaxed—because he ended up pushing himself to stand on the kitchen island, cackled, and started loudly and dramatically shouting limericks.

"There was a young lass of Madras
Who had a magnificent ass
Not rounded and pink
As you'd probably think
But was gray, had long ears, and ate grass."

Cole was giggling and moving to spot Brennan so he didn't fall and die, until Nellie pulled him down.

Another hour later, Cole started to sober up and resume the role of mom-friend, pushing water on everyone, until eventually Brennan sobered up, too, which had the effect of making the party seem a lot more gross, sticky, and anxiety-inducing. Cole was flourishing a couple of pre-rolled joints—god bless the legal state of Massachusetts—and getting a group of people to start a circle outside.

When that properly distracted most of Brennan's friends, he made his way to the bathroom for that late-party breakdown moment when you stared at yourself in the mirror and contemplated existence. Or was that a Brennan thing? But the door was locked, and continued to be for ten minutes, even after he banged on the door and finally got a pointed moan in response.

Oh. Oops. There were definitely people hooking up in there.

"Sorry!" he called through the door and paused his crisis for later. The party was winding down, people beginning to leave, either too drunk or too sober to be there.

Down the hallway from the bathroom, Nellie and Sunny were talking in urgent whispers. Brennan didn't have any qualms using his spidey senses to eavesdrop this time, catching the end of a sentence—

"—if there's new turns that we don't know about."

—before Sunny stiffened and turned to look directly at Brennan.

Nellie rushed forward with a smile. "Oh good, Brennan!" she said. "We wanted to find you, we were about to head out."

"Is everything okay?"

"Everything's super. We've got some business to deal with, so don't let us interrupt your party."

"Oh," Brennan said. "Can I help, or—?"

"No, no," Nellie insisted immediately, putting a companionable arm around Brennan and steering him toward the door. She found her bomber jacket within the jumble on the coat hooks and shrugged it on while giving Brennan a teasing smile. "Cole's great, by the way."

"Right," said Brennan. "Are you sure there's nothing I can do?"

Nellie opened the door and Cole was on the other side, pink-nosed from the late-night autumn air, a few people behind him with various levels of the giggles. Cole's hair was especially tousled, and Brennan wanted to reach out and fix it, tug the jacket around his neck tighter against the wind.

The sound of a throat clearing pulled Brennan's gaze from his weed-scented love interest, and Nellie was watching him with a completely unsubtle grin.

"What you can do," Nellie said, "is text me the details tomorrow."

Sunny said, "Retweet." And then they both disappeared into the night.

"What was that about?" Cole asked, stepping inside and into Brennan's space, the length of their arms pressed together.

"Don't worry about it," Brennan said.

The party crowd continued to thin as the morning hours crept in, and Brennan and Cole were continually in each other's orbit, catching each other's eyes throughout the night in a weird, soft tension Brennan had never experienced before. The quiet confidence that he wanted Cole, and the tentative amazement that Cole could want him back.

Mari had disappeared at some point in the night. Cole was mostly sober, helping those who weren't order Ubers home, telling everyone to have a good night and drink water and eat a big breakfast tomorrow in that disgustingly charming way of his, waving goodbye to girls carrying their high-heeled shoes and guys who smelled strongly of beer.

Then Cole was at his side again, a hand on his elbow, smiling conspiratorially.

"Let's go somewhere," Cole said.

"Yeah?" Brennan asked. "The Waffle Den's the only place open."

"Nah, I have a better idea," Cole said. He smiled, and this one seemed a little brighter, a little more private. "Trust me?"

All Brennan could do was follow.

13

SWIMMINGLY

BRENNAN'S PHONE

> **Brennan**
> Nellie I'm freaking.
> Nellie are you around?
> Can't call.

Nellie
What's up? Are you okay?

> **Brennan**
> I think I'm gonna do something not good?

Nellie
Brennan what are you talking about is
everything okay question mark question mark?

> **Brennan**
> I like this boy.

Nellie
You like a boy
You scared me! Oh my god. I know, why is that a problem?

> **Brennan**
> I'm gonna,
> Kiss his face?

Nellie
Yes

> **Brennan**
> He's really nice.

Nellie
Yes

> **Brennan**
> I just feel like he deserves better.

Nellie
No

> **Brennan**
> He doesn't really know me yet.

Nellie
Maybe
But shouldn't you give him the chance to?

> **Brennan**
> I want to.

Nellie
Then kiss his really nice face.
You're allowed to want things.

> **Brennan**
> Ugh.

It was cold, so by the time they reached the Dolson Center and stopped in front of the big glass doors, Cole's cheeks were flushed, hands shoved in the pockets of his coat.

"The rec center?" Brennan asked. "It's a little late for a workout."

Brennan wasn't a big gym rat—he loved running outside, with a route and scenery and sunlight. But, absently, he thought about returning to test his vampiric strength and speed with more accuracy.

"I used to smoke with the night janitor," Cole said. "He keeps a spare key hidden."

Brennan still wasn't sure why they were there, but he kind of liked not knowing. He'd never been big on surprises but something about Cole's smile made him want to go with it.

Cole produced a key from somewhere and unlocked the door, both of them giggling into the cold air. The Dolson Center was vast, open, and modern. A smoothie joint was at one end and gym equipment sprawled across the first floor, with a balcony that overlooked everything else. The walls were windows, looking out into the grassy quad.

Cole beelined across the gym toward a door on the far side, and when he opened it, the smell of chlorine assaulted Brennan's nose.

An Olympic-sized swimming pool stretched out in the middle of gray tile floors, light filtering through the water and making the whole room glow blue even though the overhead lights were off.

Cole's sneakers squeaked and echoed against the tile floor, and he held the door open for Brennan to walk through. He grinned. "Care for a late-night swim?"

That *smile*. What else could Brennan do but follow?

But before he could, Cole was turning, grin wavering, fiddling his fingers together.

"I mean, we don't *have* to swim," he said. "We can just put our feet in, or not at all. I just—the vibes here are pretty awesome, right?"

It hadn't occurred to Brennan that Cole could be as nervous about this unspoken thing between them as Brennan was. And that seemed wrong, as wrong as Cole crying in the library had been, and Brennan couldn't have it.

So he dropped his backpack, dropped his coat, and said, "Oh, we're swimming."

They stripped down to their underwear and Brennan kept his eyes to himself, except for when he didn't, and both of them were laughing like children. Cole reached for his hand as they jumped into the pool together.

The water was cool but not cold, and Brennan broke through the surface, Cole's fingers entwined with his. Cole had freckles on his back, Brennan noted. He was all lean muscles and delicate skin and he laughed as he pushed his hair back from his eyes.

Cole splashed Brennan, and Brennan splashed him back, and they went back and forth splashing until Cole started trying to dunk him, which devolved into Cole clinging to Brennan from behind, arms wrapped around Brennan's shoulders, somewhere between a piggyback ride and an intimate embrace, Cole's chest against his back. Brennan had mercy on his poor gay heart and gave in, dunking them both in the water instead of reveling in it.

When they resurfaced, Cole swam around to face him again and shook his hair out like a dog. It was wilder than ever from tussling in the water, and his freckles stood out against the water droplets rolling across the canvas of his skin.

"Man, I wish we had some music," Cole said, treading water, hands gliding in an entrancing pattern.

"Yeah, what's the mood?" Brennan asked, swimming lazy lines back and forth across the deep end. "More indie stuff I've never heard of?"

Cole at least looked sheepish when he said, "Fifty-fifty chance for something unbearably indie or, like, Taylor Swift, because I'm only human." He lit up, and went on, "I have this amazing record collection. You should see it sometime."

"I've never listened to music on vinyl," Brennan admitted, but he loved how Cole lit up from the inside when he talked about it. He stopped swimming at the edge, anchoring himself to the wall.

"Well, you *definitely* have to come listen, then."

"How'd you get into that? Record collecting?"

"My brother. Noah. He was a year older than me. He was, like, the rebel kid. Loud music in his room all the time, blew off school, smoked weed. The records were part of the aesthetic, I guess."

"And he . . . gave them to you?" Brennan prompted, but he had a feeling he knew the answer.

"He killed himself before graduation," Cole said, the same way he might say he was out of milk. "I kept his records, and now I add to the collection. I started out doing it for him, but it's mostly for me now."

Brennan didn't know what to say.

"Ugh, sorry," Cole said. "Talk about a mood killer."

"You apologize too much," Brennan said. Cole splashed him. "I mean, if you don't want to talk about it, that's fine, but you're allowed to, if you want. I can listen." He didn't say, *I want to know everything about you.* "Were you guys close?"

Cole smiled and his eyes turned distant. He leaned to float on his back.

"For most of our lives, yeah. He was a year older than me. Me and him and Mari were a trio, we all grew up together. He was always labeled a troublemaker, or whatever, and then Mari was this total genius-girlboss, and I was just, like, happy to be there.

"We weren't talking, when it happened. So that's always gonna feel like shit. I thought he was pushing me away but it was all, like, signs. Or whatever."

"I don't think it's fair to blame yourself. You can't let someone treat you like shit out of fear of them killing themselves," Brennan said, because talking about capital-S *suicide* always brought up a seasick sort of feeling and gut reflex for defensiveness and apology.

"It wasn't like that. You don't understand."

Brennan wanted to say that he *did* understand, but he didn't know how to explain it all. He wasn't used to people knowing him. It was safer that way, keeping the ugliest parts of himself separate.

"Yeah. Sorry."

Maybe that wasn't fair to Cole. Maybe he deserved a better friend than that, when he opened up about all his stuff, while the things Cole knew about Brennan were stumbled into by accident.

Cole deflated. "No, I'm sorry."

With a buzzing sigh, the pool lights went off all at once, and they were plunged into total darkness.

They both froze, and one of Cole's hands gripped his arm. Except—

Brennan blinked a few times, and things came into focus, clear as ever—maybe *clearer.*

"Shit. Must be on a timer," Cole said, laughing with a nervous edge.

Brennan wanted to kick his own ass for not being more honest, because now the moment was broken.

"Should we go?" Brennan asked.

"Maybe," Cole said.

Neither of them moved.

Cole edged closer to Brennan, water rippling around him, blinking somewhere past his shoulder. Cole joined him in floating near the edge of the pool, hanging on to the wall. Maybe it was the darkness, the fact that he could see Cole but Cole couldn't see him, that made it easier.

"You know, maybe I do understand." Brennan was sure it confused Cole, but he didn't say anything, just pressed his fingers harder into Brennan's shoulder and treaded water.

"Can I be honest with you?" And when that was too vulnerable, he followed up with, "Since you already brought down the mood and everything."

Cole swatted him.

"You're ridiculous," Cole said. And instead of returning to his shoulder, he reached for his hand. Oh god. Brennan must be more pathetic and starved of intimacy than he thought, because just that was heart-stopping. This was slow and intentional, not an afterthought as they jumped in the pool. He was even more grateful for the dark, because eye contact on top of it all might actually melt him down to goo.

"Are you afraid of the dark?" Brennan asked.

"Only if I'm alone," Cole said. Brennan squeezed his hand. "But come on, you can tell me anything."

Interesting. Brennan believed him.

Cole inched closer. Maybe he thought Brennan couldn't see, either. Somehow, that seemed unfair. Like he was cheating.

He closed his eyes.

"I used to want to die, like, all the time," he said. There, years of grueling depression summed up in a neat little sentence. "I know, I seem so put-together, it's shocking." Humor, to deflect, as Dr. Morris so often pointed out. "But I've kind of been depressed and anxious my whole life. I was existential. Like, 'We're all insignificant, nothing matters, life sucks and then you die' existential."

"Do you . . . still?"

Brennan flexed his fingers nervously where they clung to the edge of the pool.

"Sometimes it's worse or better. I'm okay a lot of the time now. Therapy does wonders, but for a while there . . ."

"It was bad," Cole concluded.

"Yeah," Brennan said. "I've always been depressed and anxious. I think I'll probably be depressed and anxious in some capacity for the rest of my life. Which, given recent events, will be a long time."

"There's nothing wrong with that. I have anxiety. I go to therapy. It's not a big deal."

"Yes, but what I mean is." Brennan stopped, frustrated. "What I'm trying to say is, it's never your fault. Sometimes it's the *parents'* fault, maybe, but you can't blame yourself for not being there if he pushed you away. It's brain chemicals and generational trauma, but not your responsibility."

It suddenly felt important that Cole knew that.

"Don't you think more people in the world would be okay if they saw a friendly face when they needed it? If there was a little more compassion?" Cole asked.

A possibility occurred to him that Cole was there out of pity after seeing Brennan's panic attack, that he was walking on eggshells around Brennan, scared of hurting his feelings when he was near his breaking point.

"Other people's happiness isn't your responsibility," Brennan said.

"Okay. Maybe not. I'd still like to try."

"That's a nice way of thinking, but what about what *you* want?"

"I'm right where I want to be," Cole said, so quick Brennan was dizzy with it.

"Oh? In a dark, wet room, alone with a vampire?"

"Don't forget *cold.*"

"Sounds like a nice night," Brennan said.

"It has been," Cole said. Slid closer to Brennan, the water around them sloshing. Brennan could feel Cole shivering.

"If you're cold, maybe we should go—"

"Brennan," Cole interrupted.

Brennan opened his eyes. Cole was close, one hand latched on to the edge of the pool, the other clinging to Brennan. He squinted, but his eyes must have been adjusting, because he almost caught Brennan's eye.

"Yeah?" Brennan asked, his voice coming out deep enough to surprise even himself, and Cole's eyes darkened, or maybe Brennan's night vision wasn't reliable and he was thinking wishfully.

"Can you see in the dark?" Cole asked. He unwound their fingers and slid his hand up Brennan's arm, over his shoulder, up to the back of his neck. Thank god they were submerged in water, because Brennan felt like he was on fire.

"Um, yeah," Brennan managed.

"Good. I'm afraid if I try to kiss you, I'll miss."

Brennan's stomach did a dramatic somersault. He was a computer glitching, data not computing, but there it was: Cole. Wanted. To kiss. Him? The wheels kept turning—

"Do you need me to spell it out for you?"

Cole's breath was on his face. His brain was slow like molasses, clogged up with processing new information, like, Cole smelled like old coffee and vanilla and chlorine. Like, *Cole* wanted *Brennan* to *kiss* him.

"Maybe," Brennan squeaked out.

Cole laughed against Brennan's cheek, eyes crinkling.

"Good lord, it must be exhausting inside your brain."

Cole's nose nudged Brennan's, finding his way in the dark, pausing in question.

Brennan was overwhelmingly aware of Cole's pulse—in his throat, in the hand pressed to the back of Brennan's neck, rippling through Brennan from where their skin touched.

"You have no idea," Brennan said.

But he wasn't scared. He was in control. And for the life of him, Brennan couldn't find a single reason to stop himself from what he wanted to do. He lifted a hand to cup Cole's cheek, curved their faces together.

The wheels in Brennan's head stopped spinning.

They met in the middle, soft and sure, and then pulled back, Cole's breath against his lips, their foreheads touching, and Brennan closed his eyes again, but it was okay, because then Cole was diving back in and they were *really* kissing.

The sensory difference of kissing, as a vampire, was the first thing Brennan noticed—because that romance-novel bullshit of tasting things besides morning breath on a kiss was true, and Cole tasted like mocha and ice cream. The smell of Cole's shampoo mixed with the chlorine was suddenly overwhelming, this close. But he sunk into the soft press of mouths and let himself get lost in it, letting his more human instinct take over and kiss Cole with the thorough attention he deserved.

Cole wrapped his arms like vines around Brennan's neck and shoulders, pressing forward and pulling Brennan in. Brennan followed gladly, drinking Cole in with his one free hand, cupping his cheek, his jaw, going up into his hair and down his back, wrapping an arm tight around his waist. Cole sighed a dreamy little sound and dropped his head back,

Adam's apple bobbing. Brennan pressed two hard kisses to the skin of Cole's neck, then another, tasting the salt and chlorine.

And then the sound of Cole's pulse in his ears, the feel of it rushing under his lips, sent a jolt of something feral through him, the same gut instinct that usually had him lunging after squirrels. He felt his fangs filling his mouth in that familiar, uncomfortable way.

He launched himself away from Cole in a jolt, splashing halfway across the pool, hands covering his mouth to hide his fangs.

Cole looked . . . like he'd been kissed senseless, frankly, lips red and damp hair sticking out in odd directions. Brennan wasn't much better.

Then Brennan's eyes fell to Cole's neck, where a single dot of blood pearled.

"Oh god. Are you okay?"

"I'm fine," Cole said, dazed more than anything, but Brennan scanned him for signs of pain.

"You're bleeding."

"I'm okay," Cole said again, daring to creep closer in the water. "Are you?"

"Yeah," Brennan squeaked. "But maybe we should cool down."

"Are you thirsty, do you need to go—"

"No!" Brennan said, because he wasn't going to hurt Cole, he was in control, but— "They sometimes. Come out. When . . ."

Cole's dark gaze flickered between Brennan's eyes and lips like he understood. His mouth curved into the smallest smile. He closed the rest of the distance Brennan had created and brought one hand to Brennan's face and oh-so-slowly pressed his thumb to the corner of his lip, where one of his fangs poked out. The next kiss Cole pressed to his mouth was gentle and light.

"I trust you," Cole said.

"I could have hurt you," Brennan protested, weak to his own ears.

"But you didn't."

"We should get out of the pool," Brennan suggested.

"We should go back to your place."

Brennan blinked a few times and wondered if a better vampire would have said no and gotten far away, but he was too far gone for that. Instead, Brennan made a show of pinching himself. Cole flushed beautifully.

"We should definitely go back to my place," Brennan agreed.

Brennan had never gotten out of a pool and into clothes faster in his life, even though they were giggling the whole time. Brennan was trying to help Cole not trip over himself in the dark, while Cole used the dark as an excuse to touch Brennan's chest once and his ass twice, playing innocent but laughing loud and bright when Brennan teased him.

They were still damp when Cole locked up the pool. Once the door was locked, Brennan pressed Cole against it with another searing kiss, because apparently that was something he could do and he'd take advantage of that for as long as he could. Brennan only pulled away when Cole was smiling into the kiss too much.

They threaded their hands together to weave through the gym. Outside, the cold wind was harsh against their damp skin and hair.

"Shitting Christ," Cole tugged his jacket closed and zipped it up. Damp curls dangled in his eyes, and for once, Brennan let himself push them out of his face. Cole's eyes danced with affection. "At least it's not far."

Brennan glanced around the quad. It was late now—had to be almost four in the morning, at least—and campus was empty. Just autumn leaves on the ground and a winter chill in the air.

"Could be faster," Brennan suggested, deciding in a split second that he was more than willing to risk it all for a *chance* with this boy, pathetic as it was. He crouched down in front of Cole and reached back. "Hop on."

"When I told Mari I wanted to climb you like a tree, this isn't what I had in mind."

"You wanted to—you told *Mari*—?"

"I tell Mari everything." He laughed.

Cole hopped up and Brennan situated Cole on his back, Cole's arms going around his neck, Brennan's hands under his thighs.

Jesus, Brennan hadn't thought through how much physical contact there was in a piggyback ride. Cole's whole front was pressed to Brennan's back and Brennan needed to be alone with Cole in a bed, like, *yesterday.*

"Hold on, okay?" Brennan warned, poised to run.

"Sure thing," Cole said, cheeky. "You know what this reminds me of?"

"I swear, if you say *Twilight*—"

"*Twilight,*" Cole said.

For that, Brennan took off running.

Cole's gasp cut short in his ear as they launched into what felt like flight, wind whipping around them as Brennan moved impossibly fast. Brennan kept an ear out for signs of other people, but all he heard was Cole's incredulous laugh and then whooping like he was on a roller coaster. They cut through campus, hurtling toward the block of off-campus housing where he and Tony lived.

Brennan slowed to a walk as they approached the building. Cole laughed breathlessly in his ear.

"The vampire strength is pretty hot," Cole said. "Think you could bench press me?"

Brennan wanted to do a lot more than that.

Cole hopped down as Brennan unlocked the door, and then they stopped altogether when they saw what was behind it.

Marisela, aiming a bottle of pepper spray at Brennan's face, the other gripping her phone. On the floor beside her, just next to a pile of shoes, was Brennan's freezer, lid open, contents displayed: approximately a dozen packs of hospital-grade human blood strewn across the ground. Next to the freezer was the broken lock that used to keep it shut, and a hammer.

"You know," Mari said, "at first I honestly thought it was a coincidence when we saw you the day a bunch of blood went missing from Dr. Huong's lab."

"Mari, what are you doing?" Cole started.

Mari kept the pepper spray trained on Brennan's eyes. Brennan had no clue if pepper spray worked on vampires, but that was not a theory he wanted to test out anytime soon.

"Cole, get the fuck away from him," Mari said, her voice deadly low. Something in the tone made Cole's spine straighten. He took half a step toward her, maybe on reflex, but it still hit Brennan like a stab in the gut.

"Listen, Mari—"

"Don't say my name, you literal fucking freak. Back up!"

"Freak" stung.

"Mar, take a few deep breaths, okay?" Cole said, but it was meek. He was shrinking into himself. "I feel like you're lashing out unfairly."

"I am lashing out in a perfectly fucking rational way!"

"What are you even doing here?" Brennan asked.

Mari flushed red, embarrassment mixing with anger. Which meant the answer was probably Tony. "That doesn't matter. What matters is, as Cole's best friend, it's my responsibility to make sure his crushes aren't serial killers, so it's my job to check their rooms for dead bodies—"

"Oh, my god, Mari—"

"But then it was like, who the hell has a *locked* freezer hidden in their *closet*? And, who the hell has a *stockpile* of *human blood* in their closet?"

Fuck. Shit. Mari's eyes were a dangerous blaze, daring him to try to lie his way out of it. And Cole stood halfway between the two of them, head down, shoulders drooped, infuriatingly silent.

"I know it looks, uh, not good," Brennan tried. "But I have a valid explanation for—"

"But then I realized," Mari interrupted loudly. "I don't want to know. I don't want to hear it. I don't care!" She took a step forward, thumb poised over the pepper spray's trigger. "I want you to stay away from me, and my friends."

She reached for Cole and pulled him by the hand toward her, stepping protectively in front of him with the pepper spray shielding them both. Worse, Cole went without protest, head still down, unreadable.

"I'm a vampire," Brennan blurted. Then shoved his hands over his ears as if he could shut out the response. Shit. *Fuck.*

Mari was stock-still. "Sorry. What?"

"I know how it sounds," Brennan said, forcing every ounce of desperate honesty into the words, needing her to believe it. "But it's true. It's new. I got hit by a car and a vampire turned me, and now I need blood to survive."

"Okay," Mari said, voice low, nodding slowly. Then, "You're delusional."

Brennan squeezed his eyes shut. "Fair enough," he said. "I would think the same, if it weren't happening to me."

Cole's voice was quiet but clear. "It's true." He still wouldn't look up from the floorboards.

Mari whirled around toward him, taking her eyes off Brennan for the first time since they'd arrived. "What the fuck are you talking about, Cole?"

"It's true," Cole repeated. "He's a vampire. But he isn't hurting anybody—"

"You *knew* about this?" Mari demanded, gesturing to the pile of blood, some stolen from the school, most from the vampires' blood drive.

"Maybe we can just," Cole said, "um, sit down and have a conversation about—"

"Um, this is not a *sit-down-and-talk* situation," Mari said. Cole sank further into himself at the dismissal. Mari turned back to Brennan. "If what you're saying is true, this is a fucking *priest* situation. More likely, it's a situation for antipsychotics. You need fucking help."

"I wish antipsychotics would help!" Brennan said. "But I need blood. Animals don't cut it."

"He took from the blood drive," Cole added, not helpfully.

Mari glanced back and forth between them for a long time while Brennan dared to hope with bated breath and Cole continued to study the floor like he was going to be tested on it. Brennan watched the expressions pass over Mari's face, the tentative realization that they were being serious, that this was a possibility.

"And you saw," Mari finished, to Cole. He nodded, damp and deflated, and she went quiet for a minute. "Oh my god. Cole, are you bleeding?"

At the curve of his neck was the tiniest smear of blood from where Brennan's fang had pricked him before he could pull away. It was barely anything, but he was still bleeding, and Brennan had still been the cause of it.

"It was an accident," Brennan started to defend himself, but it came out weak. What difference did that make? Cole was hurt, and it was his fault.

"Oh my god," Mari said. "And now that girl is missing. Did you hurt her?"

"No," Brennan said, barely a whisper. Because even if he hadn't, another vampire had.

"He wouldn't," Cole said.

Wouldn't he? He'd hurt Cole, after all. How was he any different from Dom?

"Do you even hear yourself?" Mari pressed her lips together for a long moment. She shook her head at Cole with what could only be described as pity. "You're doing it again, Cole," she said coldly. "Taking in strays because you feel guilty about Noah."

Cole recoiled like she'd physically slapped him, and Mari marched up to Brennan to stick a finger at his nose with her free hand while the other still brandished the pepper spray.

"And you," she said. "Stay away from me, stay away from Cole, stay away from Tony. Get a new lease, transfer universities, flee the country, I don't give a shit. If I see you again, I'll find the closest thing to Buffy the goddamn Vampire Slayer we have in this world and send them your way."

She pushed past Brennan to get out the doorway and left Cole standing in the entryway with Brennan, head hanging low.

She stopped outside and held out a hand like an owner calling a dog. "Cole, come on."

Worse, Cole went. Didn't even look Brennan in the eyes.

The door slammed shut behind them, leaving Brennan with the mess.

Mari was right. He was a freak. A monster. He was stupid to get caught up in a fantasy of normalcy with Cole, when he couldn't even *kiss* Cole without drawing blood. He'd let himself get distracted, and now he was facing the consequences.

First, he would need to clean up the blood.

He wished, more than anything, that he could collapse in his bed and sleep, but in addition to being an immortal being who was incapable of sleep, he turned on the lights of his bedroom to find his bed occupied.

"Fucking shit, Dom!" Brennan shouted, nearly dropping the pouch of blood he was sipping through a straw like a Capri-Sun. It tasted better that way, okay?

"That sounded brutal," said Dom, reclining on her elbows at the edge of Brennan's bed, arching an eyebrow as if she was the offended party here. She was wearing all black again, her hair cropped short and dyed that inky black. Whatever Goth moment she'd been working up to in the past months was in full swing. "Keeping a secret's not so fun when it bites you in the ass, huh?"

"What are you doing in here?"

"I wanted to talk to you," Dom said, smiling coyly. Brennan recognized vodka on her breath.

"You could have texted," Brennan said. He was *not* in the mood for this. His hair was still wet. He still reeked of chlorine. He still felt Cole's kiss on his lips, his nose nudging Brennan's. *Fuck.*

"I wanted to talk in person."

"I'm not in the mood. Besides, we're seeing each other in a few weeks with Sunny and Nellie—"

"I wanted to talk *without* Sunny and Nellie."

"Well, you could have at least had the lights on and not given me a goddamn heart attack."

"Noted for next time," Dom said.

Brennan desperately wanted to discourage a *next time*. He didn't need another reminder of all the ways he was a monster.

"Why did you come here, Dom?" Brennan asked, and even to his own ears he sounded exhausted.

"Haven't you heard the good news?" Dom deadpanned. "Evelyn's disappearance is no longer under investigation. Like it never even happened! Isn't that great?" She let out a dry, humorless laugh.

Brennan's hands curled into fists at his sides. "Isn't that what you wanted?"

Dom gave a cruel, wry smile. "Wow. I almost forgot what a complete bag of dicks you are."

"What do you want me to say? Congrats on getting away with murder and thanks for stopping by?"

"My sister died, you heartless fuck. She was the only good thing in my life and she's gone. Even her *memory* is gone." She stood abruptly, swaying drunkenly into Brennan's space as she lilted toward the window rather than the door. "I don't know why I came here. Stupid idea."

"Wait," Brennan said, stepping in front of her and scrubbing a hand over his face. "I'm sorry. Just—say what you came here to say."

Dom frowned, thoughtful, pale, and gaunt. She looked, for all intents and purposes, like a vampire.

"I don't know if I can keep pretending," she said. "Playing at human when I'm not."

"Okay," Brennan said, low. "Talk to Nellie. You can transfer or something. I'm sure there's a pamphlet about it."

"No, listen. You're holding on so hard to the things that make you human, but for me—that was Evelyn. And if Evelyn's gone, so am I. My old life doesn't matter. The shitty job, the shitty parents, the shitty apartment." She seemed to be realizing it as she was saying it, and laughed, childishly incredulous. "I can do whatever I want now."

Something dark swirled in Brennan's stomach. "And what is it you want?"

"I don't know. But I know what I don't want. I don't want to ever feel powerless again."

The dark thing in the pit of Brennan's stomach turned cold and solid. This time, when Dom moved to leave, Brennan let her.

"Dom." Brennan's fingers shook, squeezing around the blood packet.

Dom turned her head to look at him over her shoulder, the moonlit window lighting up her profile, an icy expression on her shadowed face.

Brennan swallowed hard. "Don't come back here," he said.

Dom's face shuttered, hard and stony, mouth set in a line. She huffed a cold scoff and turned back toward the window.

"Keep pretending, if you want. I'll do what I have to do to get by. Like I always have."

She was disappointed, he realized. She had wanted him to understand. Maybe even expected him to.

She ducked through the window, sliding it shut behind her. She moved so quietly, with hunter-light footsteps, that Brennan could barely hear her exit.

14

CREATURES OF THE NIGHT

Missed calls from Nellie [6]
Missed calls from Sunny [2]

·················

Instagram

KeepItSunny ✔ messaged you.
Call Nellie right the fuck now.

·················

Nellie
Hey don't freak out but something may have happened!
Don't panic! We're outside your apartment. Yes I'm texting him right now
is it still recording I hate this thing how do I make it

·················

EMERGENCY ALERT—Sturbridge [1 text]
Crime alert—Sturbridge University Police Department responded
to an off-campus incident involving two students and an animal

attack. Park services and animal control have been contacted and SUPD is investigating the situation. Stay on campus paths and out of the woods until SUPD gives the all-clear notice.

The street outside Brennan's apartment was blanketed with the first snow of the season, everything camouflaged white, more snow flurrying around him. Nellie and Sunny stood in front of his building, Nellie in a fluffy puffer jacket, Sunny in a long wool coat. He could have used therapy with Nellie right around then, what with Mari's threats and Cole's silent departure fresh in his mind, but he shoved it down in the face of their urgent texts and grave expressions.

"Hey," Brennan greeted them, taking the steps down to the sidewalk to get on equal footing.

"Are you okay? Is everything alright?" Nellie's hands fluttered around him, searching for some hidden injury.

"Yeah, of course, I'm fine—"

"We worried when you weren't responding."

"I'm fine. I'm good. What's going on?"

Sunny piped up without looking from her phone, "Oh, they definitely hooked up. He has a hickey."

Brennan slapped a hand over his neck, face warming.

"Oh my god, Brennan, good for you!" Nellie squealed.

"No! Stop! This is not the topic! What happened?"

Nellie and Sunny exchanged uneasy glances.

"You saw about the 'animal attack'?" Sunny said. "A vampire's involved. Two people died. Students here."

"Whoa, *what*? They died?" The alert called it an *incident,* not a fucking murder. But fear quickly replaced surprise. "Who—who was it?"

"Two frat guys. We're working on it," Sunny said, and Brennan felt a weight lifted that it wasn't Cole. But Sunny was so matter-of-fact that it only made Brennan angrier. Two people were dead, Mari knew about him, and Dom—

Oh no.

"Dom was here last night," Brennan said, realization making him sick. "Talking about doing whatever she wants and not wanting to pretend anymore. It has to be her."

Nellie and Sunny had another wordless conversation with frowns and narrowed eyes.

"What?" Brennan demanded.

"That just . . ." Nellie said, "it checks out. We were at the, uh, crime scene?" She wrinkled up her nose. "Gross, we're like Vampire CSI. But Sunny picked up her scent, and there were prints that match those vintage size nine Doc Martens she's been rocking."

"And you're sure that— Why do you know what shoes she wears?"

"I'd ask why you *don't,* but your Target-brand Vans knockoffs speak for themselves." Sunny sniffed and pointedly glanced toward Brennan's feet.

Brennan brushed off the remark. "Well, do you know where she is?"

"We're working on it," Nellie said.

"What if she does it again? What if she comes after me, or other students?" He pictured Cole, Mari, Tony, any of the kids in his classes facing down a murderous Dom, and shivered.

"That's what we're trying to do. Stop things like this from happening again."

"Are you sure? Or are you trying to cover them up?"

"Oh, come on," Sunny spat, stalking away from the conversation. "We don't have time for this."

"I get that this is scary," Nellie said, voice firm but comforting. "But if you can try to trust us, it would mean a lot. We want the same things. To protect both the humans *and* vampires."

Brennan frowned and nodded. If this was Dom's work, then it was Brennan's fault for lashing out at her like she wasn't his problem to deal with.

"How can I help?" Brennan asked.

"Don't," Sunny said.

Rolling his eyes, Brennan deferred to Nellie, but Nellie gave an apologetic smile. "We really need you to stay put."

"Are you serious? People are dying."

"Which is why you need to leave it to us," Nellie said. "Obviously, let us know if you hear anything from Dom, or see anything weird."

"Right," Brennan bit out, "or if more people die."

"Watch your tone," Sunny said, harsh, then, "Nellie. He's in one piece, you told him the news. Let's go."

"Where are you going? Do I at least get to know the plan?"

"We're gonna investigate," Nellie said. "And *you* are going to pinky promise to stay out of it."

Brennan arched an unimpressed brow at her extended pinky finger.

"I will not be doing that," said Brennan.

Nellie shrugged. "Worth a try."

Taking the train took the drama out of storming directly to Dom's apartment in a rage. By the time the commuter line dropped him in Boston and Brennan was walking up to Dom's complex, most of the rage had melted away into worry. He didn't know what he was going to say, or what he was supposed to say. He only knew that she had come to him before, and he'd messed it up, and he had to fix it.

As he came to her unit, a wind gust pushed open the door on its own. It hadn't been locked, or even closed.

Brennan stood in the open doorway and gaped at the bare apartment. The lone window in the living room was open, letting in a fierce chill.

It wasn't completely empty—the couch was still there, the TV and its stand, the appliances. But all the pictures, all the books and coats and cooking utensils and personal items, were packed up in a stack of boxes on one side, some labeled DONATE and one labeled TRASH. The trash box was on top, full of photos that were framed and loose and in albums, a hundred little Doms and Evelyns left behind.

Something was wedged in the open window, flapping in the wind. Brennan crossed to the window slowly, looking around like he might be dreaming and the apartment might transform back to the one in which he'd shared drinks with Dom a few weeks earlier. He grabbed the thing from the window—a folded piece of paper—and slid the window shut. The carpet in front of the window was damp from rain and snow.

He unfolded the paper, and it was a printed flyer, plain 8½" × 11" printer grade. Brennan had seen it before, on Facebook.

SAVE THE DATE!

CREATURES OF THE NIGHT: VAMPIRE BALL

MARCH 1, 2025

Will take place at the Old Florence Inn just outside Boston.
Vampires and humans mingle together for one mysterious night
in a historical setting.

Light refreshments. Live entertainment. Drinks available for
purchase with ID.

Formal/Gothic dress code will be enforced.
18+ event.

He flipped it around and there, in scribbled, hasty handwriting, it read:

B,
You won't want to miss this
—D

He flipped it again, hastily scanning both sides, looking for more written notes or some other clue. Was it a threat? A warning? An invitation? Or something she'd misplaced on her way out? Brennan peeked through the window, but he only saw a snowy-slushy alleyway. No sign of Dom, and no hints of what she was thinking.

He tucked the flyer into his journal and, for reasons he couldn't explain, tucked a photo of Evelyn smiling brightly in as well. Then he left Dom's empty apartment, closing the door behind him.

BRENNAN'S PHONE

Brennan
Found this at Dom's place. She's gone.

Nellie

Yikes

I thought you were staying out of it 😣

Brennan

Nope. What do you think?

Also did you just use an emoji?

Nellie

I'm learning!

And I mean it's the biggest gathering of vampires

among humans in one place of the year

Brennan

So if she were planning something around that,

that would be bad.

Nellie

Yes

Brennan

Can you cancel the ball?

Nellie

It's been the same standing date and location for over

a century and every vampire in North America knows about it.

I couldn't get the message out to the ones that don't use technology

or don't have a stable headrest

Stable address

Not to mention Quinn would be heartbroken

Brennan

So, the ball goes on?

Nellie

The ball goes on

·················

Drafts to Cole

Brennan

~~Hey, I know Mari said she'd kill me if I talked to you again but~~

~~Hey, how are you doing?~~

~~I'm sorry I'm like this and everything is hard but~~
~~I miss hanging out with you~~
~~Hope you're doing well.~~
~~Am I even allowed in the library anymore or~~
~~will I be nerfed on sight?~~

....

A Pamphlet

Protecting Your Territory: Wards and Protection Charms for the Low-Level Vampire

BY NELLIE ADAMS

While your clan and clan leaders do much of the work of protecting you and your loved ones from potential rogue vampires, we understand the desire to take extra precautions, especially in times of conflict. Not everyone can do complex protection work (see "Protecting Your Territory: Practices for the High-Level Vampire" for information about binding, banishment, and other more extreme measures of protection), but anyone, regardless of vampiric abilities, can use these small measures to enhance their safety and feel more secure.

Environmental Wards

Environmental wards can protect certain areas, such as a room or household. Commonly, these are sigils carved in entryways, but can take many forms. Below, you can see a few common sigils, their uses and functions, and how to install them into a space.

Protective Charms

Protective charms are items that can be kept, held, or worn by a human to prevent vampires from being able to bite them. These items are rare, difficult to find, and more difficult to make. Please inquire with your clan leaders for more information.

It's important to remember that these protective measures are not invincible and can sometimes be ignored by extremely powerful vampires. You should count on your clan leaders for defense, and if you need help addressing a conflict, please reach out to them for additional aid.

He rapped his knuckles on the now-familiar door and waited in the cold, the skies cloudy. He had a backpack full of materials and a stack of relevant pamphlets, and he was the kind of determined that one only got when faced with murderous vampires.

The door opened a few inches and Mari peeked through, looking equal parts frazzled and pissed. Her body blocked any view into the apartment. She was wearing an AC/DC muscle tank about four sizes too big for her, and her short hair was in a wild, stubby ponytail at the back of her neck.

"Oh, hell no" were the first words out of her mouth. "Was some part of my *flee the country* message unclear? And now there are these *animal* attacks?"

The worst thing about Mari being so protective was that she was *right* to be protective. She was doing what any person in her right mind would do, which was to keep the vampire bullshit far away, thank you very much. Now, more than ever, she was trying to take care of her friends.

"I know," Brennan said. "I know it's a lot. I can't blame you for being protective or wanting to keep all this vampire stuff *far* away from you, but now—there's a real threat out there. And I'm trying to fix it. And Cole, he's mixed up in all of this and that's on me. He is good and, and, he's worth a thousand of me. I *know* that."

But that wasn't the point. It wasn't about his self-hate, it was about a person he fucking liked and who made him feel like a human. And Brennan didn't want to let Cole down. Ever.

He finished, "I don't want him to get hurt. I . . . I wanted to put up some protective wards around your apartment. No clue if they work, but I wanted to try."

Mari did a little head tilt and the seconds passed in the quiet throb of her pulse, the sound of the TV inside, the wails of some neighbor singing in the shower. It felt like a lifetime before Mari's expression softened.

She opened her mouth as if to say something, but then a shout emerged from inside the apartment.

"Everything alright, babe?" The New York accent made it clear who it was. Brennan looked at Mari, then over her shoulder into the apartment, then back.

"All good," Mari called back, cheeks bright red, glaring at Brennan with a fire that said I *dare you to say shit to me right now.*

Brennan tossed up his hands in innocence. "Good for you," he said. Then corrected, "Hell, good for him." He couldn't even begin to understand the dynamic between Tony and Mari, but it seemed to work for them.

"Yeah, well" was all she said, but she smiled. Actually smiled. It was small, but it was possibly the first real one she'd given Brennan. She eyed his backpack, then his face. She stepped back from the door with something akin to defeat, and finally let the door swing open farther than a few inches.

"I'll only take a few minutes. Or, I can come back later? I mean—"

Mari rolled her eyes. "Fuck it. Do your thing." Then, "What, do you need to be invited inside? Is that real?"

Brennan offered a wry smile. "It will be, once I carve this sigil into all your doors and window frames."

Mari stared at him for a beat, unimpressed. "Well, we probably weren't getting our deposit back anyway."

She moved from the doorway and Brennan followed her. Tony was in the bedroom, and Mari offered to distract him while Brennan got to work, which was the closest thing to supportive Mari had been of Brennan's secret.

He set right to it, digging through his backpack to find the pamphlet for reference. There were a few different sigils he wanted to try out, and the only reason he had to believe they worked was that they were in the pamphlets, but it seemed far-fetched. Somehow, the idea of a few stray symbols being able to ward off vampires seemed more unbelievable than the existence of vampires in the first place.

As he set to work, Mari returned from the bedroom and studied him, and he felt like measly cells under a microscope with the intensity of her scrutiny. He tried to ignore her. There was one door, a few windows, and a few sigils for each, so it didn't take more than a few minutes before he was returning to his backpack to put the knife away.

Then he put on the oven mitts he brought so he could dig out another knife and a bag with a few bulbs of garlic. He handed both to Mari, who accepted them warily, squinting at Brennan.

"This is a silver knife," Brennan said. "It's the only thing that can break skin for vampires, I think, and it burns to touch, so it'd be good to have on hand. And, garlic—it stinks enough that I wouldn't want to drink anything if it were in the vicinity, so, I don't know, keep a bulb in your room or something?"

Mari turned the knife over in her hands. It was a small thing, barely sharp, because apparently silver made for shitty weapons outside of vampire hunting. She curled her fingers around the knife and nodded.

She said, "You actually really care about him, huh?"

Brennan stilled. It was wild to him that there could be any doubts. He was sure the way he felt was stamped on his forehead.

"I do," Brennan confirmed.

Mari studied him until she finally sighed. "Just," she said, with the air of giving in, "try to deserve him, okay?"

He would. He was.

Brennan nodded once, a dip of the head. When he gathered his things and passed through the warded front door, pins and needles surged over his skin.

15

CONFESSIONS OF A VAMPIRE

BRENNAN'S PHONE

Dr. Mom
Happy thanksgiving love! Wish you could be here!

••••,•••••••••••

Tony
🦃 GOBBLE GOBBLE 🦃 to all my 🐔 FILTHY 🤢NASTY 🦃 TURKEYS
👌 🦃! I'm thankful to have all you 😩😵😩 SLUTTY 🍗 PILGRIM 🦃 🐾
BITCHES 🕺🕺💜💜 in my life !!! Send this to 🔟THIRSTY🦃 🦃🐔THOTS🦃
who deserve to get 🐾🦃 STUFFED 🐾🦃 like a TURKEY 🦃🦃 🐾🙁 this
HOE-vember!!! 🦃 🐾🐾🦃

Brennan
Thanks Tony, happy thanksgiving to you too.

BRENNAN'S JOURNAL, THE BACK PAGE

Cole Apology
- I really like you and liked kissing you and want to date you. You're beautiful and kind and deserve better than me but
- But I'm a vampire and that entails weird things sometimes and you need to know that and be...not okay with it, maybe, but at least, willing to understand.

Waiting for Thanksgiving break to tick by on a mostly empty campus felt like agony, but once Sturbridge was back in full swing and on the downward path toward midterms hell, Brennan steeled himself and headed to the library, which felt like neutral ground, with no (or, less) danger of sucking blood or sucking face.

He paced in front of the library, trying to convince himself to go in. With the background chatter of stressed students and people entering and exiting in droves, it was still busy with midterm season. Brennan was, admittedly, nervous. Not the usual weighty anxiety, but the old-fashioned, middle-school-crush, store-bought variety. Wondering if Cole still liked him back seemed silly in the wake of everything else, but it mattered. *Seeing* Cole felt like the *only* thing that mattered.

God, what was wrong with him? He liked Cole so much it felt unreasonable, and he needed to know if Cole felt it, too. If Cole could see Brennan's whole picture and still feel it.

Dr. Morris would ask him why he was so afraid of rejection. Nellie would tell him that he had to communicate with Cole if he wanted to move forward. Tony or Mari would tell him to stop being a coward and do it, but with more colorful language.

Weirdly, that one worked. *Pull yourself together, Brooks.*

He straightened up and went to the door, flung it open, and—

Ran right into a walking stack of boxes. The boxes started to topple but Brennan's arms shot out reflexively and caught them, scooping up the top one and stabilizing the rest of the pile in the kid's arms.

It all happened in a second and, with the top box in Brennan's hands, Cole's face poked out above the stack, and Brennan forgot to breathe.

"Hey," Cole said, and he sounded kind of breathless, too.

All of Brennan's preplanned speeches left from his mind with an audible *whoosh*.

"Hey," said Brennan.

"Good catch," Cole said, flushing. But maybe that was from carrying the stack of boxes, which Brennan realized, glancing at the box in his own hands, were full of heavy textbooks.

"Let me get those," Brennan said, and scooped up the boxes in his other arm, stacking them on top of the box he already had. The tower of boxes was heavy, but being a vampire came in handy on rare occasions, it seemed.

Cole watched Brennan in something of a daze, eyebrows shooting up at the display of strength. He was definitely blushing now, and not just from exertion. Interesting.

In a more devastating turn of events, Cole was wearing a suit, navy jacket over white shirt with a printed bow tie.

Cole really was unfairly handsome, boyish but angular, eyebrows thick and expressive, unruly curls and old Converse the only part of his usual wardrobe that had made the cut. Was it the light, or did Cole's hair have a reddish tint?

"Can you, like, not block the door?" a disgruntled voice rose from behind them.

A cluster of students stood a few feet behind them in various degrees of annoyance, and Brennan and Cole sheepishly darted away from the door, lingering outside the library. It was starting to get dark and, as if on cue, the streetlights that lined the path around the quad flickered on.

At least Cole looked half as flustered as Brennan felt, shoving his hands in his pockets and then taking them out again and then fiddling with the sleeve of his jacket while Brennan carried the boxes.

"Where do you want these?" Brennan asked.

Cole directed him to a side storage room around the corner from the front entrance, and Brennan followed him, heaving the boxes up onto the shelf Cole pointed out, feeling Cole's gaze on him the whole time.

"Thanks," Cole said.

Without the boxes as a shield, the nerves came back full force. And there was Cole, looking every bit the sexy librarian he was, and in all Brennan's contingencies of how this might go wrong, he had not accounted for *that suit* and the way his brain short-circuited.

"What's with the suit?" Brennan asked. Did not wince, did not facepalm, but it took effort.

"I had an interview for an internship," Cole said, waving his hand dismissively.

"Oh, how'd that go?"

"Fine, it was good, it's, you know, kinda stuffy."

"Right, yeah."

This was awkward.

Then Cole said, "I'm really glad you came by. I wanted to see you." Cole searched Brennan's face for some response and Brennan didn't know what his face was doing, but it encouraged the rest of the words to spill out. "I feel so shitty about what happened with Mari. She's so insistent and protective, and I don't know how to say no to her. And I didn't know how to talk to you, after I let her say all those awful things about you—"

"Hey, you're not responsible for what she said." Not that Brennan could even blame Mari, when her reaction was the most normal response so far.

"But more than that," Cole insisted, "I fucking missed you. Isn't that pathetic? I missed having someone to shelve books with, and I missed watching you organize the pamphlets you don't even let me touch, and I kept finding *Twilight* memes I wanted to send you but wasn't sure I was allowed."

"You can always send me *Twilight* memes," Brennan said, because his brain was stuck on *I fucking missed you* and might be there for a while. And god, how casually Cole could say something that made Brennan dizzy. It made him want to be honest, too. Maybe that was why he blurted, "I'm sorry I scared Mari." *That I'm not normal.*

"*No,*" Cole said. "I'm sorry she spoke to you like that. I'll talk to her. She—you're—"

Instead of words, Cole reached out and took Brennan's hand. Brennan was flooded with relief. Somewhere during the conversation, they'd started swaying toward each other like magnets.

"Well, I care about you," Cole finally admitted. "I know the vampire things are weird and new to you, to us both. But we can figure it out together, yeah?"

"That sounds good," Brennan managed. It felt like a massive understatement when *figure it out together* was much more than *good*. "What—how can I be better?"

Cole rolled his eyes, but there was something so affectionate about it that Brennan warmed instead of getting defensive.

"You don't have to be so careful around me."

"I just don't want to mess this up," Brennan said, and it came out too honest.

The thing was, Cole deserved for someone to be careful with him. Cole was so special, and he didn't even realize it. Cole was smiling up at him, soft and sappy, and Brennan couldn't believe that this was his life. That it could be this easy. That Cole could like him, and Brennan could like Cole, and that could be enough.

"Oh, thank god, Cole! There you are!"

Brennan jerked away from Cole to see the blue-haired librarian darkening the doorway to the storage room, hands on her hips.

"We're dying in there, what are you doing?" she asked.

Cole tugged at his suit jacket and his cheeks went red. She was raising a brow, somewhere between amused and judgmental, like she had an idea of what Cole might be doing with Brennan alone in a storage closet.

"I—" Cole started, pushing a hand through his hair. "Brennan was helping me carry out some boxes. I'll be right in. One minute?"

The girl huffed. "Hurry, though. You know I can't stand crying freshmen." She disappeared from the doorway with a last meaningful look at Cole.

And they were alone again, but Cole wasn't smiling anymore, mouth twisted in a frown.

"I really should go. I don't mean to blow you off—"

"Don't worry about it. You're working, I should be leaving."

They crept toward the exit, Brennan holding open the door for them as they settled in the frame.

"Are you free later tonight?" Cole asked. "I still need to convert you to the magic of music on vinyl. I just—I *do* want to talk to you."

And that made Brennan giddy enough to tease, leaning in under the orange glow of the streetlights from outside. "Aw, you wanna *talk* to me? You might give a boy ideas."

Cole beamed. "Maybe I want you to get ideas."

"I might have a few already."

"Save them," Cole said. He rolled forward on his toes, rising an inch. "So, you'll come?"

"I'll be there."

A Pamphlet

So You Want to Date a Human: A Vampire's Guide to Interspecies Relationships and Sex

BY NELLIE ADAMS

Communication Is Key

Vampire or human, the most important part of any relationship is communication, and that takes work from both parties. Talk to your partner, and think about important questions, such as:

- What do you want to put into this relationship?
- What do you want to get out of this relationship?
- What expectations do you have of this relationship?
- Where do you see yourself in five years? Ten? One hundred? One thousand?

Do your views and wishes align? What obstacles are there, and how can you overcome them? What compromises are you willing or unwilling to make?

(For more information about communicating your unique needs as a vampire, see "How (and When!) to Have the Vampire Talk With Your Loved Ones.")

Safe Sex Practice—Frequently Asked Questions

Humans and vampires may look alike, but in addition to fangs, many bodily functions differ. You can read more about the physical changes of a vampire in the pamphlet "Your Vampire Body and You: A Guide to Vampiric Puberty."

"WHY DO MY FANGS KEEP COMING OUT?"

It is normal to experience thirst while aroused. You should always make sure you have had blood before intercourse if you do not intend to feed during. Regardless, fangs are sharp, so be aware of them.

"CAN A VAMPIRE HURT A HUMAN DURING SEX?"

It is equally as possible as a human hurting a human during sex. Positive sexual experiences are all about boundaries, communication, and consent.

"WHAT ABOUT CONSENT?"

Consent is no different for vampires than humans. It must be given before and throughout the act of intimacy, for both sex and feeding.

It is recommended that vampires have sex only with humans who know they are vampires, to avoid any consent issues regarding species and age differences.

Vampire saliva contains a trace amount of mild aphrodisiac, but it is not strong enough to impact consent.

"DO I STILL HAVE TO WEAR A CONDOM?"

Vampires cannot contract or spread sexually transmitted diseases, and they cannot impregnate or be impregnated. However, it is recommended to use a condom for clean-up and comfort.

"HOW CAN I DRINK BLOOD SAFELY DURING A SEXUAL ENCOUNTER?"

Never have sex with or drink from a human while hungry, to avoid overfeeding. Have your human partner eat or drink something sugary to maintain energy.

Make sure all parties involved know what to expect and are fully consenting.

Drink from the neck or wrists for safe access to blood flow.

Your partner will experience a sharp pain from the initial piercing before a soothing, pleasurable venom calms them. Stop immediately if your partner expresses discomfort after the initial piercing.

Pay attention to your partner's pulse and only drink a little at a time. It is better to drink too little than too much.

Remember, you can always reach out to your clan leader for additional advice or resources.

The pins-and-needles tingle on Brennan's skin told him the wards were working as Cole invited him into his and Mari's little duplex on the opposite side of campus from Brennan and Tony's place. Cole kicked off his Converse at the entrance and headed for the milk crates full of records in the corner of the living area. Brennan paused to take in the space, now that he was seeing it without a flood of drunken college kids or the vague threat of Mari's presence. It was cozy and hipstery, like Cole. It smelled like cinnamon and vanilla, like he'd been baking recently. He probably had.

"I'm gonna be honest, it's kind of intimidating to choose a perfect first record for you," Cole said, kneeling next to the crates and shuffling through.

Brennan stepped toward him but couldn't help getting distracted by the photos covering the wall. He hadn't looked too carefully at them in the dim light the other night, but they were hard to ignore. They were overwhelmingly of the same three people: Cole, younger but just as smiley; Mari, with longer curly hair and crooked glasses; and someone else, a taller boy who looked like an older, darker-haired, chain-smoking alter ego to Cole, armed in every photo with a cigarette and a permanent frown. The trio seemed to be friends from a young age—selfies and photos going back to Cole with braces and Cole with buckteeth, Mari pudgy and with wider smiles, the other boy growing his hair out into a ponytail over time. He must have been—

"Noah," Cole called from where he was on the floor, shuffling through records. "My brother."

"Yeah," Brennan said. "He looks like you."

"Well, he's older, so he always used to say that *I* looked like *him*." He had a distant look on his face as he took in the wall of photos, and then quickly pulled their attention back to the boxes of records with a sharp, "So! What do you want to listen to?"

Brennan shuffled toward Cole and crouched down to peer into the box of records. "What's your favorite?" Brennan asked.

"Let's see . . ." Cole flipped through records, humming. "Mari likes old-school punk, Tony likes Billy Joel and the Beatles and that kind of thing. I have lots of indie, and folk, and lots of old-school stuff and—"

Brennan laughed. "But what's *your* favorite?"

Cole's hands stilled on the records but his eyes stayed trained on them. "People don't usually ask that," Cole said. "Do you have a genre you like?"

"Oh, come on, is it embarrassing?" Brennan asked. "Or can you not decide?"

"Both. Give me a genre. To narrow it down."

Some of his most pleasant memories with his mom were them listening to music, working on homework together when Brennan was in elementary school and his mom was getting her PhD. And before that, when Brennan was in preschool and his mom was getting her master's, he would ask her to make up worksheets for him to do alongside her. Even then he was a nerd—desperate to do homework like his mom always was.

"My mom used to play a lot of seventies music growing up, so I like that," he said. "And, like, punk? I had an emo phase in middle school."

"I'd bet money you're still in your emo phase," Cole said.

"I would not take that bet."

"Were you an MCR stan?"

"Not a *stan*—"

"No, no. Question. Have you listened to My Chemical Romance in the last year?"

"No comment."

"In the last six months?"

"You're so judgy."

"That's a yes! You were a stan! Did you ever have the haircut, like—" He held one hand over one side of his face, covering his eye and forehead, mimicking dramatic bangs.

Brennan didn't answer.

"You *so* did! I love it. Can vampires grow their hair out? I think you could rock it."

"Are you roasting me to avoid choosing an album?"

"Nah," Cole said. "I know what to choose." He nodded at the open space of carpeting between the couch and TV. "Go sit down. On the floor. It's part of the experience."

Brennan bit back a grin and sat with his back against the foot of the couch, while Cole selected an album and slotted it into a record player with experienced ease. Then he approached Brennan, dropping to the floor next to him with loose limbs.

The first notes played and Brennan's face split in a grin. He'd expected something more hipster, but this was upbeat and familiar.

"ABBA?"

Cole nodded and scooted out to sprawl on the floor, legs kicked out, tucking his arms under his head. "*Arrival.* 1976."

Brennan slid over, following suit to lie down on his back. "Part of the proper experience?"

"If you really want to do it right, you also have to close your eyes."

Brennan did, and listened. There was the music, sure, but there was also Cole's breathing, Cole's heartbeat. The song picked up and Brennan felt Cole tapping his fingers against the floor to the beat.

After a minute, Brennan asked, "So, why this one?"

"My mom loved it, too," Cole said. "She used to complain about my brother playing his records too loud all the time, but this was the one album she let him play through the whole house. And the three of us would dance and jump around." Cole shifted next to him until their shoulders were touching. "Plus, it's, like, iconic."

"Obviously." Brennan grinned.

The first song faded and the next one began with a blare and he imagined little Cole, his brother, and his mom bopping around a kitchen filled with light. Brennan shot up into sitting.

"Not to insult this experience," Brennan said, "but I feel like we can't *not* dance to this one. It's in the *name.*"

Cole's eyes opened and he sat up on his elbows, smiling. And the way Cole looked at him—Brennan didn't want him to stop. "You're absolutely right," Cole said.

They were both up in an instant. Brennan wasn't a dancer—at the other night's party, he'd gladly jumped on the table to recite poetry and did his fair share of mingling, but when it came to the dance floor, he kept his distance. But Brennan was realizing that the rules he thought he had were different when Cole was involved.

They only bobbed awkwardly for a few seconds before they got into it, jumping around. Brennan took Cole's hands and twirled him. Cole laughed and Brennan did it again to see if it garnered the same response. When Cole stopped spinning, he landed with a hand on Brennan's chest, flushed and delighted. Brennan sang along under his breath, not caring if he was out of tune. Cole stayed close, an arm's length away, moving his hips in a way that was *very* distracting.

"You hear the difference, right?" Cole asked. "On vinyl, it's fuller. Like, listen to that hi-hat—it doesn't sound like that on Spotify!"

"Yeah, I hear it," Brennan said, and he did, a different warmth layered. But he wasn't entirely sure that it wasn't because of the present company, and the enthusiasm he spoke with.

The next song was softer, slower, and Cole's wide grin mirrored it. Brennan dared to nudge closer, the hand not twined with Cole's going to his waist, not pulling him forward but easing, asking, and Cole pressed forward in answer. Brennan was keenly aware of Cole's sharp intake of breath, the speed of his heartbeat. The hand on Brennan's chest slid up to his shoulder. Slowly, Brennan turned them and swayed to the music.

"I've never actually slow-danced with someone before," Brennan admitted. If he'd still had a heartbeat, he was sure it'd be racing faster than Cole's.

"Oh thank god, me, either," Cole said. "All the books made high school seem so much more romantic than it was, didn't they?"

"And a lot more exciting," Brennan agreed.

"Your inciting incident came a little later in life, huh?"

Brennan's mind offered a trail of breadcrumbs toward bad thoughts like, *This isn't late in my life if I'm going to live forever,* but Cole's smile was soft, his voice light, and he tapped his fingers where they splayed between Brennan's neck and shoulders. It was grounding as much as it was endearing. They swayed, slow and steady, and again Brennan wanted to kiss Cole.

Through everything, Cole had been the one thing he chose for himself, the highlight of his days. He liked to think that even if he wasn't a vampire, he would have ended up here, with Cole. They could have had squad *Bachelorette* Nights and flirting at the library without these added complications. Because it wasn't about vampirism, was it? It was late nights talking in the library, poetry anthologies and romance novels exchanged back and forth with sticky-note messages. It was Cole taking care of Brennan and Brennan taking care of Cole. Couldn't that be enough?

He wanted him and Cole to be inevitable. But it still wasn't certain. He wanted to kiss Cole, and he knew on some level that Cole would reciprocate—the searing memory of their kiss in the pool was an aching reminder—but he had things he wanted to say.

I like you, but I'm a vampire. And I want to make sure you really understand that.

Brennan had, embarrassingly, gone so far as to rehearse in the mirror.

"I like you," Brennan said, and Cole's eyes softened.

Cole ducked his chin down. Then he looked back up and his mouth curved into a smile that was half the size of the ones he gave freely but twice as bright, eyes crinkling, and Brennan thought, *Yes. That. I want to do this, every day.*

"That's good," Cole said, "I was worried for a second."

Brennan's gaze fell to Cole's lips, which were especially pink and kissable right then, or maybe Brennan had never given them enough consideration. He ended up saying, almost absently, "Yeah, no worries there."

"Good," Cole said, and then kissed him, the hand on his shoulder going to the back of his neck to pull him in—Brennan went gladly.

Brennan tugged him in by the waist without the questioning hesitation or the frantic need from last time. They kissed with the slow certainty that they had time, the quiet knowledge that they liked each other and were going to do something about it. The rest of the world stilled, and all he knew was Cole's pulse racing, his smell—vanilla, underneath coconut shampoo and sweat—his taste, and Brennan pressed in until there was no space between them, until the back of Cole's knees hit the couch and he wobbled, Brennan stabilizing him.

He'd wanted to say something else to Cole. He'd had it rehearsed, but with Cole sucking on his lip like that, he couldn't quite remember. What was it? He'd wanted to say—

"I'm still—" Brennan warned between kisses, "—a vampire."

Cole pulled back, licked his lips, eyes roaming Brennan's face. "Nobody's perfect."

With that, Cole flipped them around so Brennan's back was to the couch, pushed Brennan down to sit, and climbed on top of him. It was, admittedly, the hottest thing that had ever happened to him. Then Cole was kissing Brennan within an inch of his undead-not-life, and Brennan wondered why the hell he'd been talking himself out of this for so long.

Except, a weight in Brennan's mouth let him know his fangs were dropping again, and Brennan ripped away, flight reflexes kicking in. But he stopped himself, freezing with a few inches between them, breathing heavy against each other. Cole looked at Brennan's mouth. His fangs. What if he hurt Cole again? What if he lost control? What if—

Cole gave Brennan's hair a gentle tug and caught his eye.

"Okay?" Cole asked. He didn't seem worried about anything other than Brennan wanting to stop. Cole trusted him. Maybe that was enough.

Brennan let himself pull Cole back in, let Cole deepen the kiss, and let himself get lost in it. They pressed together until the couch stopped working for them, at which point he let Cole pull them to his bedroom, and Brennan let himself stop thinking altogether.

16

WE GO TOGETHER

r/sturbridgeuniversity

u/micahlandau

Hear me out: vampires at Sturbridge

Did everyone get the email from the SUPD about two students dying at Pike's Point? It was super vague and didn't mention anything about cause of death, just reiterated normal safety precautions and said Pike's Point would be off-limits.

I've already been on edge this semester since my last post so I couldn't write this off as a coincidence. I did some digging. The SUPD report said it was late night/early morning on 11/21, and I remembered seeing this tweet where an SU student mentioned ambulances near that end of campus around 2 a.m. that night. So I looked at the SU crime log, and apparently the only call in that time was about an animal attack in the woods.

Do you really think an animal killed two people? And why would Sturbridge take so long to say anything about it? They didn't even name the students.

These kinds of signs—dark energies, dead animals, dead people—I've seen them before and I know what it means.

There are vampires at Sturbridge University.

I don't think my herbal charm bags are gonna cut it.

>> u/tastefulnobody: The woods outside campus have black bears and freaking moose living in them. Am I the only person who paid attention during the wildlife safety presentation in orientation week? There are very much things in the woods that could kill people, especially people who are drinking, which is what people tend to be doing when they go to Pike's Point. And the news is probably vague as a request from their families. You're reading into things and, worse, you're both making a mockery of and sensationalizing the deaths of these students.

>> u/belatedmanifesto: this is coming from the person who (checks notes) was conspiracy-theorizing about dead rodents in his most recent post on this sub?
>>>> u/bratberry: Yep.

···················

Brennan
[link]
Have you seen this?

Sunny
We're handling it.

···············

Brennan
Okay I used to be team Jacob but he became
such a creep in this book?
And what's with Edward's no-sex-before-marriage thing?
Like, he's cool with killing animals and people, he's cool
with being in a relationship with a ridiculous age gap, but he
draws the line at premarital sex? THAT'S the limit?
Cole
IT'S ALL SO BIZARRE OH GOD you're gonna
LOVE Breaking Dawn

Brennan

Lucky for me I know a cute librarian

who can get me a copy.

Cole

I'll see you soon then 😶

The library grew steadily busier as the semester ramped toward a close, finals looming. Brennan waited for Cole in the storage room where the Blanket Guy Comfort Stash stuff was, busying himself with his journal, perched at a table with his legs kicked out in front of him.

The door threw itself open and Cole exploded into the room in a flurry.

"I'm *so* sorry I'm late, god, I just had the *worst* interview of my life for a job I don't even want but my dad's gonna be *pissed* because it was a *nepotism* interview and he *pulled strings* for me and I *still* couldn't stick the landing." Cole pushed hands through his hair, leaving it even wilder than usual, dropping his backpack to the ground and throwing off his coat. "I don't even want the job! I'm sorry, listen to me ranting—"

"Hey, no," Brennan said, jumping up to flutter around Cole for some way to help. He settled for putting both hands on Cole's shoulders to still his pacing. "Slow down, are you okay?"

With Brennan square to him like this, Cole finally deflated. Then he blinked a few times, tilting his head to look up at Brennan, because Brennan had drawn closer than socially acceptable for *just friends.* But they weren't quite that anymore, and the realization must have dawned on Cole, too, because a blush crawled over his cheeks like a sunrise and some tension drained out of him.

"Hey," Cole said, so soft where a moment ago he'd been a tornado.

"Hey," Brennan said. "What's going on?"

Cole pushed a hand through his hair again. "Not much. Except that I wasted two years on a business degree I can't stand, I'm moving toward a future I don't want, and I'm so terrified of the idea of graduating and dealing with reality that I'm letting it happen! And god, this must sound so, like, trivial, I know you have other problems that are way more important than my bullshit quarter-life crisis—"

"No, stop that. Tell me about your problems," Brennan said. Cole nodded, and Brennan gently steered him toward the chairs at the table. Cole, naturally, swerved to sit on the floor, flopping back onto the shag rug instead of the perfectly good chairs. Brennan followed suit, sitting cross-legged a safe few inches to Cole's side. As soon as Brennan settled, though, Cole scooted so their knees were nudging together, casually seeking him out in a way that was almost dizzying.

Brennan melted at the intimacy and said, "So then, what would you rather be doing?"

"What?" Cole's expression was blank, uncomprehending.

"If you didn't choose business, if you could do anything. What would you rather be doing?" Brennan asked.

Cole frowned. "I don't know." He reached for Brennan's hand to fiddle with his fingers in lieu of a stim toy, which was unfairly endearing.

"I'll be honest, I never pegged you for a business major, but I might be biased."

"Yeah. I wasn't sure what I wanted to do so this seemed like the responsible choice, I guess. . . . I like the library? Books, helping people, chatting—I'm good at it, but it's not exactly a permanent position." His frown deepened. "I just need to grow up. This is the path I'm on. It's the right path, objectively speaking, and it makes sense, so—"

"Okay, but in a world without parents and responsibility and capitalism, what would you want to do? I mean anything. You could join the circus."

Cole laughed, and the smile was a relief after the stormy brooding before it. "Yeah, that would really go with my ongoing theme of disappointing my parents."

"I think parents try to find something to be disappointed about no matter what. Either way, it's your life, not theirs."

"I know. I know, you're right, but it's . . ."

"Not that easy?" Brennan finished.

"Yeah," Cole said, soft and final, but he stopped playing with Brennan's hand to lace their fingers together. Cole inhaled sharply and changed the subject. "What's going on with the vampires, though? I saw about the students at Pike's Point. I mean, are we safe?"

Brennan squeezed Cole's hand instead of pulling away at the mention of the deaths, the reminder of Dom as a looming threat.

"I don't know for sure," Brennan admitted. "Dom went rogue and ditched her place. Sunny and Nellie say they're handling it."

"But?"

"To be safe, I warded your apartment, *but* I'm hoping I can check out the place where—"

"Whoa, hold on, you warded my apartment?"

"Just a few protective sigils from one of Nellie's pamphlets."

"What the hell, that's so cool, and you did it without me?"

Brennan sputtered. "My bad, I forgot the vampire stuff gets you hot and bothered—"

"Shut *up*," Cole said, laughing loud and bright, swatting at Brennan. "It's objectively cool, first of all, and second, it's not the *vampire stuff*, it's *you*."

Something about it laid out like that tugged at Brennan's chest with a dramatic swoop of affection, and gratitude that it was returned.

"Yeah?" Brennan said, drawing closer.

He wanted to kiss Cole, and he might even be allowed to.

"Yeah," Cole said, defiant, like a challenge, and met Brennan in the middle.

The kiss was slow and soft and sure, comforting but thrilling. Brennan pulled back to breathe, hands intertwined between them, and Cole's mouth curled in the way it did when he was biting back a smile. Fondness bubbled up like balloons in his stomach. It felt irresponsible to like anyone this much. He'd never felt like he had so much to lose. The thought made the balloons pop and flop to the pit of his stomach. He squeezed Cole's hand, other hand reaching for Cole's elbow, steadying him.

"Seriously, though," Brennan said. "The last thing I want is to put you in any kind of danger."

"Hence warding my apartment?"

"Yep. And, I need to research more about protection charms, and check out Pike's Point."

"The murder spot? Yeah, I don't love that idea, to be perfectly honest."

"It's the last place we know Dom was. Nellie and Sunny already investigated, so it's possible they covered up any evidence, and I doubt I can do anything they can't do themselves. But I can't sit around waiting. I should have known Dom was going this direction so it's . . . it's my problem to help fix."

Cole nodded along, then said, "Okay, then I'll come with you."

"Uh, no?" Brennan said. "What part of not putting you in danger—"

"Oh, *lord,* don't give me the Edward Cullen *New Moon* 'I'm dangerous' bullshit! I'm not letting you go to a murder spot alone, because I don't want you in danger, either, and I'm *definitely* not letting you solve a vampire murder mystery without me because that sounds cool as hell."

"It might *sound* cool, but this is serious."

"I *know* that, Brennan," Cole said, exasperated. "Sue me for wanting to be part of my boyfriend's life!"

It hung in the air for a second, Brennan's mind tripping over the word like a broken record, and it only took a beat for Cole's brain to catch up with his mouth and a blush to erupt over his face.

"Well, I mean, um—"

"Boyfriend, huh?" Brennan felt a goofy smile taking over his mouth.

"I'm realizing now that's a huge assumption and it just kind of came out," Cole said, words flowing out in an anxious flood, "and well, over break, my mom kept pestering me about whether I was seeing anyone, and I guess you came up and I'm realizing that I probably really jumped the gun on that so we can totally take this as slow as you want, obviously you have a lot going on—"

"Cole," Brennan shushed. "I'd love to be your boyfriend."

"Yeah?"

"Yeah."

"Well, then, after *Bachelorette* Night, we go to Pike's Point. Together."

Brennan sighed in frustration, but knew he would give in. He would do anything Cole asked of him, really.

"Okay," Brennan said. "We go together."

Bachelorette Night came and went in a warm blur. It was nice, weirdly. All four of them squeezed onto the couch instead of Brennan being banished to the floor, which resulted in Cole sitting half in Brennan's lap. He sure wasn't complaining. Mari was still cold to Brennan, but she wasn't threatening him with violence and reluctantly allowed his presence. They watched the actual *Bachelorette* this time, not *Love Island,* and everyone seemed avidly invested except for Brennan, who'd grown steadily interested in watching the others' reactions. How Mari privately swooned at some of the more romantic lines, how Tony got weepy any time someone mentioned their mom or grandma, how Cole found a couple to root for in episode one who somehow ended up the strongest of the season.

To be honest, Brennan was pretty happy to be there while it lasted.

But when the show ended, and Mari corked the remnants of a red wine bottle, giving Brennan some sort of meaningful look as she left, reality kicked back in.

Tony said his good nights, whether to go to bed or to stay up playing *Call of Duty* until 3 a.m., they didn't know.

But as campus went to sleep, Brennan and Cole geared up for a nighttime hike.

"Wow," Cole said, aiming his phone's flashlight in sweeping motions across the clearing at the top of the hill, panting slightly with exertion from the incline of the last mile. "This place is a dump."

It was dark, but Brennan didn't need vampiric night vision to see that was an understatement. Pike's Point was an empty clearing with an old junker car rusting with half its tires missing, grass littered with bottles and cans and red plastic cups, condom wrappers and used condoms, the odd sock or shoe. In the center of the field, a dirt patch housed a pile of wood encircled by stones—a makeshift firepit—and an abandoned cooler and lawn chair set up next to it.

"Yeah, in terms of haunted murder spots, definitely not one of the nicer ones I've been to."

Cole reached for Brennan's hand. "We can do better for our next date."

"Um, this totally doesn't count as a date," Brennan said. "Our first date can't be all vampire stuff, and I wasn't prepared, so—it doesn't count."

Cole's laugh was bright and contagious and Brennan found himself smiling.

"You don't get to call it *not* a date. A date is two people who are romantically involved spending time together and doing an activity. Look at us. Spending time together, doing an activity."

"And this is an ideal first date for you?"

"It seems pretty *us,*" Cole said. "Besides, the pool was our first date. Or when you came over and listened to records."

Brennan warmed thinking of it. He'd never listen to ABBA the same way again.

"Hm," Brennan said. "I could be okay with that."

"Yeah? Is that acceptable?" Cole teased. Then, "Come on, let's look around."

He popped up on his toes to peck a quick kiss on Brennan's lips before whirling around to investigate further, and Brennan let himself revel in the bubble of affection before following.

"Have you ever been up here before?" Brennan asked. He scanned piles of trash, trees with initials carved into them, fallen branches and rocks. Nothing of interest, nothing that screamed *scene of a murder,* but there had to be something.

"I had some friends freshman year who threw a party here once, but other than that, I think it's too far out for people to bother. You?"

"Nah, not up here," Brennan said, and hesitated before adding, "But . . . the bridge we passed on the way—that's where the crash was. Where I turned, or whatever, and Dom killed her sister."

It was also where he tried to kill himself last year, but that seemed a bit much.

"Oh," Cole said. "Shit. Do we think that's a coincidence?"

The bridge was at the base of the hill, a long, winding, steadily inclining path between there and Pike's Point. Close enough that it had reasonable connections to Dom.

"Unfortunately, probably not."

They fell into quiet as they continued searching, but the more trash Brennan rifled through, the more he was convinced that Nellie and Sunny had already buried any evidence. That, or there was no evidence to begin with. A clean kill.

"Are you guys looking for something in particular?"

The voice came from right over Brennan's shoulder and he jolted so hard he nearly headbutted the person, twisting to see—

"Travis?"

Before he could say anything else, like, *You scared the living shit out of me,* fifty pounds of excited dog barreled into Brennan in a blur of motion. Vampire instincts or not, he tumbled to the ground as Rosie the vampire dog slobbered all over his face.

"Rosie! Down!"

Rosie backed away so Brennan could sit up, wipe his face, and greet the dog more civilly, petting her all over as she wiggled and pressed closer.

"Aw, she likes you, mate!"

"What are you doing out here?" Brennan asked.

"My domain's just downhill," Travis said, Australian accent as aggressively thick as ever. "I heard voices, and with everything I've heard about this place recently, I wanted to make sure everything was okay."

"Yeah, that's why we're here," Brennan said. "We're checking it out."

"Playing detective, eh?" Travis crooned. "Reminds me of Nellie when she was your age."

Cole came from across the clearing and cooed at the dog, immediately dropping next to Brennan to pet her. Brennan tensed, unsure if Rosie would be as calm and sweet around a human, but she preened under Cole's attention and offered him a polite sniff.

"My goodness!" Cole's Southern lilt was dialed up to a ten. "And who might this be?"

Brennan cleared his throat. "The dog is Rosie," he said. "And, uh."

Travis was bare-chested under a pair of denim overalls and a heavy, worn parka. His blond mess of dreadlock-adjacent tendrils poked out from under a cowboy hat. He looked unhinged. Brennan wanted to melt into the ground to avoid having to make this introduction, but despite his best efforts, he remained solid, and had to deal with the consequences.

"Uh, this is Travis, I think I've mentioned him," Brennan said, rubbing at the back of his neck. "And, Travis, this is Cole. My, uh. Boyfriend."

His face was burning. If Cole was to be believed, he was bright blue.

"Ah, young love," Travis said. "There's nothing like it. Nice to meet ya!"

He offered a fist bump in lieu of a handshake. Brennan glanced at Cole, worried he might have noticed Travis casually dropping the L-word as if this thing wasn't *new* and fucking *fragile,* but Cole was wide-eyed and delighted, attention completely on Travis.

"Yeah, you, too," Cole said, starstruck. "You're really thousands of years old?"

Travis took it in stride, easy grin never wavering. "That I am! And you're really just, what, eighteen?"

"Twenty," Cole corrected.

"Not bad," Travis said. "When I was a kid, living past eighteen was an achievement."

Brennan forced a laugh. "Haha, yeah, anyway," Brennan said, "we should really get back to our thing, but thanks for checking in."

There wasn't really anything left to do—he'd been about to give up either way. But the strange, weird sadness of Travis felt like something that should be kept far away from the warmth that was Cole.

"Oh, well, whenever you guys finish up your investigation, you should come on down and join me for some tea! I have a kettle on, joints rolled—"

"Oh, I don't know—" Brennan started.

"That sounds amazing," Cole was saying. "It's kind of a long hike."

As if Brennan hadn't carried him on his back up the hill.

"Maybe let's do a rain check on that?" Brennan said, voice going higher-pitched. He tried to catch Cole's eye to convey some sort of message, but Cole was all eyes on Travis.

Brennan wasn't jealous because that would be ridiculous. However, Travis *did* crash what they had established was a date, so if he *were* jealous, which he *wasn't,* it would be justified.

"Alright, alright, at least sit with me for a bit?" Travis said. "I get lonely out here, it's rare I see a friendly face."

And that was kind of pathetic. Brennan deflated. Was it Dom who had said Travis didn't leave the woods? Which could be helpful, actually. He lived near here, and he'd been friends with Dom. He could know something—but it might be difficult to get a straight answer out of him.

"Okay, we'll rest for a little bit," Brennan said.

Travis cheered and went to the firepit at the center of the clearing, a sad pile of rain-damp wood. He waved his hands and, in a crackling burst of light, started a roaring fire.

"Cool," Cole breathed.

"Oi, I like that enthusiasm! This is a good one, little Brennan."

For the record, Brennan resented that.

They settled around the fire, Travis cross-legged on the ground, Cole in the lawn chair, Brennan between them sitting on the cooler. Rosie circled them, stopping to sniff at each of them in turn before resuming her pacing.

"So, you heard about the murders," Brennan said. Sure, fuck it, right to business. "I'm guessing you heard about Dom?"

"Right, the poor kid. Can't say I didn't know she had it in her." He sighed. "It's a brutal life out there, but it's hard to see people you care about choose a path you don't agree with."

Travis dug through the pockets of his coat, his overalls, and patted down his chest, before finally finding a joint tucked behind his ear.

"Aha!"

"Nice," said Cole.

Travis lit the joint with a flick of his fingers and Cole gasped as Travis inhaled deeply, the bitter smell slowly permeating the air.

Brennan tried to stay on track. "You weren't surprised? I know you were kinda friends."

"Oh, sure, we were friends for a little while. A fleeting moment, in the grand scheme of things, maybe, but a few months. Or, weeks? Or years—what day is it today?"

"December third," Cole said, but Brennan knew asking Travis about timelines was a lost cause.

"Did she tell you anything?" Brennan pushed.

"Yeah," Travis said. "I saw her the night before she skipped town."

"The day of the murders?"

"Which murders?"

Brennan bit down a growl of frustration. "The murders. Here. At Pike's Point."

"Right! Not that day, the night before. She seems lost, really, it's sad."
He extended the joint to Brennan. "You want some?"

"Uh, no," Brennan said, "but did—"

"Oh, I will if you don't mind!" Cole reached across Brennan to pluck
it from Travis.

"Did Dom say where she was going? What she wanted? Did she
mention the vampire ball, or what she had planned?"

Travis perked up. "The vampire ball?"

Did he not know?

"There was a flyer at Dom's place with a note to me. I'm not sure
what she might be planning, but that many humans and vampires together seems like a bad mix. She didn't say where she was."

"Man, I haven't been to the annual ball in decades! That brings back
memories. I used to dress to the nines with Shea, up until the vampire
ball of 1928, when—"

"She didn't mention it?" Brennan asked.

"No, she didn't," Travis said. "Though, in hindsight, I suppose I
mentioned it. I was telling her about Shea, actually. The vampire ball of
1928 happens to be where she died."

"What happened?"

"Well, you see, I can't *just* tell the story of the vampire ball of 1928,
not without telling you about Shea herself, so that you can understand."

"Okay, fine," Brennan said through gritted teeth. "Just tell us what
you told Dom."

"Okay," Travis said. "Shea was wild and free. Like a wild horse. Un-
tamable. From another time, ethereal."

Is this really relevant? Brennan wanted to ask, but Cole leaned forward
in his seat with interest, and one hand absently reached for Brennan's
shoulder, soothing without even realizing it. So he bit his tongue. The glow
of the campfire flickered, casting shadows across Travis's face. That's when
Brennan realized that, as Travis spoke, the golden glow of the campfire
danced and flickered, and slowly curled into the undeniable shape of a
woman's silhouette with wild hair.

"She was almost a thousand when I first met her as a little baby human," Travis said. "I must have been your age, even." The fire shifted,
and the delicate tendrils of orange formed mirror silhouettes of a man

and woman. "She was fearless and spontaneous and laughed freely, didn't take anything too seriously. I was pretty serious back then, so naturally we fell in love."

The figures leaned together until the flames overlapped, and for a moment the flames were just flames until Travis started speaking again.

"She turned me and we ran away together. We decided we wouldn't play by anyone's rules but our own. We would be free and in love and well-fed forever as long as we were together."

In the fire, the flames of Travis and Shea circled a screaming man. They drew closer, and then they bit him, one on each side.

"And for centuries, we were." The image fizzled out. "I think of those as our golden years. We were legends, myths, gods. Passing through towns, taking sacrifices. Killing who we wanted to kill. Drinking what we wanted to drink." Travis caught Brennan's growing horrified expression and shrugged. "It was a different time."

Travis kicked his legs out and reclined, leaning back on his hands.

"I say all this to emphasize that this is how she lived her life for thousands of years. Before me, and with me. It was her normal." In the flames, a tree sheds its leaves and blossoms and sheds them again, time passing in an endless cycle. "Why would she change what worked for her? But, after a while, I started getting interested in society again. Some cool new artists were doing some great work in Italy, and it excited me."

A silhouette that looked suspiciously like Michelangelo's *David* appeared in the campfire, and Brennan's head spun trying to make sense of that information. The Renaissance was the fifteenth century or so, and if Shea was thousands of years old before then, she could be *literally* prehistoric. . . .

The fire shifted again and Brennan tabled that existential crisis (and history-nerd fangirling) for later. The flame lovers stood at odds, shouting and waving their hands.

"I tried out the whole undercover vampire gig, the *urban* thing. Shea couldn't take it. We were pretty on-and-off for a while because of our, ah, conflicting lifestyles. So on and so forth, blah blah blah, eventually, I ran away to America." The figures dissolved into a ship cutting through waves on a rough sea. "It was all very dramatic. Sometime after the Civil War, if you're familiar with it?"

"Um, yeah," Brennan said. "I'm familiar with the American Civil War."

"Oh, good. Who's to say, you guys get so much right and so much horrendously wrong. Anyway. Shea followed me out and said she'd make the sacrifices 'cause she missed me. Most romantic thing that's ever happened to me. We fucked for six days straight after that."

The figures in the fire illustrated this with more detail than he'd thought fire capable. Ew.

"So for, I wanna say a good fifty years? I don't know, a *while,* she did the whole housewife thing. But some creatures aren't meant to be domesticated."

A house with a picket fence fluttering in flames.

"Which led to the vampire ball of 1928. This was after Sunny and Nellie had teamed up and started campaigning for all sorts of urban clan regulations, and it was the final straw for Shea. She told me one day she couldn't take it, she couldn't keep hiding. I asked if she was going to leave, and she said she'd do one better."

The house and picket fence rotted and crumbled.

"She had a plan. She wanted to out vampires to the world. She wanted to be feared again, like we were in the glory days. She wanted to be known. You have to understand—that's only human."

Even Brennan leaned forward in anticipation.

"What was the plan?" he prodded.

"She wanted to spark frenzy in the vampires, getting them to attack the humans publicly and, theoretically, start some sort of vampire uprising. The plan was hazy, admittedly, but she was gung ho about it. And I was in love."

The fire dimmed to a soft glow, as if that was the end of the story. But Brennan needed all of it.

"You helped her," Brennan pushed.

"I tried to." Travis shrugged. "Needless to say, didn't go as planned. Sunny and Nellie stopped us before the ball even started. Shea put up a fight. They killed her. They didn't have a choice, really. I don't even blame them. They bound me to these woods as punishment for helping her and, well, I've been here ever since."

Travis waved a hand over the waning fire and in an instant, it flickered out. *Storytime's over, kids.*

"Wow," said Cole.

"Hold on," Brennan said. "Why did Dom want to know about Shea? How did this come up?"

"Oh," Travis said, suddenly bashful, examining his fingernails. "She asked me what my greatest regret was."

"And? What is it?"

"That I didn't die with Shea that day."

Travis looked off into some middle distance for a moment before blinking away the memories and coming back to himself, easy smile returning slightly forced. Brennan couldn't imagine living for thousands of years, let alone losing someone you've loved for that long.

"But man, what a downer that is, am I right?" Travis said. "I must sound like an old man, rambling on about the good old days and lost love."

"No, not at all," Cole said. He was adopting his Library Blanket Guy voice, all open and supportive, extra Southern twang amping up the charm. "Thank you for sharing."

"Did Dom say anything else?" Brennan tried again. "About the ball, or about where she was going?"

"Nah. She kinda snapped at me and told me she was skipping town, and that's the last I saw her. I hope she's doing okay, murder or not."

"Skipping town is . . . good," Brennan said. "That means not bothering *us,* at least, but Sunny and Nellie won't be able to contain the murders if she's running."

"She'll be in someone else's jurisdiction." Travis shrugged. "Someone else's problem."

"Until she comes back," Brennan said. "There's still the ball. She ran away after she heard that story. What if she wants to finish what Shea started?"

"If that was the plan," Cole said slowly, "why wouldn't she wait till then? Why kill people and run off now?"

"She needs power," Brennan and Travis said at the same time.

"Hah, jinx!" Travis said, laughing, but Brennan went cold under Travis's confirmation.

"So she's going on a murder road trip to power up before the ball?" Brennan asked.

"That'd be my guess," Travis said, "but who's to say, really?"

"Great," said Brennan. "Awesome."

"Damn," said Cole. "What are we gonna do about it?"

That was the question.

"Sunny's tracking Dom," Brennan said. "Nellie's covering the blood bank. I want to hit the library and keep researching, maybe try to find a relevant pamphlet."

"Good fucking luck with that," said Travis.

"But other than that . . ." Brennan caught Cole's eye. Cole took his hand. "I think we wait."

17

DELICATE

Brennan

You seemed to like Travis.

Cole

Fucking coolest person I've ever met!!!

And so charming???? Like wow.

Brennan

Can't say I get the appeal.

Cole

Aw. Babe.

Are you jealous?

Brennan

NO!

He's super old and powerful, he kinda freaks me out, that's all.

Cole

Don't worry, I promise you're still my favorite vampire.

Brennan

~~You might be my favorite human~~

Aw, do I get a trophy? A plaque?

Cole

Don't test me, or I'll put it on a t-shirt.

....

Nellie

Thanks for the heads up hey watch where you're going ash hold

Sorry voice to text.

Sunny will keep an eye out and I'll let Quinn know to stockpile more
blood than usual. We've got this covered.

....

bloodsucking memes for immortal non-teens (new england clan)
QUINN MILLER

The annual New England clan reunion VAMPIRE BALL will take
place at the Old Florence Inn outside Boston. Join vampires and
humans alike at our annual celebration, where vampires can mingle
freely with humans in one place.

*Remember that for the safety of the clan, hunting is not permitted
in protected areas. Read more from our "So You Want to Kill a
Human" pamphlet. Humans will be present, and secrecy must be
maintained. If you have concerns about blending in, please reach
out to Nellie, Sunny, or Quinn!

8 comments / 22 💜

It seemed far too easy to be real, but the last two weeks of the semester passed with Brennan jumping at shadows without any event.
Without any disturbance in the area, in fact. Whatever strange "animal
attacks" had been causing disruption had stopped, for now.

Life dared to go on.

Brennan went to classes, went to the library, and read *Breaking
Dawn,* slowly but surely. He scoured through pamphlets for history on
the vampire ball of 1928, which didn't seem to exist anywhere in Nellie's
literature. A pamphlet on the New England vampire ball was just about
the tradition of it all, without specifics. Clan history mentioned Nellie
and Sunny assuming leadership in 1928, but not how or why.

He once stayed holed up in his room for so long that Tony knocked on his door, concerned, offering—of course—a bowl of pasta. Brennan couldn't stand to say no to the extended kindness, so he took it, swallowing down retches, and when he closed the door on Tony, he dumped the bowl out the window into the alley behind their building. He and Tony might be peripherally friends, but Brennan would not sit with Tony's garlic sauce for anyone or anything.

Even Mari seemed to tentatively tolerate him during *Bachelorette Night*, though Brennan's vampirism was something of an elephant in the room. Tony still didn't know.

Then there was Cole.

They spent their nights in the library flirting like they always did, except now their feet pressed together under the table, or they held hands, or they smiled all sappy at each other across the stacks because they knew they both felt the same way, somehow. They still ended up keeping each other company late at night, and if they weren't crashing at the other's place, then they were falling asleep on the phone talking about anything and everything.

A few things were different. Half the time their work in the library devolved into making out in the stacks, the way Brennan had always secretly wanted to.

"You have no idea how many times I wanted to do this back then," Cole had said against Brennan's mouth after dragging him to somewhere in the 600s.

Half bewildered that this was his life and half unbelievably turned on, Brennan said, "I should have known, you bringing up *Twilight* on the first day. You were practically throwing yourself at me."

Another week went by, and no attacks. Nellie told him they were keeping their guard up but they were *optimistic.*

Yet vampirism, always determined to find new and creative ways to ruin Brennan's life, continued to make its presence known.

Like, okay, when he and Cole started to get *into* it? Brennan had gotten used to his fangs dropping at that point. It was still embarrassing and weird but Cole just laughed. He called it a vampire boner, which was mortifyingly appropriate.

They were in Cole's room, a stack of records knocked over on the floor, some indie singer-songwriter playing on vinyl. Cole was starting to do the thing he did where he leaned back and pulled Brennan up over him, and Brennan pulled back to make some smart-ass comment—

And Cole looked up at him with dazed eyes. *Too* dazed, because no one was *that* good of a kisser. Whatever interest had been building in Brennan shattered with the icy realization that something was wrong.

Brennan fell off the bed in his haste to scramble away from Cole.

"Um, yikes," Cole said, and pushed up to sit with a disgruntled huff. "What's wrong?"

Brennan shot back up and crept closer to the bed he'd launched himself from, squinting at Cole for some sign of . . . what, exactly? Magic?

Cole met his gaze with confusion, and sure enough, that cloudy glaze was still there, undeniable. A chill went through Brennan. Did he do that? How?

"Do I have something on my face?" Cole asked, and giggled.

"Are you high?" Brennan asked, half-desperate.

"No?" Cole giggled some more. "I'm good! Why are you on the floor? Get back over here!"

Something was definitely wrong, Brennan realized, in a magic vampire-y sense.

"I need to call Nellie," Brennan decided.

"Wait, what?"

"You're all—" Brennan made a hand-waving gesture that clearly didn't translate.

"I'm *what*?"

"Weird! Your eyes, and you're giggling—"

"I was giggling 'cause I like you?"

"I think I *did* something to you!"

"Not yet, that's the problem," Cole grumbled.

"I'm calling Nellie."

Ten minutes later, Brennan had explained the situation, Nellie had laughed her ass off, and Cole was sitting on the bed with his arms wrapped around his knees watching Brennan pace a hole into the carpet.

"*Vampire saliva has venom in it,*" Nellie explained, her tinny voice crackling through the room on speaker phone. "*You guys were swapping spit, so, yeah, he got a teensy bit enthralled by you.*"

"So," Brennan said slowly, "I accidentally roofied my boyfriend with my spit?"

Cole had been fiddling with the strings of a hoodie, and stilled his movements at the question.

"More or less, yeah."

"Isn't that, like, a moral concern?" Brennan hissed. How was she so nonchalant about it? Cole went back to fiddling with the string.

"No offense, Brennan, but you're super weak. Nothing your trace amounts of venom can do is anything worse than, like, eating an aphrodisiac. It wouldn't make Cole do anything he didn't want to do."

"Okay," Brennan said. "Okay, thanks, I guess."

"*No problem,*" Nellie said. "*I'm gonna mail you some relevant pamphlets, 'kay? Be safe.*"

Brennan resisted a groan, hung up the phone, and turned to Cole. His face was twisted in some expression that Brennan couldn't decipher beyond *displeased.* The cloudiness in his eyes had faded by the time Brennan had gotten Nellie on the phone, and there was no giggling.

Brennan flopped down on the bed a safe distance away from Cole, who was curled with his knees to his chest, avoiding Brennan's eyes.

"I'm sorry for poisoning you with my spit," Brennan said.

Cole huffed a laugh, unfurling slightly from the tight protective ball.

"I don't care about that." He seemed to gather his courage, finally looking up to meet Brennan's eyes. "But you could have talked to me. I was right here, and I was telling you I was fine. I guess it kinda feels like you still don't trust me with some of that stuff."

Cole doodled vague patterns on his jean-clad thighs with his fingers. Brennan watched his hands skating around, and eventually convinced himself it would be okay to hold them. He did, and Cole seemed to deflate with relief. Like that gesture alone said that whatever tiff this was, they were still on the same page.

"It's not that I don't trust *you,* I don't trust myself. Or, the part of myself that's a vampire."

Cole snorted and squeezed Brennan's fingers. "Do you hear yourself?" He gave Brennan an unimpressed look, and Brennan wanted to press a thumb to the crinkle between his brows. "You sound like a *Riverdale* character."

"I've never seen *Riverdale.*"

"That's for the best, you'd hate it."

They shared a small laugh. Cole scooted to close the distance between them, tucking himself into Brennan's chest like he belonged there, and Brennan ached with it.

"You're right, though," Brennan heard himself say. "I don't always want you to see the bad parts. You've seen me have vampire-related crises, like, eight times since we met. I don't want that to be the only thing we have going for us."

Cole remained unimpressed.

"It scares me," Brennan admitted. "Dom and all her drama, yeah, but more the fact that—that could be me. That I'm a slippery slope away from hurting someone. Hurting you."

"You keep saying that. Why do you think you'd hurt me? When have you hurt me, or anyone, that you're so afraid of doing it again? Since I've known you, all you've been is *good.*"

"Because I'm trying so hard to be! But what if I slip? What if I get lazy? And then underneath it all, my nature is *that.*"

He didn't know how to say, *I've lost myself before, I've hurt people before, with my stupid brain, and I'm terrified of it happening again, this time with fangs.* So he didn't.

"I'm just. I mean. The vampire stuff is always gonna come up in weird, unexpected ways. It's always gonna be . . . an obstacle."

"Well, yeah," Cole said, shrugging. "Maybe. It's part of you. It only bothers me when you don't let me be part of it. Like calling Nellie instead of talking to me. Or not letting me read any of the terrible pamphlets."

"I don't mean to keep you out of it," Brennan said, but he wasn't sure it was true. "I just think sometimes it'd be easier if I weren't—"

Cole cut him off with a stern look and a sharp finger pointed at his face. "I wouldn't change anything about you, Brennan. Or how we met, or all the drama since then."

"Right, you're *into* the vampire thing."

Cole didn't give in to the joke and kept that stern look.

"Hey, look at me."

Brennan looked at Cole, really looked at him. The barely there freckles on his nose. The curve of his lips.

"I like you. Not *because* you're a vampire. Not in *spite* of it. I just like *you*. Got it?"

The open expression on Cole's face said he *meant* it. It knocked the wind out of him, the force of that knowledge, that maybe this thing he and Cole had was bigger than all those obstacles. Vampires, venomous saliva, depression, angst—they didn't seem so insurmountable with the brightness of Cole's smile. With the fact that Cole seemed to trust and believe in him even when Brennan himself didn't, just like he'd somehow found Brennan's venting the night they'd first met to be kind and thoughtful instead of unhinged and lost.

"I don't know that it'll ever make sense to me," Brennan said, swallowing hard around something thick in his throat. "But yeah, I got it."

Cole almost made him believe he *was* good. That he wouldn't do harm, that he didn't have it in him. He wanted to tell Cole that he made him feel like the bravest version of himself. That being with Cole brought all his good parts forward and he liked it. That Cole was probably the most good, human person Brennan had ever known, and he didn't know if he'd have gotten through half the craziness of the last semester without him.

What came out instead was "And, I mean, you know I like you, too, right? Does that even need repeating?"

He wanted to dramatically facepalm. His brain-to-mouth connection was unapologetically broken.

Cole's hand that wasn't entwined with Brennan's settled at the nape of Brennan's neck. "I know," he said. He didn't need to tug Brennan down, because he was already moving to meet him. Against his lips, Cole said, "But I could bear to hear it."

So Brennan kissed him, and told him, quite a few times and in quite a few ways.

BRENNAN'S PHONE

Brennan

Hey, wait.

What happens when I'm done with Breaking Dawn?

Cole

Lol. There's a spin-off book, and the first book from
Edward's perspective, and we'll obviously have to watch
the movies.
And there's always The Vampire Diaries, Vampire Academy—
we can move on to werewolves, if you want!
But I have endless recs to give you, as long as you'll have
them, and you can keep sending me poetry. I think it's
a pretty neat little arrangement.

Brennan
It is pretty neat 🖤

Sometimes they were so in sync it was scary. Like when they met up at the library, and Brennan had picked up coffee from the bougie place Cole liked. Except, when he arrived at their meeting spot—a corner in the third-floor stacks with a table that was rarely occupied—Cole was waiting with two coffees from the less-bougie place *Brennan* liked. That happened twice before they decided to implement a turn-taking system.

And then there were the quiet moments. Like Cole's head in Brennan's lap as he read a book for class while Brennan scrolled on his phone on his latest Wikipedia odyssey. They were in Cole's room, curtains open wide to let the deceptively bright sun in, warming up the room despite the ice outside. A record played, softly, because Cole couldn't deal with complete silence. Across the bed, his foot tapped absently to the beat. Brennan had one hand resting in Cole's curls, idly twisting strands around his fingers.

"You're comfortable," Cole said at one point, leaning into the touch like a cat.

He was right. Brennan was comfortable. *They* were comfortable. Something bright and light was expanding in Brennan's chest and he was a bit worried he might want this comfort for the rest of his life. Which, of course, was hard when the rest of his life was supposed to be forever.

He looked down at Cole, the shadow his lashes cast on his cheek, eyes scanning left and right across the page. After a minute, Cole caught him staring, but didn't say anything. Just smiled and went back to reading.

Brennan tried to memorize the feeling, the corporeality of Cole's weight in his lap, hair around his fingers, heart beating a rhythm that Brennan could hear loud and clear if ever he let himself listen.

You're comfortable, Cole had said.

"You are, too," Brennan whispered.

It was snowing the day Cole left to go home for winter break, finished with his finals a few days ahead of schedule.

Brennan approached Cole and Mari's place to say goodbye for the break, and he had a brown-paper-wrapped book in his backpack to give to Cole.

In the distance, Cole emerged from the brownstone with two hefty suitcases, struggling through the doorway and down the porch steps.

With no one else around on the street, Brennan was free to nearly teleport to Cole's side with vampire speed, easily scooping the bags from Cole and carrying them down to the sidewalk.

"Well, thanks," Cole said, wearing a bashful smile and a beanie pulled over his curls.

"Knew you kept me around for something," Brennan said.

Cole punched him in the arm, then collapsed into his chest, wrapping his arms around Brennan's middle like he was a giant, lanky teddy bear. Brennan's brain broke down a little over how soft Cole was, how lucky Brennan was, and took a beat to catch up and get his arms around Cole's shoulders.

"I don't want to go home," Cole said, voice muffled against Brennan's chest.

Brennan couldn't say he felt differently. He dreaded facing his mom as much as he knew Cole dreaded dealing with his own parents. Brennan smoothed a hand down Cole's back.

"It's just a few weeks," Brennan said.

Cole nodded, face still buried, and Brennan held him as long as Cole would let him.

Eventually, Cole pulled away from the hug.

"My Uber's gonna be here any minute now, and I wanted to—hold on—"

He started digging through one of the bags, opening the suitcase carelessly into the snow, and finally presented a well-loved green paper-back.

Brennan bit back a grin. "Oh god," he said. "We're nerds."

"I think we already knew that, babe," Cole said. "But, why?"

Brennan conjured his own package to pass to Cole.

"We both got each other books."

Cole laughed.

"Well, obviously," he said, and thrust his book out so Brennan could trade the package for it.

The little book was dog-eared, sticky notes protruding from all directions. *Fablehaven* by Brandon Mull.

"Thought you might want a break from all the vampire stuff, at least over break," Cole said.

"I appreciate that."

A car crackled over ice as it slowed to a stop next to them, and Cole cursed.

"Shit, I should—"

"Yeah," Brennan said, waving him off. "Don't worry, open mine on your own, we'll talk later."

"Yeah. I'll text you."

"Good. I'll call you."

"Good."

"Okay."

Cole's eyes were locked on Brennan, swaying into his space like an invitation, and Brennan wouldn't deny him anything.

The driver honked at them.

Cole's laugh was bright and flustered. He dropped down from where he'd pushed up onto his toes and covered his face.

They separated after a long moment and Brennan loaded Cole's bags into the car while Cole charmed the driver with small talk through the window. Brennan shut the car's trunk with a slam and Cole darted over for a last fast, tight hug.

"See you, then," Brennan said.

"Yeah," Cole said. "See you."

With the driver waiting, there was nothing else to do but let him go. Cole got into the passenger seat instead of the back, a choice made only by socialites and murderers, but Brennan knew by the time they got to Boston Logan, Cole would have befriended the driver and uncovered his life story.

There was a rush of affection, of *that's my person* that made Brennan's stomach drop. Cole gave one last little wave, then closed the door behind him, and the car drove off.

He knew this was where he had been headed all this time, but it was still terrifying. To be who he was, and to be in love with Cole.

On the inside of the front cover of *Fablehaven,* Cole had written:

> B—
> Remember being a kid when anything felt possible? We discovered new worlds in every book we read and magic was all around us. This book is like that. Childish wonder. Feeling like the world is at your fingertips.
> Needless to say, that's how you make me feel.
> I'll text you from Tennessee?
>
>   Yours,
>   Cole

A few hours later, Cole sent Brennan a photo. The book Brennan had given him, splayed out on what appeared to be an airplane tray. A hand held open the pages to where a sticky note was tucked like a bookmark, a string of lines highlighted.

The caption said, "accidentally read the whole book on the ✈."

Brennan didn't need to look at the picture to know what the book read:

The poem—

Sunlight pouring across your skin, your shadow
flat on the wall.
The dawn was breaking the bones of your heart like twigs.
You had not expected this,
the bedroom gone white, the astronomical light
pummeling you in a stream of fists.

You raised your hand to your face as if
to hide it, the pink fingers gone gold as the light
streamed straight to the bone,
as if you were the small room closed in glass
with every speck of dust illuminated.
The light is no mystery,
the mystery is that there is something to keep the light
from passing through.

And below it, a note. Brennan had annotations throughout the book, but this was the one meant for Cole:

Yeah, I know, you're probably laughing because this is that gay poet Tumblr loves, but don't dismiss it! The gays love him for a reason. His words are rambling and panicky, desperate and jarring. It's how my brain feels half the time. And then you get to this poem, and it's different. Softer.

It reminds me of that day. You know the one. Or maybe, just you, in general, and how all the noise goes out of my head when we're together.

The Waffle Den was a rare kind of quiet the night before Brennan was headed home for break, so Brennan read Cole's tattered copy of *Fablehaven* over his nth cup of coffee to the sound of the waitress's phone dinging and trilling with some game while the cook hummed and scraped the griddle.

The bell over the door jingled for a newcomer as Brennan flipped the page. The book was for a younger audience and had the magical escapism Cole promised, but more importantly, Cole loved it. Brennan read it with the reverence of something that held great secrets, because for all he knew, it did.

"Right-i-o, I'm gonna need three orders of the Deluxe Den combo, to go, and as much orange juice as a young man such as myself can reasonably carry."

The newcomer spoke in a rough accented voice that Brennan recognized immediately. He resisted the urge to whip his head toward the speaker but instead slid down in his seat and prayed into his coffee that Travis wouldn't notice him.

He didn't know why it never occurred to him that he could see Travis around campus—his forest domain was undefined to Brennan, and the Waffle Den was at the far edge of campus near the hiking path that led to Travis's clearing. But seeing an all-powerful vampire ordering an inhuman amount of takeout at the Waffle Den was not something Brennan had expected, and he didn't have the energy to deal with Travis's endless stories and holier-than-thou attitude. Not when he was going to have to deal with the same from his mom for the next two weeks. Couldn't he have one quiet night on campus without the friendly reminder that vampirism was ruining his life?

"Vampling!" Travis exclaimed, popping into Brennan's view with a wide-eyed grin. Brennan winced at the term and glanced at the waitress and cook, who didn't bat an eye. He reluctantly straightened from where he'd been willing himself into invisibility in his seat.

"Travis," Brennan greeted him. He didn't bother to hide his lack of enthusiasm.

"Fancy seeing you here," Travis said, like there was a joke hidden in his words that Brennan couldn't detect. "I haven't gotten takeout in a good few decades, thought I'd spoil myself a bit. How are you holding up?"

Travis crossed over and made to sling himself into Brennan's booth.

"You still need to pay, sir," the waitress said at the register, the tone of her *sir* implying she wanted to call him anything but.

Travis shot Brennan a wink then turned back to the register.

"No worries, right?" Travis said, and despite his casual tone, the words came out slow and deliberate. "Let's call it even, yeah?"

A chill came over Brennan like a wave, and he saw the moment it hit the woman, too—she stiffened, spine straightening, eyes glazing over where she had been glaring, and all at once she softened and warmed, smiling and ripping the paper off her notepad.

"Of course. We'll have that right out to you."

"Oh, and!" Travis perked up. "My friend's coffee is on me, too."

"Sounds good," the woman said.

Travis whirled around and dropped into the seat across from Brennan, who only realized he was sitting slack-jawed when he closed his mouth with a click. He looked between Travis and the waitress, who turned to talk to the cook, who in turn started cracking eggs.

Brennan leaned across the table and hissed, "What was that?"

"Cool, right?" Travis said. "A little persuasion action. Who could resist a face like this?" He grinned cheekily and held up his palms in a facsimile of jazz hands.

"That's—" *Illegal. A frivolous waste of power. Kind of cool.* The thought of it made anxiety rise in his stomach but he pushed it down.

He ended up saying, "This is a locally owned business, not, like, a chain, so I do not approve."

Travis barked out a laugh. "No offense, kid, but the day I start looking for *your* approval is the day I die."

Brennan pinched the bridge of his nose and put his book down in defeat, face down and splayed open so the table would hold his place amongst the pages. "I don't think there's a way to take that non-offensively."

Travis kept right on, unbothered. "So how are things? Still in a tizzy about Dom?"

His eyes scanned the wall above Brennan's head and Brennan twisted to see what he was seeing. The walls were covered in framed photos and newspaper clippings in an elaborate, Tetris-ing collage of rectangles. An article about the Waffle Den opening in Sturbridge. Old-school, black-and-white photos of when the diner was new and sleek instead of rusted and grease-stained. Newspaper clippings from events around Boston.

It took him a minute to realize what Travis was looking for, and Brennan did a double take himself when he saw it—a newspaper headline about a rally against book censorship in Boston, a crowd photo, and behind the main subject of the photo was a little group of four, huddled together laughing.

He barely recognized Travis with his hair cut short, but Sunny and Nellie both looked exactly the same, outside of outfit changes. Then there was a light-haired woman with a hand on Travis's arm as she laughed. Brennan knew she had to be Shea.

"Back when Sunny and Nellie were still fun, of course," Travis narrated. However snide, his voice had a softness to it that gave Brennan pause.

They had been Travis's friends once, Brennan realized. Up until they had killed Shea and banished him to the woods. Now Travis was left alone, only remembering his friends when he dared to scour the walls of a greasy diner.

Again, Brennan was reminded why exactly Travis made him so uncomfortable. Sure, he had weird perspectives on vampirism, and he used his powers in ways Brennan didn't agree with, and until the last few decades, he had killed people mercilessly.

That all scared Brennan, but none of it so much as this: that Travis, ancient and powerful, was utterly alone. That this was all Brennan had to look forward to in an infinite life.

The waitress arrived at their table, refilling Brennan's coffee and sliding a bagged stack of to-go boxes to Travis in one smooth motion.

"You're all set, hon," she said, then slipped away to sit behind the counter.

Travis tugged the bag toward him and started to scoot out of the booth. Without making the decision to do so, Brennan spoke up.

"You could," he started, "join me, if you want. Just while I finish this coffee." He winced internally at his own actions, but Travis perked up instantly.

"Oh, well," Travis said, "if you're in need of company . . ."

Brennan shrugged a shoulder and Travis slid off his coat, making himself comfortable. He started unloading the bag of to-go boxes onto the table.

Brennan sipped his coffee and then folded his hands in front of him.

"So," he said. "Do you want to tell me more about Shea?"

Travis lit up.

18

DISTANCE

BRENNAN'S PHONE

Brennan

You still have the pamphlet with how to
ward your house?

Cole

yep, and nellie gave me some extra tips when we
were chatting the other day!

Brennan

Awesome. Let me know when you're home safe?

Cole

you got it 🖤

·············

Nellie

You counted through the packs again, do you have enough?

Brennan

Yes, I swear, I've got everything. We're all good.

Nellie

And you know where the nearest blood drive is?
It's an hour away from you but will work in a pinch.

Brennan

it won't come to that. My only concern is my mom being suspicious

Nellie

Act natural! Eat human food!

You packed the portable freezer to keep

everything good in your room?

Brennan

I've got everything. We're good. I'll focus on

my stuff, you focus on yours.

Nellie

Don't worry about Dom!

A monthlong break is more than enough for us to handle things!

·················

r/sturbridgeuniversity

u/micahlandau

UPDATE Re: Hear me out: vampires at Sturbridge

The past few weeks have been really scary to those paying attention to the signs. I know this sub hasn't been a fan of the things I've had to say so far, but there's been more developments so I compiled a short list of sources that allude to a vampire conspiracy.

- Link: My previous posts on dark omens and the first reported deaths
- Link: Animal attacks in areas surrounding Boston have law enforcement and animal control specialists mystified, with three dead in two weeks (*The Sturbridge Journal*)
- Link: Record number of missing persons reported in December for Massachusetts! Here's what we know about the six unsolved cases (*The Daily Northeast*)
- Link: Mass General nurse describes influx of "strange" animal bites (Twitter/X)
- Link: Reddit user /throwaway217389384 reported a sexual encounter with an "unrealistically hot goth vampire" in Boston area (Okay, I know this one's a stretch)

Edited to add: I see this sub is hostile as ever and downvoting anyone who agrees something is weird. I've made a new subreddit, r/occultboston, where hopefully we can talk more respectfully about the situation at hand.

>> u/easyalpha: why is this dude so obsessed with vampires? and why hasn't a mod banned him yet?

>> u/writinganatomy: Wow, these responses are not it. These connections are legit worrying. I'm not sold on vampires, but something's definitely up. Something from your last thread stuck out to me—you said you'd seen this kind of thing before? What does that mean?

>>>> u/micahlandau (OP): The dead animals, the drained rats. This person who watched me when I was younger turned out to be a vampire. I know it's hard to believe, I've been called crazy ever since, but I know it was real. They weren't evil, but they told me others out there were.

>>>>>> u/belatedmanifesto: "My Babysitter's a Vampire"? That's the story you're sticking with?

·············

Brennan

[link]

Is Dom back in Boston? Or is it someone else?

Sunny

We're handling things.

Brennan

Awesome!

I hope so!!

A letter, Brennan to Cole

"The Truth the Dead Know" by Anne Sexton

We can joke about crying into the pages of Sylvia Plath but sometimes I think about how unreasonable it is that all great artists seem to suffer, go mad, or kill themselves. Sometimes all three.

Okay, I'm being dramatic, maybe. But it's hard not to think that way.

I thought too much about death as a kid, so for a while it was really important to me to leave some sort of mark or legacy behind. To be important. I was always obsessed with the great poets, and history, all those distant figures that people know. And then I grew up and realized

how many people there were in the world, and how everything was
ultimately insignificant in the grand scheme of the universe, so there's
no point to anything since we'll all inevitably turn to dust, et cetera,
et cetera, angst, angst, existential crisis, et cetera.

All this to say, it's weird to think that I'm not going to grow old
and die. Or, maybe, that I am dead, depending on how you look at it. And
even then, maybe I do get to grow old, but slowly and miserably and
utterly alone.

"It is June. I am tired of being brave."

It is December. I miss you.

Brennan

A letter, Cole to Brennan

They Both Die at the End by Adam Silvera

I think it's normal to think about your legacy. What people think about
you when you're not around. How many versions of me are floating
around in people's heads right now? I guess I've always hoped that my
legacy is being kind to people. That people remember me as a friendly
face, someone who is good. There are more ways to make a difference
than making history, or writing the next Great American Novel.
Sometimes it's enough to be a good friend. Or to hold the door open for a
stranger. To make little differences.

You're a nerd, so I won't bother going into the butterfly effect. It
would only be redundant for you. But things you do matter. At least,
that's what I believe, and I can only hope that karma or the Lord are
looking out for me, too.

I get it though. The call to more. My dad's mad I didn't get an internship
for next semester. He thinks he can pull some strings for me. I wish he
wouldn't. I can't imagine spending my days working on spreadsheets and
marketing plans and trying not to gouge my eyes out. I probably picked
the wrong field, all things considered. Business doesn't care much about
people, does it? I wish I could bake things and read books and not worry
about all this, about money, and making a difference. But maybe us two
idiots are cursed to forever worry about things we can't change.

Cole

BRENNAN'S PHONE

Brennan

What a depressing fucking book how DARE you???

•••••••••••••••••

Call Log 12/22

Cole > Brennan 2 hr 38 min

•••••••••••••••••

Brennan

I don't know how to talk to my mom
now that I'm a vampire.

Cole

She still doesn't know?

Brennan

Nope. I don't want her to.

Cole

I get it's a scary thing to trust someone with.

Brennan

Yeah. And she worries about me a lot,
it just seems like another Thing.

•••••••••••••••••

Call Log 12/24

Brennan > Cole 1 hr 12 min

•••••••••••••••••

Call Log 12/25

Cole > Brennan 12 min

•••••••••••••••••

Nellie

MERRY CHRISTMAS! I'm glad you became part of our
lovely vampire family <3

•••••••••••••••••

Tony

🎄 DICK my 🦯HOLES 😏 with 🅱️ows of 🅱️USSY 🎄 !!! ✨ Happy ✨ HOLIGAYS 🏳️‍🌈 to my favorite 🧑‍🦱♂️ HO HO HOES 🎅 🎅 🎅 !! Make sure you keep your 😩 HOT 🔥 TIGHT 😩 chimney open 💦 WIDE🍑 for old 🧔 saint 🎄 DICK's 🍆 CREAMY 🥛 egg ⚪ nog 🥛! Send to ✉️ 5 of 🖐️ your 🧑‍🦱♂️ NICEST😇 or NAUGHTIEST 😈😈😈 HO HO HOES 🎄 to wish them a 💚💚 SLUTTY 🍆 🍑 DICKMAS! 🎄 🎄

Btw I got a bunch of new xbox games so I'll be claiming the TV for at least 72 hours after we get back

·······················

Mari

Cole said to say merry christmas to you so this is me doing that.
Merry christmas

·······················

Dr. Mom

What was that?
Are you okay? Do you need water or something?
I have advil in my purse

> **Brennan**
> I'm good!!! Give me 5 minutes.

·······················

> **Brennan**
> My fangs came out while talking to my mom.
> How do I make them go away?

Nellie

Have you been drinking enough??

> **Brennan**
> Yes!!!
> We were talking about boys . . .

Nellie

HAHAHAHAHAHA
Try a cold shower :p

A letter, Cole to Brennan

Simon vs. the Homo Sapiens Agenda by Becky Albertalli

You're a modern queer man, so you've obviously seen Love, Simon. *But before there was* Love, Simon, *there was an offbeat gay rom-com book by the one and only Becky Albertalli. I read this thing all in one go, hiding in the school library. I was twelve years old and had barely admitted I was gay to myself, let alone anyone else, and here was this openly queer book. I didn't want anyone to see me reading it, but I couldn't put it down. And then, suddenly, it was like, I realized happy endings are possible for queer kids? Before that, all I heard about gay people was that they were going to hell.*

I told my parents I was gay when I was sixteen, and I don't think they could have been more disappointed in me.

Then the next year, Noah died, and they didn't talk about it. About Noah, or about me. Just about my future, what they wanted for me.

It's so black-and-white, between here and on campus, you know? Like I flip a switch and shut myself off to make room for all the stuff they want from me.

I'm tired of them seeing me as who they want to see, instead of who I am. Does that make sense? Like I'm their lovely hardworking business-major son, and that's all. Not that I'm a coffee aficionado, or a record collector, or GAY. I've been trying to fit into their image, afraid to disappoint them. But maybe they're the ones who need to change, not me.

I'm almost halfway through college, two and a half years away from being a full adult, and I won't be relying on them for tuition anymore. (I'm grateful for them, of course, and I know I'm privileged to have had their help this long!) I won't have to be perfect anymore.

I've been trying to think more about what you said. About what I actually want to do. I guess that seems like the obvious question, but I don't think I let myself think like that before.

A letter, Brennan to Cole

I was lucky my mom's a New England radical liberal, but I didn't come out until college. I was unpopular enough in high school without the bisexuality adding a fun new slur to people's vocabularies.

The whole vampire thing feels like being in the closet all over again.

Hanging out with Tony, or even being with my mom, is so weird because they don't know this huge thing that's changed my life. I don't know how you even break that to someone. Everyone who's found out so far has been an accident, and that's kind of a relief. If you hadn't walked out that morning I stole from the blood drive I'd have gone feral by now.

I don't know what I'm worried about. Everything, I guess. That they'll be scared of me. That my mom will go right past the bullshit toward the living forever bit and she'll get all concerned and ask if I'm okay and I don't think I could stand it!

And how am I supposed to tell my mom she's not getting grandkids? She'll kill me for that alone.

By the way, whatever you decide to do, whatever happens, I'll be there, and so will Mari and Tony, and Sunny and Nellie, and all the "Cute Library Blanket Guy" fangirls of the internet. I can only hope one day your parents will see the adorable hipster you are.

If you ever want to brainstorm potential career ideas, I'm down. I'll even start:

1. *Sexy Librarian*
2. *Charming Baker-Next-Door*
3. *Hot Teacher*
4. *BILF (Barista I'd Like to Fuck)*

I could go on.

My book rec is The Strange Case of Dr. Jekyll and Mr. Hyde:

"There comes an end to all things; the most capacious measure is filled at last; and this brief condescension to evil finally destroyed the balance of my soul."

BRENNAN'S PHONE

Call Log 12/31

Cole > Brennan 5 hr 52 min

••••••••••••••••••

Brennan

You snore. It's cute.

Cole

oh hush 🫣

Brennan

Happy new year 😊

Cole

Happy new year 🖤

·········· ··········

Dr. Mom

Okay, are you gonna tell me what's up or not?

Brennan

Nothing's up? Why do you think something's up?
And why are you texting me? We're in the same house.

Dr. Mom

First of all, I'm texting because you've been hiding
in your room all break and when you do come out,
you're staring at your phone anyway.
I figured it was my best bet.

Brennan

Okay.

Dr. Mom

Second of all, there are many reasons I think
something is up! You keep leaving unexpectedly,
and making excuses not to eat. I feel like
you're not talking to me.

Brennan

We never talked much! You're just noticing
because you're actually around right now.

Dr. Mom

I'm sorry I wasn't around before. I want to listen now.
I worry about you

Brennan

Well, don't.

Dr. Mom

Don't you think I'm a little justified?

This is how you were acting last year.

> **Brennan**
>
> This is nothing like last year.

·····················

Cole

so I was talking to nellie . . .

> **Brennan**
>
> Uh oh.
>
> Why the ellipses? What's up?

Cole

well. obviously I don't have any expectations and

I want you to be comfortable.

but she was saying how.

a vampire bite

could be, like, sexual?

> **Brennan**
>
> Lmao.

Cole

why lmao?

> **Brennan**
>
> Lmao because it's funny?
>
> Unless you're being serious?
>
> In which case, sorry, absolutely not?

Cole

wow, okay.

> **Brennan**
>
> Should this be a call thing? Can I call you?

Cole

I'm at dinner.

> **Brennan**
>
> And this is what you're thinking about??
>
> I'm sorry, I don't understand why you would want that.
>
> Why anyone would want that, really.

Cole

I get it. I'm sorry too, I'm just curious, I guess.

Brennan

Okay. I mean. If you're interested in fifty shades
type of stuff we can talk about that.

Cole

lmao. that's not it.

Brennan

Then what is it?

Cole

I would trust you to, is all.

••••••••••••••••••

r/occultboston

u/micahlandau

A New England Vampire Ball

When I first saw this flyer, I thought it was cute and could be fun to go to, get dressed up, you know? But I couldn't help being suspicious. With all of the recent deaths and attacks and rumors, could this be connected somehow?

I called the host venue, the Old Florence Inn, and I asked some questions. Discreetly. Don't ask how. But some interesting details came up.

Apparently whoever sponsors this thing has booked the same date, every year, for as far back as their records go. And they've booked ahead for the next decade, paid in full ahead of time, in cash. The hotel lady I talked to emphasized this was an exception and not normal practice.

What if this is legit? A standing holiday for the vampires?

I, for one, will be in attendance.

>> u/writhinganatomy: That is so wild, it's giving . . . cult ritual vibes? Count me in.

>> u/weepncreep: Some friends of mine attend every year, and they're definitely not vampires, but they say it's a good time.

>>>> u/willfullyignorant: "Definitely not vampires," sounds like some famous last words.

·················

Brennan
[link]
Um.

Sunny
Handling. It.

Brennan
😶

·················

Nellie
Sunny said you're being passive aggressive.

Brennan
Maybe so

Nellie
Frowny face
I mean ☹️

·················

Cole
Brennan darling my boyfriend who likes me,

Brennan
Why does this feel threatening?

Cole
no! No threats!
however
I may have mentioned to my (mildly homophobic)
parents that I have a boyfriend.
and my parents say they'd like to meet you
and I'm like haha sure, yeah
thinking that they mean *someday* like in the future
then my dad says he has a conference in Boston in January 😭 😭 😭
and how maybe they would both fly up for that weekend

now, because of how they are, they'll probably only have like. One meal together scheduled in.

but all this to say, they want to meet you, sorry???

Brennan

You had me worried for a second, but yeah,

I can meet your parents?

Unless, you don't want me to meet your parents?

Cole

I do! Really! Thank you!

•••••••••••••••••••

Brennan

We're back tomorrow, what's the situation??

Nellie

We're not gonna stop until we figure this out, okay?

I promise.

Brennan

So nothing yet?

Nellie

Nothing yet.

19

THE CALM

FROM THE STURBRIDGE UNIVERSITY PRESIDENT

Dear Students,

We understand there might be some anxiety regarding returning to campus for the spring semester due to recent events in Sturbridge, Boston, and surrounding areas. Both local and university police are looking into the various animal attacks, deaths, and disappearances, though at this time we have been told there is no reason to suspect foul play or malicious intent.

Therefore, in addition to having a new required online training on wilderness health and safety, we also strongly discourage students from exploring the woods outside campus. It's always best to stay within a line of sight of one of our blue-light safety phones, to travel with a partner or group, and to stay on well-lit paths.

Additionally we would like to emphasize the safety protocols and resources available to students who may be struggling or . . .

BRENNAN'S PHONE

[To Nellie]

Brennan
You'll update me on stuff, right?
I'm back on campus and things still aren't resolved.

....

r/occultboston

u/tastefulnobody

You guys convinced me, but now I'm scared to go back to campus

Basically what the title says. I thought all of this was a load of shit when that guy was first talking about dark omens and animal attacks, but having been in this sub for a few weeks and seeing all the weird shit over break, I am totally convinced something is going on.

But now I'm anxious and paranoid over going back to campus, especially with that bullshit email from the school reiterating the same old safety measures while people are dying and going missing.

What are you guys doing to feel safe on campus?

>> u/micahlandau: If you're open to meeting up on campus, I'm happy to give you one of my protective herb spell bags. They brought me a great sense of security on campus the weeks leading up to break.

>> u/btchywitchy: pepper spray for men. silver knife for dark creatures.

....

Cole
Just got in!!
Can't wait to see you 🩶🩶

                                                              Brennan
                                        you too! i can come over to yours?

Cole
yes!
mari isn't here yet, she took a later flight

                                                              Brennan
                                                              🏃💨

The week leading up to Cole's parents visiting, Cole gave him a crash course.

His dad was a big-shot consulting yuppie type who never learned what privilege was, believed affirmative action was "reverse racism," and buried himself in work to avoid his family and his own emotions.

His mom was a semi-popular crafting YouTuber and self-proclaimed "yarn guru" who thought gay was a curse word, cried on a hair trigger, and bowed to her husband's decisions in order to avoid conflict.

Cole warned that Brennan had the honor of first ever boyfriend to meet his parents. He'd only ever had a series of flings ("Mari calls it my slut phase," Cole had admitted), so this was new territory for all of them.

Cole's dad ("He'll insist you call him Christopher, and he'll be offended otherwise, so no *mister*s, okay?") was there for a conference and would be busy most of the time, so they'd only have a few hours to spare for their son. Brennan thought it was kind of shitty, but for Cole it was a relief.

"So," Cole said now, pulling at the edges of his jacket sleeves outside the T station, a block from the restaurant they were meeting his parents at. "They're gonna be judgy and terrible and it's gonna suck."

"Way to really sell it."

"I'm trying to be honest about what you should expect."

Brennan flicked Cole's hands away from where they were mutilating Cole's tie out of nerves. He straightened it for him, more of a weak excuse to offer Cole some sort of physical support than anything. But Brennan was way out of his comfort zone either way; he hadn't been at a restaurant nice enough to wear a tie to since high school graduation. He hadn't had to meet a partner's parent ever, so there was that, too.

He meant it as a joke but it came out limp and sad: "Do you think they're gonna hate me?"

"No!" Cole said, immediate and emphatic. "That's not it. Of course not. It's not you, it's *them*. Don't panic, please, because if *you* panic, then we're *both* panicking, and at least one of us should keep their shit together."

"Cole, there's no reason for either of us to panic, it's gonna be okay."

Cole nodded to himself, trying to convince himself to believe it. But he still didn't make any motion to move. Brennan could hear his pulse racing, and not in the fun way.

"I'm gonna be there the whole time," Brennan said. He captured one of Cole's hands in between both of his own and caught Cole's eye. "And I'm sure they love you no matter what."

Cole hummed in a tone Brennan identified as *agree to disagree*. He started walking, though, so Brennan marked it as a win.

The city was cold and gray, even windier this close to the water, as they made their way through the streets. Cole didn't take his hand, and Brennan couldn't blame him, so they walked with their shoulders brushing through thick layered coats.

"Thank you for being here for me," Cole said. "I know it's not exactly fun."

"Who said I'm not having fun? I'm having a great time."

"Yeah?"

"Oh, sure. Going on a double date with middle-aged homophobes from Tennessee is one of my favorite pastimes."

"You're the worst," Cole said and smacked Brennan's chest, which he generally did when he didn't want to admit Brennan said something funny, ducking to hide a grin.

They wove through the bustling of people rushing toward somewhere warmer, the wind whipping bare trees and chilling skin. Brennan recognized the area—it was near the blood cache Nellie had taken him to that first time, the vending machine hidden between restaurants. He hadn't been back since; a different cache was more easily accessible by commuter rail from campus.

The noise of all the crowd and clutter wasn't overwhelming anymore, not like it had been when he was thirsty and confused and drowning under all of his senses. He felt like he might finally be past that, able to focus on the here and now. On Cole.

"I have a great time whenever I'm with you," Brennan said. He meant it to come out cheeky but ended up far too sincere.

Cole grinned and said, "Cheesy."

"I distracted you, at least?" Brennan offered, because they were approaching the restaurant, two figures standing huddled near the entrance. There was Cole's mom, Deborah, waving Cole down enthusiastically, and his dad, Christopher, who stood beside her scrolling through his phone and looking bored.

Cole looked on with what could only be described as dread.

"Okay," he said, smoothing down his jacket. "Let's carpe this diem."

It was then that, down the alley they were passing, Brennan recognized that vending machine he'd visited with Nellie for blood, and a shadowy figure crouching in front of it.

Choppy black hair and all black clothes, a long skirt and platform boots. He'd recognize that overly enthusiastic Goth attire anywhere.

"Oh shi—" Brennan started, but Cole was already trotting up to his parents. Seizing the day, as such.

Brennan's ears rang as Cole started to do greetings, hugging them each in turn. But Brennan couldn't tear his focus away from the vending machine—the blood cache—that Dom was messing with. What was she doing? Maybe she just needed blood? Though she'd made it clear she wasn't exactly on a cruelty-free diet, so it didn't make sense. All signs pointed to *evil scheme.*

Dom stopped in her work, glancing over her shoulder, and locked eyes with Brennan. Brennan's veins turned to ice, and Dom recognized him instantly, panic flitting across her face.

There was one frozen moment where Brennan realized that he might have the advantage. Whatever she was doing, she hadn't planned for him to be here. For once, she was the one thrown off, and maybe Brennan could—

"Brennan?"

Cole's voice pulled him from his thoughts and he realized that both he and his parents were looking at him expectantly. They'd been doing introductions.

This was maybe one of those capital letter Important Choice moments, where he was supposed to step up and solve problems, go after Dom, prove that he had conquered his vampiric skills.

He looked up to see Dom turn the corner of the alley, disappearing. Fleeing.

He turned his back to the alley, put on his parent-charming smile, and made his introductions.

"Sorry about that, I thought I saw a friend," Brennan said, and Deborah smiled politely.

"It's nice to meet you," she said.

"Thanks for letting me interrupt your family dinner."

They went through the motions of pleasantries and small talk as they went to the host and were seated. Deborah chattered on about nothing.

Once they settled at the table, Brennan excused himself as politely as he could, pleading the bathroom. As soon as he was out of their view he picked up the pace and hauled ass to the bathroom, poking furiously at the phone to dial Nellie's number.

The ringing taunted him, and he paced the length of the empty men's room.

What could he have done? What could he do besides turn to Nellie and Sunny? This was the right choice, the logical choice. He should let the experts handle it.

"*Wait, Sunny, what did that say?*" came Nellie's tinny voice over the speaker, and then a sharp beep.

Voicemail. Brennan glared at his phone like it was at fault.

"Nellie, I saw Dom in Boston, by the aquarium," Brennan said. "Call me back."

He dialed Sunny and got the same treatment, albeit with a slightly more self-aware voicemail greeting. He stopped in his pacing to stare in dismay at his phone.

He tried Sunny again. Nothing. His thumbs tore through the feed of the Facebook group, looking for a clue to what they were up to. They were nothing if not eerily responsive. Sunny especially.

He sent a last text with the restaurant info and what he'd seen and faced the bathroom door. That had to be enough.

Brennan had a family dinner to get to.

"So what do you study, Brendan?"

Cole took a sip of water like he wished it would drown him, but this was neither the first nor last time someone had made that particular mistake.

"History," Brennan answered. "And sociology, and a minor in English lit—"

"Oh, *history*," said Christopher. "That's a tough field to get into. Tough degree to make use of."

"Oh, sure," said Deb, "Mary Bird from church, her son majored in history and now he works down at the *Publix*"—she lowered her voice like she was saying a dirty word—"slicing meats for the *deli.*"

"Mom," Cole tried to scold.

She shook her head, sniffed like he hadn't spoken. "I can't imagine it's very fulfilling."

"Or lucrative," agreed Christopher.

Christopher and Deborah McNamara looked like a stock photo portraying 1950s gender roles. Where Cole's dad wore a business-formal suit and tie, his mom was in a tea-length dress. Where Christopher seemed to wear a permanent scowl, Deb always wore a pleasant smile.

"Cole was smart, choosing something so useful. Business is really so versatile," Deb said.

"He won't have trouble getting a job, assuming he actually applies himself," said Christopher, giving Cole a pointed look that Brennan didn't care for at all. Cole shrunk into his seat beside Brennan, and Brennan reached to squeeze his hand under the table. Cole clung to his fingers with a death grip.

Dinner went on like that, Cole's parents speaking in passive-aggressive language that left Brennan out of his depth while Cole grew steadily closer to hiding under the table.

As conversation went on, Cole's voice grew tense, his words short, his grip on Brennan's fingers tight enough to hurt if Brennan were human. Cole's jaw did a rippling thing it only did when he was deeply pissed, or deep in thought. Now, it was probably both.

"What exactly do you plan to do with a history degree?" Deb asked pleasantly.

Brennan swallowed down his annoyance, his anxiety, and tried his best to sound like he had his shit together. Like he was hardworking and somewhat intelligent and even halfway deserving of their son.

"Maybe something curatorial, at a museum. But you need a lot more education, or internships, and they're really selective."

"Oh, we couldn't be prouder of Cole for landing his internship for this semester," Deb said. "He's been working so hard, haven't you, baby?"

Brennan blinked and swung his head toward Cole, who was fiddling with the edge of his cloth napkin, studiously avoiding Brennan's gaze.

"His internship?" Brennan hedged. Cole had mentioned his parents pressuring him about it, but not that he'd gotten one.

"At the Boston branch of my company," said Christopher. "I had to make some calls, but Cole will prove himself in no time."

Cole shrugged from where he'd lost another two inches slinking down into his seat. "It's not a big deal."

Of course. Cole didn't *want* it. But why hadn't he told him? When had this happened?

"Well, it may not be corner offices and executive assistants yet, but you'll work your way up," Christopher continued, oblivious to Cole's turmoil. "That's the good thing about business. It's good old-fashioned, honest hard work."

They had no idea Cole hated it. His degree, the life waiting for him after college. They didn't seem to know Cole at all.

"I think the library is pretty honest work, too," Brennan said, mouth moving faster than his brain. "And Cole's really good at it."

"Yes, I'm sure he excels at shelving books. He learned the alphabet in kindergarten with everyone else." Christopher and Deb tittered together like it was hilarious.

Brennan's grip tightened around his glass.

"You know, I've been at the library my whole time at undergrad," Cole said, tentative, "and I've been thinking I might like to finish off at least this year there, so—"

"But how would you balance that with the internship and school?" Deb asked. "You can't let your grades fall behind."

"I know, of course. I guess I thought . . . maybe I don't need to do the internship."

"Don't be ridiculous, Cole," said Christopher. "Of course you do. It's the next step if you want to succeed in consulting."

Cole's shaking fingers squeezed Brennan's under the table.

"Maybe I don't want to do that at *all*."

And, wow, okay. They were doing this now.

"What are you talking about?" asked Deb. "This is your future, baby."

"I know," Cole said. "That's why I thought I could have a say in it. And I'm not—I'm not just saying this, I *have* thought it through. I know business is not what I want to do and I feel like I was pressured to choose a path."

"What are you going to do, then?" Christopher demanded.

Cole withered. "I don't know yet."

"It doesn't *sound* like you thought it through."

"I thought maybe I would take a gap year. Get a normal job while I figure things out. Work at a coffee shop or something."

Deb gasped.

"Just for a little while! Or, I dunno, maybe making lattes is fulfilling and I stick with it. Would that really be the worst thing?"

Deb started crying.

"Cole, give it a rest," said Christopher, pinching the bridge of his nose. "You're upsetting your mother."

"You're throwing your life away"—Deb sniffled—"like Noah did."

Cole reared back like he'd been slapped.

Then something magical happened. Cole straightened in his seat, gaining some six inches of height. The defeated frown that had been on his lips all dinner hardened into a line of determination.

"Noah made his choice. And so have I."

His words hung heavy in the air for a long moment. Across the restaurant, a family erupted into "Happy Birthday." The whole song dragged by, Deborah and Christopher staring at their son with matching blank expressions.

The restaurant erupted into polite applause for whoever's birthday. And then, in the relative silence that came after, Deb's quiet sobs turned to a low moaning wail.

Cole was blinking rapidly, mouth twisting, jaw working. His lip quivered and his hand in Brennan's slackened.

He stood then, so abruptly that his chair clattered over behind him. "I think maybe," Cole said, his voice the strongest it had been all evening, "you need some time."

He turned on his heel and fled.

Brennan spared a moment to realize that most of the restaurant's staff and patrons were watching their table before he followed Cole's footsteps.

The cold air was sharp as Brennan emerged from the restaurant.

"Cole!" Brennan tried calling, but Cole didn't stop moving until Brennan had caught up with him and put a hand to his arm, at which point he stopped in his tracks so suddenly he must have been waiting for it.

"Cole," he said again, but now that he'd caught him, he didn't know what to say. His heart ached in empathy for everything Cole must be feeling.

Cole stayed facing away for a long moment, shoulders shaking almost imperceptibly.

"Admittedly, that could have gone better," Brennan tried, his voice soft even as he winced at the words. Why didn't he know what to say? Cole always knew what to say, but whenever the tables were turned, Brennan didn't know how to return the favor.

Cole let out a weak little sound, halfway between a laugh and a sob, and his shoulders shook harder.

Then he finally twisted around in a flurry of motion that Brennan barely processed before his arms were full of Cole. Cole buried his face in Brennan's chest and Brennan's hands hovered a second before settling on Cole's back, tugging him close, burying his nose in the scent of his hair.

"It's okay," Brennan soothed, but it felt cheap.

"I made a huge mistake," Cole gasped, the words muffled against Brennan's shirt. "They're my family, I can't lose them."

"Look at me, Cole. You did nothing wrong."

"I shouldn't have—"

"Hey, no. It's your life. It's on them if they can't accept the idea of you as a barista. Give them time."

"But everything was *fine,* everything was okay and I had to go and ruin it and now they'll be upset and—"

"*Fuck* them being upset. They don't get to be upset. Their happiness isn't your problem."

Brennan wracked his head for something to say that could soothe the hurt riding over Cole in waves.

"You can't change the way they react, or control the way they feel. It's their job to figure it out, and it's your job to be yourself and fuck everyone else!" He paused, wrinkled his nose. "Well, not *everyone* else, and not *literally* fuck, for a few reasons."

Cole snorted a wet laugh and pulled back to look up at Brennan. His eyes were red-rimmed, tears streaking his cheeks.

"I should have told you about the internship," he said.

Brennan said, "I wouldn't have been opposed to a bit more warning of what I was walking into."

"I'm sorry."

"You keep me on my toes." Brennan sighed, hands dropping from Cole's shoulders to his waist. "It's part of the charm."

Cole opened his mouth to respond—

And Brennan's world underwent a violent twist.

In the distance came people shouting and car horns beeping, followed by an assault on Brennan's nose by the tangy iron scent of blood. It was so much, so strong, he was nearly bowled over with the force of it.

He'd fed before dinner to avoid any fang-related mishaps, and he'd gotten good enough to not react strongly at small amounts of blood.

But this was something else. This was a *lot* of blood. More than Brennan had smelled at once since turning.

"Brennan? Are you okay?" Cole's voice sounded foggy, as if from a distance, and it pulled him back to reality.

Brennan focused on Cole, eyes still puffy but widened in concern. His gaze flickered between Brennan and the distant sounds of shouting. Brennan followed his gaze. There was lots of movement—people gathering near the harbor, or scurrying away as quickly as possible.

"What is it? Are your vampy senses tingling?"

It was such an adorably Cole thing to say that Brennan almost found comfort in it. But something cold clutched his chest, the shaky feeling of anxiety coursing through his veins.

"Come on," Brennan said, and the cold gripping his chest must have come through in his voice because Cole didn't ask questions, just took Brennan's hand.

They approached the mass of people gathering around the edges of the harbor. A few teenagers were filming on their phones, while the crowd watched the water with shock and awe.

Brennan tuned out the noise of an approaching news helicopter, as well as all the gossip behind him. He pushed through the crowd, pulling

Cole along by the hand as they shimmied between people like at a rock concert.

When they finally got to the edge, Brennan froze. Cole ran into his back and then squeezed next to him to see what everyone was looking at.

The water was a river of red, bright clouds of what was unmistakably blood, the scent mixing with sea salt and burning Brennan's nostrils. Red for a whole expanse of harbor, petering off to black in the distance. Even if Brennan couldn't smell it, even if he could fool himself into thinking it was food dye, or some other strange effect, the water was undeniably littered with floating empty plastic blood bags.

His brain spun. If this was what Dom had been doing at the blood cache, then it hadn't been *one* blood cache. It had to have been a lot of them. *All* of them. Was this her plan? To attack the blood supply? If it was, it was a good one. The urban clan's ability to lay low was dependent on it.

Brennan's mind was racing faster than he could keep track of with all the dominoes tumbling through his brain of all the ways this was very, very bad.

Cole waited to speak until they were back on the T, the train car empty save for one guy sleeping across a row of seats at the other end.

"I'm guessing this is a vampire thing." Cole sat across from Brennan on the edge of his seat, drumming his fingers incessantly on his knees, desperate to pace.

"I saw Dom earlier," Brennan confessed. "Messing with a blood cache near the restaurant."

Cole did a double take. "Why didn't you say something?"

"Why didn't you say anything about the internship?"

"You've had a lot going on!"

"Well, right back at you! I didn't want to derail your thing."

Cole laughed dryly. "I would've taken vampires over disappointing my parents any day."

Brennan winced. He might be panicking, but his boyfriend had gone through a tense experience of his own.

He wished he didn't have to deal with this shit. He wished he could ignore it, take Cole home and lie in his bed and listen to records and let

Cole be as sad as he needed so long as he didn't do it alone. He wanted to hold his hand and say supportive things. He wanted to be normal. He wanted to be a good boyfriend.

But it always came back to this: he was a vampire. Maybe that was all he could be.

"I'm sorry," Brennan offered weakly.

He finally checked his phone, but there was no response from Sunny or Nellie. He tried each of them again while Cole gradually drooped in his seat, arms crossed and leaning against the window with a crease in his brow like he had a headache building.

"No answer."

"Then what?"

"I think we should get you back to campus," Brennan said. "I mean—you've had enough drama today. I can look into it."

"No," Cole said, whipping around from where he'd curled into himself. "No, I want to help. This is the perfect distraction. Please, if I go home I'm gonna put on my sad Taylor Swift playlist or watch *Love, Simon* and cry at the coming-out scene because my mom can't be Jennifer Garner, so please, please, can we deal with the vampire problem so I don't have to do that?"

Brennan squeezed his eyes shut. Whatever Dom had done, she'd done it because Brennan hadn't stopped her. She was right there. And he couldn't do a damn thing. Still, he didn't regret for a second staying to support Cole. But maybe that meant he would never be able to have both things. To have love, and humanity, while also being part of a vampire clan. He would always have to choose.

He prayed he wasn't choosing wrong.

"Okay," Brennan said, reluctant. "I guess there's one other person we could go to for help."

20

THE STORM

r/occultboston

u/micahlandau

Bloody Demonstration in Boston

[Video]

I can't believe this happened. I can't believe I saw it! I can't believe I got video!!!

I was downtown visiting my favorite psychic and then I was walking along the harbor and suddenly red starts flowing down along with deflating plastic pint bags. They painted the harbor red with blood. This has to be part of the story. Who else would have so much blood?

But what really scares me is—what kind of message are they trying to send?

Edited to Add: Someone from the *Boston Globe* contacted me to use my video on their site. This is real. [Link]

> >> u/fittingaesthetics: This doesn't seem like a good sign. Maybe some sort of ritual? Or a warning? Do you think they know we're on to them?

THE BOSTON GLOBE

The Boston Blood Party

[video caption] A river of blood overtakes the Boston Harbor after an unknown group poured thousands of pints of stolen blood donations into the water on Sunday afternoon. . . . Police are contacting hospitals in an attempt to identify where the supply was stolen from, but as of now their origins are unknown. "How any one person could accumulate that much blood for a frankly petty prank is beyond me," said one police officer.

Cole was quiet, looking out the window as the MBTA commuter rail pulled them toward campus. The gray sky finally gave in to the building pressure to rain. Something similar was building, gray and cloudy, in the pit of Brennan's gut.

Cole hadn't spoken since they'd transferred trains. Not that Brennan could blame him. But it was so unlike him. Even on the verge of a breakdown, Cole was an open book. And here he was, the quietest Brennan had ever seen him.

"It obviously wasn't optimal, uh, back there," Brennan started, voice low, tentative. "Do you wanna talk about it?"

"No, thank you," Cole said, with the mechanical ease he might tell a cashier he didn't need his receipt.

"Okay," Brennan said. Watched the winter grays of Massachusetts streak by through the window. "I just mean that I'm here for you, whenever you *do* want to—"

"I'm good," Cole interrupted.

Brennan ignored the heat in his cheeks. Not the pleasant kind he usually had around Cole, but a hot shame. He didn't know what he was supposed to do. Bringing Cole to Travis felt weird, but Cole insisted he wanted to be there. But Brennan was powerless to take away all the pain he knew Cole must be feeling. He itched for his journal, left behind in his apartment.

He started thinking of everything he said, didn't say, and should have said during the whole dinner fiasco, which spiraled into everything he said, didn't say, and should have said throughout their whole relationship and—

Cole's hand found Brennan's and pulled it to center between them, fingers twining with his effortlessly, stilling his movement and his thoughts. When Cole squeezed his hand, he squeezed back.

Massachusetts passed them by in a blur. Cole slowly unfurled from where he'd been facing the window.

"Are you sure you don't want me to walk you to yours and Mari's before I go to Travis?" Brennan asked.

"I'm sure," Cole said. He squeezed Brennan's hand tight like that might keep him from leaving him behind. Not that Brennan really wanted to. "We're in this together, right?"

Brennan pulled their hands up to press a kiss to the back of Cole's hand. "That goes both ways, you know."

"I know."

Brennan let himself relax. He held Cole's hand the rest of the ride.

Travis's dingy shack looked like even more of a mess than Brennan remembered. With the rain coming down like it was, the building swayed slightly, ready to collapse under a stray breeze.

Cole gripped Brennan's hand and stuck close in the winter evening's shadows, his other hand holding an umbrella over both their heads. Cole had known it would rain, of course, and was prepared as ever. He was taking in the building with a sort of open curiosity, like he was at a museum. A glimpse into a different world. Brennan couldn't help the tinge of envy. He would never be able to walk away from all this. Cole could.

Nervous energy made Brennan feel twitchy, and he was grateful that holding on to Cole kept one hand occupied. Nellie and Sunny's continued absence nagged at him. He'd never not gotten a reply from Sunny within minutes of texting; he'd rarely if ever seen her not glued to her phone. And he didn't exactly like Travis.

The swaying structure that was Travis's house and the junkyard of the clearing surrounding it didn't add any confidence. Chickens clucked about in their fenced-in area by the greenhouse. The air as they approached the shack smelled like smoke and the sweet tang of blood.

Rosie was out in the yard, but she didn't run to greet him like normal. She was pacing in front of the entrance to the greenhouse, whining persistently.

The tarp-flap of a front door burst open before Brennan could attempt to knock on the frame, right as Brennan had reached the stepping stone that acted as a porch. As if Travis had been watching them and waiting.

"Vampling!" Travis greeted, throwing his hands up in a flourishing welcome. He grinned wide and nodded to Cole. "And you brought a snack! Ha! Only joking. I know you're the boyfriend!" He gave an exaggerated wink.

Cole laughed politely, putting his Southern charm back on like a mask for Travis.

Rosie barked twice, loud and pointed.

"Rosie, leave it," Travis commanded.

As well trained as she typically was, she barked again in protest and sat down in front of the greenhouse door with a heavy sigh.

"Stupid dog. But hey, good to see you again," Travis said. "Come on in, do you want tea? I was just making tea."

They followed Travis inside, Cole ditching his umbrella at the door, and Travis immediately busied himself with the teakettle. "You have a lovely home," Cole tried. Brennan held back a snort and Cole gave him a stern look like he could sense his rudeness and it upset his Southern heart.

"It's not much, but it's all I need," said Travis. He fluttered about the small corner of the building that might be called a kitchen, pulling random chipped mugs from various boxes and corners. After a moment, two mugs of steaming tea came floating over to Cole and Brennan, sloshing on the box that acted as a coffee table.

Brennan didn't love tea. He had always been more of a coffee person. But, maybe because of the long day, or the chill of the rain, the smell of it then was strong and enticing. He wrapped his hands around the mug and let it warm him.

A buzz sounded from the kitchen area but Travis made no move for whatever it was. Brennan hadn't had the impression Travis had a phone.

"What brings you guys out here into the wilderness, then?" Travis said, finally stationary. He stood across from them, leaning against a wooden crate that held mason jars filled with round buds of weed. He looked at them expectantly. Brennan looked at Cole, who looked at *him* with a face he was sure matched his own—*what now?*

Brennan told Travis about everything with Dom, and the horribly named Boston Blood Party thing, and Sunny and Nellie not responding. The sound of heavy rain on the thin roofing was a constant backdrop.

Travis started rolling a joint as he listened, nodding but otherwise focusing his attention on the movements of his hands. Once Brennan finished the story, Travis didn't respond for a long minute as he started to smoke. The buzzing sound went off again.

When Travis finally spoke, it was to extend the joint. "You want some?"

Cole considered it but shook his head, while Brennan swallowed down his annoyance and sipped his tea, letting the hot liquid scald his tongue. It was the first time he enjoyed tea, and he drained the cup in no time.

"Do you have any idea where Sunny or Nellie might be?" Brennan reiterated. "And if not, then isn't it, like, your job to help stop Dom? Shouldn't you be doing something?"

Travis's expression went steely. "First of all, my *job*," he said, "is to do whatever the fuck I want. I know you're new here, but don't ever think you can tell me what I should be doing."

Ice froze Brennan's veins under Travis's sharp gaze, and he remembered again that this was a powerful and possibly ancient creature that Brennan really knew nothing about. He'd made a mistake coming here.

But the ice thawed as quickly as it had emerged, Travis's easy grin falling back across his face.

"I'm sure Sunny and Nellie are off making out somewhere. Either that, or they're having a fight. Sometimes they go AWOL like this. Like when Sunny sold Nellie's first-edition Game Boy to get them Taylor Swift tickets. They were missing for *weeks* before they finished fighting or fucking or whatever it is they do."

"Then do you have any advice about Dom?" Cole asked, hands folded politely in his lap. "I don't mean any disrespect, but she could hurt a lot of people. Or even expose vampires to everyone."

"You guys are really killing my vibe with all this negativity," Travis said. "Can we try to fuel this energy into something positive?"

"I'm trying to fuel this energy into making sure that murders don't happen," Brennan said. "Is that not positive enough for you?"

Another *buzz, buzz, buzz*—

Rosie barked louder.

"Look, I gotta go water the greenhouse plants and check on the little Rosebud," Travis said. "It'll only be a minute. Just chill, okay? Relax. I want positive energies only by the time I'm back, yeah?"

Travis slipped through the tarp door.

"He's being cagey, right?" Brennan asked.

"I think he might just be like that," Cole said.

Buuuuuuzz—

The sound was grating. He was starting to get a headache from all the sounds around him going sharp and loud.

Brennan peeked through the window over the kitchen sink to see Travis's back retreating toward the greenhouse. Then he started digging through drawers.

"What are you doing?"

"That buzzing. I didn't think he had a phone." Brennan's words scratched against his throat.

There weren't many drawers to try. He found the phone in the far one, wrapped up in a hand towel. It was the latest model of iPhone, sleek, with a pink case and—

The lock screen lit up with a preview of 99+ notifications, including some from Brennan.

"It's Sunny's phone," Brennan said. His stomach dropped. Sunny didn't seem like the type to part with her phone voluntarily.

Brennan froze with an idea that seemed impossible but also, entirely too possible.

A slew of thoughts lined up in Brennan's brain all at once.

Travis and Dom had been friends.

Travis had killed people.

Travis had told them himself he'd helped his girlfriend with a vampire uprising in the 1920s.

Travis was tremendously powerful and more ancient than Brennan could comprehend.

Brennan had possibly fucked up.

"We need to leave, I think."

"What about the blood supply? And Dom?"

"I'll explain later, but for now let's get out of here." Brennan peered out the window and didn't see Travis. He hoped he was still in the greenhouse. He went to Cole, still on the couch, and caught his eye. "I need you to trust me on this."

Cole's frown didn't waver, but he nodded.

They moved to gather their things, Brennan tucking Sunny's phone into his jacket pocket. He was starting to feel dizzy by the time they went through the tarp and into the rainy night.

Except, at the same time, across the field, Travis emerged from the greenhouse. There was a reddish glow from the building, some sort of special lighting that cloaked Travis like a bloody halo.

"Leaving already?" he called.

"I forgot I have an essay due at midnight," Brennan lied. It was the flimsiest of excuses. He and Cole kept moving toward the exit of the clearing, and Travis kept crossing the field toward them.

"Aw, are you sure?" Travis said. "We didn't even get to the good part."

And that was enough to get him to snap. "What does that mean? What do you know?"

Buzz. Buzz. Buzz.

Travis froze. His eyes cut to Brennan, head tilting owlishly, and the buzzing sound cut straight through the rain.

"Oh," Travis said. "Oh, man. You found the phone. My bad, honestly."

"What did you do? Where are they?"

Brennan knew this was important but it was getting impossible to focus. Something smelled so good, and Brennan realized that he was thirsty. But he'd been so consistent with his regimen.

Travis clucked his tongue, disappointed. "You're still asking the wrong questions," he said. "But sure. Where do I start? They're fine. Just in thrall for a couple of days. It's unpleasant, but they'll be fine."

Rain fell down around them. Brennan hoped this was one of Travis's weird jokes.

"What?" Travis said. "There's no use keeping it a secret, is there? I mean, I don't mean to be rude, but I couldn't feel *less* threatened by you. No offense. Is that offensive? Whatever. Uh, yeah, they had a lead on Dom's plan, they wanted to stop her, blah blah blah, so I temporarily incapacitated them."

Brennan recoiled, angling himself between Cole and Travis. "You're helping Dom."

Travis rolled his eyes. "No, god! *Dom* was helping *me*. I know she's got the mysterious Goth thing going for her, but what's the obsession? You guys really think she masterminded all this? She freaked out as soon as I killed those two people in November."

"I thought Dom killed them. I thought you couldn't leave your woods."

"Oh, keep *up*. Dom turned a few people to gain power, yes, to free *me*. But as soon as I told her about the vampire ball plan, she totally pussied out."

"But Dom was back in Boston. She sabotaged the blood supply."

Travis scoffed. "Again, credit where it's due? *I* sabotaged the blood supply. I didn't know Dom was back in town until you came here and told me."

Then Dom had been—what, helping? *Fuck.* Brennan's head was getting heavy, staticky, and he dug his fingers into his temples. He was thirsty, and it was getting worse impossibly quickly.

"What did you do to me?" Brennan asked.

"Ding ding ding!" Travis cheered. "Yes! Million-dollar question! I was wondering when the tea would kick in."

The words trickled in slow motion under the haze of all Brennan's senses going haywire, the flush under Cole's skin starting to smell like freshly baked chocolate chip cookies.

"What did you do?" Brennan surged forward, out of the shelter of Cole's umbrella, but the rain was nothing next to the raging, growing burn in his throat.

"Yet another thing Nellie's curriculum doesn't teach the vamplings," Travis said. He pulled a vial from his overalls pockets, filled with something murky and black. "Vampire blood. Homemade! My very own recipe."

"Brennan." Cole's voice was quiet and urgent behind him, one hand laid on his forearm, but Brennan couldn't tear his eyes from Travis. "Brennan, let's just go."

"Oh, don't leave yet, loves, I'm giving you a very helpful hint, and the ball will be much less interesting if you don't pay attention."

Brennan didn't look at Cole, and Cole's hand dropped from his arm.

"*Vampire blood,*" Travis continued, in a tone like he was narrating a children's show. "It brings a feral thirst response when consumed by a vampire. And, of course, it's essential to the process of *turning* a human. What could possibly go wrong, do you think?"

"Why?" Brennan asked. He could barely think, he was aware he was trembling, and he knew Cole was right, they needed to move. But he had to know.

Travis laughed and drew his brows together like it was obvious.

He said, "I guess I think it'll be interesting."

Brennan went cold, and it had nothing to do with the rain. He realized that his first evaluation of Travis was wrong. He wasn't depressed or aimless with his age. He was *bored.*

And that was much more dangerous.

"Why are you telling us? Doesn't that defeat the purpose?" Cole asked.

"Uh, no. What are you gonna do about it? You can't call Nellie and Sunny to help you. It might even be interesting to see what you try to do. I'm all for a good fight."

Rage and thirst bubbled up as one. "You'll get one then," Brennan snarled, "I can promise you that."

"You might want to get going then," said Travis. He cut a meaningful look at Cole and smirked. "You'll be needing blood soon."

Brennan didn't make a conscious decision to do so, but suddenly, he had launched forward, his hands fists, Cole shouting his name.

He was yanked backward by an invisible leash as swiftly as he'd started, his whole body locked up as if restrained. Invisible pressure grabbed him hard enough to bruise, if he could still be bruised.

Of course, Travis stood in front of him with his hand outstretched in a Force choking curl.

"You know, Brennan," Travis said. Brennan's toes barely skimmed the ground as the pressure pulled him forcefully upward. "I gave you a gift when I turned you. And all you've done is complain and hide and pretend. This is a gift, too. You'll see that."

With a wave of his hand, Travis turned away in dismissal and released his grip on Brennan. Brennan stumbled forward to catch himself as Cole appeared at his side with worried, fluttering hands. Brennan almost lunged after Travis again before Cole caught him by the arms.

"Brennan, let's *go,*" Cole pleaded.

He couldn't have physically held Brennan back if he tried, but the fear in his voice made Brennan go pliant, letting himself be ushered away from Travis as hunger clawed at his throat and Cole's scent clouded his senses.

As they fled through the rain, Travis's laughter in the distance devolved into a coughing fit.

The entrance to Travis's clearing sealed up behind them, thick brush growing to fill the space, but neither Brennan nor Cole stopped to wonder at it.

Brennan ran through every centering coping mechanism in the book. He tried to focus on his breathing. He tried to focus on his environment. No matter what, he kept finding himself focused on the smell of Cole, the beating of his quickening pulse.

Cole went straight into solution mode.

"It's forty minutes' walk to campus," he was saying, using his phone as a flashlight while he charged ahead, tracking through the mud, "but I bet we could do it in fifteen if you run with me on your back."

Brennan groaned and squeezed his eyes shut against the violent brightness of Cole's phone flashlight, a wave of dizziness and hunger rolling through him.

"I bet you could do it in ten minutes, really, with proper motivation," Cole said, voice going shaky.

"I don't think I'm gonna make it ten minutes," Brennan realized. He stopped to double over with his hands on his knees, trying to center himself, trying to stay in control of the instincts dying to take over and *drink.*

"Is there a—a cache nearby?" Cole realized Brennan had stopped and doubled back toward him.

"Cole, stop," Brennan pleaded.

Cole froze a few paces away from Brennan. He was shivering from the cold. Freezing rain washed over him, umbrella forgotten somewhere along the way.

"Stop what? It's gonna be fine." Cole sounded like he was trying to convince himself. His heartbeat rang in Brennan's ears like a siren, the scent of him even this close overwhelming.

Brennan summoned every bit of logical thinking he had left and said, "You need to get away from me."

"It's gonna be fine," Cole said again, but he was wide-eyed and panicked.

"Cole, I'm not—"

"*No,*" Cole said, voice shrill. "We're in this together. You said that."

"We are," Brennan said. "That's why you're going to keep going to campus, and I'm gonna go the opposite way and see how many squirrels I can drink before I start crying."

With that, Brennan turned and sprinted into the thick of the woods, ignoring Cole shouting his name in favor of snatching a rabbit from its path.

It was like licking the pages of a cookbook. He hadn't expected it to do the trick, but he hoped it might buy him some time.

Brennan had moved onto the second squirrel by the time Cole jogged up to him, breath coming in puffs of fog in the air.

"Why the fuck are you running away from me?" Cole said, and he'd never sounded so pissed.

Brennan was so dizzy, so thirsty, so desperate he thought he was going to lose it, or die. He would prefer dying.

"Cole," Brennan said. Blood was on his lips. "You are the literal light of my life, but if you don't get far away from me right now I'm going to—"

"Bite me."

"I was going to say *go feral,* but yeah, that's basically—"

"No, I mean," Cole said, "bite me."

He was waiting for a reaction with wide eyes.

"It won't kill me," Cole continued. "And it won't turn me. You can stop and I haven't donated blood in a month, so I can totally go again."

He put it so logically that Brennan felt sick, not just thirsty.

"No," he said, with such finality that he was sure Cole would leave it there.

Instead, Cole closed the distance between them and cupped Brennan's jaw in his hands, tilting his face down toward Cole's like he was going in for a kiss but pausing an inch away. Everything in Brennan was alight, but not in the good way that happened when Cole usually kissed him. His head throbbed. Cole smelled like ambrosia and nectar. Cole's heartbeat became everything, a warm bubble around them both, one Brennan was terrified of bursting.

"What happens if you don't?" Cole asked, voice quiet, breath falling on Brennan's lips.

Brennan couldn't let himself breathe.

"What?"

"If you don't get human blood. Do you starve? Do you die?"

"I don't know." Brennan was shaking. He didn't know, and he was scared—of what would happen if he didn't do this, and what would happen if he did.

"So bite me," Cole said. He tried to be lighthearted. "It's win-win, really. I can't say I'm not curious, though I wish the situation were a tad different."

"You're serious," Brennan whispered.

"I am."

Brennan wanted desperately to tell Cole that he loved him, then. Cole was watery-eyed, a determined set to his jaw. Brennan was hyperaware of every movement of him, every shift, every breath, the fluctuating speed of his racing heart. Cole had never been more beautiful, and Brennan loved him, but it wasn't the time.

Those words should be saved for somewhere softer.

"I'm so sorry," Brennan said. His hands tentatively gripped Cole's waist, squeezing in reassurance and apology.

"I know," said Cole, and he extended his neck.

And Brennan bit him.

Sweet relief flooded every one of Brennan's senses. Cole tensed and cried out, then shuddered and collapsed into it, into Brennan's arms. Distantly, Brennan remembered a pamphlet—*a vampire's venom is soothing to its prey*—and then Brennan wasn't thinking of anything but the sweet glory of the drink, the base instinct of it, how it felt like the most natural thing in the world.

The fog in Brennan's head started to clear but didn't fade completely. Brennan drank, and thirst continued to burn at his throat.

"Brennan," Cole said weakly. A warning. And reality crashed down on Brennan again, the self-hate, the fear, the *I'm hurting him I'm hurting him I'm—*

He pulled off and staggered back, leaving Cole swaying where he stood, dazed, eyes clouded over.

Brennan wanted to throw up. He wanted to run to Cole, make sure he was alright.

He wanted to drink more.

21

THE QUIET

LOCKED

99+ notifications

[The lock screen is a selfie of Sunny and Nellie together. Sunny is posing perfectly for the camera, pursed lips, and Nellie is smiling at Sunny.]

·····················

Instagram comments:

@amiahreads270: Girl where are u!!!

@kristen.baby.420: This is the longest she's ever gone without posting lol

@themargotmyers: Hey don't listen to all these haters! Take a mental health week! We don't always need to be producing content!

·····················

A Facebook comment:

@Soon-Hee Kim: Can anyone get back to me about the dress code? I messaged Nellie but haven't heard back.

After, Cole held one hand to the spot on his neck that Brennan had bitten. He said, "I'm tired. Let's go home," and those were the last words either of them spoke for a time.

Brennan wordlessly scooped up a wobbly Cole, carrying him on his back to campus. It was the least he could do.

The worst part was, he was still thirsty.

Brennan's brain was a storm of overstimulated senses and guilty self-flagellation. Cole's shivering breath in his ears and heartbeat against his back weren't comforting anymore—they were like a time bomb, ticking down to zero before he or Brennan blew.

Twenty minutes passed before they were approaching Cole's apartment, both soaked to the bone. Brennan stopped a few buildings down to help Cole back to his feet, making sure he was steady before withdrawing completely. The street was quiet and empty, just rain on the pavement and the glow of streetlights.

Cole made no move toward the house, hunched into himself, head down. Brennan said the only thing he could think to.

"I'm sorry."

It felt so weak and small and empty next to all the self-hate Brennan was boiling in.

But the words worked like a switch, and Cole straightened up, unfurling, looking at Brennan for the first time since it happened. His face was carefully blank—or, trying to be, but not quite managing, his lower lip wavering.

"There's nothing to apologize for," Cole said, trying for a smile. "I just need some sleep. Thanks for walking me home."

It was the distant politeness Cole usually reserved for people being loud on the silent study floor of the library. It was a slap in the face, a thousand times worse than Cole being mad. This wasn't petty library drama. He'd literally gone feral and sucked Cole's blood.

"Uh, no," Brennan said, "there's a *lot* to apologize for. Why are you letting me off that easy?"

"It wasn't your fault," Cole said on reflex, and maybe it wasn't justified, but it pissed Brennan off. He wanted Cole to be upset. To yell, cry, throw shit, do anything besides hide behind a mask.

"It *was*," Brennan said. "I thought Travis was sketchy but I brought you there. I knew Dom was at the restaurant but I didn't tell you."

The pent-up energy and adrenaline made Brennan need to move, and he couldn't keep looking at Cole's face trying to act like nothing happened, so Brennan started pacing. The words raging in his head finally spilled out into the open:

"If I keep you out of things, you're at risk of getting hurt. If I involve you, you get hurt," Brennan said. "And now, you're hurt. I drank so much of your blood you almost passed out. How is that anything but my fault?"

"You didn't have a choice," Cole said, and at least he didn't sound like he was trying to convince himself this time.

"But *you* did."

Suddenly Cole stopped Brennan in his pacing, turning him around with hands on his shoulders. Brennan was overwhelmed with the scent of Cole and blood. There were pinprick scars forming on Cole's neck and once Brennan saw them, he couldn't look away.

"And my *choice*," Cole said, slow and purposeful, "was to be there for you."

"It shouldn't be. Not if it gets you hurt."

"We've gone over this before. I knew you were a vampire from day one," Cole said. "I knew what I could be getting into."

"You knew what you could be getting into?" Brennan scoffed. "I didn't have a clue, so how could you?"

Brennan ducked out from Cole's grip, pacing again, scrubbing a hand down his face.

"What happened to figuring it out together?" Cole's voice was small. "What happened to letting me help?"

"It's just—it's too much."

"For me? Or for you?" Cole finally sounded pissed, which gave Brennan vindication for about three seconds before it turned to dread.

"Both," Brennan said. "I don't know how to do this. Existing, being a vampire, being a human, being a boyfriend! I thought I could do it but I can't. You deserve better."

Cole deserved better than Brennan. That was the one thing Brennan knew to be true this whole time.

Cole was silent long enough that Brennan stopped in his tracks and faced Cole from a few feet away. It was only then, when Brennan looked him in the eyes, that Cole spoke.

"You know," said Cole. "You were the one person who didn't tell me how to feel all the fucking time."

Brennan flinched. He'd seen Cole angry, sad, exhausted, turned on, scared—but he'd never seen him so *disappointed.*

"Everything I've done, I chose to do," Cole said. He enunciated his words carefully, delivering them with force and finality. "*I* chose that. Not my parents or Mari or fate. *I* chose to give because I wanted to."

Brennan shook his head. "I didn't ask you to."

"That's the whole fucking point, Brennan!"

Brennan didn't know what he was supposed to say.

Apparently, Cole didn't have anything else to add, either. They sat in the wake of that for no more than a minute before Cole nodded once and shifted half toward his place, his profile to Brennan.

Cole said, "I'm sorry, I'm just tired."

Then he turned and headed toward his apartment. Brennan felt sick, and he felt stuck to the spot, unable to follow even if he thought he would be welcome.

He watched Cole take the stairs up to the door. He watched him fumble with the lock. He watched him disappear behind the door. Cole never looked back.

The burning smell of garlic emanated from his apartment as he barged into the room, desperate for the blood in his freezer stash.

"Hey man, I thought you'd be gone longer, how was the dinner?" Tony said, looking up from his video game, a bowl of pasta next to him smelling so strongly of garlic that Brennan briefly contemplated chucking it out the window.

Brennan shot him a dark look and beelined to his bedroom. He was soaking wet from the rain and still had blood on his lips.

"Whoa, that bad?" Tony was saying, but Brennan had already disappeared into his room.

He dropped to his knees in front of the closet, unlocked the freezer, and felt a wave of relief that his stash was exactly as he'd left it. He didn't have the energy to count them. He grabbed one, threw it in the microwave, and then bit into the plastic with his fangs, draining the whole thing in seconds.

It didn't even take the edge off. He felt blood drip down his chin.

Good.

"Um" came Tony's voice from far closer than it should have. Brennan hadn't heard him coming, everything so muted and overwhelming at the same time. He whirled around and Tony was in the bedroom's doorway. "Did you just drink blood?"

Brennan couldn't help it. He laughed. Tony finding out was so low on his radar of things he gave a shit about right then.

"Yep," Brennan said. "Old news. Talk to Mari about it, I'm not taking questions right now."

He went to close the door but Tony put out a hand to stop it, moving into the doorway.

"You know, this actually makes *a lot* of things make *a lot* more sense."

"Great. Cool. Glad we could clear that up," Brennan growled. "Now's not a good time."

Brennan tried again to close the door on Tony's face, and this time, Tony let him.

Brennan opened a window and shoved a towel under the door to help with the garlic stench, then drank another pack of blood like it was nothing, against his better judgment.

His logical side was already scheming, rationing. They had a limited supply of blood now, with the harbor stunt, and with Sunny and Nellie out of commission, who knew when there would be more? How long could he make what he had last?

Brennan buried his head in his hands. The situation presented itself in a series of failures.

Travis was still at large.

Dom was still missing.

Cole hated him.

Nellie and Sunny were in danger.

He had no one to turn to.

He'd been so close to—*something*. He had Cole, he had a tentative grip on his vampirism, he had *friends* for the first time in ages. He should have known it would all come crashing down, and that it would all come down to this.

Him. Being a monster.

Brennan got up from the floor, crossed to his desk. He found his journal, a pen, and sat down.

His hands were shaking, and as he wiped tears from his eyes, he tried to organize the frantic spinning of his thoughts.

Vampire blood, he wrote. *Triggers thirst frenzy.*

The vampire ball, he wrote. *March 1.*

Turning, he wrote, *mutual exchange of blood.*

You're a fuckup and Cole will never forgive you, he wrote.

Sunny and Nellie are gonna die, he wrote.

He clenched his hands into fists to still their tremors. He breathed in, out, in, out, like Dr. Morris used to tell him to. Then he uncurled his fingers and ripped the page from the notebook. He ripped it in half, and when that wasn't satisfying, he ripped the pieces a few more times.

Then he started a new page.

He had a lot of work to do.

22

ALONE AGAIN, NATURALLY

A Pamphlet

Protecting Your Territory: Practices for the High-Level Vampire

By Nellie Adams

While your clan and clan leaders do much of the work of protecting you and your loved ones from potential rogue vampires, we understand the desire to take extra precautions, especially in times of conflict. While everyone can do simpler protection work (see "Protecting Your Territory: Wards and Protection Charms for the Low-Level Vampire" for information about environmental wards, protective charms, and other low-level measures of protection), there are more advanced methods of protection for those with some magical ability.

Binding

Binding a vampire's ability to use their powers is one of the most extreme routes of protection and is typically used as a last-resort punishment for unruly clan members. To bind a powerful vampire, the binder or binders must be at least half as strong collectively as the vampire or vampires they are binding.

Banishment

Banishment is the practice of limiting a vampire's area of access by keeping them out of certain places, or restricted to a certain area.

While simple environmental wards keep all low-level vampires from entering certain places, banishment is effective on all levels of vampires, and is a targeted effect that keeps one or more vampires from being able to move freely past the bounds of the banishment.

Thrall

A vampire's thrall is the high-level vampire's most accessible weapon, allowing them to temporarily incapacitate an enemy or prey. It coaxes the enthralled into a dreamlike state. Mild, dazing thralls take very little power, but deeper, longer-lasting thralls require high-level abilities and ongoing focus to maintain.

It's important to remember that these protective measures are reserved for higher-level vampires and clan leaders. You should count on your clan leaders for defense, and if you need help addressing a conflict, please reach out to them for additional aid.

The thing was, when Brennan thought about it logically, they were kind of fucked.

The ball was a gathering of humans and vampires alike, so any combination with vampire blood would be bad. At best, the vampires would go berserk and start biting everyone; at worst, those attacks would also turn those humans into more vampires. Either way, vampires would get exposed. Lose-lose situations all around.

Brennan threw himself into research, trying to find everything he could on vampire blood, vampire thralls and how to break them, and defeating an all-powerful millennia-old vampire. Shockingly, the research was neither straightforward nor conclusive.

He didn't eat, couldn't sleep, and put off drinking as long as possible to ration his supply. (Dr. Morris would say that not taking care of yourself is a form of self-harm. Whatever.)

It took him two days of radio silence from Cole to work up the courage to venture into the library, partially for research, partially in hopes of groveling.

Except Cole wasn't there.

Brennan stayed holed up in the library for twenty-four hours and Cole never showed up.

Finally, he asked one of the other library aides when Cole was scheduled.

The blue-haired librarian Brennan had seen with Cole a few times smiled sadly at him. "Cole's not at the library anymore. He has some new internship. It sucks, we love him around here."

Brennan retreated to his corner of the silent floor, the one he and Cole always used to occupy, and imagined Cole was there, too. Head in his lap, reading while Brennan leafed through a pamphlet that would have all the answers.

The library was no longer the comfort it used to be. He could only think of all the nights spent here with Cole, and how empty it felt without him. He tried to ignore the stinging feeling of the absence.

He knew this was how it would end all along, really. But somewhere along the way, he'd grown the audacity to think he could cling to his humanity. He thought he could be both vampire and human, that his life didn't have to be over even though it technically ended. That he could be normal. But his vampirism was real, it was his, and he had to deal with it as it inevitably blew up in his face.

He just wished Cole hadn't been collateral damage. Even if he'd offered help, being threatened by Travis and letting Brennan bite him had clearly shaken him, and Brennan couldn't blame him.

It was *his* fault Cole was in the cross fire.

He was taking notes on a pamphlet about vampire thralls, having lost track of the time ages ago, when Mari found him in his corner of the stacks.

Brennan pulled his attention from his notebook, dread building in his stomach.

"I know I messed up," Brennan said before she could speak. "Whatever you want to say, know it won't be worse than what I'm already saying to myself."

She had her backpack on, her short hair was pulled back in a wild, stubby ponytail, and she held a mug of something steaming. Coffee, by the smell wafting toward him.

"Jesus," Mari said. "I figured you were having a pity party, but this is pretty pathetic."

Some sarcastic retort died on his lips when Mari slid the mug of coffee toward him in offering. Brennan stared at her neatly trimmed fingernails pushing it forward, at the sloshing black liquid, at the mug itself, which read TEAM JACOB.

"Thanks," Brennan said. He wasn't sure how long he'd been holed up in the corner.

"I overheard one of the library aides saying a guy has been camped out on the third floor for more than forty-eight hours," Mari explained. "I had a guess it might've been you."

Brennan blinked, rubbing his eyes, pulling himself out of his research coma and back to reality. "Guilty," he said. "What day is it?"

"Friday."

Shit. "Seventy-two hours, then." He'd skipped two days of classes. What did classes matter next to all of this, anyway?

Mari scanned Brennan, took in the stacks of books, opened and bookmarked and scattered around him. Whatever she saw, she took pity.

"Look, the comfort basket is more of Cole's thing," she said. "But it's depressing as hell that you're holed up here alone."

"Gee, thanks?" Brennan said.

Mari winced. "No, I meant—I just mean . . ."

She stopped and sat down across from him, laying her hands out flat, cards on the table.

"I know I come off, like," Mari started, mouth twisting up in obvious discomfort. "Well, I know I'm not the gentlest person. But, we're kind of friends, right?"

"Are we?" Brennan was so shocked that the words tumbled out on their own. "I thought you hated me."

Mari's head dropped, covering her face with her hands. "I mean, I was skeptical, obviously, but it's not personal."

"Right," Brennan said. "Just the vampire thing."

"Yes, obviously. But it's not just that, or you. It's me, and Cole, too."

"Okay . . . ?" He wasn't sure where Mari was going with this.

"I'm fucking terrible at this," Mari murmured into her hands, then withdrew, straightening up and staring Brennan down with determination. "Listen up, because I'm not doing this monologue shit more than once, got it?"

"Yeah, sure, got it." He said it dismissively, but he *was* listening intently.

"Cole is my best friend in the entire world," Mari said. "He's got the kindest, purest light inside him and I am *so lucky* to be near it. His parents and my parents were friends, so me and him and Noah were best friends since we were in diapers. We were like, this super awesome trio, for years. From kindergarten to graduation.

"In *preschool* this kid punched a boy for being mean to me. In middle school, when Noah was getting bullied, Cole made sure he never had to go anywhere alone. He'd sneak out of class to walk him to the bathroom. And now, no matter where I fall asleep in the apartment, at my desk, on the couch, I *always* wake up with a blanket draped over me. *That's* the kind of person Cole is.

"Do you understand what I'm saying? I'm not gonna apologize for being protective of Cole because the boy has no self-preservation instincts of his own. I get protective because there are people out there who would bleed him dry." She cringed at the words. "Fuckin' A. Well, I mean. He will give and give and give to the people he loves and that is a *gift*.

"So when I realized he was choosing you to be one of those people, I thought, he's gonna get hurt."

"And now he did," Brennan finished.

"Yeah, but not how you think," Mari said. "Not how I thought, either."

"It's exactly what you thought. I'm a literal vampire and I literally drank his blood. You saw it coming since you found out about me."

"You're not listening. That's not the problem. You can't keep Cole from giving you his all because god knows no one could stop him if they tried."

"Then what are you saying, Mari?"

"I'm saying that for as long as Cole chooses you to be one of those people he'd give anything for, you have to give him everything right back. That's what he deserves. Do it for real or don't do it at all."

She frowned, looked him up and down, and concluded, "In other words, get your shit together."

Brennan couldn't even be offended. "But none of that matters if he won't talk to me ever again."

"Oh, for Christ's sake, the *melodrama*. You really have no idea how gone he is for you?" Brennan blinked back at her and she threw her hands up in disbelief. "Since you crash-landed in the library, it's been nonstop 'Brennan's so smart' this, 'Brennan's so *thoughtful*' that, and 'Yes he's a vampire but he's a *good* vampire.'"

It didn't make sense. That Mari didn't hate him, that Mari thought he still had a chance.

"Do I have to spell it out for you? Show him you care. At least *try*."

Brennan paused in thought. Show him. Show him that he loved him and trusted him, that he wanted Cole to know and see him as a whole, vampire and human. He wanted Cole to see his mistakes and flaws and think, *Yep, that's the one for me.*

That was an even more terrifying prospect than the lingering threat of Travis. The idea of being known, of being loved, of loving in return and having to trust that day in and day out they might continue to keep loving each other—or they might not. But being willing to take the risk anyway. And really, what's more human than that?

"You're being surprisingly chill about this," said Brennan.

"Oh, I was not chill the other night. Cole had to talk me down from putting out a hit on you." Brennan hoped that was a joke. "And if you ever bite him again, nonconsensually or in a way that causes real damage, I know where you live, and I think it would suck to spend an eternity without a dick."

Brennan blinked.

"Because I would cut yours off."

Brennan gulped and crossed his legs unconsciously under the table. "Got it."

Mari eyed him.

"Now go home and take a shower, you look like shit."

Brennan went home. Brennan took a shower. Brennan drank blood.

Then he went for a run.

Muscle memory led the way, but he knew where it led. The bridge beckoned.

It felt appropriately symbolic. The bridge was where he turned. The bridge was where, almost a year ago now, he had tried to kill himself.

His shoes pounded against the path until he was there, at the center of the little stone bridge, and he slunk down to sit with his back against the rail. Looked at his scar-free wrists.

Dying would be objectively easier than dealing with all this alone, Brennan thought, not for the first time. But the familiar dark blanket of depression wasn't comforting like it used to be. He couldn't sink into a murky spiral anymore. He didn't want to die.

But he was so fucking ashamed.

Almost a year ago, he'd hurt people like this. He'd distanced himself from the few half friends he had freshman year, his family, the teachers who were concerned about him. He didn't even know when he'd last called his mom, and he felt so *tired*.

When he'd attempted suicide, he hurt the people who cared about him. It was an objective fact. His mom still couldn't look at him without crying.

He couldn't do that again—not to anyone, not to his mom or his friends, and not to Cole. He'd been so sure Cole would be afraid of him when really, he was afraid of himself. If he could hurt everyone close to him before, what could he do with those same self-destructive tendencies *plus* fangs and eternal life?

He thought, after his attempt, after his hospitalization, after *so much therapy,* he'd be fine. He thought he was *good* now.

But maybe there wasn't *good*. Maybe there was just better. Maybe there was just *trying*.

He wanted to talk to Cole.

When he was a kid, he'd perfected the art of being alone. It was almost unfair that Cole could undo all that in such a short time.

Brennan looked around at the bridge, looked at the place on his wrists where his scars used to be, and he called the one person he wanted to talk to least but needed to talk to most.

Before he could organize his thoughts, the ringing stopped and his mom's voice filled Brennan's ears.

"Hello?"

That didn't give Brennan much to work with, tonally.

"Mom," Brennan said.

"Brennan," she said. "Are you okay?"

"Oh, you know." Now that he had her on the line, this was starting to feel like a terrible idea.

"No. Not really. I kind of thought you might be dying when I saw your number."

"Okay, that's fair," Brennan said. "I wanted to talk to you. Do you . . . have time?"

A beat of quiet, something crinkling. Then, "For you? Always."

Brennan didn't tell her everything. He didn't know if he'd *ever* tell her everything, even though he couldn't imagine disappearing from her life the way Nellie had with her family. But he told her what he could. That balancing everything at school was a lot. That he was having a difficult transition, to say the least. That he'd been hating himself more than usual lately.

He told her he had a fight with Cole, and he didn't know what to do.

But more important—

"I don't think I ever apologized to you."

"For what?"

"You know what. March."

She hesitated a moment, then said, "That's not something you have to apologize for."

"No, I don't have to. I want to." Brennan swallowed hard. "I'm sorry I didn't trust you and tell you what I was going through before it was too late and I'm sorry I did the same thing again this time."

"Brennan. I'm sorry I wasn't there like a mom should be. You were so smart and so independent and . . . that's not an excuse. You're my son. You can always, always talk to me. I just want you here. Alive. Okay. That's what matters."

Silence crackled over the line and Brennan wanted to believe it. Or at least, wanted to try.

"Do you remember when we used to listen to music in the kitchen and do homework together?" she said. "When you were still in elementary school, we used to be closer. What happened?"

Short answer: Brennan got sad.

He was the saddest fucking kid ever. Brennan couldn't remember himself not being curious, morbid, depressed, exhausted. Sometimes he wondered how people didn't realize sooner, didn't get him into therapy simply for radiating sadness.

"I knew that what I was feeling wasn't good, but I thought it was my fault." He still thought that, sometimes. "And it was easier to hide than accept I wasn't perfect."

"Is that what you're doing now?"

"I think so."

"Well. What are we going to do about that?"

That was one of the things he freaking loved about his mom. You can't be an environmental activist in the face of a climate apocalypse without a recklessly can-do attitude.

"I'll let you know when I figure it out."

BRENNAN'S PHONE

Brennan

we need to talk.

Dom

agreed.

Dom was outside Brennan's window by the time he got home, sitting on the ledge and knocking impatiently.

He pushed the window up and she gave him a look.

"Was warding the place really necessary?"

"Yes," Brennan said. "You can come in."

With his permission, she ducked through the window and brushed off her black jeans, tossing her black hair back out of her eyes.

"How long did you know Travis's plan?" Brennan asked.

Dom pressed her lips together and nodded, like she expected an interrogation. "He told me after I unbound him from the forest. That's when I left town."

"Why did you come back?"

Dom shrugged. "I thought being somewhere else would make me feel better. But I felt just as bad, *and* I was letting him win. Like, I was already screwed, but I didn't have to let him screw everyone else over, too." Her nails tapped nervous circles against her thighs. "I thought I could stop him, but I only saved one cache before it was too late."

They said the enemy of your enemy is your friend. But Dom had been his friend before, too. That wasn't nothing.

Brennan crossed to his dresser and dug out two small items he'd tucked away, then stopped in front of Dom.

"Tell me if I'm overstepping, but I thought you might want these," Brennan said.

His hands, outstretched toward Dom in offering, held a photo of a smiling Evelyn that Dom had left in her apartment, and the pink scrunchie from the scene of the crash.

He half expected Dom to scoff or snarl. He didn't expect her eyes to fill with tears or her hands to tremble as she reached for them both.

But she stopped short of taking them from him, her hands hovering over his.

"It's my fault all this is happening," she said. Her hands withdrew further. "I messed up, and people got hurt. And more people *will* get hurt. I freed Travis. I turned people. I *killed Evelyn.*"

"But you're trying to fix it, right?" Brennan asked. "Can't that be enough?"

Dom was stock-still except for a quiver in her lips. Then, slowly, she took the photo and the scrunchie from his hands, holding them like they were precious.

"It's a start," Dom said. She stared at the photo for a long moment, then her eyes cut back to Brennan. "But I don't know what happens next."

Brennan offered a grin. "About that . . . Do you happen to know anything about thralls, vampire blood, or grand romantic gestures?"

23

HOW YOU GET THE BOY

BRENNAN'S JOURNAL

Operation Get Your Shit Together

- ~~Shower~~
- ~~Find Dom~~
- Get Cole back
- Figure out how to free Sunny & Nellie
- Figure out how to stop Travis
- Figure out how to stop vampires from going feral at vampire ball

BRENNAN'S PHONE

You have created a new group with Tony Esposito, Mari Vasquez, and you.

Brennan
Hey all!
I'm sure you're wondering why
I gathered you all here.

Tony
this is a group chat not an intervention

Mari

yeah but I WAS wondering that

what do u want

Tony

pls imagine she said that politely

Mari

don't undermine my tone, it was what it was.

Brennan

I was wondering if I could talk to you both.

Mari

is that not what's happening?

Brennan

In person?

Mari

make your case here and I'll decide if you're worthy

Tony

for the record I'm telling her to be nice but

she's not listening

Brennan

Look, I like to think we're friends.

Outside of Cole and outside of all the vampire stuff.

Tony

I still don't really understand the vampire stuff

Mari

cole's my main bitch. you're a side ho, at best.

but yes, technically and arguably we

would be considered friends

Brennan

Great, so glad you clarified.

Tony

don't listen to her, she's secretly rooting for you guys

> **Brennan**
> Can I get to my point please?

Mari
um yes I've been waiting

> **Brennan**
> Okay.
> I want to apologize to Cole. I also want to stop an ancient
> and powerful vampire from leading a vampire attack that
> could potentially out vampires' existence to the world.
> I need your help on both counts.

Tony
say less!!! I'm in!!!

> **Brennan**
> You don't even know what I'm asking.

Tony
consider my unquestioning loyalty an apology
for all the garlic I've cooked in the apartment
this year 🙏

> **Brennan**
> Mari?

Mari
I'm thinking about it
what exactly is your plan?

BRENNAN'S JOURNAL

THE PLAN

Me
- Get permission from library to use the comfort stash storage room
- Deck out room with fairy lights Pinterest-style. Cole loves that shit.
- Prepare apology (is a slide deck too much? Maybe note cards.)

Mari
- Get Cole to the library at the right time

Tony
- Help set up
- ~~Emotional support if Cole rejects me~~

Brennan paced back and forth in front of the storage-room door while Tony double-checked that the string lights were working. The library was busier than normal, the silent-study floor lined with people ready to give death glares to anyone who dared turn a page too loudly.

When Tony emerged from the storage room, Brennan whispered, "Do you think this is kind of—"

"Gay?" Tony finished.

"*Cheesy,*" Brennan said, rolling his eyes. "Or, I don't know, too little too late?"

A girl studying nearby with an intimidating set of colored highlighters and pens shot them a glare for whispering and Brennan offered a sheepish smile.

Tony jerked his head toward the storage room in question, and they ducked into what used to be Cole's Library Blanket Guy room, now lined with fairy lights. The table at the center of the room had a box of pamphlets, Brennan's journal, and an envelope.

"Look, man," Tony said, "it's definitely cheesy. The gesture alone was bad enough, and the string lights brought you into rom-com territory."

"Awesome. Great."

"But that's the point. It's pretty *you.* And Cole loves cheesy romantic shit, that's why he loves *The Bachelorette* and company so much," said Tony. "Mari, too, secretly. If there's one thing I learned with her, it's that if you know what you want, you gotta put it out there."

"Yeah?" Brennan said. "What's the deal with you guys, anyway?"

"Eh, you know." Tony shrugged. "She wanted to get serious, I was afraid of committing, now *I* want to get serious but she doesn't trust me, so we're kind of hate fucking. Don't get me wrong, the sex is amazing—"

Brennan cleared his throat.

"But I should have been real about what I knew I wanted from the get-go. You never know if it's gonna be too late."

"I'm sure it's not too late for you guys," Brennan said.

But that was exactly what Brennan was afraid of, with Cole. That it was too late. That he'd fucked it up beyond repair.

"Maybe it is, maybe it isn't. Live and learn, and all that."

Brennan nodded slowly, going back to the storage room's door to peek out into the library. His phone buzzed, and he fumbled for it.

Mari

incoming!

the eagle has gone rogue, I repeat, the eagle has gone rogue

Brennan blinked and read it again, still halfway through the door between the room and the library. He scanned the study space, the rows of tables and chairs surrounded by the stacks.

He angled the screen to Tony.

"What does this mean? Which one of us is the eagle?"

Tony leaned forward.

The doors from the stairwell across the floor burst open, slamming against the walls, and Cole stormed in wearing a full suit, hair wild, beautiful as fucking ever.

Rows of students twisted in their seats to show their discontent at the noisy entrance, and Brennan swiftly ditched Tony in the storage room, darting through the middle of the study space to meet Cole halfway.

Cole came to a stop in front of Brennan and crossed his arms over his chest. Brennan was distantly aware of the library-goers' eyes on him, but his senses were fully focused on Cole. He took in his skewed tie, the dark circles under his eyes, the determined jut of his jaw, the ever-lingering smell of coffee.

"Listen," Cole said. "Everyone's telling me to hear you out, but first, *you* need to hear *me* out."

A few people hissed shushing noises. Cole continued.

"You didn't want to listen before? Fine. I'll say it again. I don't regret it and I'd do it again. I chose what I did."

Brennan blinked, once again overwhelmed by Cole in his presence, by Cole so determined and fiery. It was kind of hot.

"Hey *Brokeback Mountain,* I'm trying to study," someone said. A few people snickered, followed by more shushing.

Flustered and pulled out of his Cole tunnel vision, Brennan was suddenly much more aware of the eyes on them.

"Look," he tried, "let's just step into the storage room."

"No," said Cole, and Brennan fucking loved him. "I've been letting people tell me what to do my whole life, from Mari telling me who to be friends with to my parents planning out the first eighteen years of my life to the letter to—"

"Seriously, shut up!" someone said.

"Let the boy speak!" said someone else.

A round of affirmative noises and *yeah*s, and then silence fell. Over Cole's shoulder, Brennan noted someone was pointing a phone at them, recording.

Cole stepped closer. "But you," he says. "*You* never asked me for anything. Everything I gave you, I wanted to give. I'd give you more. And if you don't—" He broke off, seemed to gather his determination, and looked Brennan in the eye to finish: "If this is too much, you need to say so."

Then Cole seemed to be aware of onlookers for the first time, glancing around, nervous.

"Let's talk in private," Brennan tried again, softer.

"Cop-out!" Another onlooker.

"Answer the question!"

"Yeah!"

Brennan's face was burning. He was probably blue.

"It's not too much. I'm sorry for freaking out so much. I've been tied up in hating . . . certain things about myself, and I didn't want you to think of me like that. Because you're the coolest, kindest person, and I'm just me. But you always saw me, right from the beginning." He blinked rapidly and glanced around the watching crowd. "So can we please go speak in the private room I set up all fancy for what I thought would be me groveling?"

Cole's face was red, but: "Yeah, let's do that."

They ducked into the storage room, people cheering and hooting and shushing one another as they did. Tony gave Brennan a thumbs-up and an exaggerated wink before the door shut behind them.

The old comfort stash room was cozier than ever before, and Brennan's journal and pamphlets sat prominently on the table. On the floor was a nest of blankets and pillows. Cole took it in, and Brennan forgot to breathe.

But then Cole's eyes fell back on Brennan, and he half smiled.

"Hey," Cole said.

"Hey."

"So." Cole arched an eyebrow. "What was this about groveling?"

Brennan laughed. "I. I had a letter."

"Well, go right ahead."

"I don't know if I can top all that," Brennan said, nodding vaguely to Cole's grand entrance and declaration.

"Mama always said I had a flair for the dramatics. I always thought she was being homophobic."

Brennan laughed. His heart was light and hopeful. "Does this mean," he said. "Do you still—?"

"Depends how good this letter is." But Cole was failing to bite back a smile.

"I'm suddenly feeling like it could have used another round of revision." Then he blurted, "Have I mentioned you look really good in that suit?"

"Brennan," Cole scolded, laughing.

"It's true! I can't help it!"

"Stop flirting and start groveling."

"Yes, sir," Brennan said. "Sit down, then, get comfortable."

Brennan grabbed the envelope while Cole settled in the nest of blankets, glancing around, still slightly pink. Brennan extended the envelope to Cole but Cole hesitated, then said, "Read it to me?"

Brennan's heart picked up with a mix of anxiety and the thrill of Cole being in his presence again. He nodded, then fumbled to open the envelope and unfold the papers that had been ripped out of his notebook. Clearing his throat, he scanned the first few lines of the letter.

"Actually," he said, "this is kind of mortifying. Do I have to read it out loud?"

"Yes."

Brennan laughed despite himself, rubbed the back of his neck, and paced, trying to center himself. Eventually he sat down across from Cole on the floor, crossing his legs, letter in his lap.

"Okay."

Brennan steeled himself, then allowed himself to be vulnerable.

"*My brain likes to make trouble when I think too much,*" Brennan read. "*All the what-ifs and maybes and questions and rabbit holes and ways something could possibly go wrong. So when I'm trying to understand something, I try to think about what I know to be true. The facts.*"

Brennan kept his eyes on his carefully inked words. "*Things I know about Cole McNamara: Cole is the legendary campus cryptid, the Cute Library Blanket Guy. Cole knows almost everyone on campus, including faculty and staff, and everyone knows and loves Cole. Cole is a coffee-loving, record-playing, 'you've probably never heard of it' hipster. All this to say, Cole is kind. Cole cares about other people. Sometimes more than himself.*

"*Things I know about myself: I'm a nobody with no friends because I push people away, and I gave up on being anything special. But, also, I'm a literal vampire. I'm an anxious, overthinking, self-destructive mess. It never made sense to me why you liked me.*

"*I hurt you. I've hurt the people close to me before. I don't—I don't mean to, but it happens. It's not fair, and I'd love to blame it on mental illness, but that's not an excuse because these were decisions I made.*

"*I thought if I worked hard enough I could handle it on my own. I thought you were way too good for me and everything I did wrong or every weird vampire thing that came up was another reason for you to realize I'm too much. Or not enough.*

"*But I know that you get enough protectiveness from Mari, enough people telling you what to do and how you feel from your parents. I was so worried about not fucking things up that I made everything worse.*

"*I want to be better. I want you to know that you have me, all of me, if you want. I mean, I understand if your feelings changed. We haven't talked since—well.*

"*But. I also know that, without me, you'll never read a word of poetry outside of Rupi Kaur, and I can't allow that. I know that you laugh seventy percent more when you're with me than with others, because I kept a tally for a full week. I know that the noise in my head goes quiet when I'm with you.*

"So . . . this is everything." He gestured to the box of pamphlets, his journal. "*All my research, all my notes and ramblings, all of Nellie's pamphlets and brochures. Everything you could possibly want to know about vampirism. And, um, you can ask me anything. About any of it. About me. In case you didn't feel like you could before. Assuming you still want anything to do with me.*"

Brennan finally forced his eyes from his letter to take in Cole's reaction. Cole's eyes were round as he chewed on his lower lip.

"Is that the end?" Cole asked.

"Yeah."

Cole surged up from his seat to his knees and leaned across the space between them, and then kissed Brennan so hard they nearly toppled back onto the blanketed floor. Brennan caught Cole the best he could and kissed back like his life depended on it, the weight of Cole's body a comfort, the press of his lips intoxicating.

"Full marks," Cole said. "Apology accepted."

Brennan pulled Cole back to him by the back of the neck, and Brennan melted into him for a moment before the other things he needed to ask nudged at his brain.

He pulled back. "Have you heard from your parents? Are you okay? Everything happened so fast afterward . . ."

"Yeah. I'm okay. I've been ignoring their calls, actually."

"Yeah?"

"It's kinda funny. For so long, I couldn't stand disappointing them. But fuck that! *I'm* disappointed in *them*. I think I'm gonna quit the internship and come back to the library, if they'll have me. I'm done doing what *they* want. I'm doing what *I* want."

Cole's eyes shone and his chin jutted out and Brennan couldn't have been more proud of the boy he was in love with. "You're amazing," Brennan said. "I hope they come around."

Brennan ducked back farther to peer at Cole. "But more important . . ." He searched for a mark on Cole's neck. "Are you okay?" He found the two little puncture marks, small but noticeable when looking for them. He touched the skin below, afraid it might be sore. "How are you feeling? Were there any side effects? Faintness, dizziness?"

"No, no, none of that." Cole tried to wave him off, but seemed pleased at the concern. He still wasn't used to being the one taken care of. Brennan wanted to change that.

"I feel fine," Cole said. Brennan dared brush a thumb over the tiny scars and Cole shivered. "And honestly, you're really hung up on the bite but . . . in a different context, I might actually be kinda into it."

"Okay, no, too soon," Brennan scolded, but he was laughing, too.

Cole's responding giggle was light. "I thought so as soon as I was saying it, sorry."

Brennan finally let himself lean in again, Cole meeting him halfway, always keeping up with him.

"Thank you for this," Cole said, barely pulling back, their foreheads pressed together. "I want to be part of your world, if you'll have me."

"Oh, I would certainly have you, just say the word," Brennan said.

"Bet," said Cole.

Cole tugged Brennan back in by the shirt, and their next kiss wasn't warm and hopeful, it was hot and explosive. Brennan kissed with all the love and desperation he couldn't put words to from the last few days and Cole kissed with enthusiasm and intention. His hands were everywhere and found their way under Brennan's shirt and—

"We're still in the library," Brennan managed to protest between kisses, but his hands pawing at Cole's waist and hips probably gave mixed messages.

Cole raised an eyebrow. "We'll have to be quiet, then."

Brennan could do that.

24

THE NEW SQUAD

BRENNAN'S PHONE

"Sturbridge University Meme Center" Facebook Group

Lana Carter: I went to the fourth floor of Folz to study as god intended for the SILENT floor and instead I saw the cute library blanket guy having a moment with some kid with bad hair and this is going to be my thirteenth reason

Comments:

> RACHEL LE: Okay but here's a video bc it was really cute [1238 likes]

••••••••••••••••••

You have created a new group with Cole McNamara, Tony Esposito, Mari Vasquez, Dom VanMeter, and you.

Brennan
Clear your schedules, highly important meeting at 6!

Cole
heck yes!

Mari

IDK might be busyyy

　　　　　　　　　　　　　　　　　　　　Brennan

　　　　　　　No, seriously, does 6 work for everyone?

Tony

Mari and I will be there lol she's just being contrary.

Mari

don't speak for me

but I will be there.

Cole

and I will bring snacks!

Ignoring the panic of all his different worlds colliding, Brennan flipped through his notebook. He'd already filled pages with possible plans and outcomes, most of them negative. But that was the point of the meeting. He wasn't alone. They would figure it out together.

"So, let's see it," Tony said as he flopped down on the couch next to him.

"See what?"

"Do you sparkle? Do you have fangs? Do you have, like, a dark form you shift into at night?"

"Uh, no," Brennan said, trying to keep up. "Well, I do have fangs."

"Fuck yeah," Tony said. "Can I see?"

"I can't call them out on command! It's, like, when I'm hungry."

"Or horny, right?" Tony asked.

"What the—" Brennan bit back a curse. "How do you know that?"

"Cole told me. He thinks it's cute."

"I'm uncomfortable with this line of conversation," said Brennan.

"Well, I still wanna see. You'll have to let me watch next time you eat something."

"I will not be doing that."

Brennan heard familiar voices drifting toward them from outside, along with a pair of footsteps, and Brennan took the excuse to dart out of his seat and preemptively answer the door. It swung open to reveal

Cole, one fist poised to knock, the other holding a tray of lemon bars. Mari was a pace behind him with a bottle of wine.

"Hey," Cole said, a closed-lip, bright-eyed smile making the rest of the room fade away. His presence alone calmed nerves Brennan hadn't realized were building.

"Hey," said Brennan.

"Yes, hi," Mari said, and pushed between them to get through the door. Moment broken, Cole laughed and darted to press the briefest of kisses to Brennan's mouth before following Mari to the living room. Brennan took half a dazed moment to stare after him with heart-eyes before reminding himself to get back to business.

"Okay," Brennan said, "so we're still waiting for—"

As if on cue, a knock sounded from across the apartment, in Brennan's room.

"And, that'll be Dom."

He ducked out while Cole set out lemon bars and Mari broke into her bottle of wine, Tony playing a game on his phone. His room was just as he left it, except for the shadow darkening the window from the outside, the pale face peering in impatiently.

Brennan unlatched the window and pushed it open.

"You know, you could use the door."

Dom perched delicately in her all-black ensemble, dark eyeliner around her eyes, black nails tapping on her knee.

"Your friends were using it."

"It's not a mutually exclusive thing."

"Whatever, are you gonna invite me in, or what?"

They did a quick round of introductions ("Wait, I thought Dom was evil," Tony said. Mari kicked him in the shin.) and then settled with too many people on the couch, Dom hovering across the room with her arms crossed.

All eyes were on Brennan.

He swallowed. Right. The floor was his. He wasn't really used to being the person people turned to for guidance, leadership, or solutions. He was used to being the problem.

Cole caught his eye and gave him a little nod and smile. Brennan could do this.

"Okay, so," Brennan said. He shuffled through his journal some more. "Travis—the *actual* evil vampire—is planning an attack at the vampire ball, in less than a week. We know they're using vampire blood to roofie everyone into killing each other. If the vampires drink it, they go feral and get desperate for blood. If humans drink it, they're halfway to getting turned. If everything goes the way Travis wants it, not only will this be a very public attack that will be really hard to explain away, but we could end up with a lot of new baby vampires.

"The way I see it, there's a few routes we can take. A, we stop Travis, which is tough, because I get the feeling no one stops Travis from anything. B, we save Sunny and Nellie, who stop Travis, which is tough because Travis's thrall is too strong to break on our own. C, we prepare for the worst. We can try to restock the blood for the caches, and try to keep the vampires from killing people at the ball."

"Prepare for the worst seems like our best option," Cole said with gracious optimism.

"Great, how do we keep vampires from going into a frenzy without killing anyone?" Dom asked.

"It's possible we can prevent it," Brennan said. "He basically spiked my tea, so maybe he's planning on tampering with the food. Maybe we can get ahead of it."

"Spiking the punch at a party?" Tony laughed. "Classic."

"I bet I can sweet-talk the hotel into telling me who's catering if no one knows but Sunny and Nellie," Cole said, "so we can make sure he can't get to the food before the ball."

"Then we get to the dance early, play the middle school chaperone, and watch everyone who approaches the snack table like a hawk," Tony said. "I love it, I know every trick in the book when it comes to slipping stuff into drinks."

"Jesus, Tony!" Mari said.

"Shit, I meant 'cause Nonna doesn't like to take her meds, so we put it in her juice!"

"Travis is powerful," Dom said, cutting in. "What if he finds a way?"

"If anything seems off, we can evacuate everyone," Cole said. "I'll get floor plans when I call about the caterer."

"We also need blood," Brennan said. "The whole clan will be low on blood after the attack. If we don't refill the caches, the vampires will come to the ball hungry whether Travis's plan works or not."

"I saved one cache before Travis got to it, but that's only about twenty pints," Dom offered.

"And there are ten caches in Boston that were all emptied out, so, we'd need 180 pints," Brennan said.

Tony let out a low whistle. "Right, so . . . where do we get a fuckton of blood?"

"I mean, I could draw from everyone here," Mari said, "but we can only give so much blood each."

"I have a bunch of friends from GSA and res life and the library," Cole offered. "I could probably get them to donate blood to a sketchy cause."

"Yeah, okay," Mari said. "We can set up an . . . underground blood drive."

"Yo, hold on," said Tony. "Me and my friends used to donate blood, and then get blasted off a wine cooler since our blood-alcohol level was wonky."

"Is that a thing?" Cole asked.

Mari pinched the bridge of her nose. "Yeah, it's a thing, but it's pretty irresponsible."

"We're already having an illicit blood drive," Tony said. "Why not bribe people with alcohol? Anyone who donates gets a free beer or something? I could get a bunch of people to come that way."

"How do we keep it secret, though?" Dom said.

"I can write an NDA and waiver for anyone participating," Cole said. "Any legit blood drive would have paperwork anyway, and if anything, people would assume it's more for the alcohol."

"Sure, but what do we tell people it's for?"

Everyone was silent.

Brennan offered, "Art project?"

"We can roll with that," Tony said.

"They're gonna think we had something to do with the harbor," Dom said. "It's all over the news."

"Art project," Tony repeated.

"Performance art?" Brennan said.

"Some sort of protest?" Mari suggested.

"I love it!" Tony said. "I'm seeing something about the Red Cross? Or AIDS?"

"If people are signing NDAs it won't matter," Cole said.

"Well that can be our backup-backup cover story," said Tony.

"No, Tony, that will *not* be our—"

"Can vampires get AIDS? It's through blood so, like—"

"We're getting off topic, I think?" Brennan said.

"No shit," said Dom. "Look, this is all well and good, but there's still Travis himself to deal with. Best case, you distract him and I find a way to kill him."

"Absolutely not," Brennan said. "Sunny and Nellie stopped him before, *without* killing him. In 1928, when his girlfriend first tried to pull this. Can't you bind his powers, or put him in thrall?"

"Are you forgetting he's massively powerful? I was barely strong enough to break his binding even with him helping from the other side, I have no chance against him alone."

"What if you weren't alone?" Cole said. "What kind of help would you need?"

"Other vampires. Other *strong* vampires," Dom said.

"That was actually another thing I wanted help with," Brennan said. "I'm trying to start reaching out to some of the vampires from the Facebook group. This person Quinn seems to do a lot with the blood drive, so they're our best hope, but there are a few people that I know Sunny and Nellie trust. I'm basically going to make an impassioned plea for help. Tell them the truth. Hope for the best."

"I can help with that," Tony offered. "I'm great at sliding into strangers' DMs."

Mari made a scoffing noise of disgust.

"Me, too," Cole said.

"It won't be enough," Dom said. "He's exponentially stronger than anyone else."

"Except for Sunny," Brennan finished. "And Sunny and Nellie are in thrall god knows where."

"They're in Travis's greenhouse," Dom said. "The real problem is the thrall, which will be near impossible to break."

"So, we can't stop Travis without Sunny, and we can't save Sunny without Sunny?" Mari concluded.

"Except, that's not right." Brennan rifled through his notebook. "God, it was in a pamphlet. What was it?" He tilted his head, spoke slowly as he recalled it. "Thralls—they take focus to maintain. If Travis is across town, wreaking havoc at the vampire ball, maybe that's the best opportunity to free them. Maybe his hold on them would be weaker. Free Sunny and Nellie, they stop Travis."

"But it'll be too late, won't it?" Cole asked.

"Unless we can put off the attack. Distract him," Brennan said.

"How?" Mari and Tony said in unison, then glanced at each other and furiously looked away.

"I would love to think he's a sad old man having a temper tantrum," Brennan said. "And I would love to believe I could convince him not to do it. At the very least, I can try to buy us time."

"I'll go with you," Cole said. "You and I can attend, keep an eye out, and you can talk to Travis. The rest of y'all can be waiting in the wings with blood if hell breaks loose."

"Uh, hold on," Mari said, putting a hand up. "Isn't that basically throwing you to the wolves? Anyone in there is at risk. Including you, Brennan. What if you're affected?"

"All the more reason I should be there to make sure he's okay," Cole insisted.

"Mari's right. Any one of you guys coming in could be in danger," Brennan said, looking apologetically at Cole.

"Oh for fuck's sake," Cole said, and everyone's heads swiveled toward him in shock. "I'm not a damsel in distress! I don't need anyone's permission to go. I'm going in with Brennan, and that's it."

He was so defiant, chin jutted out, head raised. His eyes cut to Brennan with a second of doubt, of *is this okay?* Brennan answered with the tiniest of nods, and a surge of affection. As much as he wanted to be protective, Cole was his own person. Besides, Brennan was sure he couldn't do any of this without Cole.

"I need you to know that you're super sexy when you take control like that," Brennan said instead of something sappy.

Mari groaned, outraged.

"Okay, good progress," Dom said. "What else?"

Everyone leaned forward, eagerly awaiting instruction, and Brennan was overwhelmed with gratitude. Really, he couldn't do any of this without *all* of these people who decided, for some reason, that Brennan was their friend.

He laid out his notebook on the coffee table for the group to see.

"Well," he said, "it looks like we have a busy week ahead of us."

BRENNAN'S PHONE

"The New Squad" Group Chat with you and 4 others

Mari

so, we're at 23 packs out of a goal of 180.

Tony

challenge accepted

BRENNAN'S JOURNAL

Quinn Miller
- Runs the main branch of the vamps' blood drive up in Maine.
- Most active member of FB group besides Sunny and Nellie.
- Seems to be friends with a few other vamp women, Crystal and Narrissa.
- If we can reach Quinn, maybe they can reach others?

Once he unleashed his Southern charm, it took Cole no more than eight minutes on the phone with the hotel hosting the vampire ball to convince them to send over the event space's floor plans and catering information.

Mari scheduled a few time slots over the next week to set up the secret blood drive, and between Mari, Cole, and Tony's combined friend groups alone, they quickly garnered a sign-up list.

Brennan put together a list of potentially trustworthy vampires from the Facebook group based on Sunny and Nellie's interactions with them, and with Cole and Tony's help, started sending out feelers for someone who might be able to help. So far, Quinn was the most promising lead, but they'd need more than just one other vampire if they wanted to free Sunny and Nellie.

But Brennan couldn't count on Sunny and Nellie to save the day. With or without them, they would have to face Travis.

It was past 2 a.m. when Mari and Tony went to bed, leaving Cole asleep on the couch. Dom and Brennan sat on the living-room floor with the box of pamphlets between them, Brennan leafing through one while Dom lay on her back, throwing a ball up in the air and catching it rhythmically.

"So," Dom said. "What do you plan on doing? Once all this is over?"

Brennan laughed, distractedly scanning the pamphlet. "Honestly, I'm more focused on getting through this week."

"Well, what for?" Dom said, grabbing the pamphlet from Brennan to demand his attention. "Say we pull this off, vampires stay hidden, and you get to live your little life how you want it. What are you gonna do?"

Brennan blinked away the research haze and centered himself on the new question. Without Travis and murders looming, he imagined his life, vampire and human intertwined. Dating Cole, going to *Bachelorette Night* with Mari and Tony, meeting up with Nellie and Sunny, maybe even Dom, wherever she ended up after this.

"I guess," he said, and naturally, his eyes floated to Cole, asleep on the couch. Hair messed up, shirt riding up exposing his stomach, hands curled by his chin. "Maybe I want to take life slow for a while. I'm still only nineteen, and I have nothing but time. I kinda just want to enjoy this. What about you?"

"I thought I might ask Sunny and Nellie to hook me up with other clans, maybe see the world, you know? Try out some different lifestyles."

The idea made Brennan a bit squeamish. What kind of lifestyles and clans would she explore? She seemed so much more like a real vampire than Brennan—she had powers, she had the desire to turn, to kill.

"Yeah, I guess it's harder to pretend to be normal when you have actual bona fide powers," Brennan said. "What is that even like?"

Dom scoffed. "Aw, you've read all these pamphlets and you don't know?"

"It's not the same, obviously."

"Obviously. But I know the stuff in action but not in theory. That's your area."

"Yeah," Brennan said. "Together we almost make a whole functional vampire."

They shared a laugh, but Brennan's levity wasn't long-lasting. He felt himself droop with everything they'd have to overcome for those plans to succeed.

"Are you," Brennan asked, "I don't know, *ready*?"

Dom considered the question. "I'm not sure my answer is what you're looking for."

"Try me."

"Well, I'm not ready for the whole heroic bit. Stopping the bad guy, saving the day. It's a bit cliché, you know?" Dom laughed. "No, what I'm looking forward to is beating Travis. Showing that asshole he didn't break me."

There seemed to be a lot she wasn't saying, but Brennan didn't push. Brennan had been so busy hating Dom for her mistakes that he hadn't thought of things from Dom's perspective, how Dom had lost her sister and Travis had swept in and taken advantage of her trust for his own plans. It felt far too late to realize it now.

"I know what has to be done," Dom finally said. "Do you?"

Something in her tone sent a shiver down Brennan's spine. Dom tossed another pamphlet away as she stood, and made toward the window for her exit. Brennan didn't know where she was going. He didn't ask.

BRENNAN'S PHONE

Quinn Miller

Hey Brennan! Thanks for reaching out! I'd be happy to help out. I owe Sunny and Nellie the world. I can't leave the blood drive unattended for longer than I had planned, especially with needing to replenish the supply, but I was planning on coming to the ball.

Let me know how I can help and I'll be there.

....

"The New Squad" Group Chat with you and 4 others

Mari

update! we're at 46 packs out of a goal of 180 after day 1 of illegal blood driving!

Tony

hey, 1/4 isn't bad!

Dom

1/4 won't stop vampires from starving and killing people

Cole

we have time! We've got this!

....

"The New Squad" Group Chat with you and 4 others

Mari

update! we're at 94 packs out of a goal of 180 after day 4 of illegal blood driving!

Tony

♫ whooooooooooaaaa we're halfway there!!! ♫

Dom

Living on a prayer is right. Halfway isn't good enough. We have two days left.

Brennan was scribbling in his notebook when Cole strolled into Brennan and Tony's apartment. Tony was at Mari and Cole's place making a vat of garlic sauce as a precautionary measure, thankfully far away from Brennan. But all week, people had been coming and going freely, so Brennan didn't even look up, only registering it was Cole by the smell of coffee that wafted in with him.

"Hey," Brennan said absently, finishing a thought with a flurry of his pen.

The warm press of Cole draped over him from behind where he was hunched on the couch, arms wrapping around his shoulders and kissing the top of his head.

"Enough planning," Cole said. "Take a break."

"We have less than twenty-four hours before the ball," Brennan said, scanning the list in front of him. "I'm going over the backup plans again."

Cole withdrew and started shedding his coat and bag.

"You've done everything you can at this point. You need to rest."

Brennan shook his head, even though his own writing looked like scribbled gibberish after staring at it for so many hours. But this was too important.

"If we mess this up, everything changes," Brennan said.

"You won't mess this up. I trust you. I wouldn't be going into a pit full of vampires if I didn't believe you could do this."

Brennan swallowed hard. Cole sounded so confident.

"And what if I can't?" he said.

Cole reappeared in front of him, and then Cole's hands were prying the journal from Brennan's and setting it to the side. Cole straddled Brennan as swiftly as the journal was removed, taking up the space in his lap it had occupied.

"Then I guess we'll have to flee the country and start a new life in the French countryside," Cole said.

"Well, thank god you have a plan," Brennan said, but Cole was so close with his jawline and his pink lips that Brennan forgot what they were talking about.

"I like to be prepared," Cole said.

Cole ducked down and caught Brennan's mouth in a kiss, and, like a switch, all the stresses and questions and problems swirling in Brennan's brain turned off, replaced by the feeling of Cole's lips, his hands keeping balance on his shoulders, his thighs bracketing Brennan's.

Cole pulled back.

"Everything's been so high-stakes lately," he said. "I thought we should have one calm night. Before everything tomorrow."

And Cole was right, as always. Brennan could use a break.

With a little more prodding from Cole, Brennan put away his notes and the box of pamphlets and changed into comfier clothes, letting Cole borrow a pair of sweats. They curled up on the couch together and Cole queued up some music on his phone.

And like that, wrapped up in Cole like this, Brennan felt like things might be okay.

"You know what sucks?" Cole said. Brennan hummed for him to go on. "The vampire ball would actually be so fucking dope if not for everything else."

Brennan laughed. "Oh god, you'd love it!"

"I mean, an excuse to dress up? See *you* dressed up? Vampire-themed everything? I almost can't wait."

Cole played with Brennan's fingers with both hands like Brennan was his personal fidget toy, and Brennan didn't mind at all.

They stayed up late talking, laughing, kissing, until Cole fell asleep halfway through a sentence, head on Brennan's chest.

Brennan's peace didn't last long, an undercurrent of urgency and fear surging through him as he snaked an arm around Cole. Because now he had something to lose, something worth protecting, something he needed and wanted to fight for. And it was terrifying. The idea of having this, then losing it when they'd barely gotten started. The idea of failing when Cole believed in him.

He couldn't fail. He wouldn't.

25

THE PARTY OF THE CENTURY

BRENNAN'S PHONE

r/occultboston

u/micahlandau

Thank you for believing me: a note before the vampire ball

I wanted to say, as I'm getting dressed up for this vampire ball and preparing to meet up with so many of you, that I'm so grateful to have found a community of smart, creative, open-minded people.

I don't want to get too much into history, but a tl;dr is that I spent most of my life going to therapists who told me I was crazy for believing in what I know is real after having a vampire encounter when I was really young. The vampire I met wasn't evil, and he didn't hurt me, and I have no hatred for vampires. I just need to know if they're real . . . I needed to know I wasn't crazy.

Regardless of what happens at the ball, you guys have given me that.

Thank you, and I'm looking forward to seeing all of you tonight. I'll be the girl in the fabulous red velvet dress.

>> u/weepncreep: did anyone else think OP was a guy for like, the last 3 months

>>>> u/willfullyignorant: Yep

>>>> u/hardlyahater: lmao, same

·················

"The New Squad" Group Chat with you and 4 others

Brennan

So I'll see you guys at our place before the ball
for last-minute cramming.
But everyone knows their part?

Cole

infiltrating the ball with you!

Mari

yep. eyes and ears at the entrance, ready to get people evacuated.

Tony

reporting for sauce duty cap'n

Dom

I get the fun part. Breaking Sunny and Nellie out with
Quinn and the Facebook vamps.

Brennan

Cool cool cool.

Cole

we've got this you guys!

Tony

it's go time bitches

Everyone gathered to get ready at Brennan and Tony's as if it were prom day, but the quiet nervousness as they all suited up felt more like a funeral.

Cole looked amazing in a dark green suit, but unfortunately there would be no getting distracted in a coat closet at the ball somewhere, no dancing and flirting. Those thoughts would have to be reserved for later.

Assuming there was a later.

Cole also had large, tacky glow-in-the-dark fangs. When he'd shown Brennan a few days ago, Brennan had feigned offense. "That's culturally insensitive," he teased, as seriously as he could manage, and Cole nearly believed him and started to apologize before Brennan's laugh finally broke free. Cole punched him in the arm but followed up with a kiss, so he didn't feel quite chastised.

Now, though, Brennan felt like he was going to throw up. No easy teasing and laughter.

They emerged into the living room, where Dom was already ready, perched on the arm of a chair, the perfect picture of a Gothic vampire with dark hair, pale skin, and a deep navy blue velvet gown. Brennan himself wore all black, an oversized blazer, and some old combat boots and chain accessories from his edgier high school days.

Tony strolled out of his room at the same time in standard black business casual and took in the room.

"Damn," he said. "You're all *smoking,* do you hear me? I'm in love with each and every one of you."

"We should all head out soon," Dom said. "We should get to our places early."

"Ah, geez, you sound like Mari."

Mari stormed in from the bathroom like she'd been summoned, wearing a red off-the-shoulder number, hands busy fiddling with her second dangly gold earring.

Tony gaped at Mari, and Brennan exchanged glances with Cole to confirm that he was also seeing Tony's heart-eyes.

Dom, oblivious or simply uncaring, said, "Well, Mari's right. Timing is everything. Are we ready or what?"

The room fell quiet. That nervous buzzing energy returned. Mari's earring was secured.

"Looks like it," Brennan said.

"Then let's go," said Dom. She moved to stand and the others followed suit, slowly, with a sense of dread.

"Hold on," Brennan said. They turned to him. These people, his friends, gave him their full attention and waited. "I . . ." He stopped.

He wasn't often at a loss for words—more often he had too many of them to speak or write down. But now, he had only this:

"Thank you, guys."

It barely scratched the surface of his gratitude, but maybe it was enough.

The hotel in Boston was old and classic, with white marble floors, elaborate wooden paneling, grand chandeliers, and wide-open ballrooms—the grandest of which would hold the vampire ball. Everything was lush and Gothic, black-clad employees rushing around and setting things up: an elaborate fountain of red punch that ostensibly looked like blood, vampire-themed snacks decorated with bats and fangs, a photo area with plastic fangs and other props.

They'd arrived early so Brennan could sniff out the snack table as best he could, scenting for blood or anything unusual. But everything smelled normal. So they waited.

As minutes ticked by, the ballroom began to fill with more people in dresses and costumes—Gothic steampunk, elaborate gowns, capes and coattails, an impressive group of *What We Do in the Shadows* cosplayers. Even the musicians in the corner—a string quartet that began at 7 p.m. on the dot—were sharply dressed, with fake blood placed at the corners of their mouths and down their chins. There was a small cluster of people huddled around their phones that Brennan only recognized as Redditors because Micah, the girl at the center of the huddle, wore the same velvet burgundy gown pictured in her last post. At her hip was a stake sharp enough to do real damage, vampire or not.

Brennan silently added that to his growing list of potential time bombs. He and Cole lingered at the edges of the room, watching carefully. Every few minutes, Brennan did another pass to check on the food and drink. Every few seconds, Brennan checked his phone for texts from the group chat to see if anyone had seen anything yet.

Every minute Travis didn't show up, he worried he had miscalculated. What if Travis had some other plan and Brennan had taken his bait? What if Travis ran into Dom and the others they'd recruited off Facebook when they were waiting for their opportunity to free Sunny and Nellie?

Brennan's phone pinged. His stomach dropped. He grabbed Cole's hand and squeezed, felt Cole squeeze back, and took in the message. It was from Mari.

"Travis is here," Brennan said.

He didn't need to say it. Travis's entrance had its own effect, heads turning like a tide toward the door. Like he had a magnetic pull.

He must, Brennan realized. A vampire that powerful could influence and charm humans without even meaning to.

The powerful vampire in question wore a monstrosity of a tweed suit with roughly sewn-on patches at the elbows. His dreads were pulled back in a thick bun. He was as relaxed as ever, an easy smile on his face as he took in the room.

He spotted Brennan and Cole and lit up. As if they were old friends.

"Oh lord, is he coming over here?" Cole hissed.

"It unfortunately seems that way," Brennan whispered, and then Travis was in front of them, arms spread wide, open and grinning.

"You guys made it! Looking good, eh? I know, I clean up nicely—"

"Can we skip the small talk?" Brennan asked. "If you're here to gloat or make threats or maniacally laugh, let's start with that."

"Ah, Brennan, charming as ever." Travis's eyes flitted to Cole. "And your snack. Coooo-dy . . . or . . . Clint?"

Brennan curled his hands into fists.

"It's Cole—"

"Travis, you're a dick," Brennan said. "Your accent's fake and we're not friends. Do your fucking worst."

Travis's jaw dropped. He almost—*almost*—looked hurt.

"Well then, mate," Travis said, the Aussie flair amped up, "I'll leave you two to enjoy the party."

Travis retreated.

"Um," Cole said, reaching for Brennan's arm, "I thought we were trying to buy time, not piss him off."

"Well, his accent sucks, someone had to tell him."

"Brennan!"

"I'm sorry! He started talking about you and I saw red." Travis was already talking animatedly with two people across the way. "Look, he rebounded quickly."

And so it went, with Travis chatting the ears off any guests who would listen, then moving on to the next group. Brennan kept a close eye on him for any suspicious moves, eavesdropped around the hall to make sure he wasn't conspiring, kept on his schedule of sniffing out the snack table for vampire blood every few minutes.

But nothing. It was driving Brennan insane. "He's toying with us," Brennan said.

It was 8:30 exactly when Travis made his way over to the punch fountain. Brennan and Cole exchanged looks.

"Wait here," Brennan said.

"Are you sure?"

"I'm sure."

Cole frowned but nodded. Brennan pressed a light kiss to his crinkled brow and smoothed it over.

"You've got this," Cole said. "I'm right here if you need me."

And Mari and Tony were outside the doors. And if all went to plan, Dom, Nellie, Sunny, and a few Facebook vampires would soon be on their way. Brennan wasn't alone. He knew that.

He crossed the ballroom and stopped in front of Travis, the fountain between them. For a second, they took each other in, and Brennan thought distantly of those old Westerns, a tumbleweed behind them, an ominous whistle.

"Oh, Brennan." Travis sighed. "I'll give you this: you're the most entertainment I've had in decades."

Brennan seethed. "Is this a game to you?"

"No matter how this goes, Brennan, know I'm getting exactly what I wanted."

"And what's that?"

Travis grinned, and Brennan's stomach dropped.

"A swan song."

Brennan's blood chilled in his veins.

"The vampire blood is a neat gimmick, I'll admit, but it's not a deal-breaker. If I have to do everything myself, then I'll do everything myself."

Travis straightened the sleeves of his jacket, tightened the bolo tie at his neck, and raised his hands. An older woman froze in her tracks mid-twirl on the dance floor, putting her hands to her temples and shaking her head vigorously. A man with thick black eyeliner stopped reaching for a bat-shaped truffle and started looking around frantically like a dog watching a fly. A girl about Brennan's age turned and sprinted out of the room, nearly knocking over someone wearing an impressive amount of body glitter.

At the same time, the burning itch of thirst grew in Brennan's throat.

All around him the vampires of the room *glitched,* confused and panicked.

Brennan felt ice creep up his body. How had he thought it would be as simple as stopping Travis from spiking the punch? Of course Travis could do whatever he wanted. Dom had warned him—he was scarily powerful, and Brennan had gravely miscalculated.

Which meant the next best plan was to keep shit from going south as long as he could, to distract Travis long enough for Dom to bring Sunny and Nellie.

Across the room, Cole frantically texted their chat with updates. Brennan's phone *ping*ed. He ignored it. The humans at the ball eyed the odd behaviors with judgment, not realizing what was happening.

Except for one girl, the one from freaking Reddit, Micah, who took it in with wide eyes and shaking hands.

"I knew it," she breathed.

The eyelinered vampire guy stumbled toward her, twitching, fangs bared. But she stood frozen, speaking like prayer.

"I knew it was real, I knew it—"

The guy reared back, poised to strike. But before he could lunge, Tony skidded to a stop in front of the girl, wielding an oversized water gun, which he pumped menacingly a few times before unleashing a stream of what Brennan knew to be the most pungent batch of garlic sauce Tony could muster.

The vampire hissed and stumbled back, gagging and retching. Brennan winced. It wasn't harmful, but it stung a little and smelled atrocious enough to stave off even the deepest of thirsts. At least for a moment.

"That's right," Tony jeered. "Anyone makes a move, you get a mouthful of Grandma Esposito's finest scampi. *Extra garlic.*" He pumped the water gun to punctuate the threat.

Behind Tony, Micah fumbled for her phone and started recording, her phone pointed at the twitching vampire guy, then flickering toward Travis and Brennan.

Shit. Goddammit.

"Oh, for Pete's sake," Travis said.

The grand doors to the ballroom slammed shut with a *whoosh*, and the lights flickered as wind began to rush around them. The gusts swirled violently, with Travis at the eye of the storm.

People yelled out in surprise and fear as the storm mussed their dresses and hair. Blood packs began flying from the cart and from people's hands, snacks from the food table lifting up to join a threatening tornado.

Travis burst into a laugh, and panic erupted. If some had thought this was a cute vampire-ball gimmick, now they were scared. Brennan whirled around as people started screaming and rushing toward the closed doors, as even furniture was swept up in Travis's storm.

The musicians stopped playing for less than a second before Travis shot them a grin through the chaos and said, voice laced with magical influence, "Don't stop on my account."

They obediently continued playing, if a bit more of a harried tune. The affected vampires remained cornered by Tony's garlic gun, but most of the humans yanked at the doors, which refused to budge. Then there was Micah and a few Reddit companions, valiantly filming on their phones while cowering against the walls.

The news was out, or would be soon. Vampires in Boston. Brennan had failed. Dom and Sunny and Nellie weren't coming to save them.

Brennan found Cole's eyes across the ballroom. "Get out of here!" He had to shout over the gusts of wind. Even with the roar of it, Brennan could see, if not hear, Cole's adamant "*No!*" in response.

Brennan lifted his arm to shield his eyes with the back of his hand, pressing forward toward Travis even as the wind pushed him back.

"You know, Brennan, you're really the most disappointing turn I've had," Travis said. "I thought you would understand. I thought, *there's* someone who will understand the hell I'm living. But you don't. No one does."

"You don't have to do this!" The wind carried his voice away. Brennan wasn't sure Travis heard it.

But he responded, so dry and empty, "What else is there to do?"

Brennan hesitated, wind whipping his hair into his face, and he vowed that if he survived this, he would chop it off.

"You choose humanity," Travis spat. "Don't you see? These things are like flies. What will you do, decades from now, when all these little things you care about are long gone?" Travis let out a roar and the wind picked up. He extended one hand, and in an instant, a crushing invisible force went around Brennan's throat like a fist.

Brennan struggled against it, clawing at his own neck.

"I'll find new things to keep me human," Brennan managed. "New reasons to—to try to be good. You just have to *try*."

The fountain behind Travis wobbled, wavered, and fell, sending rushing waves of red punch splashing over Travis and across the white marble floor. Travis stumbled and the wind sputtered, and Brennan gasped for air.

Behind the fallen fountain was none other than Cole.

Travis was drenched in sticky red sugar water that looked like thinned-out blood, and he straightened his jacket before turning to glower at Cole.

Travis reached out a hand. Cole went taut and was pulled forward by an invisible force until his throat was in Travis's grip.

"You're young and naive. But as soon as this one dies, you won't be." He pulled Cole toward him, Cole's back to his front, and his fangs glinted as they drew out. Brennan's heart stopped. Cole was stock-still in Travis's grip, frozen in fear or thrall, and Brennan was going to have to beg.

But then Cole leaned forward—

"I'm not a fucking *chew toy*."

And reared back to headbutt Travis with all the force he could muster. Travis was an immortal vampire, and it couldn't have hurt much, but it was enough of a shock to buy Cole a second to dart out of his grasp and sprint to Brennan. Cole took his hand at his side, where he fucking belonged as far as Brennan was concerned.

"I'm *so* in love with you," Brennan blurted out.

"Not the time, darlin'," Cole said, but he smiled like nothing else mattered.

They faced Travis together.

The wind picked back up. People were shouting. But everything seemed to slow down around Brennan, where his hand intertwined with

Cole's, and he felt unstoppable. Infinite. And understanding dawned on him, clicking into place like a puzzle piece.

He'd been so afraid of turning into someone like Travis, someone distanced from humanity, utterly alone and far too old for this world. Someone who'd loved and lost too many times. But now he pitied him.

Ancient and empty, no humanity, no purpose.

Throwing a tantrum at a party for attention.

Crying out for help.

Hurting people because he'd been hurt, just like every other human on this fucking planet.

Travis had succeeded in outing vampires and throwing a temper tantrum, but he didn't have to succeed in this. In his swan song.

Brennan needed to say something. He needed to say something *fast*.

His brain moved too fast and too slow at once, wading through information and angles and late nights of reading and what came out was—

"I'm sorry," Brennan said. "About Shea."

"Don't say her name," Travis roared. The wind lashed against Brennan's face like whips, but he refused to stop.

"It must be lonely without her," Brennan said. "Thousands of years old in a changing world."

"You understand *nothing*," Travis said.

"I understand you more than I want to."

The words hung in the air. The winds raged on. Brennan took a step closer. He didn't know why, but if he could reach Travis, he thought he might be able to get through to him.

"Okay, yeah, maybe I don't know what it's like to be thousands of years old and watch everyone you know age and die while you stay the same. Maybe I won't really understand until I've lived it."

"Brennan," Cole warned.

The wind whipped faster, but Cole's grip didn't waver.

"But this, right now? I understand perfectly," Brennan said, taking one step closer. "You're lonely, and you're tired, and you're lashing out at everything because it hurts too much not to."

The wind slowed.

"You were good once." He took another step forward. "You could be again." And another.

Travis opened his mouth. Closed it. Opened it again. Everything swirling in the air dropped to the ground, collapsing onto the sticky red floor.

He was thinking. He was teetering on the edge of believing, and Brennan was begging him to choose correctly.

The grand doors slammed open. Brennan didn't tear his eyes from Travis's.

"Travis," Brennan pleaded.

Travis's eyes caught on something over Brennan's shoulder. Something like resignation flickered over him.

"Make sure someone takes care of Rosie," Travis said.

And Brennan was so busy trying to decipher that, he didn't see the commotion behind him. He only saw the blur of motion, a flash of dark hair and a red velvet dress. He processed Dom, processed Micah tossing her the stake from her belt, processed Cole's shout—

"Dom, wait!"

Before the stake plunged into Travis's chest.

In the split second before Travis died, the only emotion on his face was relief.

Travis collapsed. There was no blood. No scream. The quartet stopped playing, and the room fell silent.

The quiet left behind by the wind was deafening.

Slowly, Dom slid to the floor, falling to her knees beside him, and sobbed quietly.

Brennan looked around. Everyone had spread out to the edges of the room, as far from Travis, Brennan, and Cole as possible. They all watched the spectacle with wide eyes, except for a few unaffected vampires watching with bored or amused expressions, like this was an average Saturday night. And there, before the doors, were Nellie and Sunny, dressed to the nines and *alive* and awake and okay. Next to them were two vampires Brennan recognized from Facebook, Quinn and Narrissa, along with Mari, who rushed in with a janitorial cart loaded with blood.

Nellie locked eyes with Brennan. She smiled, soft and proud.

Mari started doling out blood packs. An older woman ripped into one with her fangs and chugged it.

Dressed in a purple tea-length dress, Sunny didn't miss a beat. She used the silence to gracefully stride up to the microphone by the quartet of musicians who were only now looking around in confusion, released from Travis's thrall.

"A huge thanks to the Sturbridge University drama troupe for their impressive performance," Sunny said, each word crisp and pointed. The words sounded candy-coated, and Brennan realized they were imbued with magic. "And to the special-effects team that made it possible." She started a small, polite golf clap that people slowly but surely joined.

She was using her vampire powers on a huge room full of humans. Something about that would have terrified Brennan a few months ago, but now it was the ultimate comfort. She was protecting them. That was her job.

"Of course, you'll all comply in deleting any photos and videos of the performance from your phones," Sunny added, the magic laced in her words cutting hard enough that even Brennan felt a tug to clear out his recent photo album.

Around Brennan, people reached for their phones, even the Redditors. Only Micah paused, staring at her phone with pinched brows before tapping, reluctant but obedient.

"Wow," someone remarked behind him as the crowd finished applauding and started to edge away from cowering near the walls. "The budget this year must have been astronomical."

"Was that KeepItSunny from Instagram?" someone else asked.

Sunny stepped away from the mic and waved at Quinn and Narrissa, who easily picked up Travis and left the room, like they were clearing a set.

Nellie went to Dom, who was crying on the floor.

The quartet began to play again.

And that was it.

It was over.

Travis was dead.

They'd won. But Travis had gotten exactly what he wanted.

26

WHEN WE TALK ABOUT FOREVER

BRENNAN'S PHONE

bloodsucking memes for immortal non-teens (new england clan)
QUINN MILLER
PARTY! OF! THE! CENTURY!

Miraculously, it took all of three minutes for the ball to revert to full swing. Though hotel staff were furiously cleaning the food and punch from the floors while an angry manager was having words with an unintimidated Sunny.

Brennan was still in shock, shaking and numb and not quite believing it was really over.

The group came together in front of the grand doors—Brennan and Cole, hands clasped tight, Mari, and Tony.

"Are you okay?" Mari ran up to Cole and embraced him while Tony punched Brennan in the arm with too much enthusiasm.

"That was the coolest thing that's ever happened to me! Did you guys see me whippin' out sauce like nobody's business?" Tony said. "I was on a roll, the wind couldn't stop me!"

"Brennan," Cole said, voice cutting through the clamoring like a hot knife through butter. "Are you okay?"

Someone appeared at Brennan's side and pressed a blood pack into his hands. Quinn Miller, the Facebook vampire, who'd helped Dom save Sunny and Nellie.

"Forgot about yourself in the mix, did you?" they said, lips quirked in a smile. Quinn was bulky and round with buzzed hair, elaborate vines tattooed on their neck. They wore a black-and-gray suit.

That was part of it, and Brennan accepted the pack gratefully, but didn't dig in, because the other part, the more important part, was: "Where's Dom?"

Quinn frowned sympathetically and nodded toward a hallway off the side of the ballroom. "Talking with Nellie about her options," they said. "You should really drink first."

So Brennan did, while Cole made sure each and every one of their friends was undamaged, offering them Band-Aids and ibuprofen.

"Say, who's responsible for getting all this blood?" Quinn was saying. "And do you have any interest in helping with blood drives in the future?"

Tony started hooting while Mari turned flustered, and Brennan took the opportunity to slip away from the group, shaking his head when Cole caught his eye with concern. He needed to do this part alone. He headed toward the hallway Quinn had nodded to.

Outside the ballroom, music and laughter muted, Brennan could hear Dom's shaky breaths. She was on the floor with Nellie crouching beside her, next to the women's restrooms in an elaborately decorated hallway.

"So," Brennan said. "Which part of the plan was that?"

Dom sniffled. "I'm sorry. He just—he manipulated me so much. I hate him for that. I *hate* him. And then I saw him and the mess and . . . I stopped it."

"You stopped him, Dom," Nellie soothed. "He endangered secrecy. He knew the penalty would be death this time. It's what he wanted."

"He saved my life once," Brennan said. "He could have been . . . He was so *close*."

"He was always *close* to being good," Nellie said. "Never quite made it there." She shook her head. "I'm sorry, Brennan."

Fuck. "What now?" Brennan asked.

"You go back to your life," Nellie said. "Sunny covers our tracks.

I write a new pamphlet about today. And Dom . . . this is only strike one for Dom. She's getting transferred to a new clan. She'll try out a few, actually, to figure out what she wants in her life. Afterlife. Kind of a vampire *Eat Pray Love* situation. It'll be amazing for her."

"Right," said Brennan. Then, remembering, "What about Rosie?"

The clack of high heels behind him announced Sunny's presence. "You know, Rosie was actually *my* dog before Travis was banished to his domain? It was his one condition of submitting. He took my damn dog."

Nellie said, "But hey, thanks for holding down the fort, big guy."

Sunny gave Brennan a narrow-eyed once-over. "It could have gone worse."

"Aw, Sunny," said Brennan, "I missed you, too."

Sunny rolled her eyes, checked her phone, typed out a quick message, then nodded to Dom.

"You ready to go?"

Dom wiped her eyes and started to stand up.

"What, you're leaving now?" Brennan said.

"She's kind of a danger to urban clan society," Sunny said, still texting one-handed. "It's partially punishment. She can't hang out to party. And so, neither can I." She jerked her head toward the lobby. "Let's go."

Dom straightened her dress and hovered near Sunny.

"Brennan," she said. "I'm sorry about Travis. And. Thank you."

And in a move that shocked Brennan to his core, she surged forward and hugged him. Quick and tight, and then she withdrew again.

"Is that it, then?" Brennan asked. "Will you have your phone, wherever you are?"

Sunny shook her head.

"I'll find ways to get in touch," Dom said, smiling slyly, and Brennan had no doubt she would. He wasn't sure if he was scared or looking forward to it.

When Brennan returned to the ballroom, the celebration was on. Mari and Tony were dancing, twirling around each other and laughing. Now that the threat was gone, even Brennan could almost get into the upbeat tune the quartet was playing.

But Cole was nowhere to be found.

He scanned the ballroom once more before venturing into the lobby. The staff eyed him suspiciously, which was fair since the vampire ball had trashed their venue, but still. He was about to give up and return to the others when he heard from outside—

"Yes, Mama." A Southern accent, the voice that Brennan knew from beginning to end by now, distorted through walls. All Brennan had to do was follow the sound.

It took him to an exit into a courtyard at the center of the hotel. The night was dark, a few bright stars making it through the city light pollution.

The courtyard was a paved patio with lush trees and garden boxes surrounded by the Gothic exterior of the building. At the center, sitting on an iron bench with intricate floral patterns, was Cole, his back to Brennan, just a pair of suit-clad shoulders and a messy swirl of hair. He held a phone to one ear and was hunched into himself.

"Yeah," Cole said. "Love you, too."

He hung up.

Brennan sat beside him.

"Hey," Brennan said.

Cole nudged his knee against Brennan's. "Hey."

"You okay?"

"That was, um," Cole said, and his voice got thick and teary so Brennan tugged him in. "That was my mom?"

"Oh?" In all of this, Brennan had thought Cole was still ignoring their calls.

"She said—" Cole took a shaky breath. "—um, that she loves me no matter what I do with my life. And that my dad will come around."

"Well, that's . . . good, right?"

"It is. Of course. I just, I wasn't expecting this tonight. I don't even know why I answered this time. I don't really know what to do with it."

Brennan smoothed a hand up and down Cole's shoulder while he processed that, then smiled. "I don't know, it sounds like cause for celebration," Brennan said. "Luckily I know a pretty good party nearby."

"I love you," Cole said.

Brennan froze.

"You said it earlier and I didn't say it back, and I stand by the fact that that was *terrible* timing."

"I love you, too," Brennan said. "Now come inside and dance with me."

Cole smiled. "I can do that. But . . . let's stay here for a minute."

Eventually, they would go inside and join their friends and celebrate the ongoing secrecy of the vampires. Eventually, they would dance. For now, Brennan held him close. The two of them together in the night, as always.

BRENNAN'S PHONE

Brennan

Hey, you mentioned a new pamphlet?

I had another idea.

A better system than the pamphlets.

Any chance I can get involved?

Maybe digitize some things?

Nellie

Yes! Absolutely! I love that! Exclamation point!

"Everybody shut up! It's the final rose ceremony, we actually have to pay attention," Tony said.

"You've been louder than anyone!" Mari protested.

"And that's why now I'm saying I'm gonna shut up!"

"I think this is their version of flirting," Cole whispered.

It was *Bachelorette* Night. The vampire ball had been two weeks earlier, and it had taken that long for things to feel normal again. There were no murders in the news, no betrayals, no secrets revealed. Just texting Nellie, hanging out with Cole and Mari and Tony, and going to classes. Brennan had finished *Breaking Dawn*. He and Cole had a movie marathon scheduled that weekend, and he was embarrassed to admit he was looking forward to it.

They were all squished on the couch, so Cole was half in Brennan's lap. Mari and Tony were pretty cozy, too. Brennan was *pretty* sure Mari and Tony were together now, but he was afraid to ask.

Brennan sipped from his blood pouch through a straw. Everyone knew now, so he could, which he had to admit was nice. Maybe Dom was onto something with not wanting to pretend all the time.

Dom . . . Brennan hadn't heard from her. Sunny wouldn't tell him where she was, but implied she was abroad somewhere. She'd said that if Dom wanted to reach out she would. After the first week, Brennan stopped jumping at every phone notification.

The bachelorette was giving out roses, and Brennan wasn't paying attention, more focused on the small circles Cole was drawing on his shoulders with his fingertips.

"Not Mark B, not Mark B—" Tony chanted. He was on the edge of his seat.

Something crashed with a thud against the window.

Brennan jumped and Cole cursed. A shadow hovered at the window adjacent to the couch and Brennan squinted at it.

A black bird pointedly pecked at the glass.

Knock knock. Knock knock.

Brennan hopped up, sensing Cole right behind him as he went to investigate. The bird was large and fat, and had a vial with a bit of paper inside tied to its ankle.

Knock knock. Knock knock.

"You've gotta be kidding me," Brennan said, and opened the window.

The bird flew in with a flourish and perched on the coffee table, extending its leg out for Brennan obediently.

"Fucking sick," Cole said.

"Dammit, I missed who she gave the rose to," Tony said.

Brennan untied the vial and let the parchment inside fall into his open hand. The bird shook out its feathers, then started picking at the crumbs on the table from the cookies Cole had brought.

"Um, is it gonna leave now, or?" Mari said, eyeing the bird distrustfully.

"I think it's waiting for a response," Cole said.

Brennan ignored them and unrolled the note. It was on old parchment, written in black ink and curly, neat handwriting.

"What's it say?" Cole leaned against him to peek over his shoulder.

"It's Dom," Brennan said.

"Dude, she has a messenger bird?" Cole said. "Fucking *awesome*. Why don't *you* get a messenger bird?"

"Guys, the show has, like, two minutes left if you could let me watch in *peace*?" Tony said.

Mari fell back on the couch, while Brennan and Cole lingered by the window. Brennan read the note, letting Cole read along, tucked into Brennan's side.

> Brennan,
> First off, if you're reading this, you've probably met my new friend Tali. If you have any snacks you can tip her, she'll greatly appreciate it for the journey home. She likes breadcrumbs, nuts, seeds, anything like that.

Cole withdrew from Brennan and darted to the kitchen. Always reliable. Brennan warmed, and kept reading.

> Okay, raven companion aside. I'm currently in Ireland, at a really traditional vampire colony. They have a whole fortress in the middle of nowhere with this whole society. You'd have a fit about morality and how they get their blood, but there are some humans here, too, companions and family members of other vampires. It's a nice little community. You'd hate it.
>
> I've been thinking a lot about my sister. About Evelyn. She was so excited to start school. She never got to. She had her whole life ahead of her, and I took that from her. I have to live with that forever now.
>
> Forever is a long time. I guess I need to start finding things to live for.
> I think, maybe, you taught me that.
> Wishing you the best from the dark side.
>
> > Dominique

"I'll give her this," Cole said, returning to Brennan's side by the window. "She certainly knows how to keep things interesting."

"Yeah."

Brennan reread the letter with Cole. Then he studied Cole, the furrow in his brow as he read, the slight movement of his lips. Those words rang in his head.

Forever is a long time.

Life was unpredictable, and life was long, and for a vampire, both were even more true. Because Brennan wouldn't age and he wouldn't die, and Cole eventually would. And that was assuming a regular old-fashioned breakup didn't part them. Somehow, that didn't matter.

In that moment, Brennan was sure he would spend his whole life loving Cole.

Cole blushed when he caught Brennan's stare, biting back a smile.

"What?" Cole said. "Are you okay?"

"Yeah," Brennan said. "I'm good."

Forever is a long time.

For the first time, Brennan was looking forward to it.

ACKNOWLEDGMENTS

This book wouldn't exist without the help of so many wonderful people, but first, I must address my dream team: To my agent, John Cusick, thank you for answering my endless questions, and thank you for believing in me and this story at a time when I thought no one would. And to my editors, Vicki Lame and Vanessa Aguirre, thank you for being the most amazing duo of champions for this book. I truly am so lucky to have had not one but two brilliant brains fighting for me and pushing me to make this story the best it could be.

It really does take a village to bring a book to life, so a massive thank-you to the many hands at work at Wednesday Books and St. Martin's Publishing Group. Thank you to Sara Goodman, Eileen Rothschild, Merilee Croft, Melanie Sanders, and Gail Friedman for shepherding this book through the minefields of publishing with gentle hands. Thank you to Kerri Resnick, Olga Grlic, and Michelle McMillian for bringing it to life with gorgeous design and creative direction, and to Andreea Dumuta for such a perfect cover illustration. Thank you to the lovely marketing and publicity folks, Brant Janeway, Daisy Glasgow, and Zoe Miller, for helping bring this story to the readers who need it. And thank you to Elishia Merricks and Katy Robitzski for giving voice to my words and characters.

Thank you to Rebecca Hilsdon and the team at Penguin Michael Joseph for giving this story just as much love across the pond. Thank you as well to the foreign rights team at Folio, Chiara Panzeri and Melissa

Sarver White, who did so much to bring Brennan's story to other countries and in other languages.

To my parents, thank you for supporting me in every endeavor and every passion, and for letting me smoke in the house while I was drafting this. (And thanks in advance for not giving me shit for memorializing that fact in these acknowledgments.) To my best friend, Rowan Little, thank you for having loved and supported this book before you even read it. Thank you to the author mentors who gave feedback to this book in its early stages and saw the potential amid the mess: Katharine J. Adams and Daphne Dador, you both gave me hope and enthusiasm in a time when I desperately needed them. Similarly, thank you to the many communities of writers I've been fortunate enough to be part of: the Query Quarry and Submission Slog servers, as well as the 2024 and 2025 Debut groups. I simply wouldn't have survived without the collective expertise and support of the online writing community.

The poem in the book Brennan gifts to Cole is "Visible World" from *Crush* by Richard Siken. Thank you to Yale University Press and Richard Siken for allowing me to use the full poem.

AUTHOR'S NOTE

Dear Reader,

The Good Vampire's Guide to Blood & Boyfriends was born from a love-hate relationship with the early 2000s paranormal romance craze. I loved the broody, existential romantic leads with monstrous secrets, and I loved the idea of loving and being loved in spite of—and because of—monstrous tendencies.

But I wanted to blend those old tropes with the sensibilities and irreverence of modern queer rom-coms: take the broody vampire and give him anxiety and a dark sense of humor, and you get Brennan Brooks. Take the woodsy, small-town setting and transpose it to a fictionalized college town in Massachusetts, and you get Sturbridge University. Take the hundred-year age gaps and power imbalances and make them into a soft, sweet love story, and you get Brennan and Cole's romance.

More than that, though, this book, and Brennan in particular, came from a deeply personal place. Growing up depressed with undiagnosed and unsupported autism, I read stories about people who were depressed, people who wanted to die, people who killed themselves. But when I attempted suicide at nineteen and survived, I realized I had no idea what came next—what happens when you survive and decide you want to keep living.

Ultimately, that's why I wrote *The Good Vampire's Guide to Blood &*

Boyfriends. It's about existential dread and making the radical choice to live even when it's hard. And it's about deserving and being capable of healthy love despite your flaws—may those be mental health struggles, a need to drink human blood, or anything in between.

Thanks for reading!
Jamie D'Amato

DISCUSSION QUESTIONS

1. In chapter 9, Nellie says, "I've noticed you talk about being a vampire the same way you talk about being depressed. You assume they're the worst things about you." In what ways are Brennan's experiences of mental illness and vampirism similar?

2. How do Brennan's relationships with Cole and Dom affect his character development throughout the novel?

3. What do you think Travis's and Dom's arcs have to say about redemption and making up for mistakes? How do they each try to do this?

4. In romance books about mental health, it is important not to romanticize mental illness while still showing compassion and understanding. In what ways does the book succeed or fail in that?

5. The book is told from Brennan's perspective. Is there another character whose point of view you would have been interested to read? How do you think that would have made the book different? Is Brennan ever an unreliable narrator?

6. The pamphlets explain a lot about how the clan system works to keep vampires a secret, but what else does the book imply about the secret world of vampires? What do you think clans beyond the New England one look like?

7. How does the usage of epistolary storytelling such as journal entries, text messages, and social media posts affect the experience of the reader,

or the way the story unfolds? How does it reflect contemporary times? How does it reveal character?

8. The book leaves questions unanswered in the end: What will become of Dom, the clan, and Brennan's involvement with it? Will Brennan and Cole be in it for the long haul when Brennan is immortal and Cole isn't—or will Cole ever become a vampire, too? What do you think the future looks like for the characters?